Praise for *G*

"*Galileo* is the work of a mature writer who has full control of her story and characters and dares to delve deeply into the eternal moral predicaments of human experience. Ann McMan writes with a fierce intelligence and sympathetic heart. In *Galileo*, she once again elevates lesbian literature."

—Lee Lynch, trailblazing author of *The Swashbuckler*

"It took courage to write *Galileo*, to take on its controversial themes, and it took talent to write it this exquisitely—Ann McMan has courage and talent by the bucket load. *Galileo* is powerful, elegant—and in the best tradition of storytelling—a page-turner that is impossible to put down."

—Ann Aptaker, Lambda Literary Award-winning author of the Cantor Gold Mystery Series

"McMan's characters clash and smash and carom off one another as if in heavy surf. And indeed, the heavy surf is the current zeitgeist, which McMan understands and portrays adroitly. Her subplots are complex and relevant."

—Elizabeth Sims, Lambda Literary Award-winning author of the Lillian Byrd Mystery Series

"*Galileo* is a tight, well-paced, and timely mystery that handles dark subjects with a light and sure touch—Ann McMan is a wonderful writer."

—Michael Nava, Lambda Literary Award-winning author of the Henry Rios Mystery Series

"Ann McMan's newest Evan Reed mystery, *Galileo*, tackles a hard and complicated subject, one she deftly surrounds with her signature wit and humor. With a sure hand, one that leads us inexorably toward the truth, McMan creates characters we grow to love—and others we don't want to take our eyes off of for fear of what they will do next. This is another winner, not to be missed!"

—Ellen Hart, Mystery Writers of America Edgar Grand Master Award Winner

Also by Ann McMan

Hoosier Daddy
Festival Nurse
Backcast
Beowulf for Cretins: A Love Story

The Evan Reed Mystery Series
Dust
Galileo

The Jericho Series
Jericho
Aftermath
Goldenrod

Story Collections
Sidecar
Three (plus one)

AN EVAN REED MYSTERY

GALILEO

Ann McMan

Bywater
BOOKS

Ann Arbor
2019

Bywater Books

Copyright © 2019 Ann McMan

Print ISBN: 978-1-61294-159-2

Bywater Books First Edition: November 2019

Printed in the United States of America on acid-free paper.

Cover Design by Ann McMan, TreeHouse Studio

Bywater Books
PO Box 3671
Ann Arbor MI 48106-3671
www.bywaterbooks.com

This novel is a work of fiction.

For Buddha—first, last and always
(which, in retrospect, sounds like our shared understanding
of how wine should be served at every meal).

For unto whomsoever much is given, of him shall be much required: and
to whom men have committed much, of him they will ask the more.

Luke 12:48

Chapter One

Whose woods these are I think I know . . .

She ought to know. She'd cooled her heels on this low ridge at the back of her property many times before—on other cold nights, when there had been vague promises that the elusive aurora borealis would blaze a meandering trail across the Pennsylvania sky. Experts said that if you were lucky and could find a place dark enough, you'd have the best shot at witnessing the spectacular light show that was a rare enough occurrence any time in Chadds Ford, but was virtually unheard of in December.

Finding dark spaces was never difficult for Evan. Making her way back out of them was the part that caused problems.

It had snowed steadily all day. Evan assumed that meant the sky would remain too overcast to reveal anything tonight. But, miraculously, the snow had stopped an hour before nightfall and the clouds rolled back to reveal a brilliant canopy of stars. The new moon was riding low on the horizon, and Saturn was shining so brightly Evan swore she could see the glow of its rings with only her naked eye.

All good omens for getting a ringside view of the elusive light show.

With that in mind, she garbed up and trudged through the drifts of powdery new snow, equipped with an ancient wooden camp stool and a silver flask of VSOP cognac that had been a

1

gift from Julia, "For those cold nights I'm not around to keep you warm."

Tonight certainly qualified. Julia was stuck in Albuquerque for two more days, doing advance planning for the American Booksellers Association's annual Winter Institute.

Evan had complained about the trip. "You have to be out there an entire week? Why can't you just Skype in, like a normal person?"

"Honey," Julia said with exasperated patience, "I'm the committee chairperson. I cannot require all of the other members to hoof it out there, then cavalierly opt to Skype in just because it suits me better not to be away from you for a week."

That last part got Evan's attention. She wasn't used to reacting like a giddy teenager when someone addressed her with an endearment. That evolution was a change—one of many since Julia had entered her life.

And those hits kept on coming.

After her estranged husband's murder, Julia's vow never to return to their Park Avenue apartment soon morphed into her decision to move her company's head office from New York City to Philadelphia. Donne & Hale's Pennsylvania office was smaller than the publishing firm's other satellites in Boston and London—but there was precedent for making it the center of operations. Julia's father and former company board chair had always preferred to run the family business from its Market Street digs in Center City—which was especially true after he'd married Julia's patrician mother, a descendent of the Hires family. The fabled union of blue-blooded bona fides netted a lot of ink in the nation's leading newspapers, and wishful prospects for many heirs apparent tantalized readers of *The Social Register* for decades.

But, alas. The golden duo produced only one offspring—a girl, named Julia Lewis—now heir to the combined fortunes of two faded family dynasties.

First editions of Poe's *Tamerlane* and root beer floats . . .

The bizarre combination was like the question lurking at the end of an obscure *Jeopardy!* clue.

But Julia Donne lived up to the potential of all that upper-class privilege. Private school at Exeter. Undergraduate degree at Yale. Postgraduate work at Oxford. Assuming the mantle of power when her father retired from the publishing house—followed by her picture-perfect marriage to a charismatic young politician who trampolined into the United States Senate after serving one term as governor of Delaware.

It was a storybook tale that had morphed into one woman's personal nightmare.

But all of that was in the past now. A past Julia was determined to leave behind.

It was freezing out here.

The cold weather wasn't doing the aching joint in her shoulder any favors, either. Evan stomped her feet in a futile attempt to knock the snow off her boots. She pulled off a glove and uncapped her flask of cognac. Heady aromas of cedarwood, apricot and vanilla mingled on the night air, filling her with a promise of warmth ahead of her first careful sip.

The truth was, Julia wasn't the only one with a desire to let the past lie buried. Evan was doing a credible job tiptoeing around her own cranky pack of sleeping dogs. It was anybody's guess how long the two of them could keep their tentative *pas de deux* going.

She took a taste of the fragrant liquid. It slid down the back of her throat and raced out along her extremities like wildfire. She stared out across miles of rolling fields at the horizon. The landscape was dotted with small copses of naked trees. They cast long, purple shadows across the new snow. She could hear a dog off in the distance. There was always something doleful about a dog barking in winter. The lonely sound traveled along the frigid night air like a hopeless cry to heaven.

She was trying hard to keep her gaze open—not to focus on any one thing. Just to watch the sky—*all* of it—for any sudden flickers or changes in hue. For any flashes of fluorescent green or magenta. So far, nothing. Just deepening darkness and an expanding marquee of stars.

3

Let's get this damn show on the road.

The unmistakable sound of boots trudging through the snow startled her. She turned around on her stool and stared at the dark figure making its unsteady way across the field. It was a man. That much she was certain of. A *big* man. But who? And why the hell was he out here at this hour of the night, making a beeline straight toward her?

She tightened her grip on the flask, prepared to hurl it at the intruder if she needed to.

It turned out she didn't need to hurl anything—except expletives.

"Evan?" The hulking figure asked. "What are you *doing* way out here?"

It was Tim. *Father* Tim—her childhood pal and erstwhile Catholic priest. He was also her daughter, Stevie's, godfather.

"Jesus, Mary and Joseph, Tim. You scared the shit out of me. What the hell are you doing skulking around out here?"

He shrugged. "Isn't that obvious?"

"I have a damn cell phone," Evan remonstrated. "Why the cloak and dagger crap?"

"I was in the neighborhood."

"In Chadds Ford?" Evan narrowed her eyes. "Doing what? Offering last rites to wayward Holsteins?"

"Something like that." He said. "I had the night off and thought I'd head your way and beg for company."

Evan checked her watch. "It's nearly ten o'clock. By now, you should be safely locked up in your little priest cell back at St. Rita's."

"They only lock us up on weeknights."

"It's Saturday," Evan noted. "Don't you have to work tomorrow?"

He shrugged.

"What's going on, Tim?"

"What makes you think anything is going on?"

"Gee. Lemme think." She indicated the landscape. "You're forty miles from your parish, standing in the middle of a snow-covered field in the dead of night—probably freezing your sainted ass off. *Nope.* Nothing unusual about that."

4

"I just wanted to talk, okay?"

Evan smelled a rat. "About?"

Tim cleared his throat. "What are you drinking?"

"High-dollar swill." Evan extended the silver flask. "Want a sip?"

"Yeah." Tim took her up on the offer. "You're right about one thing. It's cold as hell out here." He took a healthy swallow of the cognac and proceeded to cough.

"Smooth, isn't it?" Evan asked.

"Wrong pipe." Tim cleared his throat. "Why are you out here?"

"I'm watching the heavens, looking for signs and portents."

"Isn't that my job?"

"You tell me," she quipped. "You're the one with all the letters after your name."

Tim seemed to think about what she'd said. "The aurora?"

Evan nodded.

He looked at the sky. "Think it'll show?"

"Stranger things have happened." She was tempted to add "you showed up," but thought better of it.

He handed the flask back to her. "Don't suppose you have an extra stool on you?"

"Nope." Evan started to get up. "Maybe we can find a log or something?"

Tim gestured for her to stay seated. "Don't get up. I'll look around."

A minute later, Tim spotted what was left of a rotting tulip poplar stump and dragged it over to the spot where Evan sat. He dusted its top off with his gloved hand. "This'll work just fine."

"You'll freeze your ass off." Evan rummaged around inside her backpack and pulled out a folded section of old tarp. "Use this."

Tim took the thick, green square from her. "You carry this around?"

She shrugged.

"What are these things?" Tim spread the square of canvas over his stump. "Some homage to *A Room With A View*?"

Evan made a face. "You should be happy I got something out of that damn movie—especially since you made me sit through it *four* times."

"It was Judi Dench," Tim protested.

"I *know* who it was. And that's not why I carry these."

"Why then?"

"Because I come out here a lot."

"Even on nights there isn't a cosmic light show?"

"Even then."

"You're an enigma."

"*I'm* an enigma? Don't you have that backwards?"

"Me?" Tim sounded confused.

"Yeah," Evan clarified. "You're the one who runs around wearing a medieval garrote."

Tim raised a hand to his neck. "Not tonight."

Evan didn't reply. They sat together in silence for a minute. The damn dog that had been barking must've finally given up on its lament and hunkered down beneath an obliging porch. The ensuing quiet was deep and peculiar—oddly deafening, the way silent nights in winter often were.

Tim spoke first. "I came out here because I wanted . . . *needed* to talk with you."

"That sounds ominous."

"I guess it is." He kicked at a clod of snow.

"So, you waited until the dead of night to drive forty miles? How come?"

Tim gave her a half smile. "It seemed appropriate. That's usually when you show up, wanting to talk with me."

"That's different," Evan said.

"How so?"

"For one thing," she said, "you're *working*. So, when I need to talk with you about important stuff, I have to crawl inside a box, perch my ass on a hard bench, and stare at a mesh screen."

"It's called a confessional. And you know you can come see me when I'm not 'working.' We've had this conversation."

"True," Evan agreed. "So, I suppose this nocturnal visit is some kind of quid pro quo?"

"Maybe."

"You know," she said, "I never really understood the Church's need to make a difficult process even more unpleasant for penitents." Evan considered her remark. "On the other hand, I guess that practice is pretty consistent with the rest of the methods of Catholicism."

"Normally, I'd argue with you."

"But tonight, you won't?"

He didn't reply.

Evan realized that the night air closing in around them wasn't the only example of how deafening silence could be.

"Do you wanna tell me what's going on?" Her tone was softer.

He seemed to choose his words carefully. "I'm thinking about leaving."

"Leaving?" she asked. "Philadelphia?"

"No. The Church."

Evan was stunned. "The priesthood?"

He nodded.

"What the hell?" Evan leaned toward him. "Did something happen?"

He didn't answer. She gave him a few seconds to rethink his lack of reply. He didn't.

"Do you want me to guess?" She asked. "I'm pretty good at it."

He gave her a half smile. "So I've heard."

"Tim?" Evan didn't know what else to ask.

"I know. It's . . . complicated."

"I don't doubt it." Evan rested a hand on his knee. "Lucky for you, I don't have another thing planned for the rest of this evening." She held up her flask of cognac. "Except maybe finishing this."

He stared back at her. Evan thought he looked a little lost. Uncertain. The way he used to look when they were kids, and she'd drag him off beyond the boundaries of their known world to explore the dark realm of mysteries that rumbled and steamed south of West Passyunk Avenue. Growing up, she never understood why Tim seemed so content to live his life within the confines of the potholed streets and forgotten avenues that crisscrossed the lopsided trapezoid of their South Philly neighborhood like broken threads. That dichotomy they shared had always been a paradox. Evan couldn't will the years separating her from adulthood to melt away fast enough. All she ever wanted was *out*. Tim, on the other hand, seemed only too willing to embrace a life and calling that were guaranteed to play out among the same bits of broken pavement and sagging storefronts they frequented as kids. Tim attended the parish school at St. Margherita, which everyone just called St. Rita's, for his early education. Evan preferred to call it his *indoctrination*. She, on the other hand, went to public school at Stephen Girard. He studied the sacraments. She learned how to shoplift cigarettes. He attended seminary at St. Charles Borromeo. She majored in anarchy at Penn. He returned home to West Passyunk to pursue ordination into the priesthood. She laid a patch getting away from the old 'hood, and never looked back. But at no time during their disparate life journeys did Evan ever doubt that Tim was intended for anything other than a life of celibacy and service to God. So, this? Walking away from all of that after so many years?

It made no sense.

She tried again. "You came all the way out here to talk about it. Do you want to give it a try?"

He gave her a slow nod. "So, I suppose you've been following the State grand jury report on sexual abuse by members of the clergy?"

"Kind of hard not to."

"The cases and claims are all being handled by laypeople outside the diocese."

"That makes sense." Evan felt her insides begin to knot up. "Have there been any reports at St. Rita's?"

He met her eyes. "Not yet."

"And?"

He shrugged.

"Are you protecting someone?" She knew she was flying by the seat of her pants. And she hated playing Twenty Questions. But Tim was acting like a squirrel caught in the headlights of an oncoming car—it wasn't clear which way he was going to jump, but it was certain he was poised to flee.

"Maybe." He dropped his eyes. "It's complicated."

"You already said that."

"I don't know what else to say."

"All right." Evan thought about her options. "How about we make a deal?"

He looked up at her with narrowed eyes. "What kind of deal?"

"You don't quit anything until things are uncomplicated enough that you *can* talk about them—in real sentences with verbs."

"Evan . . ."

"Hey." She raised a hand. "You came out here to talk with me and promptly realized you couldn't, or weren't ready. Therefore, I, as your oldest and best friend, invoke executive privilege and demand a stay on any actions or reactions until such time as a full and complete disclosure can occur."

"Those are some terms." He slowly shook his head. "What makes you think I'll agree?"

"I know you. You're still the same little candyass who was always afraid I'd let go of your hand and leave you stranded in a strange land full of falafel stands and tattoo parlors."

"I now love falafel. And you always led me back home."

Evan saw something strobe and roll in the distance behind him. It wasn't lightning—it was more like a phosphorescent gurgle creeping along the horizon . . . an eerie green gurgle.

Holy shit. Here it was. Right on cue.

There was another rolling flash—higher and broader. There were traces of deep lavender mixed in with the glowing green. Tim saw it this time, too.

"Well, I'll be damned." He swiveled around on his stump to gawk at the sky. "I didn't think it would happen."

Evan smiled at him. "Kind of an odd stance for someone whose job it is to believe in miracles."

9

Tim laughed but didn't disagree.

The cosmic light show continued. The way the colors undulated and swirled reminded her of the used lava lamp Sheila had given her for her tenth birthday. She and Tim would daisy-chain it to a couple of extension cords and watch it for hours—usually on hot summer nights, while they sat on the front steps of her row home, waiting on Evan's mother to roll in from . . . wherever she'd been for the evening.

Sheila hadn't been all that keen on keeping regular hours—or anything else usually attached to the word "*regular*."

"It's like old times," Evan observed.

Tim seemed confused.

"You. Me," she explained. "In the dark, watching fancy colors and waiting for our lives to change."

He gave her a sad smile. "They did."

"Yeah," Evan said. "And in my case, not a moment too soon."

"Change can be a good thing."

"Absolutely true. But as a wise friend of mine pointed out, change is a process, not an event."

Tim raised an eyebrow. "A *wise* friend?"

"He has his moments."

Tim looked back at the horizon.

Evan watched him against the backdrop of the blazing night sky. Both of them were full of charged particles. The aurora might last another few hours before dissolving back into darkness. Tim's internal disturbance was sure to last a lot longer.

It was well past midnight when Evan finally turned off the lights and trudged up the steps to bed. Tim had stayed on long after the aurora faded into the deeper recesses of the night sky. They continued to sit huddled together at the edge of a snowdrift, even though Evan suggested they head back to the house and the warmth of her living room.

Tim had deliberated.

"I can't stay much longer," he'd said. Even though he did stay longer. A lot longer.

Evan figured if it were easier for Tim to talk with her—or not talk with her—in the dark, she'd just have to roll with it. After all, turnabout was fair play. In the end, he didn't reveal much more than he had initially, although he promised not to make any final decisions until they had more time, and he had more inclination, to sort through and lay bare his nebulous issues.

When he had finally checked his watch and got to his feet, it was nearly 11:45. Evan walked him back to his car and made him promise to text her when he reached the safety of his digs at St. Rita's. They hugged good-bye.

"Let me know when would be a good time to visit with Stevie while she's home for Christmas break?" he'd asked.

"Of course." Evan nodded. "She'll want to see you right away. You're her soulmate when it comes to the finer arts of reality TV and junk food."

Tim nodded and climbed into his ancient Subaru before slowly backing out her driveway, taking care to keep within his own tracks through the snow.

Evan had watched his slow progress along Ring Road. It was a mess, with only a narrow lane traversable. But I-95 back to Philly should be in better shape than it had been when he'd made his way to Chadds Ford earlier. It always amazed her how fast the highway crews got busy after these winter storms rolled through.

Her cell phone had vibrated about twenty times while she sat outside with Tim. When she reached the solitude of her bedroom, she sat down to scroll through the messages. There were two from Julia. Those made her smile.

She glanced over at the small, framed photo on her nightstand. It had been taken just over a year ago. Tim had come over for brunch and to help them decorate for Christmas. Julia posed with Evan and Stevie out back, in the snow piled up along the perimeter of the house. They had all been drinking mimosas and hanging white Christmas lights along the eaves of the porch.

Since Julia was, by far, the tallest of them, she stood on the second rung of an ancient wooden ladder. Evan was wielding a staple gun like a six-shooter and Stevie was draped with strands of tangled lights.

She stared at Julia.

God. The woman was so damn gorgeous. She was nearly half a foot taller than Evan—even without the ladder. Her mane of dark hair was loose and blowing around her face, but her million-watt smile was easy to make out. Evan and Stevie were both staring up at her with goofy adoration.

Evan frowned at her own image. She was wearing her grandfather's wool barn coat and a clunky pair of glasses. Her short, sandy hair was sticking up at odd angles.

She looked like a myopic pygmy . . . with bed head.

Whatever.

She also had five voicemail messages and ten missed-call notifications from Dan.

What the hell?

Her panicked, first thought was Stevie—but none of Dan's messages mentioned their daughter.

"Evan, it's Dan. I need to talk with you tonight. It's about a job. Call me ASAP."

"Evan, it's me again. Pick up. I need to talk to you." A sigh on the line. *"Call me when you get in."*

"Where the fuck are you? I've been trying to reach you for two hours. Call me."

"Don't you carry your damn phone with you? Call me back. It's important."

"Jesus H. Christ, Evan. Good thing I don't need a fucking organ transplant."

Evan punched the callback option on her phone. Dan answered on the first ring.

"Where the fuck have you been? It's fucking midnight."

"Relax, Dan. I have a *life*. I was out."

"Out?" He sounded incredulous. "Without your phone? Since when?"

"Will you calm down? I was outside watching the aurora."

"For three fucking hours?"

"You know, Dan, a little stargazing might actually help improve *your* vital humors."

He scoffed. "I doubt it."

"I do, too, as a matter of fact." Evan sat back against the pillows on her bed. "What's the job?"

"We got word tonight that POTUS is nominating Cawley to the court tomorrow."

"Cawley?" Evan took a few moments to let that sink in. The high court's tenuous balance of liberal and conservative ideologies had been knocked off-kilter when its moderate-voiced justice, Abel McIntyre, had died suddenly from a massive brain hemorrhage. Everyone knew the Republican-controlled administration was salivating at this prospect to tip the high court's balance— and bias—and lists of constructionist judges were circulating in the back rooms of Congress before McIntyre's body was cold. *But Cawley?* Cawley was a judicial lightning rod—a polarizing poster child of the far right. He'd never make it through the confirmation process. His appointment to the Third Circuit had nearly torn the Senate apart.

"Are you still there?" Dan's impatience had not abated.

"Of course. I'm just taking it in."

"No shit. This is one helluva curve ball." Evan could hear Dan rustling papers. "We have to move fast. This guy has a paper trail that's nine zillion miles long. But most of the stuff was already vetted during his circuit court appointment hearings, so it's old news. We need you to go deeper to find anything *not* already in the public domain. And you gotta do it at light speed. Already, dark money PACs are lining up to pump big bucks into PR campaigns to short-circuit any efforts to block his nomination."

"Dan? There's no way this guy will make it through the judiciary committee. He's a relic—not to mention a homophobe and a bigot."

"Do you read the fucking papers, Sleeping Beauty? Welcome to the reboot of Huxley's *Brave New Nightmare*."

"Okay. Whattaya got to get me started?"

"A couple of random leads and about ten thousand reams of paper."

"Great." Evan said. "I'm gonna need some extra help on this one."

"I know. Spool up your usual geeks. We'll pick up the tab."

"Who's *we?*"

"The DNC."

Evan thought his answer was too simple. That got her antenna up. "And?"

Dan didn't reply.

"Dan? I'm not taking this job until you tell me who else is paying the freight."

"Some outside donors who choose to remain nameless."

"Is the money clean?"

"Yeah." She heard him laugh. "Squeaky clean."

Dan made her crazy, but she knew he'd never lied to her before—not knowingly, at least.

"Okay." She said. "Send what you've got to my Signal account. I'll get started tomorrow."

"Great."

Evan started to hang up, but Dan wasn't finished talking.

"When's Stevie getting home?"

"The thirteenth. I sprang for a plane ticket. I didn't want her spending eighteen hours on the train from Albany."

Dan laughed. "Tell the truth. What you *didn't* want was her dragging two hundred pounds of dirty laundry home."

"No. I pretty much rely on you to keep my life filled with that—as our previous discussion would indicate."

"Touché. Let me know when she's settled so we can iron out holiday stuff."

Evan was curious. "You and Pippi Longstocking staying in town this year?"

Dan had remarried a year ago, and his new bride was an upstart millennial who worked for *Media Matters*. Evan enjoyed reminding Dan that his ebullient wife was all of six years older than his daughter.

"Will you cool it with this shit?" He lowered his voice. "Kayla really likes Stevie. They get along great."

"I don't doubt it. They probably go out for Mochalatta Chills after their hot yoga classes."

"I'm hanging up now."

That was unusual. Dan normally just hung up without telegraphing his intentions. She attempted to make amends for her sarcasm.

"I'll look over the files in the morning and let you know what I need. And I'll have Stevie call you as soon as she gets home so you can work out your times with her."

"Okay," he said. "Thanks."

He hung up.

Before Evan had a chance to call Julia, she got a text message from Tim.

Back at the Big House and safely locked into my cell.

She texted him back.

Come over on Friday night for dinner with us?

Sure. He wrote back. *What can I bring?*

Clarity, she typed. *And if that's not possible, then pick up a bottle of something wonderful.* She reconsidered. *Make that two bottles.*

Done. Thanks for tonight.

I didn't do anything.

I know. That's what I'm thanking you for.

I always strive to do the least I can do. See you Friday.

Julia was just about to give up on hearing from Evan, and turn in for the night. She'd been up since 5:30 that morning and had been sequestered in back-to-back meetings all day. She'd also been doing some long-distance crisis intervention by trying to talk one of their marquee authors off a contractual cliff.

Correction. *Another cliff.* If those negotiations went south, she'd probably be looking at a trip to Boston as soon as she got home.

She felt tired and cranky and just wanted to get the hell out of

15

Albuquerque. The winter storm that had rolled through Pennsylvania today had dumped nearly a foot of snow on New Mexico earlier in the week. Public transportation in the Duke City ground to a halt for two days, forcing Julia to extend her stay. Enough was enough. She was tired of the meetings and tired of this hotel. It wasn't that the room was spartan or unattractive. As far as hotel accommodations went, it was downright swanky. But after several nights, even the world's plushest mattress and panoramic views of the Sandia Mountains couldn't curb her homesickness.

Two more days. Then she'd be back in Philadelphia.

Unless she had to head to Boston.

It was increasingly clear to her that this job was becoming . . . onerous. After Andy's death, it hadn't taken her long to realize that the vacuum once filled by her work was shrinking. Most days, she wondered why she still did the job at all. She didn't have to. After her father's death last year, her mother, who had never had much interest in the family business, had pulled up stakes and moved permanently to Paris. That meant Julia no longer had anyone sitting in constant judgment of her job performance—or her life choices.

No one but Evan, who seemed determined to question and second-guess everything—especially things that related to their fledgling relationship.

Fledgling. That was a ridiculous misnomer. As far as Julia was concerned, they'd long since blown past the last off-ramp en route to Something Serious. It was Evan who continually slowed them down by dragging her Allbirds-clad feet and insisting that Julia wasn't ready for anything more . . . *consequential.*

Hardly. By Julia's calculation they'd crossed the relationship Rubicon the moment she opened the door to her parents' flat in London and saw a haggard and uncertain Evan standing there. That had been *her* personal epiphany—the moment she knew there was no going back on going forward with this cranky, angst-ridden, expletive-spewing bundle of contradictions. But Evan? She couldn't speak for Evan.

16

Evan was a tough nut to crack.

So, Julia did what she did. Or what she could do. She moved her office from New York to Philadelphia and took up temporary residence in her grandmother's ridiculously opulent townhouse on Delancey Place. The company maintained the coveted, Rittenhouse Square digs as a "guest quarters" for VIP authors and visiting board members. To Julia, that simply meant the asset remained on the Donne & Hale balance sheets as a high-dollar tax dodge—one of many she'd discovered since undertaking the mercurial process of unraveling her father's estate. Her plan was to sell the place—along with three other properties in the Northeast—as soon as she could secure her mother's required sign-off. That task would entail a trip to Paris, so Julia resolved to wait until she had financial matters sorted to a point that the arduous process of commandeering her mother's attention long enough to entice her to sign the paperwork could be maximized.

Julia's mother had little in common with the modest refinements of her Quaker ancestors. She loved her creature comforts just fine. Julia knew that getting her mother to agree to let go of the luxury properties would be a hard sell.

No pun intended.

She checked her watch. Nine forty-five. She had to be up and out by 6 a.m. It was unlikely Evan would call her back tonight. She opted to turn in. Ten minutes later, after she'd turned out the lights and climbed beneath the covers, her cell phone beeped. She retrieved it from the nightstand. It was a text message. From Evan.

Are you still awake?

Julia smiled and typed back. *Of course. The question is, why are you?*

Long night. Evan replied. *Tim was here. Then Dan called with a new job.*

Julia began to type her response, then thought better of it and called her.

Evan answered on the first ring. "We don't have to talk about it tonight. I don't want to bore you with the details."

"Please," Julia entreated. "Bore me. It'll be a nice break from the rest of my day."

"Things not going well?" Evan asked.

"I'm just tired. Up at 5:30 and stuck in meetings all day."

"I know you. That's not all."

Julia debated about whether or not to tell Evan she'd be stuck in Albuquerque two extra days. She bit the bullet and chose to get it over with. "You know the winter snowstorm that hit Chadds Ford today?"

"Yeah."

"Well, it originated here. And unlike the hale and hearty types who populate southeastern Pennsylvania, high-desert folk aren't as adept at snow removal."

"Which means?"

Julia could detect the flicker of suspicion in Evan's voice.

"Which means," she continued, "I'm going to be stuck out here until Wednesday."

Silence on the line.

"Are you still there?" Julia asked.

"Yeah," Evan mumbled.

"Don't pout. I can't help it."

"I know."

More silence on the line.

"You're pouting," Julia observed.

"Sorry. It's not you. I had a shitty night. This is just a fitting finish."

"Do you want to tell me about it?"

"Yes," Evan said, "but not tonight. We both need sleep. And my shoulder is killing me."

"Evan . . ."

"Don't start."

"Honey," Julia tried again. "It's not going to get better on its own. You know this."

Evan grunted. "I don't want to have this conversation right now."

"Okay. We'll add it to the agenda for our deferred mainte-nance discussion when I get home."

"Nice try." Julia could hear the sound of Evan shifting around—probably trying to get more comfortable. "Stevie comes home on Friday. I invited Tim for dinner."

"Oh, good—on both counts."

"I'm kind of assuming you'll join us?"

"Kind of?" Julia asked. "Try and stop me."

"No. Don't think I will." Evan yawned. "Dan and Pippi are asking about dates to kidnap Stevie over Christmas."

"Evan . . ."

"I know, I know. *Kayla.*"

"You can afford to be magnanimous," Julia pointed out. "You want Dan to be happy. And Stevie seems to enjoy spending time with them."

"Not as much as she enjoys spending time with us," Evan corrected.

"That may be true. But Stevie is grown up now, and we need to respect her choices—and her instincts."

"You seriously think a sixteen-year-old is grown up?"

"When she's your daughter, I do."

Evan laughed. "You're right. She ought to get hazardous duty pay."

"No comment."

"I miss you," Evan said.

Julia smiled and leaned back against a mound of pillows. "I miss you, too."

"Tell me again when you're coming home?"

"Wednesday. Morning," she added.

"I guess I can make it."

"I dearly hope so. I promise to make it worth your while."

"You dooooooo?" Evan dragged out the word to make it sound like it had five syllables.

Julia laughed. "Do you doubt me?"

"Not usually."

"My best advice would be not to start now."

"Noted." Julia heard Evan yawn again.

"We should both get some sleep," she said.

19

"Yeah." Evan yawned. "I'm gonna have to hit the ground running in the morning. Dan is sending me my weight in background files."

"Who's the pigeon?"

"*Pigeon?*" Evan laughed. "Are you watching *Noir Alley* on TCM again?"

"Shut up."

Evan was still chuckling. "The 'pigeon' is the president's nominee for the high court."

"Really?" Julia was impressed. "Who'd he name?"

"No one yet. But it's going to be J. Meyer Cawley. Dan said he's announcing it tomorrow."

"*Cawley?* I thought he was off the list?"

"So did everyone," Evan said. "Surprise."

"Wow." Julia was still reacting to the choice. "How much time do you have?"

"Not much. Less than two weeks."

"So, you'll be finished before Christmas." Julia was grateful for that bit of good news.

"With luck. Dan said the Senate is fast-tracking the nomination. I think they want it done and dusted before the recess."

"Why the rush?"

"I can only guess. They likely don't want time for anyone to uncover any tidbits that might be disqualifying."

"You mean apart from the entirety of his judicial record?"

"Yeah," Evan said. "Apart from that."

"It sounds like you'll be pretty busy. Sure you'll have time for Stevie and me?"

"The day I don't is the day they can put me in a box and bury me."

Julia rearranged her pillows.

She had a feeling they wouldn't be hanging up any time soon.

Chapter Two

The face of Edwin Miller was the last thing Evan expected to see when she started sifting through the voluminous document dump Dan sent her in the morning. But there he was, standing on the perimeter of a photo that included Cawley and half a dozen other formally-dressed men—one wearing clerical vestments—and some gangly teenage boys. The boys all wore ill-fitting suits, clearly dressed up for some kind of special occasion. There were Christmas decorations visible in the background. The group stood in front of a carved stone fireplace in what looked like a library or study. There were polished shelves lined with leather-bound books, and an elaborately framed painting displayed above the fireplace. Miller was a lot younger, of course, but Evan recognized him right away.

She peered at the note someone in Dan's office had pinned to the scan. *J. Meyer Cawley, Christmas 1995.* That had been ten years before Evan vetted the democrat for his successful U.S. Senate run in Pennsylvania.

And *twelve* years before Miller got busted for soliciting sex from a twelve-year-old boy in a Cincinnati hotel . . .

What the hell was he doing in this photo with Cawley? And where the hell was the picture taken? The photo had no other information, which surely meant Dan's staff had no idea, either. If so, where'd they get it?

The last time Evan had heard anything about Miller, he was still doing time in Hamilton County for importuning.

He was a class act.

Which made his presence in this photo with the blue-blooded Cawley even more curious.

She sent Dan a note through her Signal app.

Where'd your staff get the 1995 photo of Cawley with the group of men in penguin suits?

Ten minutes later, he wrote back.

You don't want to know. Suffice it to say it came through a back channel.

Back channel, her ass.

Marcus.

It had to be him. That slimeball had his crooked finger in every pile of dung.

I told you I wouldn't work for him again, she wrote back. *I meant it.*

Dan's reply was quick. *You aren't working for him. He's not involved in this. I told you that already.*

Why is he helping you? she asked.

Who the fuck knows? Dan wrote back. *And frankly, I don't really care. I'm on my way to Capitol Hill right now, so get back to me later if you have any more questions.*

She sat staring at the photo for another minute. She recalled that Miller hailed from a blue-collar family of steelworkers. He went to law school at Villanova on a scholarship, and worked for two years in the Cambria County DA's office before serving one term as mayor of Johnstown. It was a short hop from that gig to the State House in Harrisburg, followed quickly—thanks to Marcus—by a quantum leap up to the greener pastures of the U.S. Senate.

Evan went to her computer and pulled up the background report she'd prepared on Miller back in 2005. It didn't take her long to find the connection. Miller had clerked for the U.S. Court of Appeals for the Third Circuit before getting hired by the DA's office back home. She logged into her LexisNexis account and discovered that he'd served as one of Cawley's law clerks from 1994 to 1996.

Bingo.

It didn't necessarily follow that this connection meant anything—but if it wasn't significant, why would that buzzard Marcus have bothered to pass this teaser along to Dan? That asshole did nothing by accident. And Miller's ability to snag a plum clerkship like that was puzzling, too. She had pulled his academic records from Villanova. He was hardly a top-tier student—and Villanova grads weren't exactly in the same league as the ready pool of candidates from Yale, Harvard or Stanford where federal judges usually went shopping for clerks.

She picked up her cell phone and punched in a familiar number. The call rolled immediately to his answering machine.

"This is Rush," a husky voice growled. "Leave your name and number and I'll call you back."

"Ben? It's Evan. I've got a job and I need your help—*today.* Call me back."

Before she could disconnect, Ben's voice appeared on the line. "What's up?"

"You call screening?" she asked.

"Hell, yeah. My ex has been dogging the shit outta me for tuition money."

"Which one?" Evan asked.

"They're both bitches." Ben had two ex-wives, and two of his three daughters were still in college—one at Drexel and one at Dickinson. "But this time it's the fat-assed blonde who flits around on the six-figure, hybrid broomstick."

"How is Carla?"

"She's a cunt, just like the last time you asked about her." He coughed and cleared his throat. Evan could tell he was smoking again.

"You know, Ben . . . you could just *date* these women."

"Fuck you. And fuck her. What's the job?"

23

She'd obviously caught him at the right time. It was clear he needed the money.

"I'm doing some oppo research for the DNC," she told him. "I've got a lead, and I need you to follow up on it for me. Fast."

"Okay." Evan could hear him rustling some papers. "Shoot."

"Name's Edwin Miller. M-I-L-L-E-R. He's a former U.S. Senator from Pennsylvania. Last known whereabouts was River City Correctional Center in Cincinnati."

"Say what?"

Evan elaborated. "He was busted in a Cincinnati hotel for soliciting sex from a minor. That was back in 2008."

"Jesus Christ." She could hear Ben firing up a smoke. "Where do they fucking *find* these guys? Creeps R Us?"

"Sometimes you wonder."

"So?" Ben asked. "You just want to know where he is?"

"Right. And how I can contact him."

"Contact him? What the fuck for?"

"I don't know yet."

"Okay," Ben said. "I'll get Ping on it. That'll be a shit-ton faster than me trying to run his ass down."

"Ping" was a cyber expert who was a staple in Ben's pantry of oddballs. For years, Evan had assumed—wrongly—that Ping was a fifteen-year-old Asian kid who amused himself by hacking into his parents' Tesla and jacking up the algorithms.

Not so much.

Ping ended up being Ben's landlady—a savvy, seventy-four-year-old grandmother who lived in the apartment downstairs. Her name was Ruby Byrd. She hailed from Macon, Georgia—and, apart from being a cyber brainiac, she also made fabulous Hoppin' John.

"Lemme get going on this," Ben said. "Ping'll be back from church by nine." He laughed. "She's one of *your* people. I'll call you back later."

He hung up. Evan sat staring at the phone.

Who the hell are 'my people'?

24

Maya was annoyed.

This job stank.

And not in the usual ways these jobs were prone to stink.

No.

This one was especially malodorous. Ironic, considering her client.

But nothing unusual there.

She checked her watch. *Three more minutes.*

This wait was interminable. *And ridiculous.* Who still used pay phones? It was absurd. The things were relics. It was even more ridiculous to have to lurk about this kiosk in 30th Street Station, waiting on the sodded call. It'd already been long enough to read the same article in a discarded copy of *Business Week* four times. There wasn't enough stomach or inclination on the planet to induce another read. Who cared about Costco's decision to open its own damn chicken farm in Eastern Nebraska?

Two more minutes.

An obese man wearing an ill-fitting suit and smelling vaguely like urine and stale tobacco walked past—again. *One more trip past this bench, asshole, and I'll send you sprawling.*

Irksome pervert. He was just like uncle Omer.

Her silver pen resumed its staccato tap-tap-tap against an open notepad.

Finally, her watch alarm beeped.

Showtime.

The pay phone rang twice before she answered it.

"This is Maya."

Evan had been speed-reading back issues of *The Washington Post* and *The New York Times* for nearly two hours, trying to reacquaint herself with every contentious tidbit that had emerged about Cawley during his last round of confirmation hearings back in 1992.

There were quite a few to get through. J. Meyer Cawley had served on the staff of the White House Counsel's Office during the Bush 41 administration. There had been, however, a dearth of documents to prove what everyone later suspected: that Cawley had had more than a passing role in brainstorming the hail of blanket pardons distributed by outgoing President George H.W. Bush to all of his former cronies implicated in the Iran-Contra affair. Bush claimed executive privilege, and none of the confirming paperwork ever saw the light of day.

In retrospect, a smoking gun in hand wouldn't have mattered anyway. The Republican Party managed to take control of both houses of Congress in the 1994 midterm elections, and any lingering suspicions the Democrats had about Cawley's ascension to the Third Circuit became meaningless.

Cawley's personal life was about as salacious as an episode of *Ozzie and Harriet*. College at Georgetown. Law school at Yale, where he was a founding member of the Federalist Society. Married to the same woman for thirty-eight years. One grown daughter. A devout Roman Catholic. Membership in all the right civic organizations. Only drove American-made cars. Yadda, yadda, yadda.

Nothing much there.

His campaign for the federal judiciary did seem to benefit from several hefty independent expenditures deriving from a nonconnected Political Action Committee. There was some lingering mystery about who the PAC members were, but after Cawley's confirmation, nobody much cared anymore.

Until now.

When the campaign finance laws changed in 2010, it became legal for PAC donors to remain anonymous—and the newest campaign to back Cawley's nomination to the high court was likely to rake in a lot of money. Evan suspected that some of the usual suspects from his last go-round in '92 would still be on board behind the nominee. If so, getting her hands on just *one* of those names would probably help her run down the names of his mystery backers. And there might be some percentage in following those leads wherever they took her.

This was a perfect opportunity to call in a marker. Even the slimiest dark money groups from thirty years ago still had to file all the requisite paperwork with the Federal Elections Commission. Their members could bask in the shadows, but some poor schmoe always got tasked with signing his name on the disclosure forms.

She picked up her phone and called a familiar number.

"FEC Inspector General's Office. This is Sandy."

"Hi ya, hot stuff," Evan said. "Long time no talk."

There was a pause. "Evan?"

"Right first time. How's it going? You still working without a boss?"

Sandy lowered her voice. "Why are you calling me here?"

"One guess."

Sandy took a moment to reply. "What is it?"

Evan laughed. "Should I thank you for cutting to the chase?"

"I'm due a break. Let me call you back on my cell phone in five minutes."

"Works for me." Evan hung up.

Sandy and Evan had been classmates at Penn. They had even dated for a while—until Sandy realized that Evan was hopelessly incapable of monogamy.

Sandy's regrettable spouse was a sometime government contractor who had an unhappy tendency to dip her fingers into other people's cookie jars. The last time she'd been caught, she was staring down her nose at some hard time. That was until Sandy contacted Evan and begged her to step in and talk her accuser off a ledge. Lucky for Sandy, that wasn't hard to do. It turned out Evan had a file full of creative accounting "oversights" the firm accusing Sandy's spouse had enjoyed during its own heyday working for a client of Evan's on Capitol Hill. She made a few calls, and Sandy's burgeoning domestic nightmare quietly went away.

That was *after* her sticky-fingered spouse repaid the hefty stash of bogus fees she'd gleaned via some creative line-item charges.

In exactly five minutes, Evan's phone rang. She wasn't surprised about Sandy's punctuality. That had been another nail in their relationship coffin. Evan had been notoriously ... *casual* ... about commitments back in those days.

Evan answered the phone.

"Look. You helped me out of a jam and I'm grateful," Sandy said without preamble. "So, just tell me what you want and let's get this over with."

"That's easy," Evan explained. "I need a name."

"Whose name?"

"Well, that's the tricky part. I don't know. There was a non-connected PAC back in 1992 called 'Citizens for Integrity in Government.' They put a lot of money into several causes that were darlings of the far right—including the nomination of J. Meyer Cawley to the Third Circuit Court of Appeals. I need to know who filed their paperwork with your office."

"Are you crazy?" Sandy sounded incredulous. "You know I can't disclose that."

"I can think of a lot of things you can't do, love chunks. But getting me a name isn't one of them."

"Fuck you."

Evan laughed. "I've been hearing that a lot lately."

Silence on the line.

"When do you need it?" Sandy asked.

"Today would be nice."

Sandy balked at Evan's request. "You don't want much, do you?"

"How long could it take? Don't you use computers in your office? Or have all these government shutdowns reduced you to storing everything on cuneiform tablets?"

"All right," Sandy said. "I'll call you back in an hour."

"Thanks."

"Evan?"

"Yeah?"

"This is the *last* time. I give you this name and we're quits. Okay?"

Evan thought that was reasonable. "Sure."

Sandy hung up.

It didn't take her an hour. Evan's phone rang twenty minutes later.

"That was fast."

"Arthur Squires." Sandy didn't mince words.

Evan was surprised she had found the information so fast. "Got a business name to go with that?" She grabbed a pad and pencil.

"Smith, Martin, Squires & Andersen, PA. That's *Andersen* with two 'e's.' The PAC was set up in Delaware by this legal firm. And before you ask, their offices are in Philadelphia—and, no, I don't have the address. You can find it yourself."

"Yeah. I can find it. Thanks for your help, Sandy."

"Go to hell. You know I could lose my job for this—and possibly go to jail."

"Relax. No one's gonna find out."

"Well, see that they don't. And Evan?"

"Yeah?"

"I mean it." Sandy's voice was like ice. "We're even now. I don't owe you anything else, so don't come asking."

"No worries. I won't. You give my regards to Nellie."

Sandy hung up.

Evan sat holding her cell phone for a second before tossing it down on her desk.

Guess I can cross that resource off my list . . .

She shrugged and studied the sheet of paper where she'd scrawled the names. *Well, Mr. Squires. I wonder what else you can teach me about the honorable Justice Cawley?*

Only one way to find out.

She called Ben Rush to arrange a little after-hours visit to the attorney's office.

Tria Café West on Spruce Street was humming. Good thing they had a reservation.

Maya was halfway through a second glass of wine. And an indifferent wine it was, for the prices this place charged. *This is definitely not a venue I'd have picked for this meeting.*

But choice of location was not an available option. Mr. Zucchetto had been clear about that when he forwarded the arrangements. And that was probably because this place was in a location where he could be sure no one would recognize either of them.

Fat chance anyone I know would be stopping off here . . .

But Mr. Zucchetto was wise to embrace one certain axiom: your sins would always find you out—no matter how hard you tried to cover your tracks.

Was that outcome ever certain to bear out with the suspects in *this* little quagmire. Zucchetto and his "client" had one hell of a mess on their hands. And it was clear that he and his associates were willing to pay top dollar to have it cleaned up. That's where Maya came in.

That's where Maya *always* came in.

She tried another sip of the wine, a Tannat that was advertised as an "unsung treasure from Uruguay."

If there actually is a god, this wine never will find its voice.

"Excuse me?" It was the host. "I believe your party has arrived." He indicated a stout man, hovering near the South 12th Street entrance. He wore a chalk stripe suit and Borsalino hat. He looked like a caricature of a movie mobster. *Fitting.*

Maya nodded, and the host gestured for the man to approach her table.

"Miss Jindal?" the round man asked. When Maya nodded, he sat down on the vacant chair. "I appreciate your punctuality and apologize for my own tardiness." He removed his hat and handed it to the host. "Will you kindly hang this up for me?"

The host nodded and walked back toward his station, carrying the hat somewhat awkwardly. Maya was amused by his predicament. It didn't seem likely that many patrons of Tria Café shared the same penchant for exotic millinery.

"Have you ordered?" Zucchetto asked.

"Just the wine."

She saw her companion's nostrils flare a bit.

"I think I'll pass," he said.

"Wise decision." Maya passed him one of the two menus. "The cheese board looks palatable."

He scanned the menu. "Lighter fare is fine," he said. "We won't be tarrying over lunch."

"I didn't expect so."

Their server arrived and they gave their orders. Mr. Zucchetto also ordered a Pellegrino with a twist. No ice.

When the server departed, Mr. Zucchetto reached inside his impressively tailored jacket and withdrew a fat envelope. He passed it across the table to her.

"This contains some additional information to get you started."

Maya took the envelope and slipped it into the outside pocket of the messenger bag tucked beneath their table.

"Aren't you going to look at it?" Zucchetto asked.

"No. I don't expect to have any questions about the contents."

"Suit yourself. I'd imagine you already have your own reliable sources."

Maya was intrigued. "What makes you think that?"

Zucchetto raised a grizzled eyebrow full of wiry, white hair. "Your ... CV made for a most elucidating read."

"My *CV?*" Maya laughed. "I suppose that's one way to describe it."

"Do you dispute its contents?"

"Not having had the privilege to examine it, I hardly know how to answer."

"It does you no disservice."

"That's an opinion sure to brook disagreement in certain sectors. Yours, for example."

Zucchetto seemed unfazed by the remark. "My 'sector,' as you refer to it, is more concerned with privacy, propriety and the preservation of decorum."

"As the impressive number of zeros tidily arrayed before the decimal point in your kind offer would suggest."

"I have not previously been led to understand that the motivational particulars of an assignment hold much concern for you." Zucchetto folded his arms. "Was I misinformed?"

31

"Oh, no." Maya took another sip of the inferior wine. "I'm just making idle chatter until our meals arrive."

"Am I boring you?" he asked.

"Not in the slightest. In fact, I find myself excessively diverted."

The flippant remark appeared to annoy him. "I suppose I should be grateful you find this all so amusing."

"That's certainly one way you can interpret my indifference to your *motive*."

"In this case, I don't have a motive. I have a client with a cause."

She smiled at him. "In this particular instance, I'd argue that's a distinction without merit."

Zucchetto's nostrils flared again. Maya surmised it wasn't related to the wine this time. That was fine. Pious hypocrites like Zucchetto were beneath contempt. They were like maggots—fattened from feasting on the decay of their self-proclaimed scruples. *And time?* Time was a great ally.

"The arc of the moral universe is long," she quoted, "but it bends toward justice."

Zucchetto seemed confused. "I don't take your meaning."

"I'm not surprised," she agreed. "But in this case, it isn't *my* meaning. It's Martin Luther King's."

Zucchetto didn't reply.

Maya was amused by their exchange. She was no expert on the moral universe. That much was well established. But there was little doubt that people like Mr. Zucchetto would one day reap their just rewards.

They all would.

Evan was just about to wrap up for the day when she got a text message from Ping.

Got some information for you. Ben said I should contact you directly.

Evan texted back. *Got time to talk right now?*

Sure.

32

Ping picked up on the first ring. "Hey, Evan. So, I got some details on Miller."

"Great." Evan pulled her notepad over. "Shoot."

"For starters, he's outta prison."

"Good for him."

"Well," Ping continued. "Maybe not."

"Meaning?"

"Meaning he's serving out the rest of his most recent stretch as an inpatient at the Warren State Hospital. He's been in there for nearly two years."

Evan was confused. "State Hospital?"

"Yeah. It's an asylum."

"Asylum?" Evan was surprised. "Was he committed?"

"Uh huh. By the prison."

"What the hell for?"

Ping chuckled. "You don't think being a serial child molester is enough of a reason?"

"For prison, sure. But an asylum? There must've been some mitigating circumstances."

"Oh, there were. Let's see . . ." Evan could hear Ping flipping pages. "According to the clerk I talked to in the warden's office at Cambria County, he was beat up several times. One time, he had his head bashed in with a plumber's wrench. He nearly died from that one, and he came out of it with a traumatic brain injury. She said that caused some kind of permanent psychosis."

"Jesus Christ. That can actually happen?"

"I guess so. The clerk said he's not violent, just crazy. And," Ping added, "don't you blaspheme when you're talkin' to me. I ain't Ben Rush."

"Sorry. Is he ever gonna get out?"

"I got nothin'. The family could decide to move him to another place when his prison sentence is finished."

"How long will that be?"

"Another three years. He was serving a five-year stretch for a third offense."

33

Good god, Evan thought. "What a prince."

"Yeah. No kidding. I went ahead and tried to find out where his wife is. *Ex*-wife, I should say. She divorced his sorry ass and moved to upstate New York during his first stretch in Cincinnati. There hasn't been any contact there—with her or with their kids."

"Hard to blame her for that. Do you know if this hospital keeps him locked up?"

"I don't think so." Evan could hear Ping firing up a smoke. The click of her Zippo lighter was unmistakable. Evan always found this habit to be a contradiction for someone who led such a Christ-centered life. "He's in a secure unit," Ping continued. "But like they said—he's crazy, not dangerous."

Evan gave a bitter laugh. "Unless you're a fourteen-year-old boy."

"Well. Maybe those beatings knocked some sense into him? Could be coming to terms with what he did explains why he went off his rocker. The Lord has His ways of correcting deviant behavior."

"I doubt it."

It was Ping's turn to laugh. "Evangeline? You doubt everything."

"You spend too much time listening to Ben."

"No. I just don't twist myself up in knots trying to *understand* everything. Sometimes, things don't have any greater meaning. They just mean what they mean."

"You learn that in Sunday School, Ping?"

"Maybe. A little bit of God's Word wouldn't hurt you, Evan Reed."

"Sadly, I think that bus has left the station."

"News flash. No bus can outrun the Word of God."

Evan chuckled. "So where is this hospital and how do I get there?"

"It's in North Warren, about seventy miles east of Erie."

Shit. Too far to drive in one day. "Okay. I can probably get a puddle-jumper from Philadelphia. Thanks, Ping. I owe you."

34

"That's what Ben said. You call if you need anything else."

"You know I will."

"You be careful at that place." Ping took a long drag off her cigarette. "It has bad juju."

"It's an asylum. I don't think any of them have great Zagat ratings."

"No." Ping added. "That's *not* what I mean. This place has *ghosts*."

"Ping . . ."

"Hey. Don't take my word for it. I did research. You know . . . what you pay me for? All kinds of paranormal stuff goes on there. That whole place is creepy. Take a gander at some of the photos people have posted online. And there've been lots of mysterious deaths, too. Tales of all kinds of torture and secret medical experiments on patients. Most of 'em are long dead and buried in the cemetery there—never claimed by their families. They say there's a whole spider's web of abandoned, underground tunnels that connect all the buildings, too. Ghost hunters *love* that place. I watched some of the YouTube videos. It's bad news."

"I won't argue that it is for Miller."

"Not just Miller. It was bad news for a whole lot of poor souls before him. They went in and never came out."

"Well, don't worry about me," Evan reassured her. "I plan to be home in time for dinner."

"Just see to it that you are."

"Yes, ma'am."

Evan heard a faint ding on the line.

"That's my oven," Ping said. "I'm baking pies."

Evan had a real sweet tooth, and Ping's desserts were legendary. "Save me a slice?"

"You don't know what kind they are."

"Who cares?"

"Okay. I'll wrap some up for you and Ben so you'll have something to eat while you're waiting on bail money."

Bail money? Evan took the bait. "Which translated means?"

"When you get busted for porch climbing."

"Oh?" Evan teased. "Ben told you about our little moonlight outing?"

"Yes, he did. And I think you're both idiots."

"How come?"

"Because neither of you two geniuses could find your own behinds with flashlights and GPS."

Evan laughed. "Come on, Ping. Have a little faith."

"Honey, I've got nothing *but* faith—and common sense."

"Well, in that case, better box up some leftovers, too."

Ping clucked her tongue. "I gave up on Ben Rush a long time ago. That man is like a fifteen-car pileup on the Schuylkill—and every bit as oily. But I'd think you'd have better sense. Especially with your little girl to think of." Evan could make out some clattering sounds—probably Ping removing her pies from the oven. "Which reminds me. Desiree wants to know if you three will come by to eat with us before Watch Night service. I think it's the only way she'll agree to go to church."

Ping's youngest granddaughter, Desiree, and Stevie were the same age. They'd become fast friends after meeting two summers ago at a graduation party for Ben's oldest daughter. Since then, the girls were in constant communication with each other. She strongly suspected the pair would end up applying to the same colleges.

Evan understood that Ping's invitation was a big deal. Watch Night service on December 31 was one of the holiest nights of the year at Ping's AME church. It commemorated the night a hundred and fifty-seven years ago, when both freed and enslaved African Americans huddled together in prayer, waiting for President Lincoln to sign the Emancipation Proclamation.

Evan recalled that Ping always put on quite a spread. "Are you cooking?" she asked.

"Yes I am."

"Then we'll be there. And, Ping? Stevie will want to be sure that Desiree is showing up, too."

"She will be if her mother has any of the sense God gave her."

That seemed like a loaded comment. "What's up with Phyllis?" Phyllis was Ping's daughter.

"Well," Ping began, "that girl just lets those children run wild."

"Ping. Desiree is nearly seventeen."

"Seventeen going on thirty. You mark my words: that girl is gonna end up in *trouble*."

"I don't think so. Desiree is a good girl."

"Good girl or bad girl is irrelevant. It's *boys* that cause all the heartache. All of 'em are out there wavin' their junk around."

"Their *what?*"

"You know what I'm talking about. You have a baby boy—you only have to worry about *one* penis. You have a baby girl—you have to worry about *all* of them."

Evan found it hard to disagree. "Check," she said. "I'll tell Stevie to expect her. And I promise to be careful, too."

"See to it that you are. And that means watching your back at that crazy house—*and* staying away from any second-story work with that fool, Ben Rush." Ping hung up.

Evan actually thought about Ping's warnings for a couple of seconds. But it was too late.

Besides . . . what could go wrong?

Ghost hunters. What a bunch of bullshit.

Chapter Three

Confession at St. Margherita was held every Saturday, and on fluctuating weekdays according to the liturgical calendar. Today was the celebration of the Immaculate Conception of the Blessed Virgin Mary, and Tim drew the short straw. That meant he was sitting for the sacrament of confession from 3:30 to 4:45 p.m. He didn't expect much of a turnout. Weekday confessions were mostly attended by octogenarians who habitually received the sacrament three or four times a month. They were what the priests called "tea baggers"—they dipped in and out with dispatch, usually so they could be first in line for blue plate specials at the Melrose Diner.

By 4:30, he'd only had four penitents, confessing to a litany of mostly rank and file "I had impure thoughts about the bag boy at Kowalski's Market" type of venial sins. That was okay. He wasn't in the best frame of mind to grapple with any grander demons.

All of that changed in a hurry when the paneled door on the other side of the confessional opened and closed.

"Bless me, Father, for I have sinned."

The voice belonged to a young man—probably a teenager. He didn't say anything else after his declaration, so Tim proceeded with the standard prompt. "How long has it been since your last confession?"

"Um. Well . . ."

"Yes?" Tim asked.

"A while. Maybe a couple of years."

"That's a long time," Tim commented. "Did something prevent you from making this confession sooner?"

"No. *Yes.* Sort of . . ."

"Would you like to explain what you mean?"

"I would. But it's hard."

Tim sat back against the narrow, padded bench. "That's okay. You can take your time. Consider me your captive audience."

The young man gave what sounded to Tim like a nervous laugh. "They told me you were cool."

"They?" Tim asked.

"People," he said. "Friends. In another parish."

"Are you from another parish, too?"

"Is that okay?"

"Of course, it is. God doesn't care about your zip code."

"No. But they say he cares about other stuff."

Tim was impressed. "'They' were right about that part. Do you want to start by talking about what you think God *does* care about?"

"Okay." Tim could see the shadow on the opposite side of the screen move as the young man shifted around on the bench. "It's my brother. He's . . . Look. I don't know about this for sure. But I think one of the priests at our church is doing shit . . ." He caught himself. "Oh, man . . . I'm sorry. *Stuff.* To him."

Tim felt sick inside. "Stuff? What kind of stuff?"

"You know. *Stuff.* Sexual stuff. I think it's happened a couple of times."

Dear God. "Has your brother confided in you about this?"

"No. And when I came right out and asked him about it, he wouldn't answer me."

Yeah. That's not a surprise. "What makes you sure something happened?"

His next words made Tim's blood run cold.

"Because he's not the only one."

Tim took a moment to try and compose himself. They'd all had training about how to handle revelations like this when they were brought forward. He knew what he was supposed to say. But the words just wouldn't come.

The young man wasn't finished talking. "The same thing happened to me."

"I am so, so sorry." Tim closed his eyes. *What am I doing?* They all had a script. This wasn't part of it. He felt like he was swimming upstream in a surging river of broken promises. A universe of disjointed words and canned phrases rushed past him as he flailed and tried not to sink beneath this flood of failures. *His flood of failures.* The Church's. It belonged to all of them. *None of the words they'd been taught were right. None of them were enough.* "Tell me what I can do to help you—and your brother," he said.

"I don't . . ." The young man hesitated. "I don't know what you mean."

"I mean I want to help you. Help *him*. I want us to find a way to make this stop. Together."

"I'm . . . I don't know."

"This should never have happened. Not to you, and not to him. It isn't right. It isn't what God wants and it isn't what the Church wants." Tim took a deep breath. "But we live in a real world surrounded by real people. Many of them are deeply flawed. And they do things they shouldn't. They hurt other people. And sometimes, they succeed in that because of a compact of silence we keep without really understanding why we do it. Speaking the truth, as you have just done, takes great courage. To reach a place where we can come forward and throw off the fear and shame that hold us hostage is a gift from God—perhaps the greatest gift." Tim stopped speaking and waited a moment to see if the young man would reply.

"What happened . . . does it make me queer?"

"Are you worried about that?" Tim asked.

"Yeah. I think that's what people will say."

"It doesn't work that way." Tim chose his words carefully. "Nothing can make us be someone or something we aren't. We just are who we are."

40

"Do you really believe that?"

Did he believe it? "Yes," Tim answered. "I more than believe it. I *know* it. I want you to know it, too—inside, where it matters. And maybe understanding that will help you to let go of some of your fear."

"Okay. I can try."

"You came here today to tell someone," Tim suggested. "To tell me. Do you think you're ready to come forward and try to change things?"

"I'm not sure. Maybe?" The young man shifted around inside the tiny space. "I don't know."

Tim knew his inquisition needed to end. He couldn't pressure the young man any more—that was the last thing he needed. What he most needed was to leave here today believing he'd found a safe place.

A safe place in the Church? What a joke . . .

"Would you like to say a prayer?" Tim asked.

"That's why I came here. To ask for forgiveness."

"I won't withhold a sacrament from you, but you have confessed to no wrongdoing."

"Not telling anyone isn't wrong?"

"Not when your silence proceeds from fear."

There was another moment of silence. "Can I come back here and talk to you again?"

"Yes. Any time you want. My name is Father Tim Donovan. You may call the Church office to find out when I am next hearing confession. Or you can just call me directly and we can find another way to talk."

"Okay. Thanks."

"Would you like to pray together, now?" Tim asked.

"I guess so."

Tim removed his purple stole and kissed it before setting it down on top of his breviary. "We will ask God to give you strength." *I am the one who needs forgiveness . . .*

Evan's commuter flight landed in Erie a few minutes after 10 a.m. She'd lucked out and got a nonstop connection on American. There were only eight or ten people on the small regional jet. Most of them looked like tired, mid-level management types. She had no idea what kind of business venture would send anyone to a decaying rust-belt town, sagging into one of the bleakest spots on the lake.

It didn't matter. The damn ticket still cost more than six hundred bucks.

But that was Dan's problem, not hers.

After her plane landed, she made her way through the small airport to the Hertz counter located inside the terminal. The place was a shithole, but at least the rental cars were on-site. In thirty minutes, she was in her Ford Escape and heading east on I-86 toward Chautauqua Lake in New York State. From there, it was a straight shot south, back into Pennsylvania and the hospital campus in North Warren.

There was a fair amount of snow on the ground, so Evan paid the upcharge to switch to an SUV. It was a good decision. The roads in and around Erie were mostly clear, but the closer she got to Chautauqua, the sketchier conditions became. The sky was looking pretty ominous, too, and the temperatures were hovering right around the freezing mark. She hoped her 5:54 p.m. flight back to Philly didn't get canceled. The last thing she wanted—after having to see Edwin Miller again—was getting stuck here overnight.

After she'd passed some clusters of little, rainbow-colored cottages dotting the access roads leading to the rarified waters of Chautauqua, she turned off the main highway and headed south on a two-lane road that had seen a lot of hard use. It was more potholes than pavement, which reminded her a lot of the streets in her old neighborhood.

What the hell is it with the roads in this part of the country? Evan veered around another crater that stretched across more than half of her lane. *Somebody's brother-in-law must be making a killing on all these half-assed repaving contracts.*

It was spitting snow when she reached the Pennsylvania line and she discovered, too late, that the driver-side windshield wiper on her Ford Escape was for shit.

Great.

She pulled over at a TrueValue Hardware store located in a mostly abandoned strip center in a small town called Sugar Grove, to see if they might have a replacement set that would fit. While she was waiting on a tall man with a badly pockmarked face to "check in back," she pulled out her phone to see if she had any messages.

She had three missed calls. One from Ben Rush and two from her daughter. It was unusual for Stevie to call her twice. Normally, she'd just text or leave a message. Evan walked to the front of the store, close to its grimy, plate-glass window, to return Stevie's calls. She hated it when people in stores talked on their cell phones—always too loudly—and only made the exception to do so herself because she appeared to be the only customer in the bleak place, which, judging by the amount of dust collecting on most of its inventory, didn't see much consumer traffic.

Stevie didn't answer, so Evan left a message telling her she was traveling, but would leave her phone turned on while she was in the car.

She hoped nothing was wrong. As soon as she'd disconnected, her phone rang. Evan smiled.

"Hey, kiddo. What's up?"

"Hey, Mama Uno. Not much," Stevie said. "Sorry I didn't get the phone before the voicemail kicked in. I'm doing laundry."

"Is that why you're calling? Did you run out of quarters?"

"As if. These machines take debit cards, now."

"And I thought cultural progress peaked with microwave popcorn."

"You're such a nerd." Evan could hear rumbling noises in the background. Probably dryers. "Hey," Stevie continued, "I wanted to let you know my flight times changed. I got the alert from Southwest this morning."

"Good change or bad change?" Evan asked.

"I guess that depends on your point of view. My flight now arrives in Philly at 2:45 instead of 5:20."

"That's a good change. Earlier is better."

"Can you still pick me up?"

Could she? Evan had to think about it. If she drove to the airport and back at that time of day, they'd be eating dinner at midnight. "How about I see if Tim can get you? He's coming for dinner Friday night, too."

"That'd be cool. He owes me twenty bucks, anyway, so I'll make him stop at Wawa and buy me a couple of Shorties."

"You want twenty dollars' worth of turkey sandwiches?"

"Duh," Stevie said. "School in upstate New York."

"Right. My bad. I consigned you to life in a food desert."

"Besides . . . didn't you say you were *making* dinner?"

"Yeah."

"So I'll need some *real* food to get me through whatever bizarre-o, free-range forage fest you have planned."

"Remind me to cut your allowance in half." Evan thought about something Stevie had said. "Why does Tim owe you twenty bucks?"

"It's a Catholic thing. You wouldn't get it."

"Right. Of *course,* I wouldn't."

"Are Dad and Kayla coming, too?"

"For what?"

"Hello? Earth to Reed. For dinner on Friday night."

"Nope. Just us. Meaning you, me, Tim—and Julia."

"Nice." Stevie's voice resonated with *that* tone—the special one she reserved for Julia. It was downright . . . reverential.

"Is that okay with you?" Evan asked.

"Is what okay with me?"

"Julia? Dinner? With us?"

"You're such a dork, Mom." Evan heard a loud buzzing sound on the line. "That's mine. I gotta go or my whites will get all wrinkled."

Evan was proud of the finite list of things she'd somehow managed to get right about parenting—but Stevie's keen load sense when it came to doing laundry had to rank as one of her greatest maternal successes.

"See you on Friday," she said. "I love you."

"Love you too, Mama Uno." Stevie hung up.

Evan walked back toward the cash register just as the gangly man, who looked like an auto store version of Ichabod Crane, emerged from behind a tattered curtain carrying an elongated box, yellowed with age.

"Found some that might work," he said. "I can put 'em on for you, but there ain't no refunds if you try 'em and they're wrong."

"How will we know if they're wrong?" Evan asked. She didn't really care about a refund. Now she was just curious.

Ichabod scratched his chin. "They might scratch the windshield glass or fly off on the highway."

That sounded like fun. Evan looked back out the dirty front window. The snow was gaining in intensity. An overnight stay in North Warren or, with luck, back in Erie was looking like a real possibility now.

What the hell?

"Let's do it. They only need to last for about two hours."

Ichabod nodded and pulled the ginormous wiper blades out of the tattered box. Evan thought they probably were designed to fit a '56 Packard.

She paid for the purchase, and followed Ichabod out into the swirling snow.

The small town of North Warren had all the earmarks of an afterthought.

It was nothing but an outpost on the Conewango Creek that had once welcomed the droves of low-wage laborers who flocked to the remote, northwestern county in search of work in the area's booming lumber and oil drilling ventures. A couple of miles downstream, where the Conewango joined forces with the Allegheny River, mill owners and oil barons reposed in rarified Greek Italianate and Second Empire mansions that lined the broad avenues

45

of Warren—the small borough's wealthier namesake to the south. That economic line of demarcation remained in force until a couple of enterprising farm families in North Warren sold off several large tracts of land that, in 1880, became the site of the Warren State Hospital for the Insane. In its heyday, the hospital housed more than 2,500 inpatients. Today, more than a hundred years after the area's once-thriving industries had played out and moved on, the asylum had only 215 residents—and Edwin Miller was one of them.

Evan navigated her way past the clusters of ramshackle houses and strip malls that peppered the small town to find the hospital's imposing main entrance on North State Street. It fronted a pretty stretch of land that ran along the west bank of the Conewango Creek. She turned in and drove up the long, tree-lined drive that led to the main building—a gargantuan, twin-towered, stone and masonry Italianate creation that gave Evan the heebie jeebies. She recalled the apocryphal tales about this joint that Ping had hinted at. At the time, she had rejected it as hyper-sensationalized urban myth. Now, she wasn't so sure.

She found a parking space near the main entrance and walked toward a building that seemed to brood over its surroundings. She looked up through the swirling snow at its pair of dark towers that scratched at the sky like bony fingers.

Jesus Christ. If you weren't crazy when you came in here, you sure as fuck would be before you got out.

Inside, the cavernous lobby was lavishly furnished with formal-looking settees and delicate antiques. There were a couple of hideous silk flower arrangements large enough to dominate the altar of a mega church. Gladiolus, snowball hydrangeas and lilies—all in vibrant colors that didn't occur naturally in any garden environment she knew about.

She guessed that nobody spent much time tarrying out here.

Across the lobby, a flashy, middle-aged woman with platinum blond hair and a very perky set of boobs sat behind a large, antique mahogany desk. Evan walked across the polished parquet floor to greet her.

"May I help you?" the woman asked. She wore brightly colored, harlequin-style glasses and had unnaturally blue eyes. Her name tag read "Shirley."

"Hello. Evan Reed to see Edwin Miller. I phoned ahead."

The woman clicked through some screens on her computer monitor and stopped on one. "Yes. I see your name here. I'll get an aide to take you to Mr. Miller. I just need you to sign in." She pushed a thick, open logbook toward Evan. "It shouldn't take long."

"Thank you." Evan signed her name to the log. The last visitor appeared to have signed in weeks earlier. *Not much traffic at this joint.* Shirley handed her an adhesive-backed visitor badge.

While she waited on the attendant to take her to Miller, she wandered away from the information desk and perused a bunch of framed photographs that dominated a narrow stretch of wall beside a set of double doors. *Locked doors.* The photos were all of middle-aged men. Generations of them—probably dating back to 1880, judging by some of the facial hair. She leaned closer to read some of the tiny plaques beneath the photos. *Ahhhh.* They were all the various directors of the hospital. The mostly black-and-white images stretched from mid-thigh height to near ceiling. She did a double-take and squinted when she noticed that one of the photographs looked strange. It was in its frame— *sideways.*

What the hell? This guy must've been a serious asshole . . .

She was about to ask Shirley about it when one of the locked double doors clicked open, and a young man wearing blue scrubs leaned around it to address her.

"Evan Reed?" he asked.

"Yes." She nodded.

"Follow me, Miss Reed." He held the door open for her. "I'll take you to Mr. Miller."

They entered a long corridor that led past a bunch of doors with small overhead signs. They all appeared to be offices. The corridor made a sharp dogleg to the right and terminated at another security door. The attendant wore an ID badge on a

47

lanyard, and passed it over a proximity reader. The door unlocked and they entered the "male" unit. It looked much the same as the office wing. Most of the doors were open. There weren't a lot of windows, except the ones she could see in the patient rooms— and none at the end of the hallway, which she thought was an odd architectural feature.

The attendant led her to a smallish lounge area that sat off to the left of the next dogleg, and another set of locked doors. Evan guessed those doors led to another patient unit. There were three men in the lounge. Two were watching *Fixer Upper* on HGTV, and the third man was sitting by himself at a small table, working a jigsaw puzzle.

Miller.

She nearly didn't recognize him. His hair had gone completely white and he'd lost a ton of weight. He also had a nasty-looking scar that cut across his forehead like a badly stitched seam.

The attendant pointed him out. "That's Mr. Miller," he said. "When you're finished with your visit, just pick up the phone over there by the water fountain. It'll ring at the desk. Tell them you've been visiting with Miller and are ready to leave. Someone will come to escort you out."

"That's it?" Evan asked. "Anything else I need to know about him?"

"Not really. He's pretty harmless. Mostly just mutters and works that puzzle he brought with him from prison. He finishes it, then takes it all apart and does it all over again." He gave Evan a short nod. "You should be fine."

Evan doubted that. She didn't have the greatest track record with the former senator.

"Okay," she said. "Thanks."

"Sure." He turned and left her to her own devices.

She took a deep breath and approached the small table where Miller sat, staring at his piles of puzzle pieces.

"Hello, Eddie."

Miller blinked up at her. Evan couldn't tell if he recognized her or not. To be fair, they'd only met a couple of times, and two

48

of those encounters hadn't been very cordial. She remembered him having bright, hazel-colored eyes. But now they just looked dull, like all the color had bleached out.

He didn't respond to her greeting.

"Do you mind if I sit down here?" she asked.

He didn't reply, so she carefully pulled out a molded plastic chair and sat down across from him. The table top was covered with little piles of puzzle pieces. There was also a bright green plastic bowl, half full of small candy bars. Snickers. Milky Way. Twix. It looked like a stash of leftover Halloween candy. A pile of wrappers littered the table directly in front of him. It triggered a memory. *Miller had a sweet tooth.* She recalled commenting about his penchant for candy bars in her vetting report to Marcus. "He's always eating candy bars," she wrote. "Probably uses them as bait to attract the kids he preys on."

Fat lot of good that insight did . . .

"What kind of puzzle are you working?" she asked him.

He held up a tiny piece and showed it to her.

Evan studied it and the section of the puzzle he'd already assembled. It looked like part of a painting—one she thought she recognized from someplace. She could make out the tops of a couple of heads, and part of a red building. The real mystery was the way Miller was working the puzzle—from the center out. Granted, she didn't have that much experience with jigsaw puzzles. But Stevie had loved them when she was a kid, and she believed that the easiest way to complete them was to work from the outside in. "The edges with the flat sides and the corner pieces are the best ones to start with," she explained. "Once you get all those in place, it's a lot easier to figure the rest out."

Apparently, Miller favored a different approach.

"Is this a painting?" she asked.

He nodded. "They're little stars."

"Really? From here, they look like people."

He regarded her like he was seeing her for the first time. "I know you."

Evan nodded. "You did once." She noticed that Miller had

something clenched in his left hand. "What are you holding onto?" she asked.

He opened his palm and showed her the tiny puzzle piece that rested there. It was sky blue and had two flat sides. "The end."

"The end? Of the puzzle?"

"Of everything," he said.

Evan wasn't sure what to say. Maybe talking with him was like playing the slots? You always stuck with a hot machine. "Do you like this puzzle?"

He nodded again. "It makes sense."

"It's good when we find things that make sense. A lot of things in life don't."

"I know you." He looked at her with a blank expression. "You found out."

Evan was surprised. "I found out about what?"

"Aquarius."

"Aquarius?"

"The stars." Miller looked up and seemed to study a nonexistent sky.

Okay. This was going off the rails. "You mean the zodiac? The constellation?"

"Aquarius got punished. He carried the water but he got punished."

Miller took another mini-candy bar out of the bowl and unwrapped it.

Evan could tell he was running out of steam. The machine was going cold. Time to try something different.

"Eddie?"

He stared at her while he swallowed the Snickers bar—apparently without chewing it. Evan watched the bulge of chocolate work its way down his throat.

"Do you remember working as a clerk for Judge Cawley?" she asked. "In Philadelphia? Right after you got out of law school at Villanova?"

Miller's expression didn't change. It was still as empty and vague as it had been when she first sat down.

"Judge Cawley?" Evan repeated. "J. Meyer Cawley."

"Jupiter punished me," he said.

Evan wasn't sure what he meant. "*Who* punished you?"

"I carried his water, and he punished me."

Evan stared at him trying to make sense of what he was saying, knowing it was probably a fool's errand. There likely *was* no sense to what he was saying.

"Who is Jupiter?" she asked.

Miller picked up a random puzzle piece from one of the piles. Miraculously, it snapped into place perfectly. It was another little chunk of the red building.

"Jupiter stole the light." He looked at her. Evan thought she saw a flicker of recognition, but it came and went so fast she wasn't sure. "Aquarius comes up in the cold."

"I don't know what that means, Eddie."

"The stars," he said. "All the little stars. Jupiter stole their light, but they all come out when it's time."

"I should look at the stars? Is that what you mean? I'll find Jupiter in the stars?"

"Aquarius got punished." He reached for another candy bar.

"Eddie?"

He ignored her.

"Eddie? I don't know what you mean."

He didn't reply.

Evan sat back in her chair while Eddie swallowed another chocolate bar. It was clear that he was finished talking to her. "He's crazy," Ping had said.

Boy, was that ever the truth.

Her heart sank. Coming here was a dead end. A colossal waste of time—hers *and* his.

What Miller had done was contemptible. He deserved to pay for the harm he'd inflicted on those kids and their families. But he never should've been reduced to this. No one deserved *this* kind of punishment.

Ever.

She looked at her watch. With the snow, it probably would

51

take her more than two hours to make it back to Erie—if she were lucky, and her damn wiper blades stayed on. She'd have to hustle to make it back in time to check in for her flight. And that was if her flight outta this little corner of hell even happened.

"I'm gonna go now, Eddie. I'm glad I got to see you."

He didn't say anything.

"Okay." Evan pushed her chair back and stood up. "Good luck with your puzzle. I hope you find all the missing stars."

Eddie looked up at her then. For a second, his eyes seemed more focused.

"Galileo," he said.

Evan wasn't sure she'd heard him correctly. "What?"

"Galileo finds the stars."

He dropped his eyes back to the table and reached out for another puzzle piece.

"The stars?" She asked. "Do you mean the children?"

He didn't reply.

She tried again. "Who is Galileo?"

No answer.

"Eddie? Who is Galileo? What did Galileo do with the stars?"

Miller ignored her.

Evan deliberated. Continuing to press him was pointless. Everything about his demeanor told her he was finished with their interview. She knew she'd be unable to get him to focus again . . . on anything.

Leaving was her only option.

"Bye, Eddie. You take care of yourself."

She crossed the room toward the water fountain and the waiting phone that would summon an escort to see her out.

Outside the hospital in the parking lot, Maya sat slouched behind the wheel of her rental car and watched as Evan Reed made her way through the falling snow toward her own vehicle.

Well, well. Score one for you, Mr. Cohen.

The DNC had obviously hired Reed to do some light-speed

oppo research on Cawley. There was no other way to explain her presence here. That little tidbit made this work a whole lot more interesting.

And challenging.

Reed was the best. If it occurred to her to come to this godforsaken place to check Miller out, it wouldn't be long before some other enterprising gumshoe figured it out.

On the other hand, it seemed unlikely that Miller would be able to give Reed any useful information—even if he were inclined to do so. According to Zucchetto's sources, he was no longer mentally fit enough to function independently, and would likely live out his days in this, or some other mental institution—probably as a ward of the state.

Not too shabby for a serial child molester.

Nice work if you can get it.

Judging by the small amount of snow visible on the windshield of Reed's car, she hadn't been inside very long. That surely suggested that her visit with Miller hadn't yielded anything significant.

That would be no surprise. The guy was certifiable. Driving up here had been a ridiculous waste of time—an entire day in the damn car. But flying was too risky and would leave too much of a trail. Witness Reed being here at practically the same time. They would've been on the same damn flight.

Wouldn't that have been cozy?

It was clear that this little jaunt wouldn't yield anything. But Zucchetto had been adamant about the need to "tie off this loose end."

The only loose ends related to Edwin Miller were the frayed ones that dangled between his ears.

Still. In for a penny, in for a pound. A job was a job. And this job promised a big damn paycheck. Half now. Half when things were . . . *sanitized.*

Once Reed started her car and had safely exited the parking lot, Maya got out and trudged through the accumulating snow toward the asylum entrance.

With luck, this errand wouldn't take more than a few minutes.

◊ ◊ ◊

Julia called her assistant to book a flight to Boston on Thursday. That would allow her to spend Wednesday night at home with Evan, take care of business in Boston, and be back in Philadelphia on Friday, in time for Evan's dinner party welcoming Stevie home.

She was forced to make this Boston trip because of failed negotiations with their current problem child: an up-and-coming fiction author whose last book had shortlisted for a PEN/Faulkner award. That was a notable distinction, to be sure. But the contract department at Donne & Hale had thrown up its hands when the escalating demands of the upstart author and her literary agent led discussions related to a new contract to grind to a halt. Julia generally tried to stay out of this aspect of author relations, but securing the rights to this next book was important for D&H—not simply because it was expected to be as well received as its widely lauded prequel. The company now was very focused on expanding its catalog of books written by women. That effort had been a particular objective of Julia's when she took the helm as publisher. Her father, and his father before him, had been more focused on continuing to churn out the same mixture of books and monographs written by and about men.

Not that this previous, myopic trend had hurt the company's bottom line. It hadn't. D&H still benefitted from the stature acquired from having published some of the most seminal works in American literature. But Julia understood that keeping the business relevant and vital meant expanding its portfolio to address the needs and interests of a more diverse reading public— and that effort included dragging the company forward to embrace new delivery technologies. For many years, D&H had been proud of its refusal to publish books in electronic format. Julia had changed all of that—much to the chagrin and umbrage of its board, a collection of crusty old men who Julia privately referred to as *Syndics of the Drapers' Guild*. But she persevered. There were new stories and different voices that deserved to be discovered and heard. This was the very argument she had continued to have with her father, ad nauseam, until he finally resigned from the board in a huff, and left full superintendence of the company in her hands.

"Disagreeing with you is pointless," he complained. "You are determined to degrade the mission of this company, one indifferent prose work at a time."

It didn't matter to her father that those "indifferent prose works" included one National Book Award winner, three Pulitzer Prizes in literature, and more than a half-dozen PEN awards. Already, D&H had politely declined lucrative offers to merge with two different companies that made up part of the Big Five in publishing. *No.* To Lewis Donne, his daughter had been and would always be, only as good as her next failure.

None of that rattled Julia. Not anymore. She'd grown up without any expectation of support from either of her parents—for anything she did. But there were times, lately, when this model for business-as-usual wore thin.

She was tired. Tired of all of it.

Within the space of twenty-four months, she'd lost both her husband *and* her father.

Last year, her father had finally succumbed to the combined ravages of gout and congestive heart failure. To Julia, it was an ironic understatement that Lewis Donne actually died stewing in his own juices.

And the surreal circumstances behind her husband's death had been so steeped in high-level conspiracy that she'd never shared all the gruesome details with either of her parents. That was just as well. They hadn't needed to understand what all had transpired. Nor did they need to know that Julia had already resolved to divorce Andy long before a sickening chain of events led to his murder.

No. His *assassination*—carried out on the night he had shown up in disguise at her apartment, intending to kill her because he believed her decision to end their marriage would ruin his bid to run for president.

But Evan had been there to stop him. Evan had taken her place at home that night. And Evan had been the one hit by the same bullet that ended Andy's life. A bullet fired from the gun held by Andy's mistress, Maya Jindal—the woman who had always been a shadowy third party in their marriage.

Thinking about the aftermath of all of that still made her cringe. It had been a waking nightmare. One she never would've survived without Evan.

But survive, she did. And she was learning that surviving was a process. It required care and loving attention—not unlike teaching an abused shelter animal to trust that you won't hurt it. Evan had her own struggles with this concept and, on some days, Julia was the one who offered the coaxing and reassurance. They were both wounded. But together, they were working their way toward something better. In fact, Julia had a few ideas about what shape "something better" might take. And she planned to share those ideas with Evan when she got home from this damn trip.

Thank god her time in Albuquerque was winding down. Her last meeting was tonight—a dinner in the hotel with other conference organizers. Then she'd be finished, and on her way back to Philadelphia tomorrow morning.

It couldn't come soon enough.

She had only one remaining errand to take care of: calling her mother to discuss selling the Delancey Place townhouse and the Park Avenue apartment. That was a conversation she'd been dreading. But it needed to happen. She was going to have to make a trip to Paris, whether she wanted to or not. So, she needed to lay the groundwork for it, and at least open the discussion with her mother.

She looked at her watch. It was nearly 3 p.m. in Paris. With luck, her mother would be between social engagements.

No time like the present . . . .

She picked up her phone and placed the call. It took a full minute for it to ring through.

"*Oui.*" Her mother sounded harried. But that wasn't unusual.

"Hello, Mother. Did I catch you at a bad time?"

"Julia. How lovely to hear from you. Is it my birthday already?"

Julia sighed. "Not for another three months. I thought I'd surprise you."

"You certainly have. To what do I owe this delightful event?"

It made no sense to try and talk around the reason for her call—it wouldn't make her mother's reaction more favorable. It was best to cut to the chase. "I need to plan a trip to Paris. I wanted to see if you had any thoughts about a good time for us to schedule a visit."

"*Schedule* a visit? With my own daughter? Why? Are we negotiating a treaty or something?"

You had to hand it to the old gal. She didn't pull any punches.

"Or something," Julia said. "I want to see you, of course. But there also are some business matters we need to discuss. I'd rather do that in person—with your permission."

"Julia. You know I have little interest in business. I always left those matters to Joey."

Only Katherine Hires Donne *ever* got away with calling Julia's father "Joey." The stalwart J. Lewis Donne disdained nicknames. He only tolerated this one because of his perfect indifference to his wife and her whims.

"I understand that, Mother," Julia said. "But 'Joey' is no longer with us, and it falls to me to manage our business and family affairs. Sadly, there are times that doing so requires your participation. This is one of those times."

It was her mother's turn to sigh—dramatically. "When were you thinking about coming over?"

"After the holidays. If that works for you?"

"I'll be with Binkie and Albert at their lake house in Annecy until the 28th. They're coming back to Paris for New Year's Eve. Why don't you plan on joining us? Gerald will be there, too," she added with emphasis.

Gerald? Seriously?

"I don't think so, Mother."

"Oh, come now, Julia. It's been more than two years since the incident with Andy. It's time for you to come out of your shell."

Incident? *That was one way of putting it . . .*

"Mother, I have no desire to spend New Year's Eve, or any holiday, for that matter, with Gerald Lippincott."

"But you grew up together. And you always had so much in common."

"Not since I quit eating paste."

Her mother didn't reply. Since she was rarely silent, this was a certain indication that she found Julia's flippant response annoying.

Julia didn't really care. She was more concerned with shutting down any ideas her mother had about rekindling a relationship with Gerald—or anyone else. And the best way to do that was to tell her mother about Evan.

"Well," she began, "this touches on another thing I need to discuss with you. I hope you'll be happy to learn that I have moved on. I'm now in a relationship with someone."

"Really?" Her mother sounded intrigued. *And suspicious.* "Would this have anything to do with your decision to move to Philadelphia?"

"Yes." Julia saw no reason to deny it.

"So, he lives in Philadelphia? Is he from a family we know?"

"Not in Philadelphia. In Chadds Ford. And not from a family you know, although that's hardly relevant."

"It is to me. What name?"

"Reed."

"Reed." Her mother took a moment to consider the information. "Is he related to the Radnor Reeds?"

"I don't think so. And, Mother? *He* is a she."

"I beg your pardon?" Her mother sounded incredulous.

"You heard me."

"Julia. You cannot be serious."

"Oh, but I am. Her name is Evan Reed. She's forty-two, single, has a sixteen-year-old daughter, and lives in what was her grandfather's house in Chadds Ford. And, yes, it's serious. Very serious, in fact."

58

"This is perfectly absurd. I refuse to discuss it."

"That's your prerogative, Mother—of course. But you need to know that I shall *not* refuse to discuss it. And before you suggest it, I am not likely to change my mind or come to my senses."

"Julia . . ."

"Mother," Julia adopted a softer tone, "I'm not sharing this with you to hurt or offend you—or to complicate your life. But this is what and who I am. I've always known it. And now I have the opportunity and the good sense to embrace it, and to find real happiness. Please don't disparage that. If you can't find your way to understand this, at least try to accept it."

"That, I shall never be able to do."

"Then make your peace with this in whatever ways you need to. And in the meantime, let me know when we can meet to discuss business matters, as burdensome as they may be to you."

Julia's mother didn't reply.

"Are you still there?" Julia asked.

"Of course, I am."

Julia relented a bit. "Please believe that this isn't some kind of whim or overreaction to losing Andy," she explained. "I think I can imagine how much of an unwelcome shock it is for you to hear this. And I apologize for dropping it on you with so little ceremony. But it would be disingenuous of me to conceal it, or pretend to be otherwise. I owe you greater respect than that—in the same way I owe it to myself."

"I need more time to digest this, Julia. I'm not prepared to say more right now."

At least that was something. It wasn't like her mother to withhold her opinions . . . about anything.

"Okay. How about you contact me when you've had time to look at your calendar, and let me know when I should plan to come over?"

"All right. Is that all?" It was clear that her mother was ready to end the conversation.

"Yes," Julia said. "For now."

Her mother disconnected without saying good-bye. It took Julia a moment to realize she'd hung up.

She slowly shook her head.

That went well . . .

"A funny thing happened on the way to the asylum."

"I'm not sure what you're talking about." Mr. Zucchetto sounded baffled. And irritated.

Maya laughed. "I was trying to be ironic."

"Please pay me the courtesy of being direct."

"Very well. Let me simplify matters for you." Maya had placed the call to Mr. Zucchetto from the car after the visit with Edwin Miller. "I spent ten minutes with him—ten minutes I'll never get back."

"Which means?" Zucchetto's impatience had not abated.

"Which means, coming here was a complete red herring. The man's completely around the bend. He's incapable of stringing enough words together to form a sentence."

"You're saying he has no recollection of events?"

"No," she corrected. "I'm saying he's incapable of coherently communicating any recollection he *may* have—about anything."

"I don't find that wholly reassuring."

"Believe me. He's harmless."

Zucchetto didn't appear ready to accept that assessment. "Is he in a secured location?"

"The unit itself is locked. The patient rooms are not."

"How were you able to account for your visit?"

"Very simply." Maya merged the car onto Interstate 80 East, and the longest leg of the drive back to Philadelphia. "They thought I was a social worker, visiting from his former home."

"Former home?" he asked.

"Cambria County Prison."

"Very clever." Zucchetto sounded impressed. "No one questioned your credentials?"

"Not at all. In fact, I found the staff to be excessively incurious."

"That is very good news."

"Hold your applause," she cautioned. "There is one fly in the ointment."

"And that is?"

"To put it simply," she said, "I wasn't Mr. Miller's first visitor today."

Zucchetto was quick on the uptake. "Who was it?"

"Evan Reed."

Maya admired the passing scenery while a very frustrated client took his time adjusting to the news.

The snow was patchier this far east of Warren. It was barely spitting flurries now.

"That is most unfortunate," Zucchetto finally said.

"I don't know how 'unfortunate' it is," she observed. "But I will agree that your situation just got more complicated. If Evan Reed was able to pull this thread, it won't be long until some enterprising journalist makes the same connection—and those will lead to other more fruitful discoveries."

"That would be regrettable. But for now, my limited interest in Mr. Miller has been satisfied."

"Well just in case your satisfaction proves premature, I have a tasty little tidbit up my sleeve."

"Which means?" he asked.

"Which means I have a made-to-order diversion to lob into Ms. Reed's path."

"Do you have confidence it will work?"

"Oh," Maya chuckled. "It'll work just *fine*."

Chapter Four

Evan was sure of two things after she woke up in her hotel room on Wednesday morning.

One: she'd never spend the night in Erie again, even if it meant hiring a dogsled to mush her way out.

And two: she was going to rip Dan a new asshole for giving out her Signal address.

At least, she *assumed* it had been Dan, after she checked her phone and saw that she had an encoded message from an unknown sender.

Of the finite number of people who even *knew* she had a Signal account, Dan was the only one she knew who would be so damn careless. He had an annoying lack of respect for communication protocols, and always had. They'd argued countless times about this very thing over the years. But he remained an unrepentant Luddite who'd rather fax documents instead of sharing them through encrypted channels. In fact, Dan was one of the only people she knew who even still *had* a fax machine.

Right now, however, she had to decide whether to allow the message to load, or not.

Before doing anything, she shot a quick text off to Ben Rush, who promptly told her he had no fucking clue, and suggested she ask Ping.

Okay. Fair enough.

Hey, Ping? she texted. *How can an anonymous person be sending me a Signal message?*

That's easy, Ping wrote back. *If you don't have that option blocked in your preferences, anybody can send you messages.*

Evan checked her account preferences. *Shit.* "Block anonymous messages" was unchecked.

Okay, she texted back. *How'd they find my address?*

They can't find it, Ping responded. *They have to KNOW it. Your Signal address is the same as your account phone number.*

So anyone with my cell phone number can send me Signal messages? Evan texted.

Pretty much, Ping answered. *Anybody who has the phone number you used to open the account can send you messages, anonymous or not. That's the main reason why so many people open their accounts with burn phones.*

Burn phones? *God. What a world.*

Good to know. Thanks, Ping.

Is this billable time? she asked.

Evan laughed. *Yeah. Go for it.*

Evan navigated back to her Signal app.

Okay. So maybe she *had* been too quick to blame Dan. Especially since it seemed that anyone who had her cell phone number could send her Signal messages. Assuming, of course, that she had used her cell phone to set up her account—which she had. And the list of people with her cell phone number was pretty endless. That meant this message probably came from someone she knew—or someone who knew someone else who had it.

But if that were the case, why send it anonymously?

She looked at the notification again. It simply read "New Message From Anonymous Sender."

What the hell? She opened it. When the message displayed, it identified the sender as someone named "Moxie."

Moxie? Who the hell is that?

The message was short. And it had an attachment.

Since we're playing in the same pond, I thought it would be useful to divide and conquer. You might find the attached helpful in your research.

63

Evan was in a quandary. Who the hell *was* this person? And how did they know what she was working on?

She clicked on the link to display the attachment. It was another photograph of Cawley. This one was plainly several years older than the previous image she'd received from Dan. For one thing, Cawley was sporting a tad more hair. He was posing with a priest and a group of boys inside a church. The kids were all wearing basketball uniforms with *Wildcats* stenciled on their jerseys. Cawley was handing the priest a check. They were all smiles. Evan enlarged the photo as much as she could on her iPhone to try and examine the background more closely. Something about the setting looked familiar to her. Then she saw him.

Holy shit.

Tim.

Tim was one of the kids. She was certain of it. That mop of untamed red hair was unmistakable. He'd been on the basketball team at St. Rita's when they were kids. Sheila used to drag her to services there on random holidays, usually Christmas and Easter, when she thought it was meaningful to be seen. Evan never paid much attention to anything during those outings, except dropping Atomic Fire Balls into the curiously long-handled offering baskets that were thrust past them about twenty times during every Mass. She also remembered being creeped out by the hideous carvings on the base of the baptismal font, partially visible in the background of this photo. Its tangled maze of bodies always reminded her of that Rubens painting included in the fat book on art masterpieces that some previous tenant had left behind in the row home they rented. *The Rape of the Sabine Women.*

The irony of that one never escaped her.

She was pretty sure the smiling priest accepting the check from Cawley also appeared in the newer image with Miller—only in that photo, he was wearing more elaborate vestments.

What the hell?

She'd have to wait until she got home to see if any of the other faces showed up in this older photo, as well. But that might be hard to determine. Most of the kids shown here would've been quite a bit more mature in 1995.

Who the hell *was* this "Moxie" person? And why send this photo to her? Apart from the obvious clue that someone else was looking into Cawley's background, too. If so, why the cloak and dagger bullshit? And what did Moxie mean by suggesting they were "playing in the same pond"? Evan found that to be an interesting choice of words, especially since her job was simply to find out if there was anything *new* to discover.

Guess we can check that one off the list . . .

The rest would have to wait until she got back to Chadds Ford.

Julia had a ninety-minute layover in Atlanta, which ended up being a good thing, because she had to schlep her bag halfway to Marietta to reach her connecting gate. The good news was that her flight to Philadelphia was scheduled for an on-time departure. *For once.* With luck, she'd be back at the townhouse in plenty of time for dinner—with Evan.

She resisted the temptation to stop at the Café Intermezzo on Concourse B for an *espresso doppio*. She knew herself well enough to understand that giving in to a simple indulgence like this would result in a sleepless night.

Not that she was at all opposed to the idea of a sleepless night—under other, more welcome circumstances.

Once she got settled at her gate, she had most of thirty minutes to kill before the boarding process began. She made use of the time to respond to a few emails. There were several from her assistant, updating her on meetings and the machinations she'd gone through to shift Julia's schedule around to accommodate the Boston trip. And there were two messages marked "high priority" from her father's estate attorney. She read both of those. It seemed there were several specific bequest documents that required her sign-off as trustee. He apologized for the short notice, but asked if she would be able to visit his office before the 15th of the month.

That meant tomorrow or Friday.

Well, that was not happening.

She wrote a quick response to him, explaining that she'd be in Boston on Thursday and Friday, and asked if he could send the documents to her via courier. Otherwise, it would be the first of the week before she could meet with him.

Another message intrigued her and made her smile. It was from Evan's daughter, Stevie. They'd exchanged email addresses when Stevie was home during the summer, and Julia heard from her once in a while—usually about something quirky happening at school or, lately, with questions about some Christmas gift ideas she had for Evan or Dan. Julia never ceased to marvel at how well Evan, Stevie and Dan managed to navigate the terrain of their curious family troika. Dan was Stevie's father—a relationship circumstance that derived from a drunken one-night stand in college. Instead of terminating her surprise pregnancy, Evan had stubbornly determined to go forward with it, and Stevie became the happy result of a youthful indiscretion.

Stevie had grown into a wonderfully tumbled amalgamation of the best of both of her parents. She was fresh, open and unapologetic. Julia adored her.

She opened the message.

Hey, J! Mom told me you were coming for dinner on Friday, and I just wanted to send you a note to say I'm really happy you'll be there. Mom was growing a tumor about asking me if I was okay with it. No matter how much I tell her I'm happy you guys are together, she keeps thinking I'm gonna freak out or something. I thought maybe you could talk to her about this? And maybe see if she'll cut Kayla some slack? She seriously needs to get over that. Anyway..... Maybe we bring it up after she's had a bottle of wine? You know how much easier she gets. I'm gonna ask Tim to help out, too. If we gang up on her it could be like one of those intervention things, only nobody has to go to rehab. Mom can be stubborn sometimes, but I

*know we both love her. If I'm butting in where I don't
belong, just tell me. Okay? See you on Friday.*
  Love, Stevie

God, this kid was incredible. It never ceased to amaze Julia
that Stevie was so often the only adult in the room. And she was
dead-on about Evan and her skittishness about relationships.
But that didn't make Evan unique . . .
  They both had been running in place for a while now. Julia was
overcautious about pushing Evan into something she might not
be ready for. And Evan was too timid to press *her* on just about
anything. Maybe resolving to confront all of this head-on really
was the best way for them to move forward.
  Maybe she *should* think about doing that?
  She smiled at the idea.
  Maybe tonight would be a good time to start?
  She clicked the reply button, and wrote back to Stevie.

Back in Chadds Ford, Evan brewed a big pot of coffee before sitting down at her grandfather's ancient desk to call Dan and give
him a summary report about the trip to see Miller, and receiving
the second photo from the anonymous Moxie person. After shutting down Dan's reflexive tirade about the expense of her overnight
trip to Erie, she reminded him of *his* collapsed timetable, sent him
a scan of the new image, and hung up.
  She scrolled though a couple of messages from Ben. He'd
managed to track down the address of the law firm that had set
up the pro-Cawley PAC. He said their main office was located
in one of the older Center City buildings on 8th Street that also
housed street-level retail space. Ben figured that all the noise and
pedestrian traffic from crazed Christmas shoppers would make
their after-hours visit a lot less risky than it might have been at
another time of year. Ben said he was planning to scope the site
out during regular business hours so he could get a sense of the
layout and what kind of security system they'd be dealing with.

Unless he ran into something insurmountable, which he doubted, he said they should plan to stage their little after-hours tour on Saturday night, between 7 and 9 p.m.

She wrote back to tell him she'd be ready, and settled in with her mug of tepid coffee-water to spend more time comparing both of the Cawley photographs in greater detail.

The coffee tasted like ass.

Her Proctor Silex had been on the fritz for about six months. Small wonder. The thing was a relic that came with the house. Her grandfather's coffee had always pretty much sucked, too. She guessed that was because her grandfather mostly drank Frank's Black Cherry Wishniak.

She stared down into her chipped mug—another castoff from her grandfather. She could see little flecks of . . . something floating in it. And there appeared to be some kind of oil slick forming on the top.

She frowned at the sketchy liquid before resolving to drink it anyway. Time was money, and she needed to get to work.

Evan took another look at the photograph Dan sent her. It didn't take much examination to figure out that the piece of artwork hanging over the fireplace was the same one depicted in the jigsaw puzzle Miller had been working. She was certain of it.

She recognized the picture, too. Something by Winslow Homer . . .

Yet another art masterpiece contained in that monster book she grew up with.

What was the name of that damn painting?

She did a quick Google image search. It only took a few seconds to find it. There it was. *Snap the Whip*. It depicted a bunch of boys playing the childhood game in a field outside their red schoolhouse. It was part of the permanent collection in the Metropolitan Museum of Art in New York City.

She studied the photograph again. The painting looked too elaborately framed to be a reproduction. If there were *any* chance it had been the original, maybe its presence in this image would allow her to figure out where the photo had been taken?

She shot off a note to Ping.

Hey. Got another little mystery for you to run down. Could you look into any exhibits that included the 1872 Winslow Homer painting called Snap the Whip? It's in the permanent collection at the Met Museum in New York. See if you can find out if it was on loan or traveled anyplace in or around 1995? And if so, where? Thanks!

God bless Ping. She didn't just keep Evan plied with savory dessert concoctions—and life coaching—she also made research a helluva lot easier.

While she waited to hear back, she spent some time examining all of the blank expressions on the faces of the kids in the new photo sent to her by the Moxie character, and trying to determine if any of them looked like they could be the same young men in the first photo from Dan. It became clear in short order that this was a waste of time. The only thing she was sure of was that the robed cleric who appeared in Dan's image was the same priest shown accepting the check from Cawley in the older photo taken at St. Rita's.

She thought his name should be pretty easy to run down. Since Tim was also in the earlier photo, he'd be sure to recognize the priest and could give Evan a starting place. Hell. This guy could *still* be at St. Rita's. A lot of priests hung around the same parishes forever. There was even a slim chance Tim might remember this occasion.

Probably not very likely. Civic groups in the area were always making gifts to the parish in support of sports teams. Since the kids in this photo were all wearing Wildcat uniforms, Evan assumed this check was intended to underwrite some kind of CYO initiative.

She shot Tim a text message and asked if he had time to meet her around four that afternoon for a drink before dinner. She told him she was heading into the city to connect with Julia later on.

Tim wrote back almost immediately, and said he was free. He suggested meeting at The Twisted Tail on South 2nd Street, because it would be a straight shot on Lombard Street from there to Julia's townhouse on Delancey Place.

Of course, Evan thought. Tim was a total bourbon snob, and he loved this joint. In fact, Tim loved anyplace that served twenty-dollar cocktails.

Evan told him she'd be there. It also occurred to her that she could ask him about Stevie and that whole "Catholic" debt thing . . .

Her phone rang. It was Ping.

That was sure fast.

"Hey," Evan said.

"Hey. I've got some information for you about that picture."

Evan grabbed a notepad. "Shoot."

"Okay. So. For starters, that Met painting wasn't on loan anyplace in 1995. It was part of a centennial show in Philadelphia in 1876, but that's the only time it ever visited the city."

"Well. Shit."

"Hold your horses." Ping wasn't finished with her report. "I did some other research, and found out that the Met copy of the painting isn't the only version Homer painted."

Evan was surprised. "No kidding?"

"No kidding. He painted several of them. The Met picture is actually one of the practice pieces he painted before creating the final painting. There are some little differences between the two if you look at 'em side by side. For starters, the final one is a lot bigger. And it has a mountain scene in the background, instead of a valley with other buildings in it. They're both dated 1872 and signed by Homer."

"Ping, you're a genius."

"Thank you. That's why Ben pays me the big bucks."

"I thought that was only so you wouldn't kick his sorry ass to the curb."

"That, too. Somebody's gotta take pity on his daughters." Ping chuckled. "But here's the best part of the story. The bigger painting isn't in the Met collection at all. It's at a place called the Butler Institute in Youngstown, Ohio."

"And?" Evan prompted.

"*And* when I called them, they told me that their version of the painting *had* been loaned out in 1995, to some big-money donor who wanted to use it at a private fundraising event."

"No shit? Did they say where?"

"One guess."

"Philadelphia?"

"You go it, sister."

Bingo. Now they were getting someplace. "Did they have the name of the patron?" Evan asked.

"Not at first. So, I sweet-talked her by asking about Youngstown . . . said I used to live there right after I got married and worked in one of the old steel mills. Said I heard it closed down and asked if she knew what happened to the man who owned it. Told her he was always *real* nice to work for."

"She fell for that?"

"Honey, white women *always* fall for my thick, Georgia accent—especially when it telegraphs that I'm respectfully black. Once I started filling her ears with stories about how much I just *loved* my ol' white overseers, we were practically sorority sisters. So, after our little love fest, when I asked her about the name of the person who borrowed the picture, she trotted it right out. Are you ready to copy?"

"Yep."

"Okay," Ping began. "His name was J.A. Lippincott. L-I-P-P-I-N-C-O-T-T."

"Seriously?" Evan asked. "As in the publishing Lippincotts?"

"I have no earthly clue."

"Was there any information about the physical location for the loan?"

"Miss Scarlett didn't have one. She said that probably meant it was lent out to Lippincott personally, meaning it likely went to his residence. She did say that wherever it went, it would have to have been to a location with adequate security. Insurance and all that."

"If this J.A. Lippincott belonged to the Main Line Lippincotts, security probably wasn't an issue."

71

"That's what I thought, too."

"How do you feel about trying to run him down and see if you can get a better trace on this—and where the fundraiser was held?"

"Already started," Ping said.

"I owe you, Ping."

Ping laughed. "Not as much as you're gonna." She disconnected.

Well, hot damn. Evan looked at the photograph again. *Well, well, Mr. Miller. Maybe you* were *trying to tell me something, after all.*

Tim arrived at The Twisted Tail about fifteen minutes early. That wasn't by design; he'd just lucked out, and all the traffic seemed to be headed in the opposite direction.

It was early enough that he was able to snag a small table near the front entrance. That way, he could watch for Evan through one of the windows that fronted on 2nd Street. He figured she'd probably have to park at least a block away, and from this vantage point he'd be sure to see her walking in.

He didn't know why that mattered to him. But it had always been that way. Evan was like an anchor in his life. She kept him grounded and never missed a chance to point out, usually in very colorful language, whenever he had his head up his own ass. The whole reason he went to see her on the night of the aurora was so he could tell the truth about his situation. But when push came to shove, he couldn't get the words out.

Not all of them anyway.

Now he found himself foundering in this unhappy middle ground of half-truths. One foot in. One foot out. It was like being stuck in a twisted dance—a Hokey Pokey of not quite confessing.

He laughed at his unwitting choice of venue for the meeting with Evan.

Talk about your Twisted Tails . . .

Back at seminary, Father O'Shaughnessy had often warned his class of aspiring priests to pay attention to the choices they made. "We do nothing by accident," he cautioned. "Therefore, it is wise to understand your motivations to act—or to react. Always consider your responses and ask if they truly derive from God."

In this instance, it was *inaction* Tim was guilty of. And that, he was persuaded, certainly did *not* derive from God. He was finding that he no longer could acquit himself of his great sin of keeping silent. The Church was changing. At least, it was attempting to change, however slow and clumsy its progress. There were systems in place now to deal with these things—flawed systems, but at least the Church was being forced to have the conversation. Perpetrators were beginning to be held to account.

At least, *some* perpetrators were being held to account.

Sadly, when it came to the Church hierarchy, Orwell was right: some pigs were still more equal than others. And that unhappy truth made his quandary even murkier. The whole thing was a supersized miasma of toxicity. Come and vape at the oasis of the Church's own demise . . . .

He ordered a double WhistlePig and sat back to savor it while he waited for Evan to join him. The small-batch rye was one of his favorites. Having an excuse to splurge on it was always a welcome indulgence.

Probably a wicked one . . .

It had been one hell of a ride the last few days. He'd been shaken to his core by the revelation in the confessional this week. So far, the young man had not tried to contact him again—and if he were completely honest, he wasn't sure if he felt more gratitude or concern about that.

What the hell am I going to do?

He'd asked himself that question so many times, the words had now lost most of their meaning.

The truth of it all was simple. He was guilty. As guilty as the priests who'd committed these unpardonable acts. The only question that remained was what he'd choose to do about it.

Choose wasn't even the right word anymore. There was no longer a choice. There was only a responsibility. One he no longer could shirk or deny. He'd come forward with his testimony. Then he would resign from the priesthood and seek dispensation from his clerical obligations. It was that simple.

Simple. Right.

It was anything but simple. He'd lived the majority of his life in the shelter of St. Rita's. To no longer be part of that—or of any—sacred community, terrified him.

But Evan and Julia would help him—once Evan got over the shock and finished ripping him a new butthole for keeping silent all these years. He knew she would offer him safe harbor until he could figure out the rest of his life. And that would start with how he'd make a living once he left the church.

Left the church . . . .

Evan would say that was "fucked up."

She'd be right, too.

He took another cautious sip of the rye. *Damn, this stuff was good.*

Something caught his eye. A flash of color moving past the front window. Blaze orange.

Evan.

You had to give her credit: she never worried about exploding into a room.

He waved at her when she entered and started looking around the bar. The place wasn't too busy yet. In another forty-five minutes, it would be standing room only. It was slow enough right now that you could actually hear the music. *Bill Evans. Nice.*

Evan joined him at the table.

"How long have you been waiting?" She was carrying a beat-up, distressed leather messenger bag that was bulging at the seams. He doubted it was stuffed with just paperwork. Likely, she had a change of clothes stuffed inside it, since she was heading to Julia's townhouse after their meeting. He was happy about that. Julia was good for Evan. They were good for each other. He wondered for the hundredth time why she didn't just leave some clothes over there.

"Not long," he told her. He lifted his rocks glass. "I've hardly made a dent in this."

"What're you drinking?"

"WhistlePig."

"Of *course*."

"What's that supposed to mean?"

"You're seriously asking me this question?"

"I guess not." He wrinkled his nose. "I know I'm kind of a snob."

Evan laughed. "Kind of?"

"Okay." He shrugged. "I'm *totally* a snob." He made eye contact with the bartender, who was looking their way. "What do you want to drink?"

Evan settled back into her chair. "Surprise me."

Tim held his glass aloft and pointed at Evan. The bartender nodded.

"This is gonna change your life," he promised.

"You promise? I could use that."

"*You?* I don't think so. You've got just about everything."

"Maybe. But having 'everything,' as you say, and still doubting it all carries its own load of baggage."

"That's always been true for you."

Evan raised an eyebrow. "Having everything?"

"No. Doubting what you *do* have."

Evan rolled her left shoulder. The gesture was becoming a familiar one. Tim knew it was mostly due to the lingering effects of being shot, and her refusal to have the surgery to finish repairs to her damaged clavicle. But he also thought the gesture now functioned like a bad gambler's tell. Her joint seemed to stiffen up whenever she felt uncomfortable.

Like right now.

The bartender showed up and deposited Evan's drink. "You folks let me know when you're ready for another round."

75

"Thanks," Tim said "We will." He raised his glass and held it out toward Evan. "Here's to you, and to having everything."

Evan looked dubious, but clinked rims with him anyway. She took a careful sip of the rye.

"This is . . . interesting."

"Good interesting, or bad interesting?" Tim asked.

Evan sniffed it. "I'm not sure."

"It's more fiery than bourbon. Not as sweet on the palate."

"I get that." She sniffed at the rye. "Bet it makes a good Manhattan."

"So I'm told."

"You don't know?"

"To quote Barry Fitzgerald, 'When I drink whiskey, I drink whiskey.'"

"Do you *only* quote other Irishmen?"

"No," Tim said. "If you pay attention, you'll notice that I also tend to quote a few ancient Hebrews . . . and the occasional Greek."

"Very funny."

"So." He set his glass down. "Is there a reason for this visit?"

"What makes you ask that?"

"It's 4:15 on a weekday. You penciled me in between appointments. There must be a reason beyond camaraderie and sampling strange brews."

Evan looked amused. "I hardly penciled you in."

"No? What would you call it?"

"I'd call it meeting for cocktails." Evan held up her glass. "But if you'd prefer more mystery, I could always show up outside your window at St. Rita's in the dead of night . . . because I happened to be in the neighborhood."

"I wouldn't suggest that *anyone* show up in my neighborhood in the dead of night."

"True. The last time I stopped by late in the evening, I lost a set of hubcaps."

"Kids these days . . ."

"Apropos of that..." Evan tugged her messenger bag closer

and opened an outside flap. "Would you take a look at this relic from your past and tell me what, if anything, you remember about it?"

She passed a photograph across the table. Tim was intrigued about what "relic" from his past she had, and why. Until he looked at it, and his blood ran cold.

"Where'd you get this?" It came out sounding like an accusation, and he regretted his tone immediately. "Sorry . . . I'm just surprised."

He could tell Evan smelled a rat.

"What is it?" she asked. "Is this part of what you came to tell me?"

Tim didn't fault her for her maddening intuition. It simply was knee-jerk, pure instinct. Always had been. This quality of hers was part of what made her so good at her job. She always knew how to pick up a scent that had gone cold.

"There goes that intuition of yours again," he said nervously.

"I told you I was born with an incredible shit magnet."

"Lucky you." He meant it to sound ironic.

Evan reached across the table and touched his hand. "Not always. Not right now."

Tim could feel his eyes filling with tears. It was mortifying. He tried to blink them away.

Evan squeezed the top of his hand. "Tell me."

He took a deep breath, followed by a sip of the rye. "I'm sorry."

"For what?"

"For being so weak."

"Believe me. You don't have a premium on weakness."

"No? It sure feels like it."

"Tim?" He looked at her. "Tell me."

Why not tell her? It was part of what he intended to do—if not today, then soon.

"I remember this. Well, maybe not exactly this—but events just like this."

"Events?" Evan asked.

He nodded. "When donors would show up and present checks

to the team. It was always a command performance. We'd have to put on our uniforms and line up for the camera."

"Do you recognize anyone in this photo?"

Tim fought the sting of tears again. He nodded.

"The priest?" she asked.

"Yeah." He cleared his throat. "That's Father Szymanski—now *Bishop* Szymanski. He was at St. Rita's for about twelve years."

"Do you recognize the other man?"

Tim nodded again. "But I don't remember his name. He was around a lot in those days—always seemed to be dropping off donations for things. I think he was some kind of city official?"

"Close," Evan said. "He was a judge." Tim looked up at her. "That's J. Meyer Cawley."

"Cawley?" Tim peered more closely at the image. "The Supreme Court nominee?"

"In the unholy flesh, so to speak."

Tim felt another surge of panic at her words. "What makes you say that?"

"I dunno. I was thinking maybe you could tell me."

Tim closed his eyes. He felt half sick. It was the same way he had felt in the confessional the other day. He always knew this moment would come. *Time's winged chariot.* It had finally caught up to him.

"Yes." He laid his hand on top of the photo. More than anything, he wished he could will himself out of the image—leave nothing but a vacuum in the spot he once occupied. A vacuum that could match the gaping hole in his conscience—and his heart. But he couldn't. *Not anymore.* "To answer your question, yes—this *is* part of what I wanted to tell you."

Evan didn't say anything. Tim knew she wouldn't pressure him now.

"I knew what was happening," he continued. "I knew and I didn't tell anyone. I didn't do *anything.* I just looked the other way and didn't try to stop it." He covered his eyes with his hand. "I didn't do anything . . ."

Evan took hold of his free hand. She waited while he wiped at his eyes.

"The boys?" she asked.

He nodded.

"Father Szymanski?"

"Yeah." Tim sniffed. "And . . . others. I think."

"Were you . . .?"

Tim cut her off. "No. *Not* me. I don't know why. Maybe I was already too . . . *worldly*." He made a futile gesture with his hand. "Once, he . . . Father Szymanski . . . he did something that made me feel . . . uncomfortable. Scared, even. I avoided being alone with him after that. And I convinced my parents to let me quit the basketball team." He met Evan's eyes. "That's how I ended up taking damn piano lessons for *five* years." He stared at the drink in his hands. "I never understood everything that was happening. Not really. Not until a lot later, when things started coming out. By then, I was too ashamed to come forward with what I suspected." He hesitated. "I still am."

"Tim?" Evan waited until he looked up at her again. "You were a child. What could you have done?"

"I haven't been a child for decades, Evan. We all know what was going on. Nothing about this is a mystery any longer. You've read the reports."

"I have."

"Then you must know that Bishop Szymanski was named in one of the reparation complaints filed with the diocese."

"No. I didn't know that." Evan said. "Were any of those offenses alleged to have happened at St. Rita's?"

"I don't know."

"Do you know if any boys at St. Rita's *could* have made complaints against him?"

"Yes."

"Would you be willing to tell me if any of those boys are in this photo?"

He stared at her for a moment before examining the picture again.

"Yes. Three that I know of."

"Meaning?" she asked.

He shrugged. "Meaning that I don't know everyone who might have reason to come forward."

"Okay," Evan said. "Could I show you another photo and ask if you recognize anyone in it?"

Tim thought about her request. It seemed like a small enough thing to do. Maybe it was a first step toward making restitution for his long-held sin of omission? A small step, to be sure. But it was something. *A place to start.*

"Okay," he told her.

Evan pulled the other photo out of her bag and handed it to him. He recognized Szymanski right away. It was clear this photo had been taken years later, because he was wearing a bishop's cassock. "That's Szymanski." He pointed him out. "When was this taken?"

"In 2005. I have no idea where. But that's Cawley in the foreground."

Tim nodded. "If this was taken in 2005, that was years after Father Szymanski became a Bishop. He'd be close to mandatory retirement age now."

"What's that?" Evan asked.

"Seventy-five. Even with a complaint against him, the Church will probably just push him into leaving active service because he's so close to retirement, anyway."

Evan was disgusted by that. "Canonical beat the clock, huh?"

"Unfortunately. It happens more than it should. Especially for people at his level."

"Tim? Do you recognize anyone else in the photo? Any of the younger men or boys?"

He looked at the image more closely. "Yeah . . . I think so." He pointed out one of the two older-looking boys, wearing a loose-fitting suit coat. He was standing in the background, near the massive stone fireplace. "I think that's Joey Mazzetta—from our neighborhood. He's in that first photo, too." Tim compared the two images. "Yeah. Right there." He pointed him out to Evan. In the older photo, he looked a lot younger, but Tim still recognized him. "That red hair is impossible to miss. Joey and I were the only two players who had it, and we got razzed about it all the time—especially when we were on the JV team. They called us *The Mallories*—you know . . . the copper top batteries."

"Do you know what happened to him?"

"I used to see him once in a while at services during the holidays. But that was years ago. I think he still lives with his mother on South Bouvier Street."

"Any idea if he's filed any complaints with the reparations committee?"

"None. There's no way to know who the complainants are." He absently rocked his glass. "There've been dozens of cases in Philadelphia alone—more than a thousand statewide. It's an epidemic. A plague. I honestly don't know if the Church can survive it." He lowered his voice. "I'm sure I won't."

"Hey." Evan reached across the table and squeezed his hand again. "One step at a time, okay?"

"I don't even know what that means anymore."

"Don't you? I know where we can find a couple of twelve-step meetings that could help out with that—and ply you with some really shitty coffee in the process."

"Evan . . ."

"Save your breath, dude. Who drug my sorry ass to about fifty of those—and hung out there with me—when I was thinking about dropping out of college because every relationship of mine had turned to shit? Give up? Lemme give you some clues. Big guy with *no* fashion sense? Red hair that could double as a shower loofah? Loves to guzzle high-priced hooch he really can't afford? Loses twenty-dollar bets with my kid? I'm not sure, but I think he used to go by the name *Mallory?*" She let that sink in. "Ring any bells?"

He gave her a sad smile. "You never give up, do you?"

"Not usually, no. And, Tim?"

"What?"

"Neither should you."

He didn't reply. There wasn't anything more to say. Not then. He drained his WhistlePig and signaled the bartender to bring them another round.

Julia met her at the door.

Evan usually parked at the back of the townhouse, where there was a small driveway adjacent to the alley that ran behind Delancey Place. Julia had taken care to park her Audi close to the brick wall of the townhouse's small patio, to be sure she left enough room for Evan to squeeze her car in, too.

Evan looked surprised when Julia opened the door. She stood on the steps, juggling her messenger bag and a green DiBruno Brothers satchel. Her free hand held an oversized brass key that had been aimed at the door lock.

"Were you waiting on me?" Evan asked.

Julia nearly quipped, "For most of my life," but opted instead to grab Evan by the arm and haul her across the threshold. She took her time demonstrating how happy she was to be back at home.

"Wow." Evan's bulging messenger bag slipped to the floor with a thunk. "You sure know how to make a girl feel welcome."

"It's the DiBruno bag."

"Of *course*, it is. Thank god I remembered how easy it is to turn your head. Wave a pound of fresh bucatini in your face and pffft! You melt like cheap mascara."

That piqued Julia's interest. "Not that I'm less than overjoyed to see you—but do you really have fresh pasta in that bag?" She tried to peer down into it, which was difficult because she still had her arms wrapped around Evan's neck.

"Yeah. I thought you wanted me to cook?"

"Oh, I do." Julia kissed her on the ear. "Eventually."

Julia felt the way she always felt when she was this close to Evan. Safe. Happy. Like everything was possible.

Her stomach rumbled.

And hungry. She felt hungry, too. It had been a long time since that complimentary packet of peanuts on the flight from Atlanta. She unwound her arms and smiled shyly.

"Did you say you bought bucatini?"

"I can always rely on you to cut to the chase."

"Which, translated, means?"

Evan lifted the bag. "Which means I knew you'd be starving, so I bought an entire pound."

"Dare I hope there's a bottle of wine in there, too?"

"Do you really need to ask?"

"I'll get the opener." Julia led the way to her grandmother's lavishly appointed kitchen.

Evan followed her and began to unload items from the bag. She had hunks of Pecorino and Grana Padano cheeses and a tin of four-color peppercorns. She also had a half pound of Licini pancetta, a bundle of fresh asparagus, and two bottles of Renieri Brunello di Montalcino. She handed one of the bottles to Julia, who stared at it with wide eyes.

"Are we celebrating?"

"You tell me."

Julia held up the wine opener. "Let's see. We're finally in the same time zone—together. You're cooking. Judging by the way your messenger bag is bulging at the seams, I'm going to go out on a limb and assume that you're staying the night." She waited for Evan to give her a nod. "So, yes. I'd say we're celebrating."

"In that case," Evan handed her the second bottle. "Open them both."

"I love how you think. I love you."

"I love you, too."

Julia commenced opening the wine. "What are you cooking for me?"

"*Cacio e pepe.* I thought we could crisp up some of this pancetta and grill the asparagus, too. I know how much you love it when your pee smells like grass."

"You do love your quirky torments."

"I consider it a prized, yet little understood perk of our relationship."

Julia poured them each a generous glass of the wine. She handed one to Evan. "I'll drink to that."

They clinked rims.

"This is lovely." Julia took another sip.

Evan had shed her coat and was already hauling pans out of a lower cabinet. "Yeah. It's generally better after it's allowed to breathe for a while—but what the hell?"

"'History is now and England,'" Julia quoted.

"Yes. T.S. Eliot. *Precisely.* That's just what I was thinking."

Julia smirked at her. "You got the inference."

"I'd say my mother didn't raise no idiot, but that wouldn't really be true."

"However imperfect her performance was, you're making up for it with your own daughter."

Evan fought not to smile at her observation. She was still rooting around in a lower cabinet, looking for something. "Where's that cast-iron skillet?"

Julia walked over to where she knelt, and peered over her shoulder. "Is that the awful black one you're so partial to?"

Even looked up at her. "Yes. The *awful* one. What'd you do with it?"

"I washed it."

"You *what?*"

Julia shrugged. "It was disgusting. It practically had barnacles."

Evan stood up. "Honey . . ."

"Don't start." Julia held up a palm. "I have no desire to eat incinerated meat that's probably older than this house."

Evan gave up. "Where is it?"

Julia pointed at the elaborate pot rack, hanging over a kitchen island the size of a billiard table. "Over there."

"Oh, this'll be good." Evan walked over to retrieve the skillet. She lifted it down from its hook and examined it.

"Well?" Julia asked.

"I certainly have to admire your industry. I've never seen a

Lodge skillet this smooth." Evan examined the skillet from all sides. "You practically scrubbed the black finish off."

"I soaked it overnight in bleach."

Evan closed her eyes. "Baby cakes . . ."

"Was that bad?" She gestured at the spotless pan. "Look how clean it is now."

"That depends. How hungry did you say you were?"

"I'm ravenous. Why?"

"Because," Evan returned the pan to its hook, "it'll take an hour to reseason this."

"Oh, *please*." Julia sipped her wine. "Cannot you compromise? Just this one time?"

Evan drummed her fingers against the quartz countertop.

"Well?" Julia insisted.

"I'm thinking about it, okay?"

"Seriously? Using a different pot is that complicated?"

"No. *Compromising* is."

Julia laughed. "I *have* missed you."

"I hope so."

"Do you doubt that?"

"No."

"Good. That'll make our next discussion a lot easier."

Evan narrowed her eyes. "Why do I suddenly smell a rat?"

Julia handed Evan her glass. "Drink up, sweetheart."

Marlene Mazzetta looked surprised, but appeared genuinely thrilled to see Tim when she opened the door to her row home. The Mazzettas lived on one of the street's more transitional blocks. Several of the sagging structures bordering their place had either been torn down or completely upfitted. Real estate in this part of South Philly was beginning to command premium prices.

"Father Donovan," she gushed. "Please come in."

"I apologize for just showing up like this," Tim said. "But I was in the neighborhood and thought I'd stop by." His lie was so bad that he had to fight a grimace as he got the words out. But Mrs. Mazzetta seemed not to notice, or care about the reason for his visit.

"Come in, come in." She ushered him inside and closed the heavy door behind them. The air inside the place was slightly stale, and he detected the scent of something frying. Scrapple maybe? Some kind of hash with onions? "Are you hungry? I'm just fixing dinner."

"Oh, no. Thank you so much. I really just wanted to duck in and say hello. I've missed seeing you at Mass. Joey, too."

Mrs. Mazzetta dropped her eyes. Tim felt like a cad.

"I've been sick," she apologized. "It's harder and harder for me to get out, my arthritis is so bad. This damp weather we've been having makes it flare up something fierce. And you know how Joey is. He just doesn't make time for things that matter."

Tim followed her back toward the kitchen at the rear of the house. Most of the interior rooms were dark, since the place only had windows at the front and back. He could hear a TV blaring from someplace upstairs. It sounded like a sitcom. The canned laugh track was pretty unmistakable.

"How is Joey?" he asked.

Mrs. Mazzetta lifted a bony hand lined with bulging blue veins and smoothed her hair. "He's okay. Out of work right now. His Kmart store closed and all fifty-two of their employees got laid off." She walked over to the stove and gave the contents of a large frying pan a stir. "That was in November. He hasn't been able to find anything else yet. Nothing that pays enough or has insurance."

"I'm sorry about that. I can imagine the strain that puts on you."

"Sit down, Father." She indicated the small kitchen table. It was littered with unopened mail and prescription bottles. "I'll make us some tea."

Tim felt like a jerk for not visiting here before now. The truth was that his parish probably had hundreds of households just like this one—filled with hardscrabble people who were barely

86

getting by. He felt ashamed and indicted by his lack of consideration and by how isolated he stayed inside his own small world of privilege. "Maybe Joey could visit the parish school? They might have something temporary for him."

Mrs. Mazzetta's watery blue eyes seemed to brighten a bit. "Do you think so? Would you talk with him? He won't go if I ask."

Tim nodded. "Sure. Is he here?"

She nodded. "Let me call him." She walked to the doorway of the kitchen and shouted up the stairs.

"Joey! Father Donovan is here. Come down and say hello to him."

It took a few seconds before Tim heard the sound of feet hitting the floor and creaking their way down the thinly carpeted stairs. When Joey appeared in the doorway, Tim was shocked by the change in his appearance. True, he hadn't taken much notice the last time he'd seen him, about three years ago at Christmas. But even with that, Joey had aged—a lot. He'd lost most of his hair, and what little he had left was stringy and tinged with white. He'd also lost a ton of weight—so much that Tim thought he might be sick.

Tim stood up and extended his hand. "Hi, Joey. It's good to see you."

Joey took Tim's hand, belatedly, and gave it a faint squeeze before shoving his own hand back into the front pocket of his baggy jeans. He didn't say anything.

"Why don't you two go sit down in the living room and chat while I make us some tea?"

Joey glowered at his mother. "I don't want any tea." He walked over to the refrigerator and took out a can of Genesee. "Want one?" he asked Tim magnanimously.

"Thanks." Tim said. "I'm going to make a couple more calls tonight so I'd better not."

Joey snapped open his beer. "Suit yourself."

"How about we go sit down," Tim suggested, "while your mom makes that tea?"

Joey shrugged. "Sure." He led the way to the dim living room and dropped into a worn armchair. They were near the stairs, and the distant TV was still blaring.

Tim sat down on the stiff cushion of a faded velour sofa. It was remarkably uncomfortable. He guessed no one ever used it. It had tatted lace doilies carefully draped over the arms and along the back.

"How've you been, Joey?" he asked. "We haven't talked in a long time."

"Okay," Joey said. "Not much new around here."

"Your mom said your Kmart closed."

"It happens. They're closing a lot of stores. Not just around here."

Tim nodded. "I heard that. It's sad."

"It's all the cheap crap from China. It's everyplace now."

"Yeah," Tim said. "It's not like the old days, for sure." He gestured toward the front of the house. "Driving over here, I remembered how a bunch of us used to shoot hoops out front."

"Can't do that now." Joey took a big swig of his beer. "You'd get run over by somebody's Mercedes."

Tim nodded. "Everything's changing."

The telephone rang. Tim heard Marlene pick it up and begin speaking in animated tones to the caller.

Joey jerked his head toward the kitchen. "I keep telling Ma she needs to sell this place. Take the money and move out to Overbrook. But she won't budge."

"I guess I understand that," Tim said. "It'd be hard for me to leave, too. I never strayed very far from the old neighborhood, either."

Joey looked at him but didn't say anything.

"I was going through some old photos recently," Tim continued. "Ancient ones, taken way back when we both were on the basketball team. I think that's what made me think about coming here tonight." He noticed the subtle change in Joey's expression. It was unmistakable—a tightening of the slack muscles in his face. That gave Tim a sick feeling. He knew asking about this was contemptible, but he was going to do it, anyway. "Do you ever think much about that time, Joey?"

Joey abruptly got to his feet. "I need another beer." He turned toward the kitchen.

"*Wait.*" Tim didn't mean for it to come out so forcefully. Joey stopped and looked down at him. "I want to . . . I need to ask you about something, Joey. Something I've never talked about with anyone." He hesitated and dropped his gaze to the old carpet that was covered with faded cabbage roses. "It's hard to talk about."

"Father Szymanski?"

Tim was shocked. He didn't expect Joey to come right out with it.

"Well . . . yeah. I mean . . ."

"Save your breath," Joey hissed. "If you're here to talk me out of turning his ass in, you're too late."

"No," Tim said quickly. "That's not what I . . ."

"I already *tried*—as soon as they announced that whole reparations thing. I went to the website and downloaded my stack of forms. The whole thing's a fucking joke. They say they care and want to make things right. It's nothing but a con. They don't give two fucks about what happened to us. All they want to do is pay us off so we'll shut up and go away," He wiped at his mouth with the back of his hand. "And they even lied about that. The only way they'll even talk to you is if you have witnesses who can back you up—or you can prove you told people about it while it was going on. Like *that* ever happens. What a bunch of bullshit. Right, *Father?*"

"Joey . . . believe me. I'm not here to protect the Church or to tell you to keep quiet. I want to help you."

"Really? It's a little late for that, isn't it?"

"I hope not."

"Fuck you, Tim—you and all the other sellouts. Fuck all of you who still want to look the other fucking way." He hurled his empty beer can across the room. It clattered against the wall and rolled behind an old console TV. "You and that bitch that came by here. You can both go to hell."

89

Bitch? Tim's mind was racing. "Who else came by?"

"That slick bitch." Joey clenched a hand in frustration. "Some foreign chick working for the diocese. She offered me twenty-five-hundred bucks to keep quiet. *Twenty-five-hundred bucks.* In cash. Are you kidding me? That's all my fucking life is worth to the Church? *Self-righteous cunt.* I threw the money in her face and told her to go get her nails done. Szymanski can rot in hell. Fuck the Church. *Fuck all of you.*"

He stormed out of the room and up the stairs with so much force it caused pictures on the walls to rattle and tilt.

Tim got up belatedly and followed him into the hallway. "Joey?" He called up the stairs. "Joey, *please.* That's not why I'm here."

There was no response. The volume on the upstairs TV got louder. Amplified sounds of laughter and applause made a surreal soundtrack for the twisted drama that had just played out.

The peculiar irony of this was impossible to miss. Tim had spent his entire adult life learning exactly how to respond to any situation. The Church had sacraments for everything . . . birth, sickness, death—and everything in between. But there were *no* rituals for something like this. He stood immobilized in the dim hallway. Useless—like a hunk of castoff furniture.

It took him a few seconds to realize that Joey's mom was in the doorway to the kitchen, holding the telephone handset against her ear. She remained rooted in place like a statue, staring back at Tim with a look of anguish on her face.

He had a feeling this wasn't the first time a conversation with her son had ended this way.

"I'm sorry," he mouthed. "I'm so sorry."

He backed toward the front door and let himself out.

Then he vomited in the street.

Evan and Julia were sitting together on a large sofa in front of the fireplace, enjoying what remained of the second bottle of wine. The weather had been deteriorating all day and the sky was now spitting snow. The hot fire felt wonderful. The fireplace in this room had an immense Federal-style carved stone mantel and was outfitted with gas logs that clearly had been patterned after sequoia limbs. Relaxing like this was wonderful. Dinner had been a success—a testament to Evan's ability to muddle through without the cast-iron skillet. She was doing her best to concentrate on how great it felt just to be here with Julia—and not to dwell on the disturbing revelations from earlier.

Julia had put some music on. Soft jazz. Probably Brubeck. It was nice—gentle and sweetly dissonant in just the right measure.

During dinner, she'd filled Julia in on her progress with the Cawley project, stopping short of sharing too much detail about Tim and his tangential connection to a potentially dark offshoot of her research. Tim's revelations about Joey Mazzetta and what he suspected had been happening at St. Rita's all those years ago was stunning to Evan. But she couldn't help him come to terms with it. He had to do that on his own. She would do what she could to pull any threads that might be connected to Judge Cawley—which probably would prove to be tenuous at best. But Tim needed to be the one to share information about his own past experiences. Evan supposed he would, in time. And even though he hadn't asked her for secrecy, she felt honor-bound to observe it until he chose, if ever, to disclose his history more broadly. And that included sharing any details with Julia or Stevie.

"You seem pensive." Julia's voice was soft and low, like a suburb of the music.

"Do I?" Evan looked at her. "I'm sorry."

"It's okay. What's on your mind?"

Evan reflexively hitched her left shoulder and regretted the gesture immediately. The odds Julia would overlook it were about as great as discovering that the frayed Powerball ticket in her back pocket contained the winning set of numbers.

Julia sat up and turned to face her. "Do you need some ice for that?"

And we have a winner . . .

"No. It's okay. Really." Evan tugged her back against the sofa cushion. "It's just a reflex. I promise."

91

"Evan . . ."

"I *promise*."

Julia looked dubious, but she resumed her former posture, leaning back against Evan.

"Okay," Julia continued. "So, you were saying?"

"I don't recall saying anything. You, on the other hand, hinted earlier that you were going to tell me something you were persuaded I wouldn't like."

"I don't think I said that, did I?"

"Well," Evan demurred. "Words to that effect."

Julia shifted her posture slightly so she could face Evan. "I called my mother while I was in Albuquerque, and we had a conversation about . . . things."

"*Things?*"

"Yes."

"Such as?"

"For starters," Julia indicated their surroundings, "I told her we needed to have a conversation about business matters. I chose not to elaborate, but those matters will include selling this place—and the New York apartment."

Evan was surprised. "Really? You don't like living here?"

"Well, once I've bleached all the cookware, there'll be no more worlds to conquer."

Evan nudged her. "Be serious?"

"All right. To answer your oddly curious question, no. I don't like living here. It's . . . absurd and needlessly extravagant. And it's not responsible to continue to carry these properties on the company books. That goes for the London flat, too, although I can't see my mother ever agreeing to part with it."

"Why now?"

Julia shrugged. "Why *not* now? I have no intention ever to live in Manhattan again, and I certainly no longer require lodging in Philadelphia on this ridiculous scale."

Evan felt a tiny surge of panic, which she tried valiantly to suppress. She prayed this wasn't a prelude to Julia telling her she was moving the company headquarters to Boston. After Andy's death, that had been a real possibility. She only opted to come to Philadelphia because . . . well . . . because of them. And, to be fair, her father had spent a fair amount of time during his tenure at the helm of Donne & Hale, running operations from the smaller Philadelphia office. So, there was some kind of precedent for the move.

Something in her expression must've tipped Julia off.

"I'm not *leaving*," she insisted with determination. "I'm just selling this townhouse."

Evan gave her a guilty look. "I guess I'm pretty transparent, aren't I?"

Julia sat forward again. "If you didn't already have a bad shoulder, I'd slug you."

That response surprised Evan. "Why?"

"*Why?* Tell me this: what in my demeanor or behavior toward you has ever suggested that I'd think about leaving here?"

Evan couldn't come up with anything but a jumble of confused feelings.

"I'm waiting."

"Nothing," Evan finally said. "There's nothing that would suggest you'd want to leave."

"Do you truly believe that?"

Evan nodded. She did believe it, too. She just couldn't always stifle the knee-jerk responses of her inner Eeyore. "But where will you live?"

Julia raised an eyebrow.

For once, Evan was pretty quick on the uptake. "Oh. Um . . ."

"I see this possibility hasn't occurred to you?"

"No," Evan said hurriedly. "That's not it. Of *course*, it has. I'm just . . ."

"Surprised?" Julia suggested.

Evan nodded. "Yeah. But in a good way."

"What if I promised to stay fifty feet away from your disgusting cookware?"

"We might consider that a condition."

"Do I get to have conditions, as well?"

"Of course." Evan narrowed her eyes. "Why do I get the sense you've had time to make a list?"

"I don't recall suggesting I had a list."

"No. But you've got that 'I've got a list' gleam in your eyes. I recognize it."

"Oh, please . . ."

"Ha! *See?* There it is again. You have a *list.*"

"Evan."

"Julia."

"Okay," Julia conceded. "Maybe I *do* have a list . . . a short one."

Evan made no effort to conceal her smug reaction to this admission. "Let's hear it."

"For starters, we need to ask Stevie what she thinks. That's the most important consideration."

Evan was moved that this was important to Julia. During the times she'd allowed herself to consider the possibility of Julia moving in with them—which had been increasing lately—this was the one consideration that always stopped her cold. *Stevie.*

What Stevie wanted mattered more to Evan than what she wanted for herself. She never wanted to do anything that would make Stevie feel like an afterthought or some kind of bystander. That was even more true now that her daughter was starting to think about college. Evan had observed firsthand how many parents couldn't wait for their kids to move out so they could coopt their spaces and redesign them as "offices" or workout rooms.

To be sure, their house in Chadds Ford was small, but Evan resolved that if she ever felt the need for more space, she'd add on rather than erase Stevie's footprint from the only home she'd ever known. Inviting a third person to share the already close quarters with them—even though it was less likely that Stevie would ever live there full time again—made this decision a big one. For all of them. Julia's sensitivity to that spoke volumes about how well she understood and respected this relationship dynamic.

"Thank you for thinking about Stevie," Evan said.

"Don't thank me yet. You haven't heard the rest of my list."

"True. What else you got?"

"Just two other things. First, we're getting a new coffeemaker. That item is nonnegotiable."

Evan rolled her eyes.

"And, I'm going to need office space of my own. I do have some thoughts about how best to accomplish that. It will entail adding on to the house. But if you're amenable, I think we can accomplish that with minimal disruption and in an unobtrusive manner consistent with the existing architecture—and I will pay for it. Entirely. No arguments."

"Okaaayyy." Evan considered Julia's suggestion. "I don't suppose you've got any sketches worked up?"

"Are you asking hypothetically?"

"Of course."

"Then hypothetically speaking, and you may not hold me to this—I might have considered committing a few ideas to paper . . . possibly."

Evan considered Julia's response. "Do you want to show me these sketches that may or may not exist now, or after we've talked with Stevie?"

"After *we've* talked with Stevie? Don't you want to have that conversation with her by yourself?"

"No. Why would I do that?"

"Um. Maybe because it would be easier for Stevie to speak freely if I weren't present?"

Evan laughed. "You *have* met this kid, right?"

"Obviously . . ."

"Then I shouldn't have to tell you that Stevie has *no* problem speaking freely, even in circumstances when she should keep her mouth shut." Evan smiled. "*Especially* when she should keep her mouth shut. I credit the Cohen end of the gene pool for this charming characteristic." She took hold of Julia's hand. "All this is to say that you never need to worry about knowing what my daughter thinks."

"That *is* among her more enviable traits."

"You think? It's always bugged the piss outta me."

"Trust me." Julia squeezed her hand. "The alternative is much worse. I should know. I was never able to be truthful—or be myself—with either of my parents."

"But you've committed to change that," Evan reminded her. "And you have been changing it. That takes real strength of character."

"Do you really think so?"

"I do."

"I'm glad to hear that," Julia continued, "because selling this place wasn't the *only* topic I discussed with my mother."

"Why do I think my name came up?"

"Probably, because in addition to being a persistent naysayer, you're also an uncommonly accomplished prognosticator."

"Those are among my more endearing qualities."

"I won't disagree with you."

Evan tugged on her hand. "So. Are you gonna tell me about your conversation?"

"In typical fashion, my mother lost no time trying to entangle me romantically with one of the hapless offspring of her blue-blooded expatriates in Paris."

"She did?"

"She *always* does," Julia replied. "It's what she has in lieu of a hobby. I think her exact words were, 'It's been two years since the incident with Andy.'"

"*Incident?*"

"Yes. And, apparently, that means it's time for me to emerge from my cocoon of self-imposed, virginal solitude."

Evan was more than a little curious. "Did she have someone in mind?"

"Of course, she did. I have to travel to Paris, anyway, to get her to co-sign some estate documents. Mother thought I should time my visit to coincide with the annual New Year's Eve celebration. Apparently, the Lippincotts are planning to be there, too—along with their hapless son, Gerald, a former classmate of mine at Exeter."

"Lippincott? As in the publishing Lippincotts?"

"Oh, yes." Julia nodded. "Albert and my father were always fast friends. At one time, they even talked about merging the two companies, but since Albert was only a distant cousin, no agreement ever developed. J.B. Lippincott eventually merged with Harper & Row in the late '70s, but Albert's branch of the family always remained close. Gerald's parents more or less adopted my mother after Dad died . . . thank god."

"Know if they're art lovers?" Evan asked.

"The Lippincotts?" Julia looked perplexed. "I have no idea. Probably. I think Binkie used to be on the board at the Barnes Foundation. Why do you ask?"

"No reason. It was just a whim . . . something random in this case." Evan squinted at Julia. "*Binkie?*"

Julia laughed. "Welcome to my world."

"So." Evan stretched her legs out and rested her feet on the edge of the coffee table. "Wanna tell me more about this Gerald guy? Does he work out? Am I gonna have to arm wrestle him for you?"

"I don't think so. And I told my mother much the same thing."

"Excuse me?" Evan wasn't sure she'd heard Julia correctly.

"You didn't misunderstand. I told her about you. About us."

"Holy shit." It was Evan's turn to sit up straighter. "What'd she say?"

"She asked if you were related to the Radnor Reeds." Julia batted her eyes. "Are you?"

Evan laughed. "I once did some second-story work there. Does that count?"

"Probably not. The upshot of our discussion was her complete refusal to entertain the prospect of me being in a relationship with another woman. So, she did what she always does, and resolved to pretend the conversation never happened."

Evan took hold of her hand and gave it a warm squeeze. "I'm sorry."

"Don't be. I'm not."

"Are you sure?"

"About us?"

Evan nodded.

Julia leaned forward and kissed her gently. "Yes. I'm sure."

Evan smiled at her. *Maybe that lottery card in her pocket would turn out to be a winner after all.*

"Me, too."

Julia tugged her closer. They spent the next few minutes in a focused exploration of how "sure" they both were. How far things certainly would have progressed was interrupted by the intrusion of Evan's cell phone.

"Is that you?" Julia muttered against Evan's neck.

"Is *what* me?" Evan was multitasking at the time and wasn't exactly sure which part Julia was referring to.

"That buzzing."

Buzzing? Evan drew back and blinked up at her. "What buzzing?"

Julia ran her hand up along Evan's side until she made contact with the hiding place of the offending object. She pulled it out of the inside pocket of Evan's jacket. "*This* buzzing." She held it up so Evan could see it.

Shit. Evan thought she'd turned the damn thing off. She took it from Julia and read the screen.

"It's Dan." She tossed the phone down on one of the discarded sofa pillows. "He can leave a message." She pulled Julia back down on top of her.

"Works for me . . ."

Exactly ninety seconds later, Julia's cell phone rang.

Julia pushed up and rested her weight on an elbow. "One guess who that is." She rolled into a sitting position and reached out to grab her phone off the coffee table. "Hello, Dan."

Evan groaned, and sat up, too.

"I'm fine," Julia was saying. "Is Stevie okay?" She gave Evan a thumbs-up. "Yes, she's here. Of course, you can talk with her. Hang on."

Julia suppressed a smirk as she passed her phone to Evan. "It's Dan."

Evan scowled and took the phone from her. "What the hell do you want?"

"What crawled up your ass?" Dan barked. "Did I cause a little coitus interruptus?"

"Fuck you. I'm not gonna satisfy your voyeuristic tendencies. This better be important."

"You tell me. I just got a call from a reporter at *The Hill*. Miller is dead."

"What?" Evan was stunned. "When?"

"The call?" Dan asked. "About twenty minutes ago. They knew I worked on his senate campaign."

"No. When did he *die*? How?"

"I don't have many details. The reporter said that hospital staff found him this morning. Apparently, he swallowed something that shredded his insides. He bled to death in his room overnight."

Jesus Christ. Evan was having trouble taking in what Dan was saying. *Swallowed something? What the hell?*

"Are you still there?" Dan asked impatiently.

"Yeah," Evan said belatedly. "I'm just taking it in."

"Well, if they called me, they're likely gonna sniff you out, too—especially since you were just up there to see him. I didn't want you getting caught off guard."

"Thanks."

"What are you gonna cite as your reason to go see him? I don't want us to wave any red flags about Cawley."

"I'll come up with something plausible. Don't worry."

"Did you get any hint that he was this unstable?"

"Dan . . . he was living in an *asylum*. What do you think?"

"Hell if I know. Your report didn't suggest that he was suicidal."

"That's because he wasn't regarded as suicidal by the hospital—not because of any assessment I made."

"Does that mean you thought he might do something like this?"

"I don't know what I thought. I need time to think about it all in a different context."

Dan knew her pretty well, and his next question did not surprise her. "So, that means you think it's possible he *didn't* commit suicide?"

"I'm not prepared to say that."

"Well, let me know when the hell you *are* prepared to say something—and soon. By my calculation, we've got another week at best to wrap this shit up. If there's nothing to report that we don't already know about this asshole, he's gonna sail right through the committee."

"I know that."

"Okay if I come see Stevie on Saturday?" It was like Dan to speak in non sequiturs.

"Sure. She'd like that." She thought about her conversation with Stevie and forced herself to issue an invitation. "Maybe you and Kayla can stop by for drinks?"

It was Dan's turn to be silent.

"Dan?" Evan asked.

"I'm here. I'm just surprised."

"Why?"

"Well, to put it bluntly, you're not usually so open to spending time with Kayla. I'm wondering if I should start looking around for giant seed pods."

"Very funny, asshole. How about two o'clock?"

"That'll work. We'll bring some wine. See you then."

"Right. Thanks for the information."

Dan hung up and Evan passed Julia's phone back to her.

"What was that all about?" Julia asked.

"Edwin Miller." Earlier that evening, Evan had filled Julia in on the visit to the asylum. "They found him dead this morning."

"Dear god . . . how awful. What happened?"

"An apparent suicide. He swallowed something and died from internal bleeding."

"But you're not convinced?"

"Convinced?" Evan asked her. "Convinced of what?"

100

"That he killed himself."

Evan sagged back against the sofa. "Right now, I don't know what I am."

"Fair enough." Julia stood up and reached for her hand. "You may be unsure about what you think, but I have no confusion about what you need."

"And that is?"

"A good night's sleep."

Evan reached for her hand. "Right behind you."

Chapter Five

The first call Evan made on Thursday morning was to Ben Rush. She filled him in on Miller and asked him to head to North Warren to see what he could find out about the circumstances surrounding the former senator's death.

"Why the fuck do I have to *go* there?" he complained. "Why not let me try to wrangle it out of the local coroner the usual way?"

"For starters, we don't know if the coroner in Warren County will even talk with you, and I don't have time to wait around for him to figure it out. *And* I want you to find out if anyone else visited Miller *after* I was there. That part is especially important. I saw the logbook when I signed in, and there hadn't been any recent visitors. See if you can get into the hospital and schmooze somebody. The woman who works the front desk seems like your type."

"What the fuck does that mean?"

"Ginormous tits and platinum hair."

There was a pause on the line. "If I leave now, I can be there by two."

Evan stifled a laugh. "Screw driving. American has a commuter flight to Erie that leaves at 10 a.m. You can rent a car when you get there. Keep your receipts. And, Ben?"

"Yeah?"

"The *only* billable expenses for this trip will be your airfare and car rental—and maybe lunch. Any motel bills are your own to sort out. Give me a call tonight with what you find out, okay?"

Ben muttered an expletive before hanging up.

Evan resolved to engage in a little spelunking of her own. *Why the hell not?*

She logged into Signal and sent a message to her new pal, Moxie. *Since we're now helping each other, I wondered if you had any useful insights into the sudden death of Edwin Miller?*

It took less than a minute to get Moxie's response.

I appreciate the compliment. But I'm sorry to report that I know nothing about the poor senator's untimely demise.

You're too modest, Evan wrote back. *But it's comforting to know you keep up on current events.*

I'd hardly be of much use to my employer if I didn't, Moxie replied. *Good luck with your fishing expedition.*

Well that certainly clarified things—*not.*

It pissed Evan off that this Moxie creature always seemed to be one step ahead. *And who the hell was their "employer?"* Why bother to reach out to Evan in the first place, unless it was to throw her off the scent of something else?

She still suspected Marcus Goldman. No one else made her scalp crawl like he did—and it was crawling so badly right now she had to fight not to claw it off.

Dan swore Marcus wasn't involved in the party's oppo project to throw a hand grenade into Cawley's nomination—which, if true, meant maybe the DNC had finally wised up and refused to work with him anymore.

It could be they had learned their lesson after the whole Andy Townsend debacle, and Marcus's role in covering up the late senator's involvement in Tom Sheridan's murder. Not to mention, Marcus had been the one who'd stashed all the nasty details of Evan's research findings on Miller in a drawer back in 2005, allowing the pedophile to win his own U.S. Senate race.

Yeah. Marcus was a real prince.

So . . . maybe the party *had* finally gotten smart?

She doubted it.

103

If Marcus wasn't working with them now, it only meant he was playing in somebody else's sandbox.

Yet . . . the scumbag sent Dan that original photo of Cawley with Bishop Szymanski. *Why?* She doubted it was for philanthropic reasons.

None of it made any sense. It wasn't like Marcus gave two shits about the sex abuse scandals tearing the Catholic Church apart. Her experience with handing him the goods on Miller was proof enough of that. So why tip them off about the connection between Cawley and Szymanski?

And why had Moxie sent her the second photo of Szymanski with Cawley?

Something occurred to her . . .

Maybe leading her to follow a connection between *them* diverted her from looking into something else. Maybe it wasn't about *them* at all. *Maybe it was something about Joey Mazzetta— or one of the other boys on the basketball team?*

They'd have no idea about Evan's relationship with Tim—and Tim's ability to identify Joey in each of the two photographs.

She had a feeling she might be inching closer to something. And the thought that maybe Marcus and Moxie were both working to toss red herrings into her path began to make more sense. If true, their respective goals could simply be to slow her down long enough to allow Cawley's nomination to move through the Senate before the Christmas recess.

Dan said they had less than a week to wrap things up. That meant this little game of beat the clock had to start working in *her* favor, instead of theirs.

Now she just had *one* problem: *how the hell to do it* . . .

"Murder wasn't part of the equation." Maya was annoyed and wanted answers.

"We've already had this conversation." Zucchetto sounded annoyed. "Your instructions were explicit at the outset. You are not to contact me at this number unless it's an emergency."

"Silly me for considering the murder of a former U.S. Senator qualifies as an emergency."

"You overdramatize the matter, surely. What leads you to believe Mr. Miller was murdered? I have seen no such suggestion of that. If anything, it's an unfortunate coincidence."

"Don't kid a kidder. I wasn't born yesterday. There *are* no coincidences in this kind of work."

"To what kind of work might you be referring? We engaged you, quite simply, to manage the unwelcome proliferation of negative public relations."

Maya laughed at his ridiculous characterization of their understanding. "Let's be clear about something. You may employ all the euphemisms you desire, but my stipulations were unambiguous. If murder is now part of your 'solution,' the contract price just went up—exponentially."

"It's comforting to see how deep your scruples go."

"Don't misunderstand me, Mr. Zucchetto. My *only* issue with the evolving objectives of your organization relates to the particulars of my compensation package."

"I can assure you that my associates had nothing to do with the Senator's death. And if our needs ever change, you may be certain you'll be informed and properly compensated. Until then," he added coldly, "please be kind enough to adhere to our agreed-upon protocols for communication."

He disconnected.

Insufferable prig. Maya tossed the 'special' cell phone down on the bed.

Miller had been murdered. There was no doubt of that. And if Zucchetto were telling the truth—which might be possible—who did it? And why?

Not Evan Reed. *That was impossible.* Reed was too much of a girl scout. She didn't have the stomach for it—no matter the power of her motivation. That thought was humorous for its irony. Reed's "Catholic" values would hamstring her at every turn.

What a supreme little ray of sunshine in this *pathetic costume drama . . .*

So, if not Reed, who?

She paced the hotel room before stopping to stare out the large corner windows overlooking Independence Hall.

There were a finite number of people who would be paranoid and opportunistic enough to neutralize a harmless, crazy man. And only one of them made sense in this context.

Marcus.

Julia got a reprieve from the Boston trip when her assistant called to tell her that their recalcitrant author had relented and consented to sign the second book contract after all—with a lengthy rider of caveats that Julia would be forced to review and either approve or reject.

At least this much progress was welcome news, and not just because it represented a very important acquisition for Donne & Hale. Julia was still tired from all the hours spent traveling yesterday, and neither she nor Evan had got much sleep last night. Evan had been too unsettled after Dan's call to wind down. Even after they took a long, soaking bath together, and snuggled beneath the covers, Julia could still feel the tension in Evan's body.

"Try to relax," she urged. "You can't do anything about it tonight."

"I know. I'm sorry." Evan rolled onto her back. "I don't mean to keep you awake, too."

"You're not keeping me awake. Do you need to talk about it?"

"It won't do any good. Not until I can get some information about what really happened."

"Why do you say what 'really' happened? Do you think Dan's account was inaccurate?"

Evan rotated her bad shoulder a couple of times. Julia made an effort not to comment on it. "Not so much inaccurate as incomplete."

"Meaning?"

"Meaning, I simply don't believe in coincidences. Miller didn't just happen to drop dead the day after I went to see him."

"I'm tempted to ask why you think you'd be the common denominator here?"

Evan laughed. "Don't tell me you're talking about grandiosity? Not *me?*"

"Well. The thought did occur to me . . ."

"I won't deny that this propensity functions as a go-to reference point on my psychological profile. But I promise, it's not what motivates me to be suspicious about the timing of whatever in the hell happened to Edwin Miller. He didn't meet an untimely end because of *me*—but I'm not persuaded that my poking around in his past connection to Judge Cawley didn't raise some nervous hackles that set some darker things in motion."

"Evan, that's terrible. Do you honestly believe that?"

"Unfortunately, yes. There are other minor key vibrations in this mess. And none of them support a theme that points toward anything good."

Julia began to grow alarmed. "Is it dangerous?"

"Not for me."

Julia sat up. "I'm not sure I believe you."

"Honey . . ."

"*No.* I still have nightmares about how things ended with Andy—and how close you were to getting killed."

Evan laid a hand on her knee. "He wouldn't have killed me. Maya stopped him."

"She nearly killed you in the process."

"That wasn't intentional."

"I'm not so sure. Maya does nothing by accident. *Ever.*"

"Honey." Evan squeezed her knee. "Let's not go down this rabbit hole tonight. Okay?"

Julia covered Evan's hand with her own. "All right. Not tonight. But you have to promise me that you'll tell Dan if this case gets any more . . . *complicated.*"

"Tell Dan? Why? So he can have Kayla run a blistering op-ed in *Media Matters?*"

"Okay," Julia reached over and snapped on the bedside light, "*enough.* This thing of yours with Kayla is no longer cute or funny. It's toxic, Evan. And it needs to stop."

Evan blinked back at her with surprise while her eyes adjusted to the sudden blaze of light. "Are you pissed at me?"

"What tipped you off?"

"Well, the floodlight, for one thing." Evan rubbed her eyes. "And it's not like you to issue ultimatums."

"I don't recall there being an 'or else' at the end of my sentence."

"It was implied by the context."

Julia took a moment to consider her remark. "I suppose that's true. I really *am* over this—and so is Stevie."

"I'm sorry."

"Are you?"

Evan shrugged.

"What's behind this, Evan? You love Dan. I know that. So why don't you want him to find happiness?"

"It's a trust thing."

"A 'trust' thing? You don't trust Kayla?"

"Not really. But that's not it. I don't trust Dan."

"Dan?"

Evan nodded. "He makes profoundly bad choices that end up hurting him. Always has." She raised a hand. "In case you're wondering, I'd be Exhibit A in that argument."

Julia was silent for a moment. "You both got Stevie out of that particular error in judgment, so I'd say it wasn't a total write-off."

"That's true."

"It's *his* life, Evan. Back off and let him live it. Without judgment or prognostication."

"Prognostication?"

"It seemed like a Catholic-enough term to apply here."

Evan laughed. "I never want to face you in a boardroom."

"Good instinct. I can promise it wouldn't work out for you."

Evan huffed in frustration. "It just makes me crazy when people do stupid shit."

"What makes you so certain that marrying Kayla qualifies as stupid?"

"Oh, come on. I *know* him, Julia."

"And I know you. This isn't about Dan."

"No?"

"No."

"Then illuminate me," Evan demanded. "What *is* it about?"

"Boundaries. And more specifically, where they should usually be found."

Evan knitted her brows. "I have no idea what that's supposed to mean."

"That would be my point."

Evan dropped her head back and stared at the coffered ceiling of the huge bedroom. Julia followed her gaze. The bedside lamp was casting ominous shadows that made the wells of the grids look as deep as caverns.

"Do you plan to illuminate me?" Evan asked, after a few seconds of contemplation.

"I don't know if I can."

"Why not?"

"Oh," Julia clarified, "it isn't that I don't want to. It's just that for you, boundaries are abstract concepts that have to be stumbled over before they become recognizable."

"Meaning?"

"Meaning, a parent can tell a child not to touch the top of a stove because it's hot and can burn them. The child then has two choices. She can accept the warning without question, or she can test the theory herself by actually touching the top of the stove, and probably getting burned in the process. So, for many children, until there is some empirical evidence to support a warning, the concept lacks integrity or a basis in fact."

"That sounds more like a trust issue than a boundary issue."

"What's sauce for the goose . . ."

Evan drummed her fingers on the rumpled bedspread. She shot Julia a sidelong glance. "How do you know all this shit about child rearing?"

Julia shrugged. "We published Piaget."

"Why didn't I think of that?" Evan said with wonder. "Yeah.

Well. Sheila wasn't much for issuing warnings. I grew up with a lot of burns."

Julia took hold of her hand. "I know."

"I'll try to change."

"You don't *need* to change. Just learn to pay attention to your impulses—especially when they relate to Dan and Kayla. If you do, I promise that what you see will begin to resemble something that can burn you if you keep testing it. And that's not good for you, or for Stevie."

"Okay." Evan lifted Julia's hand and kissed it. "I'll try."

"Wanna try and get some sleep now?"

"Nuh uh." Evan tugged Julia closer.

"*Nuh uh?* Got something else in mind?"

Evan kissed her. "You might say that."

"Am I going to like it?"

"I sure as hell hope so." Evan dropped back against the pillows and pulled Julia down on top of her. "I thought we could practice."

"Practice?" Julia began to lose focus as Evan kissed along her bare collarbone.

"Yeah. Suddenly, I feel the need to touch a few hot objects to see if they'll burn me."

They engaged in some creative experimentation before dropping off to sleep—blissfully burn-free, and wrapped around each other in a soft, snug cocoon.

As delightful as that had been, Julia knew they'd both pay for it today. Evan had been bleary-eyed when she'd left in the morning. They promised to connect with each other later that night, after Julia got settled in her Boston hotel room.

But now that trip wasn't happening.

She yawned.

At least she could get that meeting with her father's estate attorney out of the way. She sent a quick message off to the firm to say she'd be available today, after all. With luck, she could get that errand taken care of—and get the necessary paperwork started to secure her mother's agreement to sell the residential properties. If her mother balked, Julia would suggest handing the management of the high-end locations off to a leasing agent. If Donne & Hale would be forced to retain the assets, then at least the properties could begin to earn some revenue to justify their presence on the company's ledger books. That was her hope, anyway. With her mother, nothing was ever predictable.

The flashback was always the same.

Water. Running water.

He was freezing. Shivering. The water was cold. The water was always cold.

One naked bulb hung from the high ceiling. It kept flickering off and on like a strobe light. When it went out, broad, dark shadows covered the cracked tile walls. When it came back on, the sudden burst of light would blind his eyes and make it hard to see anything.

It smelled like Pine-Sol. He hated that.

He tried to hurry. He didn't want to be there. Not that night. And not alone.

The water was like sharp pellets of ice stinging his skin.

He flattened his hands against the slippery wall and gritted his teeth before ducking his head beneath the frigid spray to rinse.

Nearly finished.

The bulb went out again. Then came back on. In the sudden blaze of light, he blinked down at the iridescent pond of soap suds covering his feet. Then the darkness returned.

He waited, but this time, the light didn't come back on.

"I'll wash your back for you."

The low voice came from behind him. He recognized it right away. He closed his eyes. He knew this would happen. He knew it.

The man moved closer.

He recognized the cologne. The sickly-sweet scent of it mixing with the Pine-Sol was enough to make his stomach seize up. He thought he might get sick.

111

Then he felt hands on his shoulders. The man's touch was hot. The hands traveled down his arms as a body leaned into him.

He lurched away from the intruder in the small space—but he didn't turn around. He was glad it was dark because he didn't want to see the man's naked body—didn't want to see the erection he'd felt nudging his back.

"No," he said. He knew he sounded panicked. "No. I'm finished."

"It's okay, Tim," the man coaxed. "It'll help you relax. I do it for the other boys all the time."

The other boys? He didn't want to ask what that meant. He already knew.

"I'm finished, Father." He felt his way along the slick, darkened walls and stumbled out of the small shower, nearly tripping over its low threshold. He grabbed his pile of clothes off the bench without drying off, and tried to pull them on as he hurried out of the locker room.

Father Szymanski never called out to him, and he didn't look back as he ran.

Another endless night of wrestling with demons was enough inducement to persuade Tim that he wasn't finished with this. The third time he woke up from a nightmare, wound up in sheets as tight as a burial shroud, he knew he'd never find peace if he didn't try to make things right.

Sadly, that didn't seem like a possibility with Joey Mazzetta. *No.* Joey was too angry and too polarized—against him, and against the Church. Tim couldn't summon the energy or the moral authority to fault him for that. Joey was right to suspect Tim's motivation for showing up at his house unannounced— especially after his revelation that someone had approached him in a flimsy attempt to buy his silence.

That disclosure was a mystery for Tim. *Who would do such a thing?* Even considering all of the gross negligence and abrogation of responsibility the Church had demonstrated throughout its handling of these abuse scandals, Tim found it impossible to believe they would be behind something so—nefarious.

Who was he kidding?

Everything he thought he knew about the Church had been chipped away bit by bit. It reminded him of that Stephen King novella Stevie had lent him—the one about how a prison inmate, Andy Dufresne, managed to tunnel his way out of Shawshank prison using only a pocket-sized rock hammer. It took the unjustly convicted man twenty-eight years to chip out a hole large enough to allow him to escape to freedom.

But in this instance, the Church was the institution holding the truth hostage—and Tim was the one trying to claw his way out.

He knew he should tell Evan about his plan to seek out other members of the youth basketball team. But he wasn't going to. He knew she'd try to stop him. She'd tell him that sorting through this was not his path to salvation. That he couldn't change the past, and that the State had now set up an independent reparations commission to make it possible for victims of abuse to come forward.

If only it were that simple . . .

He knew it wasn't. And how many others had already tried, like Joey, and failed to get a hearing?

Besides. This wasn't about the Church. Not anymore. This was *his* rite of passage.

He'd already done a bit of innocuous research in the parish office. Four of the guys who'd played on the team at St. Rita's during his tenure still lived in the Philadelphia area. He had found current addresses for two of them, and he planned to reach out to them over the weekend.

But this time, there would be a big difference in his approach. This time, he wasn't going to show up unannounced. That knee-jerk idea had backfired miserably with Joey Mazzetta. Given the gravity of what Tim wanted to discuss, he resolved that it was better to make an initial contact with his former teammates by phone. That way, if the prospect of talking about Father Szymanski and their recollections of any unseemly behavior that may have occurred all those years ago was too painful or too much of a trigger, they could tell Tim so, up front, and be spared the spectacle of an unpleasant encounter.

Tim stared at their names and addresses. He'd written them hastily on a sheet of notepaper he'd borrowed from Sister Ida. It was cream-colored, and had an embossed St. Margherita crest above the inscription, *Domus Dei et Porta Coeli.* "House of God, Door to Heaven."

The records didn't reveal much information about the lives of the two boys after they'd left St. Rita's. He knew anecdotally that one of them—Mark Atwood—was now openly gay and running a bar on South Camac Street in Philly's Gayborhood district.

The other, Brian Christensen, managed a Chevy dealership in Gloucester City. Brian had been one of the high school students on the Wildcats team during the years Tim played basketball at St. Rita's. He was the team captain and most of the middle school boys, like Tim and Joey, looked up to him. When the rumors and whispering started about all the "special" perks that went to players who were favorites of Father Szymanski, Brian was the one they asked about it.

"There's nothing going on," he once told them, during the long bus ride home from their weeklong basketball camp at Trout Lake in Stroudsburg. Tim thought back about Brian's demeanor when they questioned him. He'd been defensive—nervous, even. It was clear he wanted to kill any suggestion that he was involved in anything with their priest. "I just worked hard—always showed up for practice, and never missed a game. Because of that, I got a scholarship to Temple."

Brian wasn't alone in his good fortune. Other players on the team were also singled out to attend fancy dinners at expensive restaurants in town, where they got to rub elbows with politicians and business leaders in the community. And, sometimes, like Brian, they got a better shot at access to scholarship assistance from wealthy team sponsors.

That inducement was the one that led Tim to spend so many extra hours at the school gym, practicing free throws and trying to improve his field goal percentages. The Donovans weren't a wealthy family—not by a long shot. And before he got his calling, Tim aspired to graduate from St. Rita's and study engineering at a good school with a respected program. Someplace like Columbia or Carnegie Mellon. But being able to afford to do that meant he'd have to earn the tuition money himself.

Or get a scholarship.

Tim came home from camp that summer determined to follow Brian's example. And when Father Szymanski began to pay special attention to him and suggested that he start staying late after practice to work on improving his skills, he was only too eager to agree. For a while, it seemed to be working.

Until that incident in the shower . . .

"I do it for the other boys all the time."

Father Szymanski uttered the words so softly and matter-of-factly, it seemed like he assumed Tim would know what they meant.

He hadn't gone home that night. Not at first. Not for a long while. He did what he always did when he was afraid: he went to Evan's. She wasn't at home when he got there—and her mother was never around that early in the evening—so the house was locked up tight. But he hung around there anyway, sitting on the top step of their front porch in the fading light, doing his best not to shake. *Not to cry.* It was near freezing outside and he was still soaked from fleeing the shower. His damp clothes were plastered against his thin body. They felt stiff and seemed to weigh five times more than normal. He couldn't stop his teeth from chattering as he hugged himself to try and get warm.

Evan finally showed up after he'd been huddled there for the better part of an hour.

"What the hell are you doing sitting out here?" she demanded. Then she noticed his hair. "Why are you wet?"

"I came here after practice. They didn't have any more clean towels after I showered," he lied.

"That's fucked up." Evan unlocked the front door. "Come on. I'll give you something dry to wear."

Tim struggled to his feet and followed her inside.

"Where were you?" he asked.

"Would you believe me if I said the library?"

"No."

She smirked at him. "Too bad. That's all I'm telling you."

She smelled like cigarettes. Tim could guess the rest. "Where's your mom?"

"Out." Evan gestured toward the street. "Who cares? Are you hungry?"

He nodded.

"Me, too." She led him up the narrow stairs to her bedroom and fished a pair of flannel pants and an oversized Eagles sweatshirt out of the broken bottom drawer of her old dresser. "Put these on and meet me in the kitchen. We'll make some pizza rolls and watch *Night Court*."

She handed him the clothes and left him standing in the middle of her small bedroom. He listened to her footsteps as she retreated back down the stairs.

That was it.

He never told her about what had happened that night—and he assumed he never would.

All of that changed for him on August 14, 2018, with the public release of findings from a grand jury investigation into broad patterns of sexual abuse by Catholic priests across six dioceses in Pennsylvania. Tim had already been aware that specific cases of sexual misconduct by priests in Philadelphia had been under investigation for more than a decade. But the breadth and scope of the 2018 report was devastating to him—and impossible to ignore.

How many thousands of innocent children had been victimized by his fellow priests—servants of Christ who had chosen to betray their solemn vows? And what extreme measures had the Church—*his* Church—undertaken to protect the abusers, and to conceal the truth?

The public no longer had to guess at the answers to questions like those.

It was horrible. Unconscionable. *Impossible to comprehend.*

And in how many ways had he unwittingly aided and abetted them all by keeping his own voice silent? He could never forgive himself for that. His selfish determination to ignore what was too difficult—too frightening—for him to confront and make public left him every bit as complicit in the commission of this tragedy as the perpetrators and their powerful protectors. *But now?* Now he could try to make restitution for his sins. He could speak up about what he suspected and tell the truth about what he'd experienced firsthand. He could make a public acknowledgment of his personal culpability by admitting to his own refusal to recognize what had been happening all around him. Signs he'd ignored, odd comings and goings, the looks on some of the altar boys' faces on Sunday mornings . . .

And he could reach out to his former teammates, too. Do what he'd never been courageous enough to do before: *listen to them.* Offer them support and a promise to bear witness to their experiences—all the things Joey said he didn't get when he tried to tell *his* truth to the reparations panel.

And he could make a public acknowledgment of his own complicity, and openly confess his refusal to recognize what had been happening all around him.

Would it make a difference?

He had no idea.

Mark Atwood and Brian Christensen might just do what Joey did: tell him to fuck off and burn in hell.

He wouldn't blame them one bit.

And he knew he'd probably fail—but he'd be damned if he wouldn't at least try.

It was nearly 5 p.m. when Ben Rush called from North Warren.

"What the hell are you still doing up there?" Evan checked her watch. "The last flight back here leaves Erie in less than an hour."

"I thought I'd stay on a little longer," he said.

"I guess I was right about those tits."

Ben sniggered. "She's nice."

"*Nice?* So, you're planning to start a book club with her?"

"Hey—back the fuck off. You're the one who sent me up here to this shithole town."

"To get *information*, Ben. Not as an opportunity to get your wick dipped."

"Don't get your panties in a wad. I'm off the clock. You want this report or not?"

"Yeah." Evan said. "I want the report. But, Ben?"

"What?"

"I want your ass back here no later than tomorrow afternoon. You want to make another booty call? You can do it on your own dime. Understood?"

He didn't reply.

"I'm not kidding," she added. "Tomorrow afternoon."

"I'll fucking *be* there. Jesus Christ, woman."

"Good. So, what's the story?"

"Well." She could hear Ben take a drag off his cigarette. "He's dead."

"No shit, Sherlock. What happened?"

"Shirley said he complained about a stomachache during the night, and the nurse gave him Panadol to help him sleep. They found him on the floor of his room in the morning, rolled up in a fetal position. He'd been dead more than an hour. X-rays showed that he had twenty-eight micro-pin finishing nails in his intestines—along with a cardboard piece of a jigsaw puzzle. The nails cut up his insides pretty bad. He'd bled to death before they found him."

"Holy shit." Evan was incredulous. "He swallowed *nails?*"

"*Micro pin* nails," Ben clarified. "They're like tiny brad tacks. Usually fired from a nail gun so you don't see them after they're shot into trim boards."

"Where the hell did he get those?"

"They don't know. Shirley said there had been some carpenters on his ward, remodeling a storage closet. Miller might've lifted a pack of them from a tool bucket."

"How could he even swallow those?" she asked.

"They were stuck inside some candy bars—apparently, a lot of 'em. They found a pile of wrappers on the floor beside his bed."

Candy bars? Holy shit . . . it made sense. Miller swallowed them whole, without chewing.

"How do they know the tacks were in the candy?"

"Because," Ben continued, "there was a paper bag on his bedside table that had a bunch more of 'em. After they found the shit inside Miller, they went back and x-rayed the candy in the bag. And all of it was full of tacks."

"Somebody put the nails *inside* the candy bars?"

"They think he did it himself." Ben coughed. "Jesus, it's fucking cold up here."

"You're outside?"

"Yeah. This goddamn motel is nonsmoking."

Evan closed her eyes. *Ben and Shirley shacked up at some fleabag motel was not a mental image she needed.*

She changed the subject. "Why are they calling this a suicide?"

"Beats the fuck outta me. Shirley says his family didn't give a rat's ass about his death, so maybe the coroner didn't think it was worth the time or trouble to investigate it as a wrongful death. Poor bastard."

"Yeah." Evan had to agree. "Poor bastard."

"That's not all," Ben began.

"What do you mean?"

"I did a little snooping around. Remember all that woo-woo shit Ping was going on about?"

"You mean about the hospital and all the paranormal activity?"

"Yeah." He cleared his throat. "Turns out she was right—at least about the underground tunnels. Some ass-wipe even *mapped* the damn things. There's a fucking two-hour, YouTube video tour. It's pretty goddamn creepy down there, lemme tell you."

"Wait a minute." Evan said in disbelief. "You went down into those tunnels?"

"Of course. Isn't that what you pay me for? To do the dirty shit nobody else wants to touch?"

Evan thought about Shirley. *Maybe Ben did deserve a little perk now and then.*

"What'd you find down there?" she asked.

Ben huffed. "Rat shit. Mildew. Cast-off furniture from the '50s. It looks like Norman Bates lives down there—with his fucking mother."

"Anything else?"

"Oh, yeah. One of those tunnels led to a set of stairs that went right up into the ward Miller was on. The door at the top had a busted padlock on it. It looked like somebody used a pair of bolt-cutters on it—and recently. The metal shavings were clean."

"Holy shit."

"Yeah. The door opened into some kind of tiny-ass linen closet. There was a set of metal shelves loaded with sheets and shit in front of it, but it was easy to force out far enough to squeeze past. So if somebody *did* decide to wax your buddy Miller, they had a way to get inside without being seen."

It was a lot to take in. Evan had no doubt now that Miller had been murdered.

But why?

Her mind was bouncing around like a rental car on one those goddamn back roads.

"Are you still there?" Ben asked, impatiently.

"Yeah. Sorry." Evan took a second to try and clear her head. "Should we tell the local cops?"

"That I broke into the hospital and now have a cockamamie theory about how Miller got taken out by some fucking ghost? Sure. They'd totally believe it—*not*. They don't give two fucks. And if you ask me, the crazy schlemiel is better off dead. It's not like he was gonna get outta this place any other way."

"I guess so." *But did she agree with Ben? Was it right not to share what they suspected about Miller's death?*

"Maybe I'll run it by Dan, and see what he says."

"Yeah. You do that." She could hear Ben take another deep drag on his cigarette. "Now if we're finished here, I've got some other business to take care of—and it's costing me eighty-five bucks an hour."

Evan blinked. "She's charging you by the hour?"

"Not *her*, asshole. The motel. Jesus."

"Sorry. Yeah. You go do . . . whatever it is you plan to do. And Ben?"

"What?"

"At least buy her dinner, man."

"Hey? What kind of cheap bastard do you think I am? There's a dog-n-cat delivery joint about a mile up the highway from here."

Dog-n-cat was Ben's offensive shorthand for Chinese takeout.

"You're a class act, Rush. Make sure you use protection."

He snorted. "I don't need 'protection.' Her tits ain't the only thing on her that's been fixed."

"TMI, man." Evan closed her eyes. "I'm signing off now."

"Later."

The line went dead.

Evan sat holding her cell phone against her ear, staring at— *nothing*—for the better part of a minute.

Then she took a deep breath and called Dan.

Chapter Six

Tim waited for Stevie outside the security screening area at Terminal E. He was glad he had arrived early because her flight from Albany landed fifteen minutes ahead of schedule. That was good news—and not simply because they'd have a better shot at getting a jump on Friday night traffic heading out of town. The simple truth was that he was anxious and impatient to see her.

Stevie was more than just his goddaughter. She was a confounding and beautiful amalgamation of the best parts of Evan—Evan, who had always been his confidant and defender. But there was a big difference between them. Stevie was blissfully untainted by the darkness that sometimes clung to Evan like a second skin. Much of that darkness derived from Evan's childhood, and the fractious nature of her on-again, off-again relationship with her mostly absentee mother. The lingering damage she sustained from the dysfunctional roller coaster ride she'd endured during her formative years colored nearly everything in Evan's life—everything but Stevie.

And now, Julia's sustained presence was adding even more proof that Evan's darkest days were behind her.

It was ironic. Growing up, Evan always teased him with the nickname "Sunny," because his family was, in her words, "so damn boring and predictable." That never bothered him—not until his interior life became murkier and a lot less certain. But Tim never shared that change with her—or with anyone else.

Instead, he poured his heart and all of his energy into nurturing the first stirrings of his calling. Once he realized he'd never be in a position to benefit from any of the "special assistance" Father Szymanski and his business associates dangled before the other boys like unholy idols, he spent more time internally focused—brooding about his own mortality and purpose. In his youthful mind, the decision to pursue a vocation existed on an entirely different plane than the frightening glimpse he'd had of what surely had been taking place between Father Szymanski and some of his classmates. After he'd willfully turned his face away from those horrors, he quickly became desensitized to any evidence of impropriety in the Church. That led him to stumble blindly toward his future in a burlesque imitation of Lot, who fled his own land of decay and debauchery with his eyes shut tight.

Tim had unwittingly sworn obeisance to an unholy pact of silence—but, somehow, he understood that if ever he dared look back, he'd be immobilized for all eternity.

A useless pillar of salt.

Stevie though? Stevie wasn't like that at all. Stevie faced her demons—*and everyone else's*—with wide-eyed candor and unbridled optimism. She was confident. Opinionated. And blessedly unspoiled.

Tim prayed she'd always remain that way—even though he knew such an outcome wasn't likely. She'd be heading off to college soon, and her world, along with her choices, would increase exponentially. In the meantime, he was determined to spend as much time with her as he could, and to treasure their sweet and playful interactions. If Evan was like the sister he'd never had, then Stevie was the closest thing he could imagine to a daughter.

One he now owed twenty bucks . . .

He felt inside his front pocket for the folded bill. He knew she'd expect him to pay up right away.

What a stupid bet. He should've known that Holy Cross would never beat Boston College.

A throng of tired-looking travelers began to file past him. Most of them were lugging rollaboards and carrying overstuffed bags. There were quite a few teenagers—all in a hurry. He supposed that Stevie wasn't the only one making her way home for the holidays.

He saw a flash of lime green. It was attached to the arm of someone who was energetically waving at him. She bobbed in and out of sight as she made her way up the concourse.

He waved back.

One thing Stevie had in common with Evan was her bizarre fashion sense. In most other ways, she took after Dan. Tall. Dark hair and brilliant green eyes.

He stepped forward to greet her. She dropped her backpack and hurled herself at him.

"Hey there, Papasan."

He hugged her back. "Howdy, shortstop."

Stevie buried her face in his jacket. "You smell like tacos."

"Sorry. I had a late lunch." She bent down to retrieve her backpack, but Tim picked it up. "I'll carry that. Do you have a checked bag?"

"Nope. Just this."

"Really?"

"Yeah. I have enough stuff at Mom's to manage." She gave him a wry smile. "She didn't fool me with the whole plane ticket thing. I knew she didn't want me to lug all my dirty laundry home."

They were making their way toward the terminal exit.

"Maybe she just wanted you to get home sooner."

Stevie shrugged. "Maybe." She elbowed him. "Where's my money, Bucko?"

Tim laughed and dug the bill out of his pocket. He passed it over to her. "I swear. You could have a great career as a bookie."

Stevie snatched the bill from him and held it in front of her nose. "Ahhhhh. The sweet scent of victory."

"What-*ever*. Do not spend that on riotous living."

"What the heck is *that?*"

"Ask your mother."

"Right. Ohhhh. *Pretzels.* Can we get one?"

Tim followed her gaze. "Why the hell not?" He took hold of

124

her arm and steered them toward the vendor cart she'd spotted. It was set up next to the tenth Starbucks they'd passed since leaving Terminal E. "Are you hungry?"

"Duh."

He chuckled. "Me, too."

"I thought you just had tacos?"

"Yeah. And your point would be?"

"Right. Mom *is* cooking tonight. We should both load up." They ordered their pretzels. Stevie got extra mustard on hers. Tim was surprised when she used his twenty to pay for them.

"I'd have gotten those for us."

"Forget about it." She collected her change from the mustached vendor. He looked a lot like Luigi from Super Mario Bros. "You can share the wealth when we stop at Wawa."

"We're stopping at Wawa?"

Stevie looked at him sideways before taking a big bite of her soft pretzel. The smear of mustard left a yellow trail along her upper lip. "Don't you wanna get something that's actually edible for later? I thought I'd get a couple of Shorties."

Tim thought about it. Evan actually was a *great* cook, although her choices tended toward the exotic. Lately, she'd been on an Ethiopian kick, and the last few meals he'd had with her had been somewhat . . . eclectic.

"Good idea. We'll pick up some Doritos, too."

They resumed walking toward the exit.

"She'll be pissed," Stevie observed.

"What else is new?" Tim held the door open for her.

"Wonder if we should pick up something for Julia, too?"

Tim laughed. "That's exactly what I was thinking."

It took them fifteen minutes to navigate their way to his car and begin to corkscrew their way out of the airport. Stevie used the time to devour the rest of her pretzel. When she finished, she looked around for a place to stash the wad of waxed paper. Tim pointed to a plastic ShopRite bag hanging from the back of her headrest. It was overflowing with discarded food wrappers.

Stevie made a face. "This car is gross."

125

"I intentionally saved all of that so you'd have something to complain about."

"Sure you did."

Once they had cleared the airport campus and were headed toward Route 1, Stevie tucked her legs beneath her and rotated on her seat to face him—not an easy maneuver in his Subaru.

"So, what else going on with you?" she asked. "Besides eating too much junk food."

Tim was surprised by her tone. It was . . . serious. Not conversational. He panicked for a moment and wondered if Evan had said something to her about his . . . dilemma.

"What do you mean?" He tried to keep his voice neutral.

"What do you think I mean? You just seem different."

"I do?"

She nodded.

"Different—how?"

Stevie wiped at some dust that had collected on his dashboard. She always nagged him about taking better care of his car. That had become especially important to her since he'd begun giving her driving lessons during her stays at home. "You're skinny," she said. "And you don't look like yourself."

"I don't?"

"Nope. Where's your collar thing?"

Tim reflexively raised a hand to his throat. "I just didn't put it on today."

"Seriously? Mom says you practically sleep in it."

"She's nuts. I don't *sleep* in it."

"You know what I mean. How come you're not wearing it?"

Tim stole a glance at her. The expression on her face surprised him. She was looking at him intently—*really* looking at him. *From the mouths of babes . . .*

He knew he was busted. Why did he always have to be so damn transparent?

"I'm . . . struggling with some stuff right now."

"What kind of stuff?"

Jeez, kid. Cut to the chase much?

126

"It's complicated." He thought about how he'd used that same phrase with Evan the night of the aurora. It sounded even lamer right now.

Apparently, Stevie thought so, too. "Maybe if you talk about it, it'll get less complicated. That's how it's supposed to work, right?"

"Who taught you that?"

She smiled at him. "You did."

Tim stared through the windshield at the line of cars in front of them. *Don't cry in front of the kid. Don't cry in front of the kid.*

"Is it something about the Church?" Stevie wasn't going to give this inquisition up.

Tim exhaled the breath he'd been holding. "What makes you ask that?"

She shrugged. "I figured it either had to be that or something about sex."

"What?" Tim looked at her with a shocked expression.

She laughed. "It could happen. You're *still* a guy."

"You say that like it's supposed to mean something."

"Trust me. Mom thinks that sending me to an all-girls school was supposed to protect me from being 'ravaged by the male species.'" She made air quotes. "Yeah. Not so much."

"Now *I'm* the one who wants to ask *you* what's different."

"Nice try, Papasan. It's your turn to spill the beans."

Tim deliberated. If part of his resolution was to tell the truth and stop hiding from his past, why not start that process now? Besides, Stevie would find out eventually . . . especially after he took up residence on their living room couch.

"Okay. I've been thinking about leaving the Church."

Stevie's eyes grew wide. "St. Rita's? *Why?* Are you moving?"

"Not exactly. But, yes. Leaving St. Rita's . . . and the priesthood."

"*No way.* Did something happen? Are you okay?"

He reached out to touch her hand. "I'm okay. And yes, something happened. But it was a long time ago, and I'm finally ready to come to terms with it."

Stevie took his hand between both of hers. "Can you talk about it? Do you want to?"

127

"I'm working on being able to talk about it. But it's a process." He gave her fingers a squeeze. "I promise to tell you everything as soon as I can. Okay?"

She nodded. "Does Mom know?"

"Yeah. Mostly."

"How about Julia?"

"No. But I thought I'd tell her tonight." He tugged on her hand. "I was going to tell you, too. It's just that it's like having to confront a problem I never thought I'd have."

"Okay." She seemed to think about what he'd said. "So, I guess this is like the priest equivalent of having marital problems?"

"What do you mean?"

"You and the Church. I mean . . . you're kind of married to the Church, right?"

He had to hand that one to her. "Yeah. I guess."

"So, it sounds like maybe one of you is cheating, and you feel like the vows you took are broken. Is that why you want to leave? Because you think you won't ever get past the problem or find forgiveness? And that makes you believe a divorce is the only solution?"

Tim gaped at her in amazement. In less than one minute, she had managed to summarize his entire crisis of faith with a single, stunningly simple analogy.

"Yes," he said, when he could find his voice. "That's exactly what this is like."

"I get it," she said.

Tim waited, but Stevie didn't say anything else for another minute or so.

When she did speak again, her words surprised him. But they shouldn't have. Everything he was learning about this kid was like waking up in a new world order.

"I think I might be bi."

"Bi?" He wasn't sure he'd heard her correctly.

"Sexual," she clarified. "I like girls. And guys," she added. "Sort of . . ."

Tim fought to keep the car between the lines on their lane. "Oh. Wow. I mean . . . that's . . . *okay* . . ."

Stevie actually laughed. "You're so full of shit."

"Hey," Tim said with umbrage. "*Be fair.* You did kind of spring that on me."

"Well? I thought that's what we were doing. Telling each other secrets?"

He considered her observation. It seemed reasonable enough. "I guess so."

"Do you think Mama Uno will freak out?"

"About you being, um . . ."

"*Bi*," Stevie repeated. "It's okay. You can say it."

"I know, I know. I'm just a nerd, okay."

"Duh. News flash."

Tim thought about her question. How *would* Evan react? He really had no idea. On the one hand, she'd have every reason to be understanding. On the other? Her knee-jerk response could easily be to blame herself because her kid grew up to walk a path similar to her own—one that was sure to be fraught with challenges. That unwelcome possibility remained, even though the cultural landscape today was so much more open than it had been when they were kids.

"I don't know what she'll think," he said. "What I *do* know is how much she loves you, and how much your happiness means to her."

"Yeah. That's what I thought, too. It's probably Dad who'll freak out."

"You think so?"

"Don't you?" Stevie all but snorted. "He'll lose his shit and blame Mom for making me queer."

Queer? Tim was confused. "I thought you said you were bi?"

Stevie shrugged. "It's kind of a moving target."

He wondered what that meant? It was clear that he had a lot to learn.

"Are you going to tell her?" he asked.

"You mean tonight?"

"Well." He considered. "If not tonight, then soon? Like over the holidays?"

"Yeah. I thought so." Her reply did not clarify her timetable. She bent toward him and socked him on the arm. "So, how about those Eagles? They ate your pansy-ass Crusaders for *lunch.*"

Tim looked over at her. Were they really going to talk about basketball now?

Stevie winked at him with confidence, and a trace of humor.

Yeah, he thought. *This was gonna be* some *night at the Chadds Ford chaparral . . .*

It had been easier than expected to get Christensen to play ball—even though he'd had the temerity to string them along while he waited on a higher offer.

Maya was entertained by the irony.

It was always entertaining to discover how far righteous indignation would go when a big damn payoff was lurking nearby in the shadows. In the case of Brian Christensen, that distance proved not to be very far.

After he'd agreed to Zucchetto's terms, Maya paid a second visit to his dealership in Gloucester City. Brian made an elaborate pantomime out of demonstrating the improved refinements of the souped-up Camaro they sat in while they ironed out the particulars of their understanding.

"The deposit has already been made to your bank account. It should post before 2 p.m. today." Maya ran a hand over the leather-wrapped steering wheel. "All that remains now is for you to abide by the terms of our agreement."

"I won't say anything," he promised.

"Oh, I'm confident you won't. But just in case you should ever feel tempted to break your solemn pledge, you should know that my client has a very long reach—and an unforgiving nature."

Christensen looked wary. "What's that supposed to mean?"

"You're a bright guy, Brian. I don't think you need me to spell it out. Do you?"

He began to fiddle with the sound system set into the faux-wood paneled dash. It was impressively equipped with a slew of brushed steel control knobs. "This has built-in Bluetooth and Sirius XM. You can toggle back and forth between those features and the navigation system just by turning this dial."

Maya honestly did not give a toss about the technological attributes of this overpriced GM street rod.

"Impressive. Does that dial also have a setting that gauges how small the driver's dick is?"

Brian's face turned red.

"No?" She asked. "Pity. How about the depth of his discretion?"

"Look," Brian hissed with impatience. "I accepted your offer, okay? I took the money. You think this has been easy for me?"

"Which part?" Maya asked with feigned innocence.

"Jesus Christ, you're cold. *Any of it.* What the hell did you think I meant?"

"I honestly had no idea. You could've been ruminating on these pathetic attempts to interest me in test-driving this ridiculous vehicle."

His face was now a lovely shade of puce. "I was just trying not to attract attention."

"Well, then, having us sit inside a flaming-red muscle car would seem to be an ill-advised approach, wouldn't it?"

He drummed his fingers on the console between them. "*Yes.* I'll keep my damn mouth shut. Okay? Now if we're finished, you and your stuck-up opinions can get the fuck outta my showroom."

"My pleasure." Maya reached for the door handle. "One last thing. This is for you."

Brian took the small card. "What's this?"

"It's a phone number. Use it if anyone else approaches you about your extra-curricular activities with the sainted Bishop. And I do mean *anyone.*"

"Why?" He smirked. "So you can have them erased or something?"

God, this guy was a pissant.

"Or something," Maya repeated. "Just make the call, Brian. It'll be in everyone's best interest."

She climbed out and left the pathetic little weasel perched inside his macho ride.

"This looks gross." Stevie had lifted the lid on a simmering pot of—*something*—and peered down at its contents with a wrinkled nose. "It stinks, too."

"Yeah." Evan walked over to where she stood and took the lid from her. She dropped it back into place. "That's because this *isn't* dinner. I'm dyeing some socks. Dinner," Evan pointed across the room, "is in the oven."

"*Socks?* For real?" Stevie looked incredulous. "Socks are cheap. Why would you *dye* them? Just buy new ones."

"For your information, Paris Hilton, some of us choose *not* to be profligate consumers."

Stevie crossed the kitchen and turned on the light inside the wall oven. "What's in here?"

"Moroccan pot roast."

"Seriously?" Stevie sounded impressed.

"See?" Tim spoke up from the doorway. "I told you it might not be bad."

Julia laughed from her post at the counter. She'd been chopping dried cherries for the couscous. "You two really are cut from the same bolt of cloth."

Evan raised her hands toward heaven. "Did I not already tell you that? They're the reason my hair is falling out."

"Your hair is not falling out." Julia handed her a glass. "Drink your wine, dear."

Stevie laughed and Julia winked at her.

Evan narrowed her eyes. "What's going on?"

"Nothing is going on except that I'm starving." Tim began opening cabinets. "You got any nosh in this joint?"

"Why? Did you run out of Doritos?" Evan walked over to the small kitchen table and picked up a stoneware platter covered with hunks of cut-up cheese and a couple bunches of grapes. "Here." She handed it to Tim. "Don't they feed you at that monastery?"

"Just gruel, and the occasional glass of vinegar mixed with gall," he said.

"That figures." Evan shooed him. "Take this into the living room. There's a basket of cut-up pita bread already in there on the coffee table."

"You don't have to ask me twice." Tim took a bite of one of the cheeses. "What's this? It's great."

"Robusto," Evan answered. "And the other one is truffled Gouda."

Tim tried a hunk of that one, too.

"How are they?" Stevie asked.

He leaned toward her and lowered his voice. "They don't suck."

"Okay," Evan said. "Will you two get the hell outta here and let me get the rest of dinner going? At this rate, we won't be eating until midnight. And put some music on," she called after them. "And not that *fusion* bullshit, either."

After Tim and Stevie disappeared with the appetizers, Evan joined Julia at the counter.

"Fusion?" Julia asked.

"Tim likes alternative jazz."

"I don't mind it if I'm dressed for it."

Evan bumped into her. "I prefer you undressed."

Julia gave her a skeptical look. "Do I know you?"

"Not as well as you're going to later on."

"Exactly how much wine have you had?"

Evan laughed. "It's not that. I'm just ..."

"Just?"

Evan shrugged. "Happy."

Julia leaned into her. "Me, too."

Evan plucked a cherry from the pile Julia was chopping and popped it into her mouth. "Think we should tell her tonight?"

"Tell her what?"

"The pitfalls of withdrawing from the nuclear test ban treaty, of course. What did you *think* I meant?"

"Boy, you don't waste any time."

"What's that supposed to mean?"

"Evan. She's been home about twelve seconds."

"So?"

"So. I think we could at least wait until after dinner."

"Okay, okay."

Strains of hard-driving music blared out from the living room. Evan grimaced. *Foo Fighters. Great.* "Stevie!" she bellowed.

"What?" Stevie yelled back.

"Not that head-banger crap, either!"

"Oh, come on, Mama Uno!"

"*Stevie* . . ."

The music abruptly changed. Evan listened to it for a moment before fixing Julia with a look of resignation.

"What on earth is *that?*" Julia asked.

"Unless I miss my guess, it's Lawrence Welk."

Julia laughed. Evan started to holler something again, but Julia reached out and stopped her. "Don't," she said. "Trust me. Neither of them will be able to stomach this for more than ten seconds."

Evan wasn't so sure. "You think so?"

"I'd bet my last bottle of Geritol on it."

"God, I love you." Evan bent forward to kiss Julia. "Did you really pack your Geritol?"

"Why?" Julia asked. "Think you might be needing an energy boost later?"

"Not thinking. Hoping."

Julia kissed her back. "I promise to hook you up."

As soon as she finished speaking, the music changed again. Mongolian throat singers this time.

"See?" Julia beamed at her. "Told you."

"You think *this* is an improvement?"

Julia tugged Evan closer. "Who cares?"

Part of Stevie's mission during the time she was home for the holidays was to work on narrowing down the list of colleges she wanted to apply to, and which ones she planned to visit. So, after dinner, the four of them sat around the big farm table in the dining room, drinking wine and talking about possibilities. Evan even allowed Stevie to have a small glass of the Douro Tim had brought. The gesture appeared to be a significant concession on Evan's part—one Stevie accepted happily and without comment.

Julia found this simple exchange of give-and-take to be emblematic of the ways their mother/daughter social contract played out. At dinner, Stevie had humored Evan by eating two helpings of the savory Moroccan pot roast—without editorializing on what she consistently viewed as her mother's penchant for extrinsic cuisine. So, it didn't surprise Julia that when Tim opened the second bottle of wine he'd brought, Evan quietly got up to retrieve a fourth glass, and set it down in front of Stevie.

Tim appeared to take all of this in stride, too. Although it was clear to Julia that he noticed the exchange. He winked at Evan as he filled Stevie's glass.

Across the table from Julia, Stevie lifted the wine to her nose and took a cautious sniff.

"This smells . . ."

They all waited.

"Like oranges," she said. She took a small sip and let it roll around on her tongue before swallowing. "Orange flowers. And maybe vegetables? It's nice." She took another small sip. "I like the kind of soft, fruity thing it has going on when you swallow it."

Tim stared at her with wide eyes. "Did you read the label in the car or something?"

Stevie looked back at him with confusion. "No. I didn't even know you brought this."

"Well, who knew?" He sat back in his chair. "Evan? It looks like your kid got the palate."

Evan laughed. "This surprises you because?"

"It must come from the Cohen side of the family," he teased.

"I doubt that." Evan took a healthy swallow from her own glass of wine. "Normally, I'm only too happy to cede responsibility for any aberrant tendencies to Dan's DNA. But the Cohen clan's appreciation for fine wines pretty much tops out at Manischewitz."

"Aberrant?" Stevie tossed an uneaten chunk of toasted pita bread at her mother.

"Hey!" Evan promptly flung the bread projectile back at her. "Don't start something you can't finish, munchkin."

"Girls. Really?" Tim snagged the basket of ammo and moved it out of harm's way before hostilities could escalate. "Don't make me stop this car." He faced Julia. "I apologize for their juvenile behavior. Now you see why our dining options are usually limited to places like Sonic Drive-In."

"No need to apologize to me." Julia said to him. "I've been sitting here feeling smug because I thought I'd made a bold choice by not wearing my flak jacket tonight."

"Why?" Stevie observed. "I bet you'd look smokin' hot in that, too."

The easy flow of conversation ground to a sudden halt. The report from Stevie's offhand remark hung in the air like the aftermath of a cannon blast. Nobody said anything for the better part of ten seconds.

Julia did her best to try and stifle the blush she knew was creeping up her neck.

Tim became mesmerized by something fascinating on the table in front of him.

Stevie closed her eyes in mortification.

Finally, Evan cleared her throat, folded her arms, and leaned toward her daughter with a raised eyebrow.

"Yeah. Okay." Stevie faced her mother and held up her palm in a clear gesture of resignation. "So, I guess we're going to have this conversation right now?"

"You think?" Evan asked.

"Honey . . ." Julia touched Evan's forearm.

"It's okay, Julia," Stevie interjected. "I'm sorry I said that. It was rude."

"No, Stevie," Julia said. "You don't need to apologize. I wouldn't call it rude."

"Seriously?" Evan looked at her like she'd just morphed into an alien species. "I'd hardly call it polite conversation."

"Cool your jets, Mama Uno," Stevie said. "I was going to tell you tonight, anyway."

"Tell me?" Evan asked. "Tell me what?"

Stevie shrugged. "About Desiree and me."

"Desiree?" Evan sounded perplexed. "What *about* you and Desiree?"

"We like each other." Stevie said it like it was a foregone conclusion—which, in fact, it pretty much was.

Evan still seemed confused. "This is news, how exactly?"

Stevie shot Tim a look.

"Don't look at me," he said. "I can't bail you out on this one . . . *you* brought it up."

"Hold it." Evan raised a hand. "Would one of you two kindly fill me in on what all I missed in last week's episode of *This Is Us?* I'm clearly out of the loop, here."

Stevie made a face. "For starters, Mom—nobody watches *This Is Us*. It sucks."

Evan allowed her exasperation to show. "Forgive my woeful ignorance of Nielsen ratings."

"Whatever," Stevie continued. "So . . . remember when Des came up and stayed with me at Emma over fall break? Well . . . we kind of figured out that our friendship is maybe . . . *more* than friendship. You know?"

Evan dropped back against her chair. She looked in turn at Stevie, Tim and Julia. "I don't know what to say."

"Are you pissed?" Stevie sounded genuinely worried.

"Pissed? At *you?*" Evan was confused. "Why would I be pissed?"

"I don't know . . ." Stevie seemed to think about her question. "Okay. Maybe not *pissed*. Disappointed?"

"No. Not that either." Evan polished off her wine and thrust her glass at Tim. He took her cue and immediately poured her a generous refill.

"Could I have some more, too?" Stevie asked him.

"Yeah . . . I don't think so." Evan answered for him. "Stevie? Are you sure about this? You don't have to be. It's fine to take the time you need to figure these things out."

Julia discreetly extended her hand beneath the table and gave Evan's thigh a gentle squeeze.

Stevie seemed to think Evan's question over before answering. "Is that what you did?" she asked her mother.

"Me?" Evan pointed a finger at herself. "Well. No . . . not really."

Tim laughed. "*That's* for sure. You kind of exploded out of the closet and took most of the house down in your wake."

"Yo, Chuckles?" Evan gave Tim the finger. "*Not* helping."

"Why do you need *help?*" Stevie complained. "It's not that big of a deal, is it?"

"Not for me," Evan pointed out. "But it can be for you. That's why you need to take your time before you decide."

"Why does anybody have to 'decide' anything? Why can't we just be however we are and be done with it?"

Evan looked at Julia with an unspoken question: *Will you please help me out here?*

Julia didn't really feel like it was appropriate for her to wade into anything this important between the two of them, but she gave it a shot anyway.

"Few things in life are binary," she said. "The more we live and grow, the more we all realize how fluid most things are. What we know. What we believe. What we desire." She glanced at Evan. "Who we love. So, Stevie, if you're sure—if you and Desiree are both sure—then for right now, that's the only thing that matters."

"Amen." Tim raised his glass. "I'll drink to that."

Evan shook her head in resignation before raising her own glass. "Me, too."

They all clinked rims.

"Wow." Stevie collapsed back against her chair. "That sure went a lot better than I thought it would."

"Yeah?" Evan asked her. "Well, hold your applause, because I have a revelation of my own."

"You do?" The way she asked the question made it clear that Stevie knew her mother well enough to be suspicious.

"Oh, yeah." Evan reached over and took hold of Julia's hand. "How would you feel about Ms. Hottie McFlak-Jacket coming here to live with us?"

Stevie's mouth fell open. She looked back and forth between them. "*No way . . .*"

"Way," Evan said.

"With your permission," Julia quickly added.

"*My* permission?" Stevie looked incredulous. "Are you kidding?"

Evan held up a hand. "Don't get too excited. She's not sharing *your* room."

"Ex-*cuse* me?" Julia glared at Evan. "For your information, I am not a commodity. Nor will I be sharing *anyone's* room until Stevie says it's okay."

Evan looked at her daughter. "Is it okay?"

"Of course it's okay!" Stevie jumped up from her chair and rushed around the table to hug Julia. "This is totally awesome."

Julia hugged her back. "I'm glad you think so."

Evan was all smiles. "She has a few conditions."

Stevie loosened her stranglehold on Julia. "What conditions?"

Evan began to tick them off. "We have to get a new coffee-maker," she began.

"Praise God, hallelujah." Tim raised both hands toward heaven.

Evan glowered at him.

"What? he asked. "We haven't had a bona fide miracle in this parish for more than two centuries."

"Wherever would you be without your fantasies?" Evan faced

Stevie again. "And we will be adding on to the house. Julia needs her own office space."

"Cool." Stevie was plainly jazzed by the news. "When we do that, can we tack on a new bedroom for me, too?"

"Why the hell do *you* need a new bedroom?"

"Because," Stevie regarded her mother with wide eyes, "when Des comes over to spend the night, I'd rather not be across the hall from you two."

"Wait a minute, Miss Thing." Evan was stupefied. "*You* are not gonna be hittin' it with *anybody* under *this* roof. Not for at least another couple of years."

"Mom! Gross!" Stevie sounded horrified. "I wasn't talking about *me*—I was talking about you and Julia."

"Julia and me?" Evan sounded confused.

"*Duh. Yeah.*" Stevie looked over at Tim. "Trust me . . . nobody wants free tickets to Pound Town."

"And on *that* note . . ." Tim pushed back his chair. "Got any more wine in this dump, Evan?"

Evan rubbed a hand across her forehead. "Good idea."

Julia didn't know whether to laugh or slide beneath the table.

Stevie returned to her chair and sat down. "So, now that we've settled all of *that*, how about we start talking about my college applications?"

"Okay," Evan agreed. "Where's your list?"

"What list?"

"The one we discussed," Evan reminded her. "The one you're supposed to have worked on."

"I *did* work on it. It's in my head."

"Your head?"

Stevie nodded.

"Were we all supposed to intuit it?" Evan asked. "Or did you think we'd receive it through osmosis?"

Stevie looked at Julia for support. "Mom doesn't think anything has value if it's not written down someplace."

"Sorry, Stevie," Julia said, apologetically. "You're preaching to a publisher, here. Writing things down is kind of my life's work."

"It's a conspiracy, kid." Tim had rejoined them and was opening another bottle of wine.

"You, too?" Stevie asked him.

He shrugged. "At least I come by it honestly. My people started with the Dead Sea Scrolls."

"How about we compromise?" They all looked at Evan. "How about we *each* make lists? Then we can compare and look for common denominators."

"*Great* idea," Stevie said morosely. "Are you sure I can't have more wine?"

Julia laughed and got to her feet. "I'll go get some paper."

"I've got a new pack of notepads on my desk," Evan called after her. "Bring some pens, too."

Julia could hear them continuing to banter and barter about the wine as she made her way to Evan's small office. As she crossed the living room, she thought for the millionth time about what a charming house this really was.

She loved it here. It was such an inviting place—a simple, fieldstone farmhouse that had sat on this unspoiled swath of rolling land for generations. Evan once explained that her grandfather had inherited it from his father, who had operated a ferry on the Brandywine River until the area's first bridge was constructed in the early 19th century. After that, the Reeds mined clay for the kaolin processing mills that had sprung up all over Chester and Delaware Counties. As a consequence, the house was filled with white porcelain and stoneware dishes, all made from clay mined by Evan's ancestors.

She heard renewed peals of laughter from the dining room. That was the real magic here: *laughter*. Something that had never been part of her everyday life: not until she found Evan. And Stevie.

She grimaced when she reached Evan's old rolltop desk and saw the piles of folders and papers stacked on top of it—likely all of her research on Judge Cawley. What a nightmare that job was turning into. Especially after Evan related the new information Ben Rush had given her about poor Edwin Miller.

She tried to be careful as she sifted through the piles of paper to search for the notepads. Finally she saw them, squirreled away in a tidy stack behind some files. Her sleeve caught on the edge of a manila folder when she reached back to retrieve a few of them and the contents of the folder spilled out and landed on the wide plank floor.

Great . . .

The folder had contained sheets of lined paper, all filled with notes in Evan's characteristic, all caps handwriting—and a couple of photographs. Julia collected the items and tried to restore them to order before placing them back inside the folder.

That's when she saw it. *What the hell was Evan doing with this?*

One thing was certain: however it had made its way into her research, it couldn't be good news.

Should she take it back into the dining room with her?

No. That wouldn't be appropriate. She could ask Evan about it later, at the end of the evening—after Stevie had gone to bed and when they were alone together.

She rethought that scenario in the light of recent revelations.

Alone together—being quiet . . .

She was slipping the photograph back into its folder when she heard Evan's voice from the doorway.

"Hey? What's taking so long? I was afraid maybe you got lost—or came to your senses and laid a patch getting out of here." Then she noticed what Julia was holding. "Are you okay? You look like you've seen a ghost."

"Close," Julia agreed. "I accidentally knocked this folder off your desk while I was trying to reach the notepads." She opened it and withdrew one of the two photos it contained. "Can you tell me where you got this, and why you have it?"

Evan took it from her.

"This is a picture Dan sent me when I first got the vetting assignment." She met Julia's eyes. "Do you recognize anyone in this?"

"Oh, yes." Julia didn't say anything else, but Evan could sense her mounting agitation. "Why did he send you this?" she asked.

"Because this is Judge Cawley." Evan pointed him out. "And this man is Edwin Miller."

"Oh, dear god." Julia peered more closely at the image.

"I haven't been able to identify anyone else except Bishop Szymanski," Evan pointed at the cleric, "and this young man. The photo was taken in 2005. I have no idea where."

"I can help you out with that." Julia looked at her. "I know exactly where this was taken."

Evan appeared genuinely flummoxed. "You do?"

Julia nodded. "This is a private room at the Galileo Club on South Broad Street."

"Are you certain about that?"

"Absolutely certain. I've been there more times than I care to remember."

Evan took some time before asking her next question. "Do I want to know why?"

"You tell me." Julia pointed at a bearded man dressed in an immaculately tailored tuxedo. He stood just behind Judge Cawley. "That's my father."

Chapter Seven

Once he got home, Tim had time to think about how the evening in Chadds Ford had gone. All things considered, everything had gone extremely well.

Better than well, actually—at least, for Stevie. And even for Evan and Julia.

It was remarkable what a little bit of openness and honest discourse could accomplish.

And how easily, too. That was the perverse part.

If only the Church could embrace that behavior. How much better and richer could all of their lives be? How much more relevant, purposeful and effective a ministry could they achieve?

Tim didn't understand why so many people were consigned to hobble through life, dragging monster-sized loads of fear and shame behind them like ship's anchors. They lived and died without access to hope—never finding release from the twin shackles of shame and self-recrimination. And that curse was perpetuated because they had never been shown the power that derived from speaking their truths aloud, as Stevie and Evan had done this very night.

My name is Legion, the man answered, when Jesus asked his name.

Jesus wanted the possessed man to *name* his demons. *Because Jesus understood that naming them took away their power.*

Why were so many denied the wisdom of these simple truths?

Why had he denied himself?

Fear and shame. These were the greatest deterrents to grace. For too long, they had been his constant companions. For too long, he had pampered them . . . hidden them away and protected them like private treasures. His pearls of great price.

Stevie had told him he was struggling like someone trapped in a broken marriage. How profound that insight was. But between Tim and the Church, it was a toss-up to determine which one of them had been unfaithful. Hadn't they both broken their vows?

And was there any way out—for either of them?

He looked around his tiny apartment in the rectory at St. Rita's. It was spartanly furnished—mostly appointed with just his books and some reclaimed pieces of furniture. Some of those belonged to the Church, but most of them were things Evan had helped him collect through the years. That had always been a favorite pastime of theirs, especially during their graduate school days. They spent countless Saturdays together scouring junk stores and flea markets, looking for bargains and rare finds. Well-used mission-style tables. Worn woven rugs. Chipped but still serviceable bits of mismatched pottery. Even after Stevie had been born, the three of them would take off for daylong jaunts to farmer's markets in Middletown or Carlisle. They'd find shady spots along the road to park and eat the enormous picnic lunches Evan would pack. They'd splurge on fresh raspberries, apples, or peaches—whatever fruits were in season and on sale by roadside vendors. Tim would rock Stevie and croon old torch songs to her in what Evan called his "lame-ass baritone."

How familiar all these souvenirs of that time were. And yet, how unfamiliar they now seemed. And how perfectly they encapsulated the patchwork quilt of his life. These disparate relics and mismatched mementos of *other* people's histories—all stitched together in a jumbled pastiche of . . . what? Anonymity? Isolation? Confusion?

For the first time, he understood what it must be like for witnesses in criminal cases who were given new identities and placed in relocation programs. They surrendered their pasts and became strangers to their futures. And not because of anything they had *done*—but because of things they had borne witness to.

Because of things they told the truth about.

Was that the end of this? Was becoming a stranger the penalty for making things right? For making amends to God and to the people he'd wronged by his silence?

He honestly had no idea.

And he knew he wouldn't find the answers to these questions tonight. Yet he tarried, and continued to find things to do. Busy-work. Anything that could stave off his fear of sleep—of the nightmares certain to become his companions in the hours remaining before dawn.

He was actually relieved when his phone rang. As late as it was, he knew it was probably a Church matter. Likely, the call would be about some kind of family emergency—somebody sick or in need of other pastoral care. He practically sprinted across the room to answer it, feeling ashamed for the rush of adrenaline he got from the distraction. He didn't recognize the number.

"This is Father Donovan," he said.

"It's Joey," a man's voice said. Tim could hear other sounds in the background. Beeping noises—like trucks backing up.

"Joey? Are you all right?"

Disgusted laughter. "Oh, yeah. I'm *great*." He coughed. Tim thought he could hear him spit.

"Where are you?"

"I'm . . . some fucking place." The beeping sound stopped. It was followed by an engine noise and a loud bang.

Tim jerked the cell phone away from his ear. "What was that?"

"Dumpsters." Joey coughed again. "They're picking up the trash."

Tim's mind raced to come up with the right things to say—things that would keep Joey on the line. There could only be one reason for his call at this hour . . .

"It's cold tonight." *How lame. That was the best he could come up with?*

"Not where I'm headed."

"You're going someplace?"

"Aren't we all . . . *Father?*"

"You can call me Tim, Joey. I'm just a guy, like you."

"*Like me?* Oh, yeah? You wanna count the ways you're just like me?"

"I can if you want me to." Tim could hear Joey's labored breathing. It sounded almost like he was panting. There were sporadic traffic noises, too. Cars. A siren in the distance. *Two sirens.* Joey was walking someplace. "Do you want to come here? Come inside and get warmed up?"

"Not there." Joey bit off the words. "I'm never coming back there."

"Okay. That's all right. Someplace else, then? Anyplace you want."

Joey snorted and spat again. "Pancakes."

"What?"

"I said I want fucking pancakes."

"Okay," Tim said. "I could eat." He looked at his watch. How many places that weren't bars were still open at midnight?

"I thought about what you said."

Tim was unprepared for Joey's comment. "You did?"

"I'm tired of this bullshit. I don't give a fuck about the money. I just want to be done with it."

"You don't have to live with it anymore, Joey. I'll help you. I'll go with you. You won't be alone."

"They don't give a shit about us, Tim. They don't care about what he did—what they *all* did. They just want to cover it up."

Tim closed his eyes. "I know, Joey. I'm sorry about what happened to you. I care about what happened to you. I want to help you. I *promise* to help you."

"I'm ready to talk." He gave a bitter-sounding laugh. "I tried earlier tonight. It didn't work out."

"What happened?"

"I went by their high-class hangout. Some of their hired goons tossed me out on my ass. That's what happened."

147

Tim wasn't surprised. He could tell Joey had been drinking. Probably a lot.

"Let's meet someplace," Tim said. "Let's get some food."

"Now?"

"Now is good for me."

Tim heard voices and laugher. The blare of a car horn. Joey must've been walking past a bar. *Where was he?*

"How about the Melrose Diner?" Joey suggested.

That would work. With no traffic, Tim could be there in five minutes. "That's perfect. When?"

"I'm walking, but I can be there in about ten minutes."

"I'll get us a table. Joey?"

"Yeah?"

"I'm glad you called me tonight."

"Really?" he said. "You won't be."

He hung up.

What Joey had just done took courage. Now it was Tim's turn to step up.

He grabbed his jacket and keys, and headed out to meet him.

Evan and Julia talked for the better part of an hour after they made their way upstairs to bed. Stevie was shut up in her room across the hall—probably on the phone gabbing with Desiree.

She wondered if Ping had a clue about the two girls. The pair had spent a ton of time with her during school vacations—learning how to bake and sometimes helping her out when she had bigger catering jobs.

That was a topic for another day.

They finally were alone, and could discuss the photograph Julia had discovered in Evan's office.

The photo of Judge Cawley with Bishop Szymanski—and Lewis Donne . . .

Julia had been mostly quiet while Evan tried to fill her in on everything she knew—and some, but not all, of what she suspected about Judge Cawley. To be fair, she knew next to nothing about the Judge's actual involvement with Bishop Szymanski—other than the photographic evidence that the two men knew each other and that the Judge had some connection as a benefactor to the St. Rita's basketball team. And she knew nothing about Julia's father—except the new information that all three of the men were members of the same exclusive club. It made sense that Evan didn't recognize Lewis Donne in the photo. She'd never had an opportunity to meet him before his death. And Julia said she likely wouldn't have recognized him, anyway, because of the beard.

"He only had it for about eighteen months," she explained. "Mother despised it and made his life hell. She said it made him look like a hooligan. Finally, he shaved it off just to shut her up."

She went on to reveal that her father had been a member of the Galileo Club for more than forty years. The family made obligatory appearances there to attend formal dinners on occasional holidays, although Lewis Donne was a more frequent visitor. Julia surmised that his club membership and the close-knit fraternity of colleagues he had there were among the incentives that led him to spend so much of his time working out of D&H's Philadelphia office.

Her mother, Katherine Donne, all but despised the club—which always seemed strange to Julia, since her mother was such a social gadfly—and did her best to spend as little time there as possible.

Julia surmised that this was another reason why her father loved his private retreat so much.

Evan debated whether to share details of some of the things Edwin Miller had rambled on about when she visited him at the asylum. What she had earlier interpreted as nonsensical ravings now seemed to take on some greater, more ominous meaning. Was Eddie trying, in his broken way, to tell her something about Cawley? Were his comments intended to be symbolic?

Or was he just plain crazy?

Galileo, he'd said when she was leaving. Then he muttered something about Galileo studying the stars.

No. That wasn't right. He said Galileo *found* the stars.

The stars. He called the children playing in the puzzle of the Homer painting "little stars." And when he recognized Evan for a moment, he said, "You found out." When Evan asked him what he meant, he'd looked up toward the sky and said, "The stars."

Had he been talking about the boys at the Church? Were they the "little stars" he meant? Or was he talking about his own victims?

Shit. She was the one reaching for the stars on this one.

They had taken the photograph showing Julia's father upstairs with them so Julia could examine it more closely. Her inspection clarified one more thing: the Homer painting. Julia remembered it well—and what a big deal her father made of it when the club had it on loan.

"Albert Lippincott was able to borrow it from some private museum in Ohio," she explained. "Dad said he was on the board there. I don't know why they were all in such a dither about getting it. That must've been in 2005 when this photo was taken."

"It took some digging to track that thing down," Evan pointed out. "Apparently, Homer painted quite a few of these as studies before crafting the final version the club borrowed."

"I recall Albert being insufferable after he'd managed to arrange the loan. I think they used it as a prop in some fundraising campaign."

"Is that 'Albert' as in *Binkie* and Albert?" Evan asked.

"The same. Father of the regrettable Gerald."

"Do you recognize any of the other men in this group?" Evan asked.

"That's Albert." She pointed him out. He was a rather paunchy man with a big handlebar mustache. "And I think this is one of the Cadwaladers . . . maybe Bryce? I'm not really sure. This man, I'm pretty sure, was a former ambassador. To Belgium, if memory serves." She examined the image another minute. "I don't recognize anyone else—and I never met Judge Cawley or the bishop personally, that I recall. But that's not really surprising. I only ever went there under duress about twice a year."

"Did Andy ever go there with your father?"

Julia raised an eyebrow. "A few times, when we both lived in Delaware. It wasn't his style."

That surprised Evan. "No?"

"Oh, don't misunderstand," Julia clarified. "Andy loved his refinements and all connections to privilege. He just didn't care for *this* club."

"Did he ever say why?"

"You're awfully curious about this."

Evan shrugged. "Just doing my job, ma'am."

"As I recall, he said it wasn't his taste. In fact, he said he found it creepy."

"Creepy? That seems like an odd observation."

"Not really. Most of the members are octogenarian men who subsist on diets of Cuban cigars and thirty-year-old scotch. They don their Harvard ties and caucus around those grand fireplaces to spread the gospel of supply-side economics."

Evan laughed. "What about the women?"

"Women?" Julia asked.

"Well, yeah. I assume there *are* some."

Julia laughed. "Expensive ones."

"Oh?"

"The Galileo Club is very 'traditional.' Women are only admitted as guests or as chattels of their male sponsors."

Evan was disappointed by that revelation. "Well, that's a pisser."

"I agree. Although I'd be hard-pressed to find any thinking woman who would wish to become a member."

"No," Evan clarified. "That's not what I meant. Now that I know what it is, I need to find a way to get in there."

"Seriously? Why?"

Evan shrugged. "To do what I do. Ask questions. Chat up the

staff. See what I can find out about the judge, and maybe what it is that makes the place 'creepy.' You know?"

Julia looked dubious.

"What is it?" Evan asked.

"My father. Do you think he had any connection to Cawley and the bishop?"

Evan answered carefully. "Do you mean other than the fact that they all were members of the same club?"

"*And* the fact that they all appeared together in this photograph," Julia added. "With Edwin Miller."

"Do you ever remember your father *mentioning* Judge Cawley? Or Bishop Szymanski?"

"Not that I can recall."

"How about the St. Rita's basketball team? Did he ever say anything about that—or about athletic programs at other schools?"

"No. But since he wasn't Catholic, that's probably not significant. He loved sports, of course. But his tastes were always a bit more rarified. Cricket. Rowing." She rolled her eyes. "Golf, of course. But basketball?" She thought about it. "Not that I can recall."

"What about philanthropy?" Evan asked. "Might he have contributed to any scholarship programs in the community—possibly ones favored by other club members?"

"I suppose that's possible. I really don't know." Julia took a moment to think more about it. "Why do you ask about sports teams?"

"All of the boys in this photo were on the St. Rita's basketball team—with Tim. He recognized them."

"You showed this to Tim?"

"Yes," Evan said. "I got a second picture from another source. It showed Cawley and the bishop with the team at St. Rita's. They were wearing their uniforms, and Tim was one of the players. It had been taken several years earlier than this one. I showed both photos to him to see if remembered Cawley or could identify any of the other boys in the pictures."

"Could he?"

Evan nodded.

"You haven't answered my other question," Julia said in a quiet voice.

"What question?" Evan pretended to be clueless. She knew exactly what Julia had asked.

"Do you think my father had any connection to Cawley or the bishop?"

Evan was a shitty liar, and knew it. "I honestly have no idea." She did her best to sound convincing.

"Would you tell me if you did?"

Evan didn't answer her right away. *What could she say when she genuinely had no idea herself?*

They were sitting side by side on Evan's bed, and Julia leaned toward her and rested a hand on her thigh.

"Evan?"

Evan met her eyes. "The truth?"

Julia nodded.

"I don't know."

Julia sat back. But she didn't remove her hand.

"That's what I thought you'd say."

"I'm sorry about this," Evan said. She meant it, too—and tried to infuse the simple statement with everything she felt.

"Me, too."

Evan took hold of her hand. "It might not mean anything," she said.

"Or it might mean everything."

Evan didn't reply.

Julia had made it a habit to always sit on Evan's "good" side. That way, when the spirit moved, she could rest her head on Evan's shoulder without causing her any discomfort from her persistent neuritis. Julia scooted closer now, and tucked her head beneath Evan's chin. The two of them sat together in silence, listening to the faint murmurs of Stevie's continuing conversation with Desiree, until Julia fell asleep.

Evan stayed awake much longer, praying to any god who

might be listening, to please not allow this nightmare revelation to terminate in the unholy place she suspected everything now was leading.

Tim was on his second cup of coffee—a decision he knew he'd live to regret. He'd been there for more than twenty minutes and Joey still hadn't arrived.

The cranky waitress lumbered by again and asked if he wanted to go ahead and order. For the third time, he assured her he was waiting on someone who should be there any minute.

She tapped her pen against her fat order pad a few times, before walking off without saying anything.

Hard to blame her. He didn't imagine the tips were very good at 12:30 a.m. And maybe her feet hurt?

He fought the impulse to keep checking his watch.

The place actually had more patrons than he had thought it would. There were a couple of cops sitting at the counter, drinking coffee and eating big slices of pie. It looked like cherry. It also looked pretty good.

What the hell was up with his appetite? He'd eaten like a horse at Evan's, and now he was hungry again.

Stress. He'd always been that way. He'd had a weight problem in high school.

No mystery about that one . . .

But Stevie had said he looked skinny to her.

Maybe his metabolism was changing?

He finished his coffee. This was getting weird. *Where was Joey?*

Tim started to worry. *Maybe he'd changed his mind?* He'd sounded drunk when he called. And where had he been? And why was he out walking in the middle of the night?

This time, he did check his watch. Joey was now half an hour late.

Okay. What to do?

Tim rolled the dice and got out his cell phone. He pulled up Joey's number from his call log and punched the call button. The phone rang and rang. No answer, and no voicemail. He double-checked the number to be sure he'd pulled up the right one before trying the same number again.

Same result.

He put the phone down on the table and drummed his fingers on top of it.

Ten more minutes. He'd wait ten more minutes. Maybe Joey had changed his mind and gone home? Tim didn't want to wake up Mrs. Mazzetta at this hour to find out. But he could always try stopping by there tomorrow . . .

The cranky waitress glared at him again—this time from the cash register.

I should've worn my damn collar . . .

He held up his mug and pointed at it.

Why the hell not?

At this point, one more cup of coffee couldn't make things any worse . . .

Tim finally gave up. He paid for his coffee and left the cranky waitress a ten-dollar tip. He figured it probably wouldn't improve her disposition—in fact, he wasn't sure if *anything* could—but he knew it was the least he could do after holding a table for so long and not ordering anything to eat.

He drove home to try and get some sleep—or at least to lie down in the dark to try and keep his nightmares at bay. He tried calling Joey several more times. No answer. After an hour of tossing, he gave up on any idea of trying to rest and got in his car to head toward South Bouvier Street. He was pretty sure Joey wouldn't still be out walking. It was now nearly 2 a.m., and nobody who was up to anything good would be out on the streets.

Most of the stoplights were flashing red, so the drive to the Mazzettas was quick—only about four minutes. He didn't know what he'd do when he got there—maybe just see if an upstairs light was on or look for any signs Joey was back at home. Maybe invent a plausible reason to wake his mother up?

155

There was a little bit of traffic on West Passyunk, but Snyder Street was all but deserted. When he turned east on Mifflin Street, he saw the first dazzle of flashing blue and red lights.

Great. Just what he needed . . . *Probably somebody got stopped for a DWI.*

It was when he got to the turn for South Bouvier Street that he saw the police cars—several of them—pulled up in front of the Mazzettas' row home.

Oh, God. No . . .

He parked at the end of the street and grabbed the satchel he always kept on the floorboard behind his seat. It contained his breviary, missal, stole, rosary and an extra collar and rabat that he could quickly don when needed. Once he'd put the garment on, he drove closer to the house and pulled over behind one of the police cars. A middle-aged, uniformed officer met him as he got out. Tim could see sergeant's stripes on his sleeve as he approached. He held up a beefy hand to halt Tim's progress.

"You can't park here, buddy," the officer said. Then he noticed Tim's collar. "Oh. Sorry, Father."

Tim held up a hand. "That's fine, Sergeant. I'm here to see Joey Mazzetta. Is he at home?"

The officer shot an anxious look toward the steps of the Mazzettas' house, where a younger man in a tan-colored coat was talking on a cell phone. Tim could see the shiny badge hanging from his jacket pocket. Blinding flashes of blue and red reflected off it like strobe lights. Tim assumed he was a detective.

"Wait right here, Father," the sergeant said. "Somebody will be right with you, okay?"

Tim felt his heart pounding. Something had happened— either to Joey or his mother. That much he was certain of.

The detective lowered his phone while the uniformed officer spoke to him. He glanced over at Tim while he listened. Then he nodded at the officer and returned to his call.

The sergeant called Tim over.

The man in the suit finished his call and stashed his phone as Tim approached.

"I'm Detective Ortiz," he said. "You're Father . . . who?"

"Donovan. Tim Donovan. St. Margherita Parish."

"You know the Mazzettas?" he asked.

"Yes." Tim nodded. "I'm their priest. Well . . . one of them," he added.

"Kind of late for you to be making a pastoral visit, isn't it, Father?"

"That's not why I'm here. Joey called me about two hours ago and asked me to meet him. When he didn't show up, I came by here."

"Two hours ago?" Ortiz looked at his watch. "He called you at midnight and asked you to meet him? Is that typical?"

"No . . ."

"Did he say where he was when he called?"

"No. He just asked me to meet him. I said I would." Tim made an effort to maintain eye contact with the detective. "It's what we do."

Ortiz seemed to accept that. "Where were you supposed to meet?"

"The Melrose Diner. Look . . . what's happened? It's clear something's wrong. Is he okay? Is Mrs. Mazzetta okay?"

"Mrs. Mazzetta is inside with another officer. She'll probably want to see you. Her son was killed tonight. Shot in an alley over off 15th Street."

Tim's mind was spinning. Shot? Joey was dead? *Killed tonight?* Killed while he sat in the diner, drinking bad coffee?

He felt the ground lurch beneath his feet.

Ortiz quickly reached out a hand to steady him. "Hey—*hey.* Steady. You okay?"

Tim gazed at him blankly. "Joey is *dead?*"

"Yeah. He is."

"Why?"

"We don't know yet. Maybe a robbery. His wallet was on the ground beside him. Come over here. You still don't look too steady." Ortiz led Tim over to one of the iron railings flanking the steps so he could lean against it. "Lookit, Father. Take a minute to get your bearings, okay? And then if you wanna go inside and speak with Mrs. Mazzetta, I'm sure she'd appreciate it. After that, we'd appreciate it if you gave us a statement. Okay?"

A statement? Tim wasn't thinking clearly. *Joey was dead* . . .

"Father?" Ortiz asked again. "You good with that?"

"Yes." Tim stared back at him through a fog. "Yes. I'm good with that."

The soft dinging of Evan's cell phone woke her up.

She fumbled for it and tried not to wake Julia.

"Reed," she said.

"Evan? It's Tim."

"Tim? What the hell?" She struggled to sit up. "What time is it?"

"I don't know . . . maybe 6:30."

Evan blinked at the window blinds. Not a trace of light yet. "What's going on? Where are you?"

"I'm . . . in your driveway. I didn't want to bang on the door and wake everyone up."

Julia stirred beside her. "What's wrong?" she asked, sleepily.

"It's Tim," Evan whispered. "Give me two minutes to grab some clothes," she said into the phone. "I'll be right down."

"Okay," he said. "Thanks."

Evan tossed her phone back on the nightstand and turned to face Julia. "He's out front, in the driveway."

"The *driveway?* What time is it?"

Evan was already up and grabbing the clothes she'd worn last night off a chair. She glanced at the clock. "Nearly 6:30. Get dressed and come down when you're ready."

"Is he okay?"

"I don't think so." Evan struggled into her sweatshirt and headed for the door.

"I'll be right behind you," Julia said.

When Evan reached the front door, Tim was already standing

there. Sunrise was still a ways off, and in the fading light cast by the setting moon, his pallor looked downright ghoulish.

Evan took him by the arm and hauled him inside.

"What the hell is wrong?" she asked.

"It's Joey Mazzetta. He called me last night after I got home. He wanted to meet—to talk with me about . . . *things*. About Father Szymanski."

Evan ushered him toward a chair so he could sit down. She perched on the arm of the sofa facing him.

"Joey from the photograph Joey?" she asked.

Tim nodded. "I went to see him that night after you showed me the picture." He looked at her morosely. "I didn't tell you that. I wanted to talk with him. To apologize."

"Tim . . ."

"He threw me out. He told me I was no better than the rest of them." Tim ran a shaky hand across his face. "He was right."

"Hey. Hey, man." Evan rested a hand on his shoulder. "Take it easy."

Julia came softly down the stairs and hesitated before approaching them where they sat.

"Julia is here," Evan said. "Is that okay with you?"

"Yeah." Tim raised his head and looked toward the doorway where Julia stood. "We're family."

Evan squeezed his shoulder.

"Honey?" she addressed Julia. "Would you please get Tim a glass of bourbon? No rocks."

"Of course." Julia headed for the kitchen.

"Hold tight, Sunny. We're right here with you," Evan said.

Tim looked up at her. "I know you are."

"Wanna take your coat off?"

Tim nodded and shrugged out of it.

"Are you hungry?"

"No."

"That's a first." She gave him a faint smile. He actually tried to smile back, but didn't quite succeed.

159

Julia joined them with a big tumbler of bourbon. She sat down in the chair beside Tim and handed it to him.

"Drink this," she said, gently.

He took the glass from her and took a swallow. "Joey called me at midnight last night, and said he was ready to talk—to be done with it all. We were going to meet at the Melrose Diner."

"What happened?" Evan coaxed him to continue.

"I went there and waited. He never showed. I waited for him. Called his cell phone a few times. No answer. Finally, I drove over to their house on South Bouvier. And . . ." He stopped.

"And . . . what?" Evan asked.

"There were police cars all over the place. A detective talked with me outside the house. Joey had been killed. Shot in some alley off 15th Street."

"*What?*" Evan was stunned.

"Yeah. It was horrible. *Surreal.*" Tim met Evan's eyes. "They took me inside to see his mother. She was . . ." He couldn't continue. Julia reached over and rested her hand on his arm. "I don't know what'll happen to her. Joey was out of work. They have no money."

"Did this detective say what they think happened to him?"

"Robbery, maybe? Detective Ortiz said Joey's wallet was found on the ground beside his body. *His body . . .*"

"Drink your bourbon, Sunny." Evan smoothed her hand over Tim's unruly red hair. "Was that J.C. Ortiz?"

"I think so."

"Okay. Once you're finished with that, we're gonna go into the kitchen and make some breakfast."

He lifted his head and looked at her. Then he nodded. "Okay."

"Good." Evan nodded at him. "Stevie will smell the bacon and be down here in two seconds. You wanna go splash some water on your face? Put your game face on for the kid?"

"Yeah. That's probably a good idea." Tim drained his glass and got shakily to his feet. Julia stood up, too, and without asking, stepped in to wrap her arms around him. Tim hugged her back.

"Don't get carried away," he said into her hair. "I might not let go."

"You don't have to," she said.

Tim patted her back and released her. "I'll be okay," he said.

"I know you will," Julia added, "because you have to be."

Evan understood that Julia's observation had a double meaning. When Tim kissed the top of her head, Evan saw that he knew it, too.

"I'll be back in just a minute," he said. He left them and headed for the downstairs bathroom.

Julia faced Evan. "This isn't good."

"No," Evan agreed with her. "None of it is."

"You think this was related to Cawley and those pictures, don't you?"

"I don't know. Maybe." She gave Julia a half smile. "*Probably.* You know me and coincidences."

"Evan . . ." Julia didn't finish her statement.

"Sweetie? There's *no* reason to jump to any conclusions here. We just don't know enough."

"Yet?" Julia asked.

"Yet."

Julia lifted her chin. "I'm going to ask you the same question I asked last night."

"Will I tell you if I find out?"

Julia nodded.

"I don't know. Ask me later today."

"Why later today?"

"Because," Evan stated, "after breakfast, I'm gonna go see my old pal, Detective Ortiz."

Chapter Eight

Evan and Julia had been pretty insistent that Tim head upstairs and try to sleep for a few hours.

"There's no way we're letting you drive back to St. Rita's right now," Evan insisted. "Not until you prove that you can stand up straight without assistance."

He tried to protest, but it was pointless. He knew she was right.

And Stevie chimed in, too.

"C'mon, Papasan. When you get up, you can take me driving. I'm going to Dad's later today, and he won't let me near his precious Bondo bucket."

"For good reason," Evan added.

"What's that supposed to mean?" Stevie demanded. "I never hit anything."

"Oh, really?" Evan asked. "What about that row of mailboxes at his condo?"

"Hey. That was *totally* not my fault."

"Right." Evan crossed her arms. "Lemme guess. They ran right out in front of the car?"

"Like anyone would even know if *that* happened," Stevie complained. "That Chrysler is, like, nine miles long."

"Okay, okay, you two." Tim raised a hand to halt the discussion. "Retreat to your corners. I'll *stay*, already."

Stevie brightened up at once. "And take me out for a lesson?"

"Yes, God help me. That, too."

"Sweet." Stevie resumed her perusal of the sports pages in the morning paper. "Yo? Timbo? I see here that Villanova is playing St. Joe's tonight. Up for a little wager?"

"*And*," Evan began, "while we're on the subject of your shared new lives of crime, maybe it's time for the two of you to come clean about all of these *little wagers?*"

Stevie and Tim exchanged glances.

"No," Tim said. "I really don't think it is."

Julia laughed. "Give it up, Sergeant Friday. These two canaries are never gonna sing."

"Why does it seem like I fell asleep and woke up in a Dashiell Hammet novel?"

Julia patted her hand. "Drink your juice, dear."

Tim appreciated Evan's obvious attempt to lighten the tone. The easy banter worked to push some of the darkness that threatened to overwhelm him off to the periphery—at least for a little while.

"On that note," Tim got up from the table. "I'm going to go take a shower and lie down for a while."

He went upstairs after making them pledge to come get him if he didn't reappear after a few hours. They all promised they would—so he wasn't surprised when he woke up a little after 10 a.m. to find Stevie perched on the end of the bed.

"Are you awake?" she asked, when he opened one eye.

"I am now."

She smiled. She looked so much like Evan had at that same age, he felt almost giddy inside. He figured it probably was an emotional response to the events of last night—and being so overtired.

"Did you get your shower?" Stevie asked.

"Yeah. Before I came in here to nap."

"Cool. So? Ready to go driving?"

He laughed. "No flies on you."

"I just don't wanna waste time. Dad gets here at two."

Tim yawned. "Are your mom and Julia still downstairs?"

163

"Nope. Julia went to Wegmans in Glen Mills, and Mama Uno had some kind of errand to run in the city. She said she'd be back before Dad and Kayla get here."

"Okay. Looks like it's just you-n-me, kid. Lemme go use the facilities and I'll meet you at the car."

"Sweet." Stevie took off for the stairs.

When Tim joined her, she was already strapped into the driver's seat. He climbed in and adjusted the seat to give himself a bit more leg room. He handed her his keys. "Where are we headed?"

"I thought maybe we could drive over to St. Cornelius School and practice three-point turns and parking in their lot."

"Anything going on there today?" Tim put on his seatbelt.

"I don't think so. It's Saturday."

"Sounds good to me."

Fortunately, Tim had backed into Evan's driveway that morning, so that took any immediate drama off the table. Stevie started the Subaru and did a good job negotiating the turn onto Ring Road. When they were underway, she asked him how he was feeling.

"Mom didn't say much about why you showed up at our house this morning. I figured that meant I wasn't supposed to ask."

"You can ask," he told her. "There's a stop sign up ahead."

"I see it." She slowed the car down but didn't quite come to a complete stop before rolling on through the intersection.

"Hey," he said. "You have to actually *stop*—even if there's nobody coming."

"That's kind of a stupid rule."

"Most rules are. But they exist for a reason."

"Now you sound like Mama Uno."

"Who, as far as I know, has been driving for twenty-nine years without ever getting ticketed for a traffic violation."

Stevie held up a hand. "Okay, already. I'll stop next time."

"Stop *every* time," Tim added. "Stop and count to three before rolling on. Trust me. This is exactly the kind of stuff they ding you for when you take your driving test."

They approached the turnoff for St. Cornelius. Stevie dutifully put her left blinker on.

"Do I have to stop here, too?" she asked.

"Not if there are no cars coming," Tim said.

"Duh." Stevie made the turn. "I was joking."

"Smart-ass."

Stevie drove along the access road to the school parking lot, promptly pulled into a space, and stopped.

"Before we start," she said, "could you tell me what was wrong this morning? Or am I not supposed to know?"

Tim was surprised by her question. Not that she asked it—but that she thought he didn't want her to know what was happening.

"No. You can always ask me anything. I was really rattled because a man I was going to meet with last night ended up getting shot in an apparent robbery." Tim hesitated. "He was killed."

"*Oh, man.* That totally sucks." Stevie turned off the engine.

"Yeah," Tim nodded. "It does."

"I'm really sorry, Papasan. Are you okay?"

"I will be."

"I guess I should've asked you about that before we came roaring out here. We didn't have to do this today."

"It's okay." Tim did his best to sound reassuring. "It's good to talk about it."

Stevie nodded. "I'm like that, too. Talking about stuff makes it easier to deal with. Mom almost never talks about stuff—even though she always makes me do it."

"She's pretty bossy," he agreed.

"Who was this man? A friend?"

"He used to be. He was a guy I went to school with at St. Rita's." *Was a guy?* Tim was having a hard time talking about Joey in the past tense. "He was . . . having a hard time with some things, and he asked me to meet him to talk. That happened last night, after I got home."

"Last night?" Stevie asked. "He called you pretty late, didn't he?"

"Yeah. He did. He'd been out someplace, and whatever happened there made him decide to call me. I went out to an all-night diner to wait on him, but he never showed up. I went by his house on my way home and saw all the police cars there. That's when I found out what'd happened to him."

"Wow. That's a nightmare. Was he married?"

"No. He lived with his mother. Joey was an only child."

"That's a drag. Will she be okay?"

Tim never ceased to be amazed by Stevie's ability to ask exactly the right questions.

"I hope so. I'll make sure the Church looks after her."

"Meaning, you'll look after her, right?"

He shrugged. "We'll both look after her."

"Yeah? Well, I think the Church is pretty lucky."

"Lucky?" Tim didn't quite understand her observation. "Lucky how?"

Stevie started the car. "To be married to such a good guy."

Jesús Correa Ortiz was the younger brother of a girl Evan had dated off and on in high school.

It actually was mostly *off*—at least as far as the actual "dating" part went. They really were more like occasional fuck buddies than anything else. Sofia wasn't really queer—or so she said. According to her, her interest in Evan was more exploratory than anything. But they spent enough time together that Sofia's mother, who once caught them mostly naked in the back seat of the family station wagon, never stopped blaming Evan for making her son "turn" gay.

Evan never quite understood Mrs. Ortiz's calculus on that one. But Jesús, who wisely changed his name to J.C., never let Evan forget it, either. Especially when he got beat up every other week at school because he tended to wear pirate shirts and kept posters of Prince tacked up inside his locker.

How any of that was *her* fault never exactly became clear to her.

She knew J.C. had joined the Philly P.D. after college, but didn't realize he'd made detective until Tim had mentioned him this morning. That was quite an accomplishment for a kid from

J.C.'s background—particularly in a south Philly precinct not known for its tolerance.

It didn't take her long to locate J.C.'s desk on the second floor of the 1st District Station on 24th Street. She knew he'd be working. Homicide detectives didn't tend to get weekends off. Not in this town, anyway.

She crossed the big, noisy room toward the desk where he stood, scowling at something he was reading. When he looked up and saw her coming, she could tell that he recognized her right away.

He tossed whatever he'd been reading down on his desk, which was covered with papers, photographs, and about five empty coffee cups, all emblazoned with logos from sports teams and different area restaurants.

He took a moment to look her up and down. Normally that would piss her off, but she hadn't seen J.C. in a while—not since he'd been a rookie beat cop. She was pretty sure he already had an idea about why she was there.

She fluttered the fingers of her right hand at him in her best pantomime of a feminine salute.

"Evangeline Reed." J.C. knew that using her full name would piss her off. It was clear this interview was going to be . . . fun. "What're you doing in *this* neighborhood? Your Lexus break down or something?"

"Very funny, Officer. You should try out for Spring Frolics again. Bet they'd finally let you in—what with that big gun and all."

"Yeah? Suck my dick. You see this gold shield?" He pointed at the badge hanging from his belt. "It's *Detective* now. You got some actual business here, or is this strictly a social call?"

Evan pulled out a chair and sat down beside his metal desk.

"I don't recall asking you to sit down," J.C. said.

"Funny. I don't recall asking for permission."

"Look. You lose your Pomeranian or something? If so, file a report downstairs. We do real work up here."

"Who fucking pissed in your corn flakes, J.C.? I just need some help with a case I'm working on."

He continued to stand there, glowering at her.

The ambient noise around them was ridiculous. Phones were ringing off the hook, and nobody in his shared bullpen of an office appeared to be breaking a sweat to answer them.

Their little standoff gave Evan time to make her own assessment of how the years had treated J.C. She was impressed. He was a good-looking kid—always had been. Muscular build—looked like he probably worked out four or five times a week. He still had those ridiculously long eyelashes that any woman would kill for, amber eyes and perfect, white teeth. Evan supposed he was a *very* popular boy these days—at least, in his off-duty hours.

Finally, J.C. yanked his ancient desk chair out and dropped down into it. That seemed like a courageous move to her. The thing groaned like it was on the verge of collapsing beneath his weight.

"What do you want?" he asked, in a more conversational tone. "Make it snappy. I got shit to do."

"So, you were working a homicide last night. On 15th Street. Guy named Joey Mazzetta."

"Yeah. So what?" She noticed J.C. slide some other papers over to cover up what he'd been looking at when she showed up.

"The priest you interviewed," she reminded him. "The one who showed up at the Mazzettas' house on South Bouvier? He's a friend of mine. A *good* friend."

J.C. held up his hands. "Again, I ask, so what?"

"*So* . . . what happened to Joey Mazzetta? I know he was shot and killed. Was it a robbery? Gang related? Drugs? What?"

He leaned toward her. "You know I can't discuss any of that with you—even if I did know what happened. And I don't."

"C'mon, J.C. This ain't your first rodeo. Joey was an out-of-work loser. Unarmed. Probably drunk. He was walking south on 15th Street in the middle of the night to meet a goddamn priest for pancakes at the Melrose Diner. He wasn't a gang-banger, he wasn't a drug dealer, and he wasn't out lookin' for love. What do you *think* happened to him? Were there any clues at the scene?"

He sat back in his chair. "So, you're asking me to speculate?"

"Yeah. I'm asking you to speculate, J.C. It's *Joey Mazzetta* we're talking about. I know you remember him. He shot hoops with your brother, Luis."

"Okay, Reed. Since we share such a sacred bond, I'll tell you what I *do* know for sure. You might wanna take notes on this so you can remember it in the future. I'm a half-black, half-Puerto Rican fag named fucking *Jesus*, who's managed, after six and a half years of bigoted bullshit, to make Detective in this shithole precinct. And what *that* means is that there's no fucking way I'm going to blow all that up to help you jack off some rich, white politician who doesn't give two fucks about the people who are stuck in this neighborhood because they're too poor, too stupid or have the wrong goddamn skin color." He grabbed one of the empty coffee mugs. "Now get the fuck out of my office and go play golf. I've got real work to do—for people who can't afford to pay me."

He pushed his creaking chair back, and stormed off—leaving her alone in a sea of ringing telephones.

That went better than I thought it would . . .

She pulled a small card out of her jacket pocket and tossed it on his desk before walking out.

She'd made it halfway to her car when her cell phone rang. She was relieved when she read the caller ID.

"What took you so long?"

"Hey," J.C. said. "The walls in this fucking place have ears."

"Yeah. I gathered. Nice performance. You always were a good actor."

"It comes in useful sometimes. Listen . . . you wanna meet me someplace? Like in half an hour?"

"Sure. Just say where."

"You know Stargazy?" he asked. "On East Passyunk?"

"No. But I'll find it."

"See you there."

He hung up.

Good ol' J.C.

She wondered if he still wore pirate shirts.

Stargazy was a storefront, bangers and mash kind of place in what could only be called a "transitional" block on East Passyunk. It wasn't quite lunchtime, but the joint was doing a steady business—mostly takeout, although the place had a few metal tables with mismatched chairs. Evan ordered a Pimms & lemonade, and sat down to wait on J.C.

Cops. They always knew the best places to eat.

J.C., for all his youthful fashion excesses, had always been a good kid. His father had been a beat cop in the same district where Joey earned his gold shield. Officer Alfonso Ortiz had been killed when he was dispatched to respond to a domestic dispute on McKean Street, only a few blocks from where Joey Mazzetta met his untimely end.

J.C. arrived exactly thirty minutes after his call. That impressed her. Most gay men she knew weren't exactly punctual. In her experience, "Gay People's Time" was more than just a charming expression.

J.C. pulled out a chair and sat down at her small table. Evan noticed that he was carrying a couple sheets of folded-up paper.

"Did you order anything?" he asked.

She held up her bottle. "Just this."

"Trust me to order for you? It'll save time."

"Sure."

"Cool." He swiveled on his chair and signaled to the big man behind the counter. "Hey, Sam? Bring us two of those beef and onion pies with mash and parsley liquor. Same tab."

Sam gave him a thumbs-up.

J.C. turned back to face Evan. "I assume you're buying?"

"It's the least I can do for making you queer."

"Yeah. Mom still talks about that, you know."

"How is Sofia?" Evan asked.

"Pregnant. She's on her fourth one."

"Damn, four kids?"

"Fuck no." He laughed. "Fourth husband."

"That girl never could commit."

J.C. laughed.

Evan thought that if J.C.'s detective gig didn't work out, he could always make a living as a Differio model. He really looked great.

"You know," he said, "Mrs. Mazzetta cooked food for our family for more than a month after Pop was killed—longer than anyone else. Even after the women's guild at the Tabernacle stopped coming, she kept at it. Every couple of days, she'd show up in that POS car of hers and unload shit. Lasagna. Casseroles. Even cakes. And she had to be doing all of that at night, after she got home from her job at the Acme." J.C. drummed his fingers on the table. "Joey was always a total asshole. He used to call me 'butt plug' in school. But I'll never forget how nice his Mom was to us. She didn't deserve this."

"Nobody does," Evan said.

J.C. stopped drumming. "I suppose we should save our reminiscing for another time." Sam brought J.C.'s complimentary tea over and deposited it on the table. "Thanks, man," J.C. said to him. He dipped his Darjeeling tea bag in and out of the steaming cup. "So, you wanna know about Joey?"

"Yeah. Tim Donovan is my best friend."

J.C. raised a perfect eyebrow. "A *priest* is your best friend? What the fuck? You get religion or something?"

"Or something," Evan said. "But Joey also happens to be tangentially involved in another case I'm working on. So it's possible that his death was related to that."

"You wanna say more about why you think that?"

"I will after you tell me why you might think I might be right."

"I never could fool you." He unfolded the papers he'd brought along. "Joey was shot twice at close range—in the back. No gun at the scene."

"Tim said his wallet was lying beside his body."

"That's right. It was empty—meaning no cash. But his Discover Card and driver's license were still in it." J.C. shrugged. "He also had a couple of prepaid Visa cards. No way to know if they had any balances left on them, but whoever capped him didn't seem interested in those."

"Meaning you don't think it was a robbery?"

"No. For starters, muggers don't usually shoot people in the back."

"Anything else?"

"Yeah." He pushed what looked like a ballistics report across the table toward her. "We recovered two shell casings at the scene. Both of them were rimless, bottlenecked shells. You can see them here." He pointed out the scans of the casings. "They're stamped S&B—Sellier & Bellot—pretty distinctive shells. They were unusual enough that when the M.E. removed the rounds from Mazzetta, we rushed them over to the local ATF office. They did us a solid and ran an integrated ballistics ID report. Turns out we had a perfect match for a Tokarev 7.62."

"*What?*"

'Right." J.C. nodded his head. "Not the usual sidearm favored by your common junkie who's out looking for quick cash."

"Isn't that a Soviet-era firearm?" Evan asked.

"Good guess. The TT30 is a single stack, suppressed pistol that was the weapon of choice in Soviet bloc countries back in the '30s. They're not common around here, but you can get them from collectors. And the M.E. who removed the rounds from Joey said the fabric tears and powder burns were consistent with this type of weapon—fast and powerful. They tore Joey up pretty good."

"Jesus."

"You rang?" He smirked at her.

Evan laughed before taking a moment to assess everything J.C. had shared. "Shit. This wasn't what I thought you'd say."

"Yeah. It's pretty much a goat fuck. And that's not all. Apparently, your pal Joey had a busy night—before he ended up face down in that alley."

"What do you mean?"

J.C. flipped to another page in the papers he'd brought along. "It seems he broke into some high-brow private club on South Broad Street and stumbled his way into the dining room—where he proceeded to start popping off at some of the bluebloods who were in there, stuffing their faces with Beluga caviar. Somebody called the cops, but by the time they got there, club security had already tossed his drunk ass out on the street."

"Did they press charges?" Evan asked, knowing full well they probably hadn't.

"Nope. Surprised?"

"Not really. What time did all that happen?"

J.C. consulted the copy of the police report. "About 8 p.m."

"That's four hours before he called Tim."

"Yeah. That's what Donovan said when he gave his statement." J.C. drank some of his tea. "Mazzetta must've used that time to keep bar hopping."

Evan didn't want to ask her next question, but she knew she had to.

"What's the name of the club?"

"Let's see . . . The Galileo Club. It's on a corner of South Broad Street." He gave a short, bitter laugh. "Corner? Shit. It's the whole fucking block."

Evan felt sick, and it wasn't the Pimms.

Sam was headed their way with two heaping plates of food. *Great.*

J.C. picked up his papers, refolded them, and tucked them into his jacket pocket. "Sorry. Can't let you keep these."

"No sweat. Thanks for sharing."

Sam left their plates and some silverware wrapped in paper napkins. "Lemme know if you need a refill, J.C.," he said.

"Will do. Thanks, man." J.C. slid the grease-stained check across the table toward Evan. "Yours, I think."

"Yeah." Evan picked it up and tucked it beneath the edge of her plate. The steam rising off the parsley liquor was making her feel woozy.

Who was she kidding? It wasn't the food. The food was fine.

It was this whole damn mess. This case was an ongoing nightmare showing no signs of ending any time soon.

And now Julia's father was right in the goddamn middle of it.

J.C. was already digging into his food.

"So, Evangeline," he said. "It's your turn to share. Tell me why you think Joey was murdered."

"Yeah. About that." Evan sat back and ran a hand through her short hair. "How much time do you get for lunch?"

Dan and Kayla arrived at Evan's house about fifteen minutes early. Tim and Stevie had already returned from Stevie's driver's ed lesson, but Evan was still a no-show. Before leaving, Evan had tasked the pair with sweeping off the back porch, in the event it warmed up enough that the party might be able sit outside. Temperatures were rumored to reach into the low fifties.

Julia doubted that would happen.

After greeting her father in the driveway, Stevie informed him that they only had about five minutes' more work to do before joining the group inside.

Evan's not being at home was like the ring of a coffin nail for Dan.

Julia wasn't worried, although Dan rarely missed an opportunity to grouse about anything related to Evan's behavior.

"She knew we were getting here at two, right?" He handed a bottle of nondescript wine to Julia. "This is pretty shitty."

"Relax, Dan." Kayla nudged him. "She probably got held up."

He huffed. "Held up. That's about right. Where the fuck is she?"

"I'm not sure," Julia said apologetically. "She had a meeting in town. Why don't you two go sit down? I'll get us some glasses."

"Let me help you, Julia." Kayla followed Julia into the kitchen.

"I'll go out and hang with Tim and Stevie until Evan gets here," Dan said.

Julia had only met Kayla twice before, and both occasions had been fairly abbreviated encounters. But she liked her. Kayla was smart and vivacious—but not in an obnoxious, millennial way. Kayla's energy was more about her personal drive and determination to work hard enough to earn the notice of a more mainstream news outlet. She'd been at *Media Matters* for about eighteen months when Dan first met her. She'd been assigned to a team of environmental impact reporters tasked with promoting green energy policy initiatives, and Dan was working with a couple of congressional campaigns where fossil fuel debates were hot-button issues.

The first time Dan asked Kayla out, he'd had the very great misfortune to run into Evan and Julia at CHIKO, a Chinese-Korean fusion restaurant on 8th Street near Capitol Hill. Evan later laughed like hell at Dan's obvious embarrassment about being busted on what clearly was a date with someone young enough to be his daughter. Thankfully, she managed to behave better than expected, and the two couples chatted amiably for a few minutes before they were seated at different tables. Julia had to kick Evan beneath the table—*twice*—to get her to stop snickering whenever she looked over at Dan's table.

"Stop it," Julia hissed. "Behave yourself."

"Will you quit kicking me?" Evan rubbed her chin. "It's going to leave a mark."

"You're the one who's going to leave a mark if you don't start acting like a grown-up."

"What's that supposed to mean?" Evan was still rubbing her leg.

"It means they're obviously on a date. Judging by Dan's mortification at running into us, I'd venture a guess that it's a first date. If you keep acting out, there probably won't be a second."

"I'm not acting out."

"Oh, really?" Julia leaned forward across the small table and rested her chin on the back of her hand. "How would you characterize your demeanor?"

"I'm just . . ." Evan fiddled with her water glass. "Curious."

"Curious? If I didn't know you better, I'd be jealous."

Evan looked shell-shocked by her comment. "You're not, are you?"

175

As tempted as Julia had been to let her twist in the wind a bit, she relented. "No. I'm not."

"Good," Evan seemed to relax. "It's nothing like that. It could never be."

"It's comforting to hear that. So if your nose isn't out of joint because Dan's actually out on a date with someone, then what *is* bugging you?"

Evan seemed to balk at Julia's question. "You're kidding me, right?"

"No," Julia said "I don't believe I am."

It was Evan's turn to lean forward over the table. "Did you *see* her?" she whispered.

"Of course I did. There's nothing wrong with my eyesight, except a bit of early-onset presbyopia."

"And?"

"And, what?"

"Come on, Julia. She's practically Stevie's age."

"That's an overstatement, and you know it. Besides, what possible relevance does it have? I should be shocked that you, of all people, would display such churlish prejudice."

"Churlish?" Evan appeared miffed by Julia's comment.

"That's what I'd call expressions of baseless ageism."

"Ageism?" Now Evan simply looked baffled.

"Are you going to continue to repeat everything I say?" Julia said. "If so, this is going to be a very dull evening."

Evan sat back and stared at the tabletop for a moment. Then she cut her eyes up at Julia and gave her a sly smile.

"It's really sexy when you get pissed. It's like getting dressed-down by Dixie Carter."

"Except for the accent . . ."

"Well," Evan said. "There *is* that."

Julia stared at the ceiling. "I love you, but sometimes you act like a sophomoric frat boy."

"Oh, yeah?" Evan waggled her brows. "I can think of a few occasions where that behavior was actually to your liking."

"Don't prevaricate. Let's try to stay in the moment."

"Oh, I'm in the moment, all right. If I were any more in the moment, I'd slide right off my chair."

Julia laughed. "It's good to see that your sense of humor has returned. Now can you try to focus that good energy and fucking leave those two alone for the rest of their meal?"

"Ohhhh. Profanity. That ain't helpin' your cause, Miz Julia."

Julia raised an eyebrow. "Keep it up. I'm sure you and the rest of your *Designing Women* will enjoy a night on the sofa."

"Okay, okay." Evan reached a hand across the table to take hold of Julia's arm. "I'll behave."

"Promise?"

"Cross my black heart."

To be fair, Evan had managed to constrain herself for the rest of that evening . . . mostly. But ever since, she'd been engaged in a nonstop diatribe about the root of Dan's foolishness. And that editorializing shifted into high gear when he and Kayla had got married last year. This gathering today would give Evan her first real shot at exercising her recent pledge to be more understanding and less judgmental.

It was anybody's guess how successful she'd be sticking with her recent resolution when she finally got home.

Julia stole a surreptitious look at her watch. Evan was now twenty minutes late. It wasn't like her to be tardy—and even less like her not to call or text if she were running late.

"What can I do?" Kayla asked.

Julia handed her a corkscrew. "How about you start by opening the bottle you and Dan brought? I've got some hors d'oeuvres ready, too."

"Sure." Kayla took the corkscrew from Julia but immediately set it down on the kitchen counter. "This one has a screw cap." She held up the bottle. "I'm sorry. But as hard as I try, Dan clings to his proletarian tastes when it comes to wine."

"Don't apologize. I'm certain it'll be delicious."

"I admire your optimism." Kayla cracked open the bottle.

Julia studied her without being too obvious. She really was a pretty young woman. Striking, actually, with her long, fair

177

hair and athletic build. It was easy to see how she'd turned Dan's head. The bigger surprise was how much gravitas she had. Julia felt confident that Kayla's journalistic aspirations would pay off eventually—especially with a boost from the powerful connections Dan had on Capitol Hill.

It was that very suspicion that kept hamstringing Evan. As much as she tried, Evan said she couldn't shake her fear that Kayla—whether wittingly or unwittingly—was using Dan as a stepping-stone to greener pastures. She didn't want that for Dan, and she certainly didn't want that for Stevie, who seemed genuinely to be forming an attachment to Kayla.

Julia chose to adopt a more sanguine point of view. She saw no evidence that Kayla was not genuinely attached to Dan— although she was the first to admit that she'd spent little focused time with either of them since they got married. She hoped that would change now that she'd be living here with Evan and Stevie.

That thought made her smile.

Kayla noticed. "You seem lost in thought."

"Do I? It's my turn to apologize for allowing myself to be distracted."

Julia carried a tray loaded with wineglasses over to the counter where Kayla had set the open bottle of wine. "Maybe we should go ahead and fill these?" she suggested. "Give it a chance to breathe a bit."

Kayla laughed. "Are you kidding? Mouth-to-mouth resuscitation wouldn't help *this* wine. Want my advice?"

"Sure."

"I say let's fill Dan's glass with this vinegar and open something else. He'll never know the difference, and I have reason to suspect that you and Evan have better palates."

Julia was amused. "Did some little bird tell you that?"

"Oh, yeah." Kayla nodded. "My hope is that this is not a characteristic Stevie inherits from her father."

Julia went to Evan's small wine refrigerator and drew out a nice Cotes du Rhone. It was a good drinker—a Vacqueyras.

Jammy, but not too spicy. It was one of their favorites. She held it up for Kayla.

"How about this one?"

"Hell to the yes." Kayla nodded energetically. "Gimme." She fluttered her fingers toward the bottle.

Julia passed it over to her. "We've got a few more of these, too, should we need them."

Kayla was already cutting the foil. "Trust me, we'll need them. He's in a mood today. It's this damn Cawley business."

"Evan said the timetable is pretty compressed."

"That's one way to describe it. It's probably the world's worst-kept secret that Cawley was making the rounds on Capitol Hill all last week. The judiciary committee is planning to vote on his nomination as early as Thursday or Friday."

"Next week?" Julia was surprised. This would not be welcome news to Evan.

"Uh huh. Those fossilized assholes want to be sure to get their hand-picked ideologue on the court before they blow town on the 17th."

"Does Evan know this?"

"The date?" Kayla asked. "I think so. I know it's part of what Dan plans to talk with her about today. That's why he acted like such a jerk when we arrived and she wasn't here."

"I really do expect her any minute," Julia reiterated. "It's not like her to be late . . . for anything, really."

Kayla nodded. "Stevie talks about that proclivity of her mother's with fondness."

"Fondness?" Julia quoted. "I don't doubt she talks about it, but I suspect it's with something other than fondness."

"You're right. I lied." Kayla began pouring the Vacqueyras. "Good god, this is *gorgeous.*" She gave Julia an intent look. "Can we just keep this for ourselves?"

"Works for me."

The door to the back porch opened, and Stevie erupted into the room with her customary flourish. Tim, Dan *and* Evan followed behind her more sedately.

"Too late," Julia whispered to Kayla. "We're busted."

"Busted about what?" Stevie promptly began counting wine-glasses. She looked at Julia with disappointment. "There's one missing."

"Yeah," Julia held up a hand. "You'll have to ask your mom about that one."

"Seriously?" Stevie sighed dramatically. "Beloved Mama Uno?" She addressed Evan. "May I please have a glass of Dad's wine, too?"

Evan walked over and gave Julia a quick kiss. She shook Kayla's hand warmly. "I'm so sorry I'm late. It's really good to see you, Kayla."

Kayla handed Evan a glass. "No sweat. Stuff happens."

"Mom? *Hello?*" Stevie snapped her fingers between the two women. "May I *please* have some of Dad's wine?"

Evan examined the two open bottles. Then she chuckled and looked slyly at both Kayla and Julia. "Sure, honey. You're welcome to have a small glass of your dad's wine. Right, Kayla?"

"Absolutely. *Stellar* idea, Evan." Kayla picked up Dan's nine-dollar bottle of . . . *something*, and held it aloft. "Grab a glass, young lady."

"Yeah," Dan groused. He faced Evan. "I hate to be the one to break up this little love fest, but since you've finally consented to join us, I need about twenty minutes of your time to talk shop."

"Can it wait two seconds, Dan?" Evan asked.

"No. It fucking cannot wait two seconds. If it could, I wouldn't need to talk to you right now, would I?"

"Geez, Dad. Throw a rod, why don't you." Stevie sniffed her glass of wine and promptly made a face.

"Drink your wine, Stevie," Dan said dismissively. "We'll be right back."

Kayla handed Evan a glass. "You'll need this," she said. She also handed Dan the glass she'd poured from his bottle.

Dan took it from her, then grabbed Evan by the elbow and steered her out of the kitchen.

"I guess we'll be in my office," Evan called over her shoulder. "Don't say anything important until we get back."

180

Tim munched on some canapés Julia had made. "These little blended family gatherings are always so much fun."

"This smells like piss." Stevie put her glass down, then shoved it another two feet away. "Like day-old potato salad that's been left out in the sun." She faced Julia. "Mom did that on *purpose*."

"Hey." Kayla took Stevie's discarded glass to the sink and dumped it out. After giving it a good rinse, she brought it back and refilled it with the Rhone. "You saw *nothing*," she cautioned.

"Yeah." Tim laughed. "No worries, Kayla. When it comes to hooch, she's a regular Sergeant Schultz."

"Who's that, Timbo?" Stevie sniffed her new glass of wine and made happy sounds. "This is more like it."

"Sergeant Schultz was a character on . . . Who cares? You still won't know what it means." He picked up another canapé. "These things are great. Where'd you get 'em, Julia?"

"Prepare yourself for a stunning revelation, Tim. I *made* them."

"Really?" Tim seemed genuinely surprised. "Evan says you can barely boil water."

Julia rolled her eyes. "Evan thinks anyone who cannot properly dice an onion is some kind of simpleton. But however challenged I am in the culinary arts, I do have some modest claims to fame when it comes to the preparation of appetizers. Credit my miserable youth and the endless weeks I spent at summer camp."

"You went to summer camps that taught you how to make *appetizers?*" Stevie was incredulous. "We just learned how to roll joints and use condoms."

Julia laughed. "You say tomato . . ."

"Nothing beats a Catholic education," Tim commiserated. "So, is there any more wine that Dan *didn't* bring?"

It only took Evan about five minutes to bring Dan up to speed on what had happened since they last spoke after Ben Rush's trip to North Warren. She could tell he was concerned about the Joey Mazzetta development, but he was unwilling to pass any of the information about her suspicions along to the senators leading the opposition against Cawley's nomination.

"At this point, it's nothing but supposition," he said. "Without any kind of corroboration or hard evidence, it's nothing we can use."

Evan was as frustrated as he was. "You think I don't know that? I'm trying to follow these leads, but they keep expanding so fast, I can't keep up with them. It's like playing Vatican whack-a-mole."

"What do you mean?"

Evan ticked the items off. "The bishop. The relationship between the boys on the St. Rita's basketball team and Cawley's club. The odd coincidence that Edwin Miller showed up in the photo of Cawley at the club with both the bishop *and* some of the team members. The fact that the only people who might be in a position to clarify any of this keep managing to turn up dead. And while we're on it, let's not forget the special insights I got from my anonymous little pen pal, Moxie."

Dan held up his hands. "What's your point?"

"My *point* is that this stinks, Dan. There's some way Cawley is more involved with the bishop and those kids that extends beyond his dropping off the occasional check for new sports equipment or bus rides to basketball camp. *I know it.* We're talking about kids who were routinely targeted for sexual favors by their damn *priest*—and God knows who else. Szymanski used this parish like it was some kind of private game preserve. And let's not diminish the fact that this reprobate is now a bishop in the Philadelphia archdiocese—one who probably has a lot of motivation to keep his extracurricular activities under wraps. And that's especially true now, after the grand jury report came out and started naming names."

"I get that. But what has this got to do with Cawley? And don't tell me about your fucking women's intuition. That shit won't stop his nomination, and you know it."

She did know it. And that made her angrier than she was already.

"Screw you, Dan. I'm doing my best to try and nail it down. But it's a little tough when all the damn witnesses end up dead."

"Will you fucking sit down?"

Evan dropped into her desk chair with a huff. "The homicide detective I talked with this morning told me that Mazzetta went to Cawley's private club before he was killed. He was drunk and started mouthing off in the dining room about some of the members." She glared at Dan. "You think it's some kind of happy coincidence that Szymanski happens to be a member of the *same* private club as the judge?"

"Look." Dan's tone was a tad more conciliatory. "I agree that this stinks. And if you ask me, the slimy fucker is in it up to his comb-over. But unless or until you can get somebody on the record, or come up with photos of some kid sitting on Cawley's face, he's gonna sail through that senate committee less than a week from now, and take his seat on the high court—forever and ever, amen."

Evan was sickened by Dan's comment. Even though she knew him, it was still possible for her to be shocked by such a callous demonstration of his empathetic myopia.

"These were *kids*, Dan. Kids who were betrayed and sexually abused by someone they should've been able to trust. Their lives were changed forever. Some of them will never recover. Some of them, like Joey Mazzetta, will never even get the chance to try. You might think about that the next time you decide to dismiss their lives out of hand because they can't be useful to your cause."

"Hey. *Back the fuck off.* It's not just 'my' cause. You think any of their lives will be improved if assholes like Cawley get lifetime judicial appointments? To be good at this job, I *have* to have 'empathetic myopia,' as you call it. Otherwise, we'd never win at anything. And, P.S? Don't bite the hand that fucking feeds you."

"Right," Evan said, sarcastically. "You've got a great track record, Dan. Except for a few tiny lapses now and then—like back in Pennsylvania, when you didn't stop Marcus from concealing the unsavory truth I'd uncovered about Edwin Miller."

Dan was plainly beyond pissed at her. His face was turning

purple. He slammed his glass down on an end table so hard the stem snapped and cheap wine went everywhere—including all over his trousers.

"*Godfuckingdamnit!*" He jumped up and brushed wildly at his pants.

Evan bolted to her feet and rushed over to where he stood. All she could see was red liquid flying all over the place, and she wasn't sure if he'd managed to cut himself in the process of dropping what was left of the wineglass.

"Jesus, Dan! Are you all right? Did you cut yourself?" She reached for his hand. There were no visible signs of cuts. "God. Let me go get some towels."

She turned to head toward the downstairs powder room, but he caught hold of her hand to stop her.

"I'm sorry, Evan." He looked like he meant it. "I do care about what happened to those kids. If somebody did that to Stevie, I'd kill them with my bare hands."

Evan gave his soggy fingers a squeeze. "I know that. I'm sorry, too. This business is really getting to me."

She hadn't even told him the part about Julia's father—or Tim's struggle with leaving the Church.

And now she was nearly out of time. *Four more days?* It was insane. She'd never be able to deliver any hard proof before the Senate voted to send Cawley on his merry way.

Hard proof? That was a joke. *Hard proof of what?* That was the confounding part. She didn't even know what questions to ask to find what 'hard proof' there was to find.

But she agreed with Dan about one thing: Cawley *was* wrapped up in all of this.

And she was running out of time to prove it.

"Screw this mess," she said to Dan. "Let's go get more wine."

The rest of the evening was pretty uneventful.

Tim stayed on for another hour after Evan and Dan rejoined the group, then made his excuses and headed back to St. Rita's.

"I gotta work tomorrow," he said. "And it might be a good idea to shave before I show up for Mass."

"Yeah," Stevie nodded. "That whole Wolfman Jack thing you've got going on ain't a-workin'."

"Wolfman Jack?" Tim asked. "You have no clue who Sergeant Schultz is but you know about Wolfman Jack?"

"Of course," Stevie declared. "We stream him on Spotify."

Tim squinted at her. "You're joking, right?"

"Nope. That voice kept meat and potatoes on Mrs. Wolfman's table for years."

"And with *that*," Tim said, "I am outta here."

"Shoot us a text when you get home?" Evan asked.

Tim nodded at her. "Thanks," he looked at Julia, "*both* of you. I mean it."

Stevie's cell phone rang as Tim was leaving.

"It's Des," she said. "I'm taking this one upstairs." She answered the call. "Hey. Lemme call you right back—I'm saying good-bye to Dad and Kayla."

"You are?" Dan asked.

Stevie disconnected. "Well, yeah. Aren't you picking me up on Tuesday?"

"Yes, we are," Kayla replied. She nudged Dan. "Say good-bye to your daughter."

Dan got to his feet so he could hug Stevie. "Why am I always the last one to know what's going on?"

"Because you're clueless." Stevie hugged him back, before walking over to kiss Kayla on the cheek. "See you on Tuesday. We're still doing Alice Glass, right?"

"Oh, yeah." Kayla nodded. "I've already got the tickets."

"Sweet." Stevie headed for the stairs, which she took two at a time.

Dan faced Kayla. "Who the hell is Alice Glass?"

Evan answered for her. "I think she's the musical love child of Joan Jett and Morrissey."

Kayla leaned forward and high-fived Evan.

Dan still looked confused.

"More wine, Dan?" Julia asked.

He looked at his watch. "No. Thanks, Julia. We need to shove off, too. I gotta be on the Hill by seven."

Kayla stood up beside him.

"I'm so happy you both got to come by today," Julia said. "I know it meant the world to Stevie."

Dan looked up the stairs. "All appearances to the contrary."

"Stop sulking." Kayla elbowed him. "She's going to be staying with us the rest of the week. You can put her cell phone in the freezer . . . with mine."

"I don't put your cell phone in the freezer."

Kayla looked at Evan. "This is my struggle."

Evan laughed. "Been there, bought the T-shirt."

"I never put anybody's cell phone in the freezer . . ." Dan continued to complain.

Kayla took him by the arm. "Let's go, Heathcliff."

"You let me know what you find out tomorrow night." Dan said to Evan. "Time is money."

She nodded. She'd earlier filled him in on the after-hours visit she and Ben had planned to the office of the attorneys who set up the pro-Cawley PAC.

Dan and Kayla made their way outside and climbed into Dan's ancient Chrysler. The big engine nagged a few times before thundering to life and belching a dense cloud of black smoke into the air.

Evan grimaced. "That thing is a damn menace. I don't know how it keeps passing inspection."

"I guess he knows people in high places," Julia mused. "Or there's always the classic approach men are prone to take to protect the things they love."

"What's that?"

"They change the laws." Julia shrugged. "Call an environmental menace a 'classic,' and presto: it becomes exempt from all compliance with clean air regulations."

"You ought to be in Congress."

"*No thank you.* Talk about T-shirts *I* never want to wear again."

Dan slowly backed down Evan's driveway. It wasn't much of a trip. The car was already a third of the way out before he engaged the gears.

Evan and Julia stayed in the yard and watched the big hunk of silver steel crawl along Ring Road like an armadillo. When it disappeared over a hill, Julia turned to Evan.

"What, exactly, is this job you and Ben Rush are doing tomorrow?"

"You really don't want to know." Evan said.

"Is it dangerous?"

Evan thought about how to answer. "Not if we don't get caught."

"Evan . . ."

"Honey? Let's not go there, okay?"

Julia folded her arms. "I agree with you. Let's *not*. I watched you tonight. You tried to hide it, but I saw how much your shoulder was hurting. You could barely pick up that scrub bucket Stevie and Tim left on the porch."

"That was my fault. I grabbed it with the wrong hand." After she said the words, Evan realized what a mistake she'd made. Julia didn't miss a trick.

"See? I rest my case."

Me and my big mouth . . .

"Baby, come on. I'll take some Tylenol and it'll be fine."

"You're *not* taking Tylenol," Julia corrected her. "You've been drinking."

"Okay then, I'll take some Advil."

"You're probably destroying your liver."

That comment surprised Evan. "I haven't been drinking that much."

"Not the wine. The analgesics. You pop them like Tic Tacs. It needs to stop. We both know there's a remedy for this. You're just too scared or too stubborn to take care of it."

"I promised you I would," Evan insisted.

"When?"

"When did I promise?"

"No." Julia said with trace of exasperation. "When are you going to take care of it?"

"After Christmas?"

Julia seemed to consider that offer.

"Okay," she said. "I'll stop haranguing you under one condition."

"And that is?"

"You make an actual appointment for the surgery. No arguments. At this rate, you'll be lucky to get a date within the next six months."

Evan beamed at her.

She loved it when a plan came together . . .

Chapter Nine

"Shaken On Camac" was Mark Atwood's personal gold mine. The upscale bar and private club was located on a quiet, cobblestone side street in Philly's Gayborhood. Mark had opened the club six years ago, and it didn't take long for the place to stake out a top-five listing on websites like Yelp and TravelGay.

Tim was surprised at how willing Mark was to meet with him. He didn't even ask what Tim wanted to talk with him about. "Sure," he said. "It'd be great to see you. Why don't you come by on Sunday evening? We open at five, and there's not much of a crowd until after eight. We should be able to talk without too much interruption."

Tim wondered if maybe he wasn't the first guy from the old team to reach out to Mark for the same reason. After what had happened with Joey, he wasn't sure about anything anymore.

He figured the conversation with Mark would be binary: he'd either be open to discussing the time with Father Szymanski, or he wouldn't. Tim recalled that Mark had been one of the coterie of boys who palled around pretty regularly with team captain, Brian Christensen. By itself, that fact didn't mean anything. But Tim had more than an inkling that Mark had been one of the priest's "favorites." That had been remarkable, in part, because Mark was small in stature and not that accomplished as a player. He'd always been more of a team mascot than anything. From the outset, all the guys knew Mark was gay. But Father Szymanski always had a zero-tolerance policy for any razzing or name-calling.

Tim fervently hoped Mark had escaped any of the abuse boys like Joey had endured—but he kind of doubted it. Still, he knew he'd need to tread carefully and not go too far with his queries if Mark showed any signs of furtiveness or distance from the topic. Thoughts about what happened to Joey would likely haunt him for the rest of his life.

After Mass, he made another condolence visit to Mrs. Mazzetta, and sat with her for more than an hour. She wanted her son to have a Catholic funeral, and Tim consented to do the service. It was the least he could do. Joey's faith might have lapsed, but at the tragic end of his too-short life, he'd been determined to speak out and make things right. Tim wanted to honor that—for Joey and for his grieving mother.

Tim's second call to request a meeting date with Brian Christensen didn't go as smoothly as his first conversation with Mark Atwood.

"Why?" Brian asked him, without preamble.

Tim was nonplussed, but concocted a response he hoped sounded reasonable. He didn't want to go into everything in a phone call. "I'm reaching out to a few of the guys from the team. It's been a long time, and I thought it would be nice to reconnect." He left it at that.

"You're a priest now, right? At St. Rita's?"

"Yes," Tim said. "I never strayed too far from home base."

"Okay. Sure," Brian said. "When do you wanna connect? I'm in Gloucester City now."

"I know. I heard you have a pretty successful car dealership there."

"I do okay," Brian said. "You in the market for something different?"

Yeah, but I won't find it on a car lot, Tim thought.

"I wish. This is just a social call."

"Too bad." It sounded like Brian was in his car, driving someplace. Tim could hear a car horn and some other traffic noises. "I sometimes do bookwork at the dealership on Sunday afternoons. Do you wanna come over and meet me there this weekend? Maybe I can tempt you with a new ride?"

"You never know." Tim knew that leading Brian on, even in this offhand way, was dishonest, but he did it anyway. "What's a good time?"

"Any time after noon. How about 1:30? Does that give you time to get over here after Mass?"

"That should be just fine. Thanks for being willing to get together."

"Do you need directions?" Brian asked. "It's just off the Whitman Bridge on Black Horse Pike. Crescent Chevrolet."

"Great. I'll use GPS."

"Okay. See you on Sunday. Hey," Brian added. "Bring your title and insurance papers with you. Like you said, you never know. Right?"

"Right," Tim said, without much conviction.

There were a ton of things Tim had no clue about, but buying a new car wasn't one of them.

But there he was anyway, pulling into the big lot full of shiny new and "gently used" cars at Brian's dealership. Tim noticed that all of the recent snow had been cleared from the lot. That wasn't unusual. They would either dump it on some vacant lot or put it in the river.

His visit with Brian was early enough in the afternoon that he'd have plenty of time to get to Mark's club by five, when the place opened. Depending on how long his talk with Brian lasted, he might even have a couple of hours to kill before heading to the Gayborhood.

Maybe he could stop by Twisted Tail and get a WhistlePig? After this visit, he'd probably need one.

Brian must've seen him drive up and park. He walked out of the big, plate-glass enclosed showroom to greet him.

Tim recognized him right away. He looked exactly like an older version of his younger self—still blond, still trim, still . . . *slick.* Just like the salesman he'd always been. He was chewing gum, too. That hadn't changed, either.

Tim climbed out of his embarrassingly beat-up Subaru to greet him. He cursed himself for not even stopping at Sheetz on his way over to run the damn thing through a car wash.

He'd chosen to wear his collar today. He thought it might add some gravitas to their conversation.

"Hi there, Brian." Tim extended his hand. "It's good to see you after so many years."

Brian shook hands with him. Tim was surprised that his handshake was so . . . lame. He thought that seemed odd for a car salesman.

"How've you been?" Tim asked.

Brian indicated the impressive inventory of cars and trucks on his lot. "Great, as you can see."

Tim always found it remarkable when people equated how they *were* with what they *did*.

"Are the wife and kids doing well?" Tim asked.

"Fine." Brian didn't elaborate. "Normally, I have the kids on Sundays, but they're in Florida this week with their mom. Disney World."

"School out for the holidays?" Tim asked.

"Yeah. It seems to get earlier every year." Brian led them toward the showroom. "Let's go inside and sit down. It's freezing out here. We can look at cars later, if you're game."

"Sure." Tim followed him inside, past a haphazard array of brilliantly colored muscle cars. Most of them had their hoods up to show off their impressive engines. He tried to avoid looking at the sticker prices. He knew the information would just depress him. There were "no money down" and "bad credit, no problem" posters all over the place.

That depressed him, too.

He resolved to give his Subaru a bath on the way back to town.

Brian ushered Tim into a glass-walled office. It had a couple of shelves lined with trophies. Most of them commemorated sales milestones, but some of them recognized victories by athletic teams. Softball. Soccer. Lacrosse. There were a couple of plaques with Big Ten logos on them, too. He didn't see any basketball trophies.

192

"These are impressive." Tim pointed them out. "Does your dealership sponsor all these teams?"

"Yeah." Brian took a seat behind his big desk. "We do patronage for a quite a few of the Rutgers teams."

"That's a great thing to do for the community."

"It's good for business, too." He gestured at a leather chair that looked like it had been taken out of a car. It had "Camaro" stamped in cursive writing on its headrest. "Have a seat."

Tim sat down. The chair was surprisingly comfortable. He ran his hands over the soft leather on the armrests. It was a saddle brown color, and had bright orange stitching.

"Like that?" Brian asked. "It's an exact replica of the seats in that car right *there*." He pointed at one of the flashy cars they'd walked past en route to his office. It was electric blue in color.

"It's pretty . . . plush," Tim observed. "I'd be afraid I'd fall asleep if I tried to drive sitting in one of these."

"Yeah," Brian said. "They're pretty sweet."

Brian had some framed photos on a credenza behind his desk. They were mostly pictures of him, posing with beefy, uniformed athletes or buxom, pretty girls holding Crescent Chevrolet banners. Tim didn't see any photos of younger kids who'd be the right age to belong to Brian and his . . . what? Estranged wife? Ex-wife?

He found that omission sad.

"So." Brian cut to the chase. "You came all the way over here to reminisce about the good old days at St. Rita's?"

"Kind of," Tim said. "Mostly."

Brian leaned back in his impressive chair. "I figured you'd want to hit me up for some kind of donation. I get those mailings from the parish all the time."

Tim nodded sadly. "They are pretty relentless."

"You think? I haven't set foot in that place for at least twenty years."

"Why is that?"

Brian shrugged. "No reason to go back."

"You had a lot of friends there, though. All the guys on the team? Father Szymanski?"

Tim noticed the shift in Brian's expression. The change was slight, but certain. All of the fine lines around his mouth tightened.

"We haven't kept in touch," he said.

"That's too bad. I guess you know Father Szymanski is a bishop now? He left St. Rita's a few years after you graduated."

"Like I said, I don't keep in touch." Brian's tone had changed, too. It was noticeably colder. "Why are you asking me about him?"

"Who?"

"Szymanski."

Tim didn't answer his question. "I saw Joey Mazzetta last week," he said instead.

Brian got to his feet. "Okay. We're done here."

"Why?" Tim stared up at him.

"Give me a break. It's obvious why you're here. And I'm not talking. Not to you, and not to anybody else—so don't waste your time."

Tim got belatedly to his feet. "I'm sorry I upset you, Brian."

"I'm not upset. Don't flatter yourself. I just don't give a damn about any of that. Not Szymanski. Not any of it. So save your breath."

"I'm still sorry." Tim turned around and left the office.

He was halfway across the showroom when Brian called out to him.

"Let me know if you change your mind about a car."

Tim kept walking and didn't look back.

Maya wasn't surprised when the number for Crescent Chevrolet displayed on the iPhone screen.

"Yes?"

"It's Brian Christensen."

"So I see. What can I do for you, Brian?"

"You told me to call if anyone came asking questions about Szymanski," he said.

"Yes, I did. Is that why I have the pleasure of hearing from you on this gray Sunday?"

"Somebody just left here."

"Did that somebody have a name?"

"Tim Donovan. Father Tim Donovan. He's a priest at St. Rita's. And he was on the basketball team there when I was. He went to school there, too."

"I gathered," Maya observed. "Is there any other reason I should care about this?"

"He wanted to talk."

"What about?"

"What the fuck do you think he wanted to talk about?" Brian was losing patience.

"Oh, I don't know. Maybe he just stopped by? The Eagles game isn't on until four."

"Yeah . . . nobody 'stops by' fucking Gloucester City. He called and asked to meet with me. When he got here, he started asking questions—about Szymanski, and some other guys on the team. He wondered if I knew that Szymanski was a bishop now."

"What did you tell him?"

"I didn't tell him anything—and I made it clear I wouldn't. I threw his ass out."

"Oh. That's *very* smooth, Brian."

"What do you mean?" Brian was becoming more agitated. His voice had gone up at least half an octave. "Isn't that what you said you wanted? Isn't that what you said you were paying me for?"

"I don't recall suggesting you *do* anything other than call me. But your little exercise of initiative will be certain to create more problems than it solves."

"I don't know why you'd say that."

"Don't you?" Maya tsked. "Allow me to clarify matters. Your ill-advised attempt to manage the situation has probably confirmed, rather than allayed, any suspicions Father Donovan had about your involvement with the regrettable former priest. Careless missteps like this are expensive, Brian."

"What's that supposed to mean?" Brian's voice was now tinged with alarm.

"I honestly can't say what it means . . . for you. I can assure you that my client won't be happy with this news."

"I'm not giving the fucking money back."

"There might be other remedies."

"Are you threatening me?"

Maya laughed. "Not at all."

"Look . . . I kept my mouth shut. I did what you asked. I won't say anything about what that bastard did to me or the other guys. I earned this money."

"You're preaching to the choir, Brian. I'm not your enemy."

"So, what am I supposed to do?"

"*Now* you want my advice?" She asked. "I don't know what actual good it will do you. You don't have the best track record when it comes to following it."

"Yes," he snarled. "I want your goddamn advice."

"It's simple. Stay off the phone."

She hung up on him.

Stupid jock. Now Zucchetto would have a fucking brain hemor- rhage and ruin his ridiculous hat.

This job was growing too many tentacles. It was becoming impossible to wrangle them all.

She walked over to the desk, opened a browser on her silver laptop, and quickly typed a query into the search field.

Father Tim Donovan, St. Margherita Parish, Philadelphia.

Evan met Ben at Ping's apartment so the three of them could discuss logistics for their extracurricular outing later that night. Ben explained that Ping had done a bit of advance work, hacking into the servers at the law firm, and had come up with some use- ful information that she thought should change their approach to their fact-gathering mission.

When Evan got there, she was surprised to see Phyllis and Desiree, who had stopped by after church to have lunch with Ping. They were both dressed to the nines. Evan was impressed by how grown-up Desiree looked in makeup and fancy clothes.

She was used to seeing her in skinny jeans and loud T-shirts emblazoned with political slogans. Today she just looked . . . chic—like she could be a model in an H&M ad.

Desiree had turned into quite a looker. Stevie had great taste. It bothered her that she felt irrationally pleased about that . . . *It was messed up.*

Desiree gave Evan a warm hug. It lasted longer than the friendly hugs they normally exchanged when they saw each other, so Evan suspected that Stevie had wasted no time filling Des in on her accidental "outing" at dinner the other night.

"It's *so* good to see you," Des gushed. "Stevie said you were doing great."

"Did she?" Evan teased. "Well, as you know, that girl is just full of surprises."

Des looked worried for a few seconds, until she realized Evan was pulling her leg.

"I get it," she said with obvious relief.

"I'm glad *you* do," Evan smiled at her. "That makes one of us."

"What are you two going on about?" Ping asked. She was loading some GladWare containers into a Trader Joe's freezer bag. "This should be enough. Not that many people show up for Sunday night supper," she said to Phyllis.

Phyllis filled Evan in. "It's Mama's turn to cook—but since she can't go tonight, I'm dropping everything off."

That seemed unusual. Ping rarely missed church.

"Why aren't you going, Ping?" Evan asked. "Not feeling well?"

There was the sound of some half-hearted knocking at the door and Ben Rush sauntered in.

"Hey Phyllis. Hey Des." He nodded to Evan. "I see you're right on time."

Ping zipped the big bag closed and handed it to her daughter. "I'm not going to service tonight because I have some work to do with this reprobate."

"Hey!" Ben protested. "*Reprobate?* That's kind of harsh."

Ping looked at him over the rim of her half-eye spectacles. "Have you seen a mirror lately? You look like something my cat hacked up."

"I thought you said pets weren't allowed in this building?" Ben asked.

"Seriously?" Evan asked him. "That's the part of her analogy that bothers you?"

He shrugged. "Got anything to eat, Ping? I didn't have lunch."

"What else is new?" Ping gestured at her stove, which was loaded up with pots. "Help yourself. But wash your damn hands first."

"Why?" Ben made a beeline for the stove. He opened a top cabinet and got out a dinner plate. "I'm not dirty."

"Do *not* even go there. If you ask me, you should dip yourself in Purell before you set foot outside your apartment."

Phyllis laughed and made her way to the door. "Nothing ever changes between these two, does it, Evan? C'mon, Des. Let's go. I wanna get home before the Eagles game."

"I'm TiVo'ing it," Ben said as he loaded a plate with stew meat and creamed potatoes. "But I don't know why I bother. That Agholor is a pussy. They should've traded his sorry ass to Buffalo when they had a shot last year."

"Yeah." Ping turned to face Ben and worked the flat of her hand around in exaggerated circles. "I'm gonna need you to check *all* of that. My granddaughter is standing right *there*."

"I *know* that," Ben said. He gestured at Desiree with a big serving spoon. "Hey, Des? Am I wrong? How much does Agholor suck?"

Desiree looked at her grandmother. "Sorry, Gran . . . he pretty much bites the big one."

"And we're outta here." Phyllis guided Desiree out the door. "Later, Mama. Evan? If she kills his ass, I'm not helping you clean up the mess, capeesh?"

"Don't worry, Phyll." Evan held the door for her. "I'll call ServPro."

The pair left in a swirl of coats and bulging bags of food.

Evan closed the door and faced her "team."

"Does one of you two plan to fill me in on what's going on?"

"Yeah." Ben sat down at Ping's kitchen table. "Pull up a chair. Ping has some news."

Evan eyed Ben's ridiculously overloaded plate. He'd somehow managed to perch two biscuits on top of his mound of stewed beef and gravy. "That food looks pretty good."

Ping shook her head. "Go get a plate. I swear . . . the two of you are like a mobile bread line."

Evan beamed at her. "I didn't get any lunch, either."

"Go, go." Ping jerked her head toward the food. "It'll take me a minute to boot this thing up."

Ping grabbed her laptop off a pile of advertising circulars from the Sunday paper.

"Ping did a little recon for us and tried to bust into the servers at Smith, Martin, Squires & Andersen." Ben laughed. "She thought maybe she could get what we needed and keep us outta the joint. Ain't that right, Ping?"

Ping was busy logging in to her computer. "Everything but that 'us' part."

"Whattaya mean by that?" he asked.

Ping glared at him. "I'd like to keep *her* fanny outta the joint. She's got her little girl to think of. *You?*" She dropped her eyes back to her screen. "I'd be doing society a favor to let you go up there and bungle your way into getting busted."

"Hey." Ben shoved a big forkful of meat into his mouth. "I've got three girls, too."

"Don't talk with your mouth full, fool. Nobody needs to see that."

Evan chose to stay out of their argument. Ping would fill her in when she was ready. Besides, Ping's food was just too damn good to have divided loyalties. Evan hoped there was pie hiding someplace, too.

"Okay." Ping found what she'd been looking for. "I tried several brute force phishing attempts earlier and discovered that for such a highfalutin' place, this joint has a pretty wide back door. All I had to do was call in and pose as a help desk technician.

Once I got patched through to one of the senior partners, it was easy to talk him into changing his network password as part of a security update. He was only too happy to oblige—just so he could get off the damn call. Once I had that changed, it was pretty much smooth sailing."

"No shit?" Evan was intrigued. *Maybe they wouldn't have to break in there tonight, after all?*

"Don't get your hopes up," Ping said, quickly dispatching that fantasy. "Data related to certain top tier clients isn't stored on their servers—and it's not in the cloud, either."

"Which means what?" Evan asked. "Paper files? CD-ROM drives?"

"Could be. But doubtful. I think the data is probably too sensitive to be kept on any network—or on any kind of portable media. Especially if they're managing work for powerful people who want to stay anonymous."

"That's sure as shit the case here," Ben added.

"So, where would they keep it, then?" Evan asked.

"My poking around proved that they used to have a robust Intranet that interfaced with a gateway computer connected to the outside Internet. But, the gateway computer got removed about seven months ago, give or take, when the firm upgraded their security protocols and access privileges—probably in response to those leaked Panama Papers that made buttholes at every law firm on the planet pucker up."

"Which means what?" Ben asked impatiently.

"Which means," Ping continued, "it's now not connected to *anything*. So, the company transitioned to a work flow management system called Clio, and then archived old data to offline storage. So unless I'm wrong, they're probably still running their Intranet like a private network with independent storage. A setup like that wouldn't show up on the firm's public-facing network."

"Can you still get into it?" Evan asked.

"Probably. Dumbass used the same password for everything."

Ben snorted. "Wonder if they have Hillary's emails, too?"

Ping squinted at him.

"Okay. If you're right," Evan pondered, "how do we find it? And if we do find it, how do Ben and I hack into it?"

"*You* don't," Ping declared.

"Say what?" Ben asked.

"I'm saying *you* don't—as in the two of you. I wouldn't trust either of you to open a box of crackers."

"I appreciate the vote of confidence, Ping." Evan pushed her empty plate away. "But that doesn't help us. How're we going to get the information we need to go forward on this? I only have a couple more days before Dan pulls the plug on our work and the Senate votes to move Cawley's nomination to the floor."

Ping looked back at Evan with narrowed eyes. "I do it."

"You?" Ben scoffed. "How? You just said you couldn't hack a private server."

"Not *remotely*," Ping said. "I can't do it from here. But if you get me *inside*, and we can find it—I can get you in. Guaranteed."

Ben sat back and laughed. "No fucking way. Take you along on a B&E? That's the stupidest thing I've ever heard. What's your Plan B?"

"There *is* no Plan B, fool." She shifted her gaze from Ben to Evan. "You don't take me along, you got no shot at cracking this. End of story."

All three of them sat in silence for a few moments. Evan tapped an index finger against the edge of her dinner plate while she thought about Ping's suggestion.

Ben broke the standoff first. "It's a fucking stupid idea."

Evan gazed at him, but didn't reply.

"There's no way in hell it would work," he added.

Ping crossed her arms.

"We'd have to have our heads examined even to consider it." Ben was running out of arguments and his frustration was evident. "You're both insane." He flopped back against his chair in defeat.

Evan picked up her plate and headed to the stove for seconds. *They had several hours to kill—why not enjoy it?*

Eventually, Ben got up and followed suit. She handed him a serving spoon.

"We're actually gonna do this, aren't we?" he asked.

She nodded at him before reclaiming her seat at the table.

"So, Ping?" she asked, as she speared a hunk of beef. "You got any pie?"

Mark Atwood had been right. The place was nearly empty when Tim arrived at five.

The reviews he'd read on Yelp were not exaggerated. Shaken was quite a place. The interior walls were all paneled with polished mahogany. The booths were upholstered with dark green leather and the light fixtures mimicked Victorian-era gaslights. The bar exuded more of a cozy *let's meet for intimate conversation over twenty-dollar cocktails* vibe than a pickup joint.

Not that things didn't get livelier later in the evening—or on Friday nights, when Shaken was lauded for hosting some of the best drag shows in Philly. Tim supposed the venue for those must be located on the other side of the bar, which wasn't open to view during his visit. The establishment took up space in what had been several storefronts on Camac Street. It was clear that Mark had sunk a lot of money into improvements on this place. Judging by the things Tim had read about the popularity of the bar, he was probably getting a good return on his investment.

Mark seemed genuinely happy to see him again—unlike the awkward reception he'd got earlier from Brian Christensen. But then, Tim recalled that Mark always had been outgoing and friendly. Tim was impressed with how well he looked, too. He was an attractive man, although he still had a slight build and almost porcelain-like features.

As they sat down and started exchanging some easy gossip about their time at St. Rita's, Tim began to wonder if he'd made a wrong assumption about Mark's potential involvement with Father Szymanski. Maybe Mark hadn't been one of the "other boys" Szymanski had referenced the night he propositioned Tim in the shower. He started feeling a twinge of nervousness about even broaching the subject.

Face it, he said to himself. *I don't have the greatest track record with this . . .*

He probably should've listened to Evan. She had pretty much ripped him a new one for striking out on his own to talk with Joey Mazzetta. And she'd been more than a little bit curious about the mysterious woman who Joey said had offered him $2,500 to keep silent about Szymanski.

"Who was she?" Evan asked.

Tim told her he had no idea, and neither had Joey. He assumed she was working for the Church.

"Did he describe her in any way?" Evan dug in. "Offer any clues about how to find her?"

"No," Tim said. "Other than to note that she was 'slick'-looking. I even asked his mother about her when I had a few minutes alone with her on Saturday night. She didn't recall much, except she said the woman looked 'foreign' and dressed very well."

Evan hadn't asked any other questions about Mrs. Mazzetta, and she didn't make any judgments about Tim's blundering into this part of her case—other than to warn him not to try it again.

And yet, here he was. He didn't look forward to their conversation when she found out.

Evan always found out.

Tim had been quiet for too long. Mark must've noticed some kind of change in his demeanor.

"Are you okay, Tim?" he asked. "Is the drink not good?"

Mark had poured Tim a generous tumbler of Basil Hayden's before they headed to one of the more remote booths in the bar to sit down and get reacquainted.

"No. The bourbon's fine. I'm sorry. I'm just . . . preoccupied." He took a deep breath. "Part of that concerns you."

"Me?" Mark looked perplexed. "How so?"

"It's kind of a long story. But I've talked with a couple of our other friends from the basketball team—about their interactions with Father Szymanski."

He could tell by the immediate change in Mark's expression that he knew exactly what Tim meant by "interactions."

"Look, Tim," he began. "I think I know where you're headed, and you need to know that I have no desire to come forward with any allegations against him. I'm done with all of that. I made my peace with it years ago. I mean no disrespect to you," he added quickly. "I just think it's better to short-circuit any concerns you might have about me right up front."

"Concerns?" Tim wasn't sure what Mark meant. "Why do you think I wanted to talk with you about this?"

Mark shrugged. "It makes sense that you'd want to do what you can to protect the Church. I'd have to be an imbecile not to be able to connect the dots between everything that's happening now with all the grand jury findings and your sudden appearance here today."

Tim felt ashamed. "I apologize that I haven't reached out to connect with you before now. I have no excuse for that and I'm sorry."

"Why *would* you contact me?" Mark asked. "It's not like you're on the lookout for a safe gay bar. Which, by the way," he added, "this is."

"No," Tim nodded. "You're right. My visit is not about that."

"Yeah. I didn't think so." Mark said. "If that ever changes, though, you know who to call. I hope my saying that doesn't offend you."

"No. I'm not at all offended by that, Mark."

"I didn't think you would be. You always seemed pretty cool about me being gay."

"We're all children of the same God," Tim said. "As far as I know, He doesn't play favorites."

"No. But Father Szymanski sure did."

"I think I knew that," Tim confessed. "But I never did anything about it. I can't forgive myself for my silence."

"What could you have done, Tim? He'd have just denied it. You were only a kid, like the rest of us. Nobody would've believed you." He made a dismissive sound. "Nobody believes half of the

204

stories now. Have you seen what they expect you to have as proof—even before they'll sit down and talk with you?"

"I know. Joey Mazzetta told me about his experience when I went to see him last week."

Mark seemed surprised. "You saw Joey *last week?* Before he got killed in that robbery?"

Tim nodded.

"Man. That was some awful shit. Poor guy." Mark was silent for a few moments. "Did he file a complaint with the reparations committee?"

"He tried," Tim said. "But he didn't have the corroboration they required so he gave up."

"I don't doubt it. As many cases as there are that go forward, there probably are five times as many that just go away—for those exact reasons." He finished his glass of iced tea and beckoned to the handsome young man who was busy restocking the bar. "Hey, sweetie? Will you bring us another round?"

"I probably shouldn't," Tim said.

"*Trust me.* You'll need it when you listen to *my* story."

"Your story?"

Mark nodded. "That's why you're here, right? To find out what I know about Szymanski?"

"I suppose so. But not because I'm trying to protect him," Tim said. "Nobody sent me here to talk with you."

"Oh, trust me," Mark laughed. "*That's* already happened."

"What do you mean?" Tim had a sinking feeling he already knew what Mark meant.

"Some classy dame wearing four-inch stilettos came waltzing in here and offered me a big settlement to keep my mouth shut—a *cash* settlement. I didn't take the money. I told her I wasn't going to say anything about that pervert—*or* his pals." He fastened the top two buttons on his pullover. "Do you think it's cold in here? Hey, Santino?" He addressed the bartender again. "Would you ask David to turn the damn thermostat up—*please?* I already asked him twice." He faced Tim. "Sorry. That dude has perpetual PMS. I swear he gets more hot flashes than my aunt Gladys."

Tim was confused about something. "Why did you turn down the money if you already knew you weren't going to go forward with anything?" he asked. Then he quickly thought better of his question, and how rude it probably seemed. "I'm sorry, Mark—that was inappropriate. I shouldn't have asked about it."

Santino delivered their refills and affectionately squeezed Mark's shoulder.

"Thanks, amore." Mark patted Santino on the derriere before shifting his attention back to Tim. "I don't have any problem talking with you about *any* of this. I made my peace with it all years ago—long before any of this other stuff became public. I didn't take the money because I was stupid." He shook his head. "Santino bitched me out later because we could've used the cash to upfit the kitchen in this place—which would finally allow us to offer better food options. Right now, we're doing good to manage decent appetizers. But, oh well . . . What's done is done. Besides," he took a drink of his iced tea, "I don't want to be beholden to anybody. What if they came back later and tried to extort us? That shit happens in this town all the time—especially to small clubs like this."

"I think you made the right decision, too," Tim acknowledged. "Did this woman tell you who she was representing?"

"No. I just assumed she was working for the Church. It's no secret how invested they are in keeping all of this quiet. Look at what we now know they've done over the years to hush it all up and protect the priests. It's pretty disgusting, if you ask me."

"I agree with you. It's intolerable and very . . ." he didn't finish his statement.

"Very . . .what?" Mark asked.

Tim met his eyes. "Unforgivable."

"From their perspective, I can see that."

"What other perspective is there?" Tim asked.

"The Church is a thing, not a person. A 'thing'—like an organization—can't be responsible. Only the people who run it and make bad decisions for it are responsible. It's a baby and bathwater kind of thing, you know?" He shrugged. "You don't throw one out because the other got dirty. That's how I see it, anyway."

"The Church is the bride of Christ." Tim responded in the only way he understood: *by rote.* It's what he'd been programmed to do. It's what they'd *all* been programmed to do.

Mark regarded him with a raised eyebrow. "Then Christ is in a pretty fucked-up marriage, if you ask me."

Tim was blown away by Mark's analogy and how perfectly it dovetailed with Stevie's simple summation of his dilemma. He had no idea what to say.

In that moment, he had no ideas about anything.

Mark stretched a hand across the table and pushed Tim's tumbler of Basil Hayden's a tad closer. "I really think you need to drink this," he said in a softer voice.

Tim took a careful swallow of the Kentucky bourbon. When he found his voice again, he asked Mark another careful question.

"You said you made your peace with what happened to you a long time ago. Do you mind telling me how you did that?" He lowered his eyes. "I seem to be struggling with it myself."

"Therapy, dude. *Lots of it.* I know everybody's process with recovery from this stuff is different. And that's if you're even lucky enough *to* recover. For me, it was simple: I didn't really have a choice. My life was in the shitter—and so were all of my relationships. There wasn't enough coke in Philly to make me forget. Not enough sleeping pills. I could either stay on the path I was on and lose everything, or I could get some help." He rested his elbows on the table and leaned forward. "Believe me, Tim. There are people out there who get this stuff. Who know how to help you find your own way through it. You just have to make up your mind to *find* one—and then be brave enough to tell the truth when you do. It's not easy, but not many things worth having are."

Tim didn't dispute Mark's advice. He knew he was right. "This is what got you to a place where you didn't want to speak out about Father Szymanski?"

"Hell, no," Mark corrected him. "That was something else altogether. Therapy just helped me to stop throwing my life away with both hands."

"I don't understand. What made you decide not to go public about what happened to you?"

Mark sat back. "In a word: commerce."

"Commerce?"

"Sure. You think we make a great living running this little storefront fag bar? Think again. It's what happens *upstairs* that pays the bills."

Tim felt out of his element. "I don't know what that means."

Mark smiled. "There's no reason you *should* know what it means. Santino and I run a second business out of this location—a very specialized one that caters to a specific clientele."

Only one possibility occurred to Tim, but he was reluctant to suggest it.

Mark seemed to read his mind. "Before you ask, it's not 'rent-a-boy' services. We operate a legitimate private club—members only. It's a place where the city's closeted rich and powerful can come to kick back—be who they are, dress how they want, behave how they want, be *with* who they want—all without fear of disclosure. They pay us a *lot* for this privilege, and in exchange, we guarantee their privacy. The financial security this venture provides us would evaporate if I blew the whistle on the bishop—and attracted a nonstop media circus to our doorstep in the bargain." He shrugged his narrow shoulders. "Like I said . . . sometimes, your choices are simple."

It was a lot for Tim to take in. He knew he'd probably think about little else once their interview ended and he was alone to consider everything Mark had shared. But there was still one thing he wanted to follow up on.

"Earlier, you said Father Szymanski played favorites. What did you mean by that?"

"Are you sure you want to know?"

"I think so," Tim nodded. "No—I *know* so."

"Okay," Mark said. "It was all pretty gruesome. Let's just say that Szymanski and his colleagues had some pretty eclectic tastes."

"His colleagues? Other priests?"

"Not usually. It was mostly other members of his fancy private club."

"I heard the stories about how some of our team members got to go there for special dinners," Tim asked. "Is that what you mean?"

"*Special dinners?*" Mark considered Tim's comment. "I guess we got dinner . . . *sometimes*—if we performed really well." He gave a bitter-sounding laugh. "We mostly went over there as trophies. Tidy little presents for the fat cats who gave so much money to the parish. We got passed around a lot on those nights—just like basketballs in practice." He stared at Tim. "You get my meaning here? They took turns with us—sometimes, two at a time. They even had some special rooms upstairs for it—places that weren't open to other club members. And all the while, they told us what *good* boys we were and how well we'd be rewarded for being 'nice' to them. *Nice?* Like choking while you sucked some old codger's dick was being nice? Or letting some skeevy perv in a black mask fuck you up the ass without lube or a condom? Nice? I don't think so."

Tim could feel the bile rising in his throat. What Mark was describing was worse than anything he'd imagined—and what he'd allowed himself to imagine had already been repugnant.

"I don't . . . I can't . . ." Tim couldn't finish his statement.

"Later on," Mark mused, "there were people who told me I became queer because of this. Can you believe that shit? Like being raped by someone can *make* you gay?" He scoffed. "Funny how nobody ever suggests that getting raped can make you *straight*. I wonder how they square that part of their stupid equations?"

Tim closed his eyes. He wanted to flee. He wanted to run away from this place as fast and as far as he could—to run to a place where he'd never have to hear this again. Never have to know this again. To find a world that had no space for such cruelty—no 'special rooms' where the innocence of children could be sacrificed in perverted acts of illicit and godless pleasure.

Enough. It was all enough.

"Yes." Mark said quietly. "It is."

Tim opened his eyes and looked at him. He didn't realize he'd spoken the words aloud.

But whether he had or hadn't didn't matter.

Mark had managed to find a way out of his personal horror. And he'd given Tim a path to find his own.

This wait was becoming interminable.

Maya snapped up the iPhone tucked into the console of her rental car and checked the time again.

Tim Donovan had now been inside Shaken On Camac for more than an hour.

What the hell was taking so long? Whatever they were talking about, it couldn't be good news for her client. Atwood had refused to accept Mr. Zucchetto's generous offer two weeks ago. His response to the offer had been almost . . . blasé—as if a sudden infusion of $10,000 in cash meant nothing to the small businessman.

Maya was anything but naïve. Atwood's insistence that he had no desire or inclination to become involved with the bishop's problems seemed credible. His face had been completely open when he'd said it. There was not the slightest reason to doubt the veracity of his statement.

So why was his conversation with Donovan taking so long?

It probably wasn't due to the quality of the cocktails served here. Maya's fairly broad experience with gay bars could attest to that. Most people didn't seek these places out to titillate their palates by sampling their impressive inventories of fine spirits.

Ten more minutes, and I'll have to move this sodded car again. A traffic cop was already chalking tires on the opposite side of the

210

street. The meter maid stopped behind a black Ford and pulled out her citation book. Some poor bastard was getting a ticket. No ... the driver was still sitting in the car. He opened his door and got out to go talk with the cop—clearly in an effort to avoid the citation. The hard-boiled public servant seemed unimpressed.

Welcome to Philadelphia, asshole.

The traffic cop calmly finished writing up the ticket, and then pointed out some other empty spaces farther down the street.

Cheap bastard. Just pay the sodded ticket, already.

The ill-humored man snapped the ticket from her extended hand and stormed back to retake his seat behind the wheel of his car.

Jesus fucking Christ. Maya recognized him.

He was one of Marcus's flunkies. Marcus had about a dozen goons like this who did his shit work. Their list of duties was pretty varied. Most of them worked as "cleaners." Some of them, like this guy, did whatever the hell Marcus needed to make problems go away. The fact that he was here, parked on the street outside this innocuous bar in Philadelphia's Gayborhood, could mean only one thing.

Tim Donovan had become a problem that needed to go away.

Well, well. We live and learn. Maya wondered if this ill-tempered thug had enjoyed his little jaunt to North Warren? There was no doubt now that Marcus had arranged for Senator Miller's creative demise. He got extra points for that one.

Joey Mazzetta's murder, however, had not been carried out in as laudatory a fashion. In fact, it was downright clumsy. And the special signature Marcus chose to append to the commission of Joey's last act was unabsolvably sleazy—even for him.

It was personal, too. Marcus made sure of that.

The street door to Shaken opened and Tim Donovan stepped out into the cold. Maya watched him hike up the collar on his black wool coat and walk toward a Subaru that had seen better days.

She waited to see what Marcus's Big Bad would do. If he started his car and followed Donovan, it would certainly result in some very bad news for Evan Reed this evening. If, on the

211

other hand, he got out of his car and went inside the bar, the good Father might get a reprieve to preach another day.

Either way, it was clear that things were about to get a whole lot murkier.

Donovan started his car and pulled out of his space. Maya watched him rumble and rattle his way along the cobblestone street, headed for god knew where.

Big Bad did not follow him. Instead, he climbed out of his car and walked toward the entrance to Shaken. That had to mean that for right now, his objective was to gather information—not to shut down the conduit.

How long that would remain his job was difficult to determine. It, like everything else associated with this tiresome business, was a floating decimal point.

The second thing that surprised Evan was how easy getting inside the actual office of Smith, Martin, Squires & Andersen turned out to be.

The first thing that surprised her was the physical location of their office building.

Ben had said the highbrow Center City firm was located in a building on 8th Street. Evan didn't give that a second thought until they arrived at the scene and she realized that the actual building was on the *corner* of 8th and Market Streets—with entrances on both sides.

It was the same damn building where the Philadelphia offices of Donne & Hale were located.

Fabulous.

Julia's firm used the Market Street address, so it never occurred to Evan that both businesses would be housed in the same damn building. She prayed that no one in Julia's office—like, for example, *Julia*—would decide that Sunday night might be the perfect time to get caught up on some extra work. Evan didn't make a habit of visiting Julia at work, but the Philly office was small enough that everyone on the staff there knew who she was.

Once they'd entered the building—from the 8th Street door—and taken the elevator to the second floor, Ben Rush approached a large potted ficus tree that stood in front of an imposing art deco window located at the south end of the hallway. He dug around beneath the Spanish moss that covered the soil and withdrew a plastic card attached to a blue lanyard.

"Behold," he said, holding it up. "The key to the kingdom."

"You've got to be kidding me." Evan was astonished. "A key card?"

"Yep. It's all-access, too. We use it, then drop it right back here when we're finished."

"How the hell did you get that?" Evan asked.

"Never underestimate the persuasive powers of Benjamin Rush, PCI." Ben buffed his nails on the lapel of his jacket.

Ping clucked her tongue and faced Evan. "Which, translated, means he had to pay somebody half a stack to get this."

"I resent that," Ben retorted. "I didn't have to pay *anybody* five hundred bucks."

"No?" Ping asked. "How much, then?"

Ben looked at Evan sheepishly. "Three hundred."

Evan wasn't surprised. "*Whatever.* Now what?"

"Now we head for the maintenance closet around the corner and get suited up."

"Suited up?" Ping's voice was tinged with suspicion. "What *kind* of suited up?"

"We have to look like we have a reason to be in there. So we're gonna put on maintenance jumpsuits, and you," he pointed at Ping, "are gonna have to dress like a housekeeper."

"Yeah?" Ping wagged a finger in Ben's face. "I don't *think* so."

"You got any better ideas, Madame Curie?" Ben hissed. "You weren't supposed to *be* on this mission, remember? There are only gonna be two sets of coveralls hanging in there."

"Well, I guess you'd better try ransacking a few more supply closets, homeboy, 'cause I am *not* dressing up like a damn char-woman."

"How about you two take it down about a thousand decibels?"

213

Evan herded the pair into the nearby stairwell, where they'd be less likely to attract attention from anyone who might still happen to be hanging around this late after 5 p.m. on a Sunday. "Okay. Ben? If we have a damn key card and a credible reason to be in there, then why can't Ping just be . . . I don't know—an IT person? In there to fix some malfunctioning cyber-gizmo kind of thing?"

"I suppose that could work, too," he muttered.

"That's more like it," Ping nodded her assent. "I have mad skills fixing cyber-gizmo kinds of things."

"Right. Let's go and get this over with." Evan held the door open for them. "I want to get in and get out, lickety-split."

Fifteen minutes later, they were suited up and back in the elevator. Ping carried a messenger bag containing her laptop. She'd also donned a pair of black horn-rimmed glasses for the occasion.

Evan thought she looked very IT—right down to the requisite scowl of intolerance that usually clung to the countenance of people in that profession.

Ben also nabbed a ladder and a tattered box of fluorescent light tubes from a corner of the storage closet.

"Fool." Ping tutted when she saw what he had. "What are you gonna do with *those*?"

The ladder was hooked over Ben's shoulder, and when he swiveled to face Ping, it barely missed hitting Evan in the face.

"It's so we can look busy if anyone stops by to chat," he explained.

"And what makes you think they even *have* light fixtures like that?" Ping pointed at the box.

Ben looked baffled by her question. "Whattaya mean?"

"It's an *attorney's office*, not a damn dollar store." Ping grabbed a tool bucket. "Leave those damn things and take this instead."

Evan finished snapping the front of her coveralls. "Are you two ready?"

They both nodded.

"Okay, let's hit it."

They took the elevator to the seventh floor. Evan groaned.

Donne & Hale's offices were on the sixth floor. She saw the name of the publishing firm on the directory plaque displayed inside the elevator above the bank of buttons.

Ben noticed it, too. "Cozy." He chuckled.

The key card worked just like it was supposed to and the three of them were inside the office in a flash. The firm had wooden louvered blinds on the windows on either side of its big oak door and, mercifully, they were shut tight.

"Okay, Ping." Evan faced her. "Where do we start?"

"I need to find Dumbass's office. That's where *I* start. You two should go find their file room and start looking for hard copies of anything. If you're in doubt, make a copy of it. One of these reception desks," Ping gestured toward the two big desks that anchored the firm's foyer area like moored ships, "should have a cassette to unlock their office copier."

Ben was already opening drawers. "Bingo." He held up a small cartridge and a set of keys. He jingled the keys. "Wanna bet these are to all of the office doors? This place's security is for shit."

"Lucky us," Evan noted. "All right. Let's get busy."

It didn't take Ping long to find the office she was looking for. And when they unlocked it, there were two computers sitting on a console behind the impressive desk.

"There you go." Ping began unpacking her messenger bag. "I can guarantee you that only one of these is on their corporate network. *Amateurs.*" She sat down on the big leather chair before fluttering her hands at Evan and Ben. "Go on, go on. I don't need the two of you in here gawking at me."

They left Ping alone and went in search of greener pastures.

Evan found the file room at the end of the hallway near the entrance to the firm's canteen. Ben followed her inside. It was a narrow space. One wall was lined with standard-sized file cabinets and the other wall was shelved from floor to ceiling. The shelves were filled with rows of brown document boxes. The room was small enough that they had to stand sideways when they opened any of the file cabinet drawers.

"Ben?" Evan asked.

"Yeah?"

"I don't think we need that ladder in here with us. How about you leave it outside?"

Ben took umbrage at her tone. "Hey, wiseass? What if we need to look at shit on the top shelf?"

"*Then* we bring it in?"

He grumbled, hauling the ladder back out into the hallway.

"What are we looking for?" Ben asked when he rejoined her.

"Anything with the acronym 'PAC,' the words 'Political Action Committee,' or 'Citizens for Integrity in Government.' Also look for anything from 1992. Incorporation papers, tax records, anything like that. Arthur Squires was the attorney who managed this, so his name would probably be tagged, too."

"Roger."

They both worked in silence. The only sounds came from the opening and closing of metal file drawers. After twenty minutes, Evan gave up.

"Okay." She closed the drawer she'd been looking through. "There's nothing in here."

"Yeah," Ben pushed another drawer shut. "All I am seeing is run-of-the-mill probate shit—and most of it dates back before 1992."

Evan nodded. "Let's check these boxes over here and then be done with this. I hope to god Ping can find what we're looking for."

"Trust me. If anybody can, she will. That woman never gives up."

"Lucky for you."

Ben scratched behind his collar. "These fucking jumpsuits really gig you on the back of the neck."

"I don't think they're supposed to be comfortable."

"Yeah. The assholes who probably order them have no fucking clue how it feels to put in an honest day's work."

Evan laughed. "You mean like we're doing right now?"

He shrugged. "Why not? It sure as shit pays my bills."

They rotated and faced the phalanx of brown boxes that filled the shelves. In some sections, the boxes were stacked two deep.

216

The front of each container was tidily labeled with a card that detailed its contents and inclusive dates.

"At least this is easier to search." Evan ran her finger along a lower shelf. It seemed to her that the older stuff would be stored higher, in the harder to reach areas.

"Yeah. Imagine the potential for blackmail with all this shit."

"Don't even go there, Ben."

"Hey, I can dream, can't I?"

Evan took a second to muse about Ben's dreams, and quickly regretted it.

Something else occurred to her.

"Hey," she asked him, "do you know anything about Soviet-era pistols?"

Ben didn't seem to think her question was random. But then, nothing ever seemed random to Ben. It was part of what made him good at his job.

"Some," he said. "Which one in particular?"

"The Tokarev TT30. How common are they around here?"

"You tell me." He snickered.

Evan was confused. "What do you mean by that?"

"It was a Tokarev round they dug outta your shoulder the night Townsend was murdered."

"*What?*" Evan was astonished.

"Yeah," he said, "I shoulda kept that damn piece after I knocked that bitch out. I thought about it. Those fuckers are hard to come by—especially the Russian-made models. If I hadn't been sure it was hot, I'd have taken it from her."

"You mean Maya Jindal used a *Tokarev* to kill Andy?"

"Yeah." Ben shrugged. "Makes sense, if you think about it. They're noisy and high-powered . . . just like her." He chuckled at his own simile.

Evan's head was reeling. *Maya Jindal had a Tokarev?*

What were the fucking odds?

"J.C. Ortiz told me Joey Mazzetta was shot with a Tokarev."

"No shit?" Ben seemed impressed by that. "She must be branching out."

"Wait a minute. You think *she* killed Joey? We don't even know where the hell she is."

"I dunno. Seems like her calling card. Didn't you say some 'anonymous' person was sending you Signal shit about Cawley?"

"Yes. But . . ." *Holy Christ.* Was Ben right? Could *Maya Jindal* be masquerading as the all-knowing Moxie?

That made *no* sense. Why would Maya Jindal be involved in *any* of this?

Unless . . .

"You know," she said. "Dan admitted to me that the first photo of Cawley—the one taken at the private club with the bishop—was given to him by Marcus Goldman."

Ben lowered a couple of document boxes so he could read the labels on the ones stacked behind them. "I thought you said you'd never work for that scumbag again?"

"I'm *not* working for him. He's just the one who gave Dan that image."

"Out of the goodness of his nonexistent heart?" Ben asked.

Evan couldn't explain it, but it seemed like all of the disconnected puzzle pieces of this mystery were starting to fall into place. *All but one: a motive.*

"The end of everything." That's how Edwin Miller had described the single puzzle piece he held clenched in his hand during her visit with him. Evan had no doubt that this was the same piece they removed from his intestine during his autopsy.

"Moxie is the one who sent me the second photo of Cawley—the one with the basketball team from St. Rita's."

"Who the fuck is *Moxie?*"

"Sorry. That's the name of my anonymous Signal 'helper.'"

Ben laughed. "Somebody is fucking with you."

"That's hardly breaking news. But why do you say that now?"

"Because," he restored the boxes he'd lowered back into place, "the Signal app was invented by some dude who went by the name Moxie Marlinspike."

Evan sagged against a filing cabinet. She felt like a moron for missing so many obvious clues.

"Hey," Ben added in an upbeat tone. "Don't be depressed. If that Jindal bitch is your pal Moxie, then at least you know what you're up against."

"Great. Is that supposed to make me feel better?"

"No." Ben shifted some more boxes. "Just smarter—and a lot more careful." He halted his search and abruptly stepped backward, which wasn't easy to do in the cramped space. "Well, I'll be goddamned."

"What?"

He pointed to a slim box. "Take a gander at this."

Evan walked over and peered at the label.

Ganymede Irrevocable Trust: Estate of J. Lewis Donne.

"Oh, holy shit." Evan stared at the box like it contained a bunch of angry cobras.

"Well?" Ben asked. "Aren't you gonna take a look at it?"

"I honestly do not know."

"Well, if you won't," Ben reached out and grabbed the box, "I sure as shit will."

"Wait." Evan touched his arm. "I don't know about this. It's Julia's damn *father*, Ben."

"So what? Isn't it a little late for you to get religion?"

"We don't even know if this has anything to do with Cawley."

"That's right," he pointed out. "And we won't know until we open it."

Evan continued to deliberate. Once they opened this, there'd be no way to put Pandora back inside. And what if they found something incriminating to link Lewis Donne to Cawley and Bishop Szymanski?

Something more than the photograph she already had . . .

What then? How could she go forward with something that might have the potential to ensnare Julia's family—and her business—in what was beginning to smell like an eerie offshoot of the grand jury investigation into sex abuse scandals in the Catholic Church?

She couldn't. Not if she wanted to protect Julia.

She thought about Tim. And Joey Mazzetta. And the thousands

219

of other innocent kids who had been victimized in these scandals. None of them had a choice. None of them had the wherewithal or the resources to protect *their* good names—or even to salvage what was left of their shattered lives.

She looked up at Ben with resignation.

"You're right. Let's make copies of this and I'll go through it later."

Ping appeared in the doorway to the file room. "I got what we need. Are you finished?"

"Yeah." Evan said. She pushed past Ping and headed for the photocopier. "I'm finished."

After they'd stashed their props back in the storage closet and returned the key card to its hiding place in the potted plant, they left the building and headed for the City Diner & Cocktail Bar on South Broad Street.

Ben was hungry—again—and Evan confessed that she could use a stiff drink . . . or three.

While they waited on their orders, Ping filled them in on what'd she'd been able to glean from Dumbass's computer.

It seemed her home phishing expedition had paid off. Once she used Dumbass's password to log in to the second computer—the one that functioned as the firm's de facto Intranet—she found a treasure trove of juicy data related to all of the firm's top clients. She connected her laptop to the free-range computer in Dumbass's office, and set about ghosting the server. Once it finished copying, all of the data was compressed and backed up on her destination drive.

"What about you two?" Ping asked. "What'd you find?"

Ben answered for Evan. "We found some shit, but we don't know how useful it is yet."

Ping nodded. "It's gonna take me some time to sift through everything I got, too. I'll use whatever set of search criteria you give me to narrow it down."

"Got a sheet of paper?" Evan asked. "I'll make you a list right now."

Ping dug a notepad out of her messenger bag and handed it to Evan.

"I'm gonna ask you to do the impossible, Ping." Evan began jotting down the list of search terms and names.

"Why should tonight be different? I'm guessing you want my report by tomorrow morning?"

Evan nodded.

"It's going to cost you plenty," Ping cautioned.

"Money we have," Evan clarified "It's time we're running out of."

"Where are those fucking cocktails?" Ben got up from their table. "I'm gonna go ask what the holdup is." He strode off toward the bar.

Ping watched Evan make her list. "You wanna tell me what's on your mind?" she asked. "And don't say this timetable, because that's no different than it was two hours ago."

"It's nothing." Evan tried to avoid meeting her eyes. "I'm just tired."

"Tired?"

Evan didn't reply.

"So whatever has you looking like somebody just told you there was no Santa Claus wouldn't have *anything* to do with whatever was inside that brown box?"

"Ping . . ."

"Listen up, little girl," Ping lowered her voice, "before that fool, Ben Rush gets back. Your life is gonna go on a lot longer than anything related to whatever happens or doesn't happen with this damn judge."

Evan put her pen down and looked up at her. "Meaning?"

"Meaning, you don't have to pay for stopping this man's nomination by sacrificing your own peace of mind. This right here," she tapped the black bag that contained her laptop, "is just a *job*—not a quest for some holy grail. And there ain't gonna be no happy endings in this—for anybody. Sure . . . we might manage to blow this one up—but none of these guys are gonna lose anything. They never do. They just keep getting reborn. So, you take my advice. If what was inside that box is gonna damage something you care about—then you just let sleeping dogs lie."

"Can I do that?" The question wasn't rhetorical.

"You can," Ping nodded. "But you probably won't."

Over Ping's shoulder, Evan saw Ben returning with a tray containing their drinks.

She met Ping's brown eyes. "You're right," she said. "I probably won't."

It was just a few minutes after nine when Evan got back to Chadds Ford.

The house smelled great when she opened the front door and stopped to shake snow off her coat before hanging it up. It had started spitting flurries when she'd left Center City. By the time she made the turn onto US 322, it was snowing steadily enough that she had to use the wipers to keep the windshield clear. She was glad when she saw Julia's Audi in their driveway—but concluded it would be a good idea to leave the folder containing the photocopies of the trust documents in her car until morning. She'd go through those records after Julia left for work. Then she'd be able to figure out whether or not she needed to share any of the information with Julia—or could just burn it all in the fireplace.

Finding those documents had been a complete shock. Lewis Donne's name was literally the last one she'd hoped to see. In retrospect, it made sense that Julia's father would retain an attorney with offices in the same damn building as his own company. It was also probable that, as her father's executrix, Julia already knew about the Ganymede bequest. If so, that surely meant the fund had no relationship to anything involving Cawley or the club, and could be forgotten.

That was her hope, anyway.

Scents of warm vanilla and nutmeg met her as she headed toward the living room. Julia sat on the sofa reading something—probably a manuscript, judging by the pages she had spread out on the cushion beside her. She had music playing. It sounded like a Bach partita.

Clearly, she'd won the Pandora debate with Stevie.

Evan heard sounds coming from the kitchen—water running and cookie sheets clattering against the sink.

Stevie must've been baking. Evan was gratified that she also appeared to be cleaning up.

It was amazing how the simple scent of hot cookies could supersede anything else. She allowed herself to stand in the doorway and enjoy inhaling the intoxicating aromas.

Julia smiled at her from the couch. "Good timing." She nodded her head toward the kitchen. "Stevie promised samples when she finished."

Evan crossed the room and flopped down onto the end of the sofa. She leaned across the pile of discarded pages to give Julia a kiss. Julia smelled great, too. But that wasn't unusual. Evan wished sometimes that she could bottle Julia's scent and carry it around in her pocket like an inhaler.

"I missed you tonight." Julia cupped the side of Evan's face. "Where were you?"

Evan debated about how to answer. "I had a little . . . business to take care of in town."

"Oh? That sounds ominous."

"It wasn't," she lied. "What have you been up to?"

Julia held up her stack of pages. "In a rare moment of weakness, I consented to read an unsolicited manuscript one of our agents sent my way."

"Did you say a moment of 'rare' weakness?" Evan teased.

"You don't count."

"Good to know." Evan propped her sock-clad feet up on the coffee table. "So how is it?"

"The book?"

Evan nodded.

"It's—interesting. A cross between fantasy and cli-fi. Not the kind of thing we normally publish."

"*Cli-fi?* What the hell is that?"

Julia showed Evan the cover. "Climate fiction. It's an up-and-coming genre."

"Oh. For a minute there, I thought you were reading porn."

"Don't get your hopes up, Kemosabe."

"When there is no hope, the people perish."

Julia squinted her eyes. "Is that a quote?"

"Yes."

"What from?"

"I'm not a hundred percent sure, but I think it's from that great literary classic, *Sweet Savage Love.*"

Julia swatted her. "Can you be serious?"

"Not when you're sitting here looking all soft and snuggly."

"I did mention that Stevie is going to be bringing us some cookies, right?"

"Uh huh. Last time I checked, they traveled pretty well."

"Wait a minute." Julia gave it another shot. "Before we get too distracted, I need to ask if you're free tomorrow evening."

"Tomorrow?" Evan thought about it. "Sure. What do you have in mind?"

"I made us a dinner reservation."

"Oh? Are we celebrating?"

"Not really. But you said you needed a way to get into the Galileo Club to ask questions about Tim's friend, Joey."

Evan nodded.

"I neglected to tell you that since my father was a member in good standing, I have lifetime access to the club and its facilities. So if you're game, we're all set to go tomorrow night at seven."

"For real?" Evan was unprepared for this windfall. "That's great. You never cease to amaze me."

"Is that a good thing, or a bad thing?"

Evan ran a hand along her leg. "Let's take some cookies upstairs and I'll explain it to you."

"I get the upstairs part, but what do cookies have to do with this process?"

Evan didn't get a chance to elucidate, because Stevie appeared bearing a tray containing a plate of the hot confections—along with a bottle of wine and *three* glasses.

"Hey, Mama Uno. Good timing. I baked these to take to Dad and Kayla's, but I saved a few out for us." She set the tray down on the other end of the coffee table.

"How thoughtful," Evan observed. "Why are there three wineglasses?"

"Oh, come on, Mom," Stevie whined in her best, most exasperated tone. "We've already been through this."

"Define 'this' for me, please," Evan said. "I tend to get confused when we do these little recaps of everything we've already discussed."

Stevie plopped down on an ottoman. "I think I've already demonstrated my ability to manage a glass of wine now and then."

"I suppose that's true." Evan conceded the point. "Although I'd have to argue that yesterday is hardly remote enough in time to qualify as a 'then.' So that just leaves us with a 'now.' Wouldn't you agree, Julia?"

"I am *so* not the right person to ask about this." Julia held up her hands. "That whole space-time continuum thing has never made much sense to me."

"Thanks a lot," Evan said.

"But, if you're asking me for my opinion, simply in the abstract," Julia offered, "I'd say, what could it hurt? It's late. We're all at home. No one is going back out. Stevie has parental supervision. And she made us these fabulous-looking cookies, which are losing their fresh-baked appeal with the passage of every second we sit here, debating this academic argument about the limits of propriety."

"Nice out." Evan considered Julia's summary. "Okay, kid. Open it up."

Stevie beamed at Julia. "I knew having you move in would totally work out."

"Yeah. Don't get cocky." Evan reached out for a cookie from Stevie's platter. There were two kinds—sugar and Toll House—

arrayed in tidy rows. She snagged one that looked crammed with chocolate chips. "The night is still young."

Stevie opened the wine with dispatch, which piqued Evan's curiosity a bit. True, Stevie had always been a quick study, but something about her proficiency with a corkscrew raised a red flag.

She deferred that discussion for another day. Tonight, she needed to enjoy this easy camaraderie. She needed that more than just about anything.

Stevie poured them each a respectable amount of wine. It was clear to Evan that her daughter wasn't going to push the envelope. Evan examined the label of the bottle she'd selected. A Mascota. She was forced to give her daughter grudging credit for her choice.

Maybe Tim was right and Stevie did get the family palate?

"These cookies are divine." Julia took another bite.

Evan was tempted to say, *So are you.*

It was intoxicating to watch Julia chew.

Hell. It was intoxicating to watch Julia do just about anything. Watching Julia was better than Netflix.

Stevie held her glass of wine aloft. "How about a toast?"

Evan and Julia both raised their glasses.

"Here's to getting what we want," Stevie said, "and to loving what we have, even when we don't."

They clinked rims.

Evan allowed herself to relax into the guilty pleasures of great wine, home-baked cookies, and the healing companionship of two remarkable women.

Chapter Ten

On Monday morning, Julia paid an unannounced visit to the office of her father's estate attorney. She didn't bother making an appointment. If Arthur Squires wasn't available to meet with her, she'd simply insist that a junior associate provide access to the documents she wished to review. She recalled from earlier conversations in the immediate aftermath of her father's death that his will had made provision for some specific, continuing bequests to support various nonprofit groups. She had paid little attention to those when Art reviewed them with her. He stipulated that all of the funds would be disbursed annually from the trust account. All Julia would have to do is cosign the disbursement checks during each cycle of payments. It was *pro forma*.

But Julia's curiosity about the identity of the specific beneficiaries of her father's benevolence had increased after her discovery that his private club, Galileo, was becoming the nexus of Evan's research on Judge Cawley. She had no idea what she expected to find, but she felt some trepidation about the exercise of looking into the bequests, nonetheless. Her father had, for all practical purposes, always been a stranger to her. His peripheral role in this developing "Six Degrees of J. Meyer Cawley" narrative disturbed her. And she could tell that it was disturbing to Evan, who seemed to be doing her best not to say more than she had to about any part Julia's father played in this mystery.

It took her less than five minutes to take the elevator up to the seventh floor and walk the long corridor that led to the offices of Smith, Martin, Squires & Andersen. As expected, Art Squires was out of the office, meeting with another client. But the receptionist, who was very deferential and even more apologetic, ushered Julia into a small conference room and assured her that Mr. Squires' associate, Erskine Robbins, would be right with her. She also offered Julia refreshment, which Julia politely, but gratefully refused.

She wasn't sure how many hurdles she'd have to jump through to actually see the files she needed. Squires generally made her feel like access privileges to estate papers were precious commodities that could only be doled out after significant advance notice—and during certain phases of the moon.

Erskine Robbins hurried into the room less than a minute after the receptionist departed. He was a youngish man who exuded a frenetic air. He had a head full of wiry brown hair that looked wind-blown. Julia suspected it probably always looked that way—likely because Mr. Robbins was always in such a hurry.

"How may we help you, Ms. Donne?" he asked.

Julia was tempted to look behind him for other minions in his wake. His use of the royal "we" was quaintly old-fashioned.

"I appreciate your willingness to take time away from your other work to see me on such short notice." Julia turned on the charm. She already topped the younger man by more than six inches. why not work the corners a bit before moving in to land a real punch? She took a step closer to him. "I'm really very grateful."

Robbins took a half step backward and nearly fell over a chair.

"No. No," he stammered. "We're here to, um . . . meet your needs. In . . . in whatever ways we can."

"That's so comforting," Julia beamed at him. "I won't trouble you for long. I simply need to review some estate documents."

"Oh. Of course, Ms. Donne. I'm happy to retrieve those for you." He pushed his glasses up. "What, specifically, do you need access to?"

Julia pressed her advantage.

"I'd like to review the list of regular disbursements from my father's trust. I was silly when Mr. Squires first shared those with me, and neglected to make a copy." She rested a manicured hand on his skinny arm. "You know how silly we girls can be when we're distracted."

"Y-yes. Of course. I'll, uh . . . I'll go and get those for you right away." He backed toward the door and promptly ran into it. "It's . . . it won't take but a few minutes."

He disappeared down the hallway.

Julia felt like a sleazy imitation of Mata Hari—flashing her gams to try and gain release from Saint-Lazare.

It was a blessing that Squires had been out of the office this morning. Julia had always despised having to work with him because his demeanor toward her was always so . . . dismissive. Squires made it clear from the outset that his duty was to accede to the wishes of his client—J. Lewis Donne. Even in death, Julia's father continued to preempt her right to manage just about anything.

Robbins returned, carrying a brown box. He set it down on the small conference table.

"I believe all of the trust documents are in here," he said. "Would you like me to help you locate the names of the beneficiaries?" He gave her a look tinged with so much trepidation, Julia could tell he was praying she'd say no.

"Thank you, Mr. Robbins. I think I'll do just fine. Might I trouble you for a pen and paper?"

"Oh. Of course." He backed into the same chair again in his haste to turn and retrieve a pad of paper and about a dozen pens from a console near the door. He all but threw the items down on the table, and the pens scattered like jackstraws. Julia could see the muscles in his face tighten as he hurriedly bent to try and collect the pens.

Julia stopped him by touching his hand. "That's just fine, Erskine. I'll take it from here."

He pushed his glasses up and nodded at her without speaking. Julia waited for him to leave and close the door before she opened the box labeled *Ganymede Irrevocable Trust: Estate of J. Lewis Donne.*

The first thing she learned was that her father had established the trust more than twenty-five years ago. She'd had no idea about that, and found it odd that Squires never clarified that for her.

The list of trust beneficiaries was shorter than she expected. The largest sums of money were paid to two groups: a political action committee called "Citizens for Integrity in Government" and a philanthropic group described as a community service arm of his private club, Galileo. The latter group had enjoyed the longest history of support. She flipped through page after page of disbursements. The amounts of the donations escalated at different times. There were peaks of support during the decade of the 1990s and continuing until her father retired from the board at D&H, and her parents moved their primary residence to Paris. Still, his philanthropy to that group continued at what she considered to be a robust level. Annual, continuing disbursements from the trust were scheduled to continue at a rate of $25,000 per year. The group was earmarked as a 501(c)(3) organization, so all of the trust donations were considered tax deductible.

Good ol' Dad. Even his best deeds were guaranteed to earn benefits.

There was another, older roster of personal trust disbursements that dated back decades. Julia flipped through those pages. They were mostly payments, made to individuals, churches or colleges. Some were marked as scholarship contributions to underwrite the tuition fees of numerous recipients. Others were noted as "booster" donations to support public school athletic programs.

No. That wasn't right. Julia examined the names more closely. These weren't public schools; they were parochial schools. *All of them.* And St. Margherita's Parish led the pack in dollars of support.

Julia began to feel sick.

None of this proved anything. It could all be coincidental . . .

She continued to scan the lists of names. None of them meant anything to her.

Then she saw one she recognized, and her heart skipped a beat.

Joseph R. Mazzetta.

According to the ledger, her father's trust had made six cash payments of $500 each to him between the years of 1995 and 1998. These were noted simply as "St. Margherita summer basketball camp tuition assistance."

Julia closed her eyes and pushed her chair back from the table.

Oh, dear god . . .

It took more self-control than she knew she possessed to stand up, straighten her skirt, and calmly exit the conference room. She took nothing with her. No papers. No notes.

She didn't need to.

She understood that the rest of her life would now be a process of trying to forget what she'd just discovered.

She left the firm, rode the elevator down to her floor, and entered the offices of Donne & Hale without stopping to speak with anyone. Once she was securely back inside her own office, she entered her private bathroom and cried for half an hour.

After composing herself, she walked to her desk, picked up the phone, and called her travel agent to book a flight to Paris.

"Things are simply getting too hot. We're shutting this operation down."

Maya wasn't surprised by the call from Zucchetto. Especially after he'd had time to share details about Tim Donovan's visit to Brian Christensen in Gloucester City. It was easy to predict that his "client" would start running scared and decide to pull the plug.

These boys didn't have the stamina to go head to head with the big dogs.

"We've already transmitted your final payment," he continued. "The funds should show up by end of business tomorrow."

"Is that it?" she asked. There was no reason to prolong their conversation.

"Other than to thank you for your efficient service. We are pleased that your recommendations did not overstate your abilities."

"How kind of you to say so. I'll be out of the hotel by tomorrow morning."

"There is no need to feel pressured," Zucchetto said magnanimously. "The room is paid for through the weekend. Why not take some time to enjoy the sights of the city?"

Maya's curiosity was piqued by Zucchetto's sudden burst of collegiality.

"I *have* always wanted to see the Liberty Bell."

In fact, Maya couldn't think of anything less enjoyable, with the possible exception of getting another root canal.

"Well, then," Zucchetto said heartily. "Here is a golden opportunity. My client is happy to allow you to remain here as his guest until Sunday. That includes the use of your rental car."

"How very kind. Please convey my gratitude to your client."

"There is one last detail." Zucchetto's tone had resumed its customary brusqueness.

"And that is?"

"Once we terminate this call, every aspect of our business will be concluded. This phone number will cease to exist."

"I perfectly understand your meaning."

"I was certain you would. I wish you a very good day. Enjoy your time in this historic city."

The line went dead.

Maya laughed before tossing the phone into the trash bin, along with the keys to the rental car.

She'd already placed the "do not disturb" tag on the outside of her door. Her suitcases were headed via courier to a hotel near the airport. She'd also reserved a new rental car.

There were still one or two loose ends that needed to be tied off.

Was Zucchetto really naïve enough to imagine that Maya

would be content to sit here and flip through tourist brochures until his hired gun came calling?

Zucchetto's bogus phone number wasn't the only thing they planned to terminate.

Idiots.

Zucchetto and his "client" might have determined that things had gotten too hot—but that wasn't the case for everyone.

Like most reptiles, Marcus tolerated the heat just *fine*.

"Tim? This is Mike Duffy. I don't know if you remember me. We played basketball together at St. Rita's in the mid-'90s."

When Tim answered the phone, he didn't recognize the number on the caller ID. But that wasn't unusual. Many parish members who weren't among his regular contacts would call his landline to request hospital visits or ask for information about services or activities at the church.

"Yes," Tim said to the caller. "Of course, I remember you. How are you, Mike?"

Mike Duffy had only been at St. Rita's for a year or two, but Tim remembered him. The Duffy family had five kids. Mike's father had been an airplane mechanic who seemed to move around a lot, and their time in Philadelphia had been fairly short—only a couple of years. Tim had found no current contact information on Mike, or his family, when he'd gone to the parish office to do his research on the whereabouts of former team members.

"I'm okay," Mike said. "I live in Phoenix now, but I'm in town for a couple of days on business. I wondered if maybe you'd have time to see me. So, we could talk about . . . things."

Things? Tim knew immediately what Mike wanted to discuss. After the revelations from Mark Atwood yesterday, Tim wasn't sure he had the fortitude to take in any more—at least, not right now. Already, his stamina had commenced a slow leak and its steady drip, drip, drip was lowering his level of resolve with each passing hour.

But he was still a priest. And refusing to help someone in need was a betrayal of his vows.

"Sure," Tim responded. "I'm happy to get together. It will be good to see you." He hesitated before asking his next question, but put it out there, anyway. "What things did you want to talk about?"

Mike seemed to understand Tim's question. "I've read some of the articles about the Church and all the men who are speaking up about the priests, and what they did. And I went to see Mark Atwood at his bar last night. He told me about your visit and what you talked about. So I figured it was okay to call and ask you about it—about Father Szymanski and the team?"

"Did Father Szymanski behave inappropriately toward you, Mike?"

"*Inappropriately?* I guess that's one way to put it."

Tim closed his eyes. "I'm sorry, Mike. I don't mean to diminish anything that happened. I'm really sorry."

"It's okay," Mike said. "Look. I don't really want to talk about this on the phone. Can we meet? Maybe tomorrow night, after the conference wraps up?"

"Of course. Where would you like to meet?"

"I'm in Center City at the DoubleTree. My flight back to Arizona leaves tomorrow night at 10:15, so I have to check out of here as soon as the last session ends. Could you meet me at the hotel around six? Maybe we can talk in the lobby bar there? It's pretty decent."

"Sure," Tim said. "I can do that. Where should I look for you?"

"The hotel has temporary parking for conference guests set up in the garage on level two. I'll wait for you by the hotel elevators there with a pass for your dashboard so you won't get towed. We can go down to the lobby together."

"Okay." Tim wrote down the hotel information and the time. "I'll see you tomorrow evening. I'm . . . glad you called, Mike."

"Yeah," Mike said. "Me, too. Oh—one last thing. My phone has to be turned off during the meetings, so I won't be able to answer it if you call or have to cancel."

"I won't cancel. I'll be there."

"Great. Thanks for doing this, Father."

"You don't have to call me that, Mike. Tim is fine."

"Okay. See you tomorrow."

"Bye, Mike."

Tim hung up,

After the call, he began to pace back and forth across his small living room.

What now?

He needed to tell Evan what he'd learned from Mark Atwood. He knew that meant she'd want to go to Shaken and interview Mark herself. But even if Mark named names, his determination not to go forward with any of what he knew would just make his information hearsay. So nothing he shared with her could be used to stop Judge Cawley's nomination—and that was even if Cawley *had* been one of the perpetrators Mark referenced in his nightmare revelations about the Galileo Club.

If. If. If. There were just too many ifs.

His pacing continued.

This is ridiculous.

He grabbed his jacket and headed for the church. If he was going to be awake all night, he could at least spend the time in prayer.

Ping called Evan a few minutes after Julia left for work. Evan had just returned from retrieving the papers she'd left in her car overnight. She wasn't looking forward to the errand ahead of her . . . not at all.

"Great timing," Evan said, when she picked up her phone. "I just sat down at my desk."

"Yeah? Well lucky you. I've been at mine most of the night."

"Great will be your reward, Ping. I appreciate the hustle."

"You might not when you hear my report."

"Okay." Evan sat back in her chair and picked up her mug of bad coffee. "Let's have it."

"I'll make it short and sweet. First, the Citizens for Integrity in Government PAC has nine primary donors, and all of them are members of the Galileo Club. There are one or two outliers, but the majority of the big money the PAC commits to support its marquee issues comes from the same group of men."

"Any names we know?" Evan asked.

"Oh, yeah. This list reads like a *Who's Who In the Harvard Tie Club*. Let's see." Ping shuffled papers. "I'll give you the high notes. We've got our art-loving friend, Mr. Lippincott. Followed by Bishop Frederick R. Szymanski, Former Ambassador Louis K. Girard, Alderman Stephen P. Jonas, Former District Attorney Richard P. Hardison, and—wait for it—The Honorable Judge J. Meyer Cawley."

"So Cawley is paying the freight on PR campaigns to support his *own* candidacy?"

"So it seems," Ping said. "I'm guessing that fact alone violates about twenty campaign finance laws?"

"It might if he actually were a candidate running for public office. That's not the case, here."

"Too bad. Still," Ping mused, "his little PAC promotes a lot of partisan agendas I think the Democrats in the Senate would like to know about."

"True," Evan said. "So? Are there any other PAC members whose names I might recognize?"

"Maybe."

"Ping . . ."

"All right, already. One other—a Mr. J. Lewis Donne."

"Yeah," Evan said. "I figured as much."

"Well brace yourself then, because his name shows up a lot—and not in any good ways."

"Okay. I was just about to start combing through the trust papers we copied last night."

"I can save you the trouble," Ping said. "I'm pretty sure there are scans of all the hard copies you found saved to file."

"You reviewed it all?"

"Yeah. And I felt like I needed a shower when I finished."

Oh, Jesus. "It's that bad?"

"It is," Ping answered. "I won't lie to you. Do you need a minute to prepare, or should I just summarize it all for you?"

A minute to prepare? *A lifetime of preparation wouldn't be enough time.*

"No," Evan said. "I'm as ready as I'll ever be. Go ahead."

"Okay. It turns out that the same mess of scumbags who run the PAC created a second pet project. About twenty years ago, they started up a nonprofit philanthropic committee. As far as I can tell, it's really a cover for some kind of private slush fund they all make regular deposits to—and at pretty big levels of support. We ain't talkin' pocket change here, either. I found records for the fund—ledgers of payouts it made over the years. A lot of the money went to some colleges as scholarship aid for students. They also gave a shit ton to fund some area athletic programs—and a lot of that cash went straight to St. Rita's—and I suppose we can thank the bishop for that. But it got stranger."

"What do you mean?" Evan asked.

"The further back I went, the more I started seeing payments to individuals—*cash* payments. There were enough of them that I created a database to look for commonalities. I wanted to be able to crosscut the data in a couple of ways. Names. Dates. How payments were categorized. Dollar amounts. Organizations' names, if relevant. That kind of thing. Oh, and by the way: all of the recipients were men, even in cases where the payments went to parents."

"Parents?"

"Yeah. Some of the cash was paid directly to parents of these kids—at least in the few cases I could verify. I don't think it's any accident that those payments were always a lot heftier than the other ones."

Jesus Christ. People took payoffs to keep silent about what had happened to their kids?

Evan's head was swimming. "How were you able to verify *any* of this?"

"It wasn't real scientific—and it would never hold up in court. But I went to The Google. And I cross-checked names on Facebook, LinkedIn and some other social media outlets. Most of these guys listed schools they attended in their user profiles.

Some even had photos posted from their childhood years—family pictures, school reunions, siblings. Sports teams. And," Ping added, "guess what *else* a bunch of them had in common?"

"St. Rita's?"

"You got it. Your boy Joey Mazzetta was on the all-star list. He got what appeared to be regular payments—not from the committee, but from one of its members through a private trust."

Evan's antenna went up at that revelation—especially if it linked Joey directly to Cawley. It might also provide a motive for Joey's murder taking place on the same night he'd showed up drunk at the Galileo Club.

"Was it Cawley?" she asked Ping.

"No."

Well . . . there went that *smoking gun.*

"Who was it, then?" Evan asked.

"One of the other men," Ping said vaguely.

Evan knew Ping was sandbagging. There could only be one reason for it.

"Who was it?" she asked again.

Evan could hear Ping exhale before she answered. "You know who it was."

Dear god . . .

"Tell me anyway," Evan insisted. She needed to hear Ping say the name.

"It was Julia's father." Ping gave Evan a few seconds to absorb what she'd said before continuing. "Tell me what you want me to do with this."

"I have no fucking clue."

"Listen," Ping said. "I don't have to include this in my report. Remember what I said to you last night."

"No. No . . . It'll all come out anyway. I'll . . ." Evan searched for the right words. There weren't any. *Not for this.* "I'll figure something out."

"Are you gonna be okay?"

Would she be?

"I honestly don't know." Evan thought about Julia. "Probably not."

Evan and Julia had already arranged to meet at Julia's townhouse before leaving for their dinner reservation at the Galileo Club. Julia didn't keep any clothing suitable for a venue like this at Evan's house, so it made sense to connect in town.

These arrangements led Evan to express concern about the dress code for the occasion.

"What the hell am I supposed to wear?" she lamented.

"Something," Julia offered.

"*Something?*" Evan quoted. "Could you maybe narrow that down a skosh?"

Julia was plainly amused by Evan's wardrobe dilemma.

"Just select something that isn't buffalo plaid or flannel and you'll be fine."

"Very funny." Evan sulked. "I'm clueless about this kind of shit."

"Oh, come on," Julia teased. "You must have some garments that are dressier than your customary outfits."

"I have 'customary' outfits?"

"I'd say so," Julia offered. "Your style is generally on the casual side."

"The casual side of *what?*" Evan asked. "Compared to you, I look like I shop at the Salvation Army." She took a few seconds to consider her remark. "Hell," she amended, "compared to you, half the damn population looks like it shops there, too."

"Honey? Will you please relax? It's not that complicated. Just wear dark slacks and a nice shirt."

"Shoes?" Evan said the word like it was an accusation.

"Shoes would be preferable," Julia suggested.

"Yeah. Okay. Yuck it up." Evan sighed. "Oh, well. I suppose they won't throw me out if I'm there as your guest."

"I'd say that's a reasonable expectation," Julia observed.

"I guess you could always tell them I'm your driver."

"I could. But I think I'd prefer to tell them nothing. They won't care about who you are, so we shouldn't spend any more time worrying about explanations we don't owe them."

"I suppose that's true."

As it turned out, Evan did have one outfit that halfway qualified as dressy. She'd actually forgotten about it, but when she was at home, fretting about getting ready, Stevie hauled it out of her closet.

"Why don't you wear this?" Stevie held up the tailored Hugo Boss suit Evan had worn to student convocation at Emma Willard last year.

"I can't wear that," Evan said. "Are you nuts?"

"Why not?" Stevie looked it over. "It's badass and you look totally hot in it."

"Hot?"

Stevie shrugged. "That's what half my classmates said."

"It's a *suit,* Stevie. I'll look like a guy."

"And the problem with that would be? Come on, Mama Uno. Gender fluidity is the shit right now."

"Oh, is it? Do tell . . ."

"You know what I mean." Stevie walked over and held the garments up in front of Evan. "See? This looks *so* great on you. And it's totally girly because it isn't, you know?"

"Are you speaking another language?" Evan asked. But she had to hand it to her daughter. The thing did look pretty good on her. It had cuffed trousers and a matching, loose-fitting jacket with peak lapels. It was light brown, and she wore it with a self-tying silk blouse she'd found in a darker shade of the same color.

"Okay. I guess it's my best option," Evan conceded. "Got any shoes I can borrow?" It was a godsend that she and Stevie wore the same size. "Nothing too girly!" she bellowed. Stevie was already on her way to her room to ransack her own closet.

Evan was already undressed when Stevie returned with a pair of low-heeled dress Oxfords and some kind of belt that looked like the business end of a bullwhip. Evan took the shoes from her.

"No pumps?" she asked.

Stevie shook her head with energy. "You're not authorized to wear those, Mama Uno. You'd come home in a body cast."

"Very funny." She put on the shoes and was pleased at how comfortable they felt. "What is *that* thing?" Evan pointed at the belt.

Stevie handed it to her. "It's a skinny belt."

"For?"

"Duh. *The pants.*"

"I don't need a belt to hold up these pants." Evan took it from her. "Besides, this thing couldn't hold up a sheet of Kleenex."

"Mom? Just humor me, here. This is a fashion thing. It's not about functionality."

"Yeah. Okay. *Whatever.*" Evan started to dress.

"Why are you so nervous about this?" Stevie perched on the end of Evan's bed. "You've been out with Julia before."

"Yeah? Not on a night like this."

"Hmmmm . . ."

Evan eyed her with suspicion. "What's that supposed to mean?"

Stevie shrugged. "Just wondering if maybe you're planning something special tonight."

"Like?"

"You tell me. A *proposal*, maybe?"

Evan had been in the process of threading the "skinny belt" through the loops on her trousers. She stopped in mid-thread and stared at Stevie with an open mouth.

"Well?" Stevie shrugged. "It could happen."

"Yeah," Evan stated. "It *totally* could happen. But it won't be tonight."

"Okay. Then why are you so freaked out?"

"Maybe because I have some other things on my mind. And none of them have anything to do with dinner. Okay, nosy?"

"Sheesh, Mom. Take a chill pill." Stevie watched her in silence for a moment. "Want me to get you a little something to take the edge off?"

"*Excuse* me?"

Stevie quickly held up a hand. "Forget I mentioned it."

Evan nodded. "Good idea." She held out the two ends of the tie on her blouse. "You wanna help me with this thing?"

241

"Sure." Stevie hopped up and walked over to face her. "We need to leave one end a lot longer, so it really looks like a man's tie."

"Of *course*, we do."

"That's perfect." Stevie stepped back to admire her work. "Okay. Now put on the jacket."

Evan shrugged it on. Stevie promptly stood the collar up so the lapels would flare out.

"Let me guess . . . you want me to look like Fonzie?"

"Am I supposed to know who that is?" Stevie asked. "Now you gotta roll up the sleeves."

"Forget it."

"Mom . . ."

"*No.* I'm not rolling up the sleeves. I hate that shit."

"Mom. You *have* to roll them up. Otherwise, you'll look like a dork."

Evan took a few seconds to consider Stevie's warning.

"Trust me? Please?" Stevie pulled out the big guns. "Julia would tell you the same thing."

In the end, Stevie won all of her arguments and Evan showed up at Julia's townhouse equipped with a hard-earned, Gen Z seal of approval. If Julia's wide-eyed reaction when she opened her townhouse door and got her first look at Evan's outfit was any indication, Stevie had made the right choice.

But that was nothing compared to Evan's reaction to what Julia was wearing.

Julia was stunning in a simple but entirely elegant mid-length, sleeveless black sheath dress. It had angled shoulders and was open from the neckline to well below the waist, and fastened with loops and covered buttons.

At least, *some* of the front was fastened. Julia had left a tantalizing number of the fasteners open.

"Holy shit . . ." Evan was mesmerized. All she wanted to do was stand there and count tiny buttons.

Julia pulled her inside and closed the door. "You look beautiful," she said.

Evan thought her eyes looked happy and a little sad, all at the same time.

"Is that a good thing?" she asked.

"Oh, yeah." Julia nodded. "Why do you keep staring at my . . . décolletage?"

"Because it's gorgeous, just like the rest of you."

Julia took Evan by the hand and led her toward the living room. "Let's sit for a minute before we go. I need to talk with you about something."

"That sounds ominous."

Evan followed her. They sat down on the sofa and faced each other.

"What is it?" Evan asked. She was growing alarmed by Julia's demeanor. "You look terrified."

"I, um . . . I made an unannounced visit to my father's estate attorney today."

"Oh?" Evan tried to quell a rush of panic. She had a feeling she knew what Julia was about to share with her, and she was pretty sure it wasn't anything good.

"After our conversation on Saturday morning, I made the decision to look into my father's estate. Just to see if there were any specific mentions of the club or any bequests from his trust that might shed some light on his relationships with Judge Cawley and the bishop. I realized that his attorney had always been pretty careful not to share any details with me—especially about the trust. I wanted to find out why that might be the case."

Evan was reluctant to pose her next question, because she knew what Julia's answer would be.

"Did he explain his reasoning to you?"

"No." Julia explained. "Because I went up to their offices so early, and without an appointment, he wasn't available. I'm afraid I behaved pretty shamefully with the poor junior associate who got tasked with 'handling' me."

"What do you mean?"

Julia met her eyes. "You might say I used a charm offensive. As soon as he entered the room, it became clear to me that he was intimidated. So, I used that to rattle him as much as possible."

"Were you wearing this outfit?" Evan asked.

Julia looked confused. "No. Why?"

Evan tried to smile. "Because they'd probably have had to scrape him off the floor."

Julia took hold of her hand and squeezed it. "Promise you'll keep saying things like that to me? I need to hear them right now. I need to believe them right now."

"I promise." Evan tugged her closer and kissed her on the forehead. "Honey, what happened?"

"He got me the paperwork I asked for and left me alone so I could go through it. Evan . . ." Julia closed her eyes. "It was horrible. The things I saw. The bequests. The payments he'd made through the years. To colleges. To schools—parochial schools. Including St. Rita's. And many other disbursements to men . . . young men. Some of them in cash. Others funneled through a tax-exempt committee at his club." She held Evan's hand tighter. "Even then, I tried to rationalize it all—tried to imagine that I'd find a perfectly reasonable explanation. I had to let go of that fantasy when I saw Joey Mazzetta's name in the record."

It was Evan's turn to close her eyes. She didn't want to see the pain on Julia's face.

"Oh, baby. I'm so sorry . . ."

"Don't be," Julia said forcefully. "I needed to know. *We* needed to know." She took a deep breath. "Now we do."

"I won't use this," Evan told her. "It doesn't have anything to do with Cawley."

"How can you say that?" Julia was incredulous. "It might have *everything* to do with him."

"We don't know that."

"Not yet."

"Honey . . ."

Julia absently checked her watch. "I need to tell you something else before we go."

"Okay." Evan didn't waste time trying to imagine what it might be. "Tell me."

"I booked a flight to Paris."

"You did?" Evan was surprised.

"I need to see my mother. To find out what she knows. What she *knew*." She laced her fingers with Evan's. "I *have* to."

"Okay." Evan raised their linked hands to her lips and kissed Julia's fingers. "Do you want me to come with you?"

Julia's eyes softened. "Yes. But you can't. And I need to do this by myself."

"I understand."

"Thank you," Julia whispered. She released Evan's hand and stood up. "Are you ready to go now?"

"Are you sure?" Evan asked.

"Am I sure about what?"

"Tonight," Evan clarified. "We don't have to do this tonight."

"It's *fine*," Julia said. "Don't worry about me. Not about this. Believe me—this errand tonight is one thing I know how to do."

"Okay." Evan got to her feet. "Promise?"

Julia gave her a sad smile and kissed her gently. "I promise."

Evan thought she'd been inside some swanky, over-the-top places before, but nothing compared in scale or refinements to the Galileo Club. An immaculately dressed doorman greeted them at the entrance after the valet whisked Julia's car away.

"What a pleasure it is to see you again, Miss Donne." He held the door open for them. "Miss Reed, welcome to the Galileo Club. I hope you enjoy your evening."

They entered a round, marble-floored foyer that was roughly the size of a ballroom. The walls were paneled in gleaming dark wood. Multiple mirrors reflected the light from an overhead chandelier that probably weighed a thousand pounds. Evan wondered whose job it was to keep the thing cleaned. It looked like a relic from Versailles.

Another perfectly groomed man glided toward them from . . . *somewhere* . . . and took their coats. He didn't ask their names, so Evan assumed his entire reason for existing was simply to know which garments belonged to what guests.

Julia seemed to take everything in stride, so Evan did her best to follow her lead and not gape at anything.

That proved harder than expected.

Julia guided them toward one of the five doorways that opened off the foyer. It led to some kind of reception area. There were other couples milling about, laughing and chatting. All of them held cocktails in crystal tumblers or stemware. Classical music played at exactly the right level: loud enough to be heard, but soft enough not to interfere with conversation.

Another well-dressed drone appeared, wearing the short white jacket of a steward.

"Miss Donne? Miss Reed?" He bowed to them. "Would either of you care for a cocktail before dinner?"

Julia answered for them.

"That would be lovely; thank you, Sebastian." She faced Evan. "What would you like, Evan?"

Evan was half-tempted to order a Bud Light, but she thought better of it. "I'll have what you're having," she said magnanimously.

"Excellent." The steward glided off.

Evan leaned toward Julia. "He didn't ask what *you* want," she whispered.

"Oh, he already knows what I want."

"Are you kidding me?"

"I wish I were."

"How many years did you say it had been since you came here?"

Julia thought about it. "I don't think I did say. But it's probably been at least six."

"Six years?" Evan was amazed.

"Give or take."

"Jeez. I get carded if it's two weeks between visits to the liquor store."

"Don't make me laugh," Julia said. "It'll ruin my veneer of icy reserve."

Evan looked around the room. It was lavishly furnished with baroque sideboards, upholstered chairs, and settees ornamented with brightly colored pillows. There were Chinese vases containing tasteful displays of fresh cut flowers everywhere.

So far, no one seemed to notice that they had joined the assembly. Evan found that surprising. Several of the dozen or so couples sharing the space were seated in comfy chairs that were arranged around small tables.

"Do you know any of the people in here?" Evan asked.

Somehow, Julia managed to inventory the room without moving her head one iota.

Damn, Evan thought. *I need to get her to teach me how to do that.*

"Yes. I recognize a few people," she said.

"Why have none of them descended upon you?" Evan asked. "Aren't they overjoyed to welcome you back into the fold?"

"It's not that," Julia explained. "Initiating contact that might be unwelcome is considered classless."

"Seriously? Why?"

"To put it bluntly," Julia regarded her with a raised eyebrow, "not everyone may choose to end the evening dancing with the one who brung 'em."

Evan's eyes grew wide. "Well, I'll be damned. I've lived a sheltered life."

"Need any more explanation for why I hate this fucking place?" She shifted her gaze and looked past Evan's shoulder. "Ah," she said in a singsong voice. "Those look *perfect*. Thank you."

The steward presented them with their cocktails and bowed to Julia before backing away.

Evan held her tall glass up to examine it. "What the hell *is* this?"

"It's a reverse martini." Julia sipped hers. "Perfectly made, by the way."

"Okaaayyy." Evan sniffed it. "What's a reverse martini?"

"It's one part gin and seven parts Noilly Prat French vermouth, finished with a gin floater and a twist of lemon."

Evan tried hers. "*Hell-o*. Where have *you* been all my life?" She took another sip. It was even better than the first. "Damn. Don't ever let Stevie try one of these."

Julia did laugh then, and the silvery sound lightened Evan's heart like nothing else could.

"Where'd you discover this wonderful thing?" she asked Julia.

"I didn't discover it. This was Julia Child's favorite drink."

"That figures. She probably downed six or eight of these before every meal."

"Apropos of that," Julia took hold of Evan's elbow, "how about we make our way to the dining room and get this show on the road?"

"You don't have to ask me twice."

As soon as they reached the threshold of a door that opened into an even larger room, a tuxedoed maître d' met them. He carried two oversized menus with leather covers bearing the embossed crest of the Galileo Club.

"Miss Donne? I have your table ready. If you'll please follow me?"

He led them to a small table, already set for two with gleaming china that bore the same crest that adorned the menus. It was located in a quiet-looking corner. Evan noted that the entire space seemed to have a plethora of quiet corners—which, by itself, must've presented a remarkable architectural challenge. The room was decorated in dark tones—coffered ceiling, walnut wainscoting, flocked wallpaper in gold and hunter green. There were no chandeliers in here. Instead, the room had low-contrast lighting coming from wall-mounted gaslights. There were ornately framed paintings everywhere—mostly hunting scenes. Men in shooting parties, surrounded by servants carrying bags filled with game birds. Epic fox hunting scenes. There was even a giant Constable-type landscape hanging over the largest field-stone fireplace she'd ever seen. It was all very refined and tailored toward a decidedly masculine clientele.

Evan supposed this was one of the club's smaller venues, since it only boasted about thirty tables.

The maître d' graciously pulled out Julia's chair for her, but left Evan to fend for herself.

Guess he tagged me as the butch in this equation . . .

She took her own seat.

Once he presented their menus and assured them their attendant would be with them shortly, he departed.

"What are you smiling about?" Julia placed her unopened menu down on the table.

Evan shrugged.

"Come on," Julia coaxed. "Tell me."

"I guess I found it insightful that he pulled out your chair, but left me to my own devices." She shrugged. "I told Stevie this suit would make me look like a guy."

"Believe me, you don't look anything like a guy."

"No?"

"No."

"I guess maybe he got the memo that the prodigal daughter had returned," Evan mused.

"I think it's less complicated than that."

"How so?" Evan deconstructed her origami swan of a napkin and placed it across her lap.

"I did rather advertise that you were my escort by clinging to your arm like a starstruck prom date as we walked in here," Julia suggested. "I think he correctly interpreted the nature of our relationship."

"Well damn." Evan looked over at Jeeves, who had returned to his post at the podium near the dining room entrance. "I guess we have to tip him 30 percent now." She held up a hand before Julia could respond. "I know, I know. There is *no* tipping at this joint."

"That would be correct. I always knew you were a quick study." Julia took another sip of her drink.

"Are you going to want another one of those?" Evan asked. Her own had gone down fast. *Too fast.*

249

"I don't think so." She looked at Evan's glass. "Would you like another one?"

"Trust me. I'd like about a dozen more. But I think it's better if I keep my wits about me. It's going to be harder to scope this place out than I realized."

"How much of a diversion do you need?"

"Enough of one that I can disappear long enough to chat up some of the staff."

"They won't talk to you." Julia stated. "Discretion is their mission in life."

"Not *this* staff," Evan corrected. "The staff nobody gets to see. Kitchen workers. Busboys. Washroom attendants. Custodians. The little people who are probably invisible at a place like this."

"That might be harder to negotiate." Julia seemed to consider the challenge Evan had presented. "I suppose I could give you a tour? Show you some of the private sitting rooms and grander public spaces? If they're not in use tonight, that might make it easier to wander astray and explain how I managed to get us lost—if we're discovered wandering around where we're not supposed to be."

Evan grinned at her. "Have I told you lately how much I love you?"

"I hope it's a lot," Julia said enigmatically. "I need it right now."

To hell with the conventions. Evan reached across the table to take hold of her hand.

"It's a lot," she promised.

Julia held her gaze. They sat quietly until an attendant approached their table to take their orders.

They dined on Chateaubriand en Croute with warm, wilted winter greens and Dauphinoise potatoes. Their exceptional meal was rendered extraordinary by the addition of a superb Bordeaux. They had both been taken aback when the sommelier showed up at their table with a bottle of Chateau Pontet Canet Pauillac and two glasses.

"What is this about?" Julia asked.

"A gift, madam," he announced as he set about opening the wine. "With all best wishes, and the fervent hope you both will enjoy your meal tonight."

"Might I ask to whom we owe thanks for this extraordinary gift?"

"Someone who wishes to remain anonymous, madam." He poured a soupçon of the wine into one of the glasses. Julia indicated that he should offer it to Evan, who did her best to avoid swooning after she tasted it.

He filled Julia's glass, then Evan's, and departed after leaving the bottle on their table.

"What the hell was that about?" Evan asked.

"I have *no* idea. But I suppose we shouldn't look a gift horse in the mouth."

"I'll drink to that."

They clinked rims. Evan thought some of the tension was beginning to leave Julia's body, but she wasn't really sure. As Julia had said many times before, she was very good at disguising her true emotions when the situation called for it.

"How are you holding up?" Evan asked her.

"All right, I think. But I can tell you I won't be sorry to never come back here again."

"I'm sorry we had to do it tonight. I'm sorry we had to do it at all."

"Don't be. It'll be over soon enough."

They both made an effort to keep their conversation light throughout the rest of the meal.

Evan noticed that no check was ever presented. She supposed that would be considered classless, too.

When the attendant came to ask if either of them cared for a dessert offering or a digestif, Julia politely declined.

"Is it possible to go for a stroll outside?" she asked. "It would be lovely to show Miss Reed the grounds and tour some of the other wonderful facilities here."

"You certainly may do that, Miss Donne. Would you like for me to arrange an escort for you?"

251

"Oh, that's not necessary." Julia smiled at him. "I know my way around."

"Of course." He bowed. "I'll have the valet meet you in the reception area with your coats. I hope you both enjoy the rest of your evening."

Julia watched him walk off before facing Evan.

"Okay," she said. "It's showtime."

Evan sedately got to her feet and walked around to Julia's side of the table to pull out her chair. After Julia stood, Evan offered her arm with exaggerated gallantry.

"No flies on you," Julia quipped.

They exited the dining room with all the practiced airs of regulars who belonged there.

Apparently, the rules governing social discourse at the Galileo Club were as varied and specific as the zones within the facility. Once they had begun to stroll through some of the seemingly endless verandas and pavilions that ringed the exterior of the building, Evan noticed that other like-minded guests who were perambulating outside began to nod and wave at them with great collegiality.

Evan was impressed by the grandeur of the club campus. The landscape design and exterior appointments were every bit as luxurious as the interior, but they, at least, seemed to pay homage to the club's Main Line heritage. Serpentine walkways lined with carved stone balustrades wove in and around manicured hedges and ponds the size of small lakes. It was more like strolling through a public park in Merion or Haverford than meandering around the grounds of a Center City club.

As they walked, Julia did a credible job of acquainting Evan with the location of various access points that should allow entry to areas where she could expect to find some of the club employees she hoped to chat up about Joey Mazzetta's appearance there on Friday night.

Evan finally got her chance to break free and duck into an

obliging doorway after a portly man and his blue-haired wife recognized Julia and stopped to renew acquaintance. Evan listened politely as Julia good-naturedly egged the couple on, inviting them to fill her in on the whereabouts of all *five* of their exceptional grandchildren. After getting the update on grandchild number one—some creature named Muffy, who was now a junior at Bryn Mawr—Evan politely interrupted to ask for directions to the nearest ladies' room.

The portly man pointed out a nearby door and rattled off a sequence of turns it would've taken a cartographer to keep up with. Evan thanked him profusely and promised Julia she'd return in short order. Julia gave her a quiet smile before returning her attention to Mrs. Portly, who was now rhapsodizing about grandchild number two, a young man who crewed at Vesper, one of the snobbiest clubs on Boathouse Row. The last thing Evan heard as she departed was that *this* was the lauded club where the Kellys rowed . . .

Once she was safely inside the building, Evan followed her nose. The kitchen was her target.

She knew they had wandered close to the building's loading dock, because Julia had pointed it out to her, just before they ran into the Portlys. Evan had speculated that this was probably the way Joey managed to get inside the building, since it would be the only area not supervised by regular club personnel. As they'd earlier tarried near the innocuous industrial entrance, Evan could make out a couple of food service and linen trucks parked behind a low stone wall separating the service area from the rest of the campus.

She knew the kitchen had to be close by. So instead of taking a left when she entered the building, she took a right and walked in the direction of the loading dock. She heard some voices and the rattle of what sounded like rolling carts, and when she rounded a corner, she saw several uniform-clad kitchen workers pushing trolleys loaded with dirty dishes toward a set of double doors.

They looked up with a bit of wariness when they saw her approaching.

"Hey, there," she said. "I'm Liz Bennet, with Sysco. We got reports there were some problems with condiments served here on Friday night. I've been trying to track down any of the bussers who might have been working that shift to help me find the culprits. The maître d' told me to come back here." She made a dramatic eye roll. "He said he was too busy to be bothered tonight."

The men seemed to relax a bit.

"That sounds like him," the taller of the two men said.

"You can follow us," the shorter guy said. "I'm pretty sure Jorge was working that shift. He's here tonight."

Evan followed the two men and their creaking trolley down a short passage that ended in the club kitchen. It was a pretty impressive affair. Chefs worked a line beneath large computer monitors and barked orders at under-chefs and kitchen associates who delivered sauces and other prepped components of final dishes. She caught a glimpse of coated attendants waiting outside a pass-through area, where completed and dressed plates were presented before being cloched for transportation to diners.

They passed that station and proceeded to another area of the kitchen where a hive of dishwashers and bussers worked in a frenzy to keep up. Evan hadn't paid much attention to how many people were dining with them, but she supposed it was fewer than fifteen or twenty other tables. She also supposed that on any given night, this place probably served meals in any number of private dining rooms, as well. There would be no way to anticipate how many of those might be engaged, or where Joey chose to make his guest appearance.

"Jorge?" The taller trolley guy called out to a much younger guy, who was busy unloading another cart of dirty dishes. "Ven aquí."

Jorge wiped his hands on his apron and walked over to where they stood.

"This lady needs to talk with you about Friday night, okay?" He proceeded to push his trolley along toward a queue of parked carts.

Jorge nodded at him and faced Evan.

"Okay," he said.

It was loud as hell in there. Evan didn't want to have to shout her questions.

"Look, is there any place we can go to talk that's quieter?" she asked him. "I promise it won't take more than just a minute or two—I know you're busy."

He looked nervously over at his station.

Tall guy spoke up. "It's okay. I've got this."

Jorge nodded at Evan, and led her into a pantry filled with shelves containing spices and other dry ingredients.

"I'm working for a couple of club members," Evan said. "People who were in the dining room the night the drunk man broke in and disrupted their evening. They're upset and don't think the management is doing enough to beef up security." She tipped her head to indicate the two guys who'd led her into the kitchen area. "They told me you were working on Friday night. Bussing tables. Is that right?"

"Yeah. I was there."

"Did you see what happened?"

He nodded. "Look, I need this job. I don't want to say anything that will get me fired, okay?"

"Nobody will know I talked with you," Evan assured him. "That's why I came in through the service entrance tonight. They don't even know I'm here, okay?"

"That's how he came in, too."

Evan perked up. "He?"

"The drunk dude. A couple of guys were out there unloading stuff to setup for some banquet Saturday morning. They said he walked right in off the platform and took off down the hall like he knew where he was going. They figured he was probably working for somebody, so . . ." He shrugged.

"But you saw him when he got to the dining room?"

"Yeah. I was bussing that night and just got back with an empty trolley. It was pretty busy in there, too. Fridays are always packed."

"Can you tell me what happened?"

255

Jorge made a face. "He went in through our service door, so nobody saw him. Any other way, he'd never get that far. He pushed right past me and Roger."

"What'd he do once he was in there?"

"He started yelling." Jorge blew out a breath. "All kinds of crap, too. Cursing. Knocking shit off tables."

"Was he just yelling in general, or was he yelling at somebody in particular?"

Jorge thought about it. "It seemed like he kept popping off about the same two people, so I guess he was looking for them."

"Did he use any names?" Jorge began to fidget a bit. He kept shifting his weight from foot to foot. Evan could tell he was getting antsy—probably about how long their conversation was lasting. She reached out a hand to reassure him. "I promise we're almost finished, okay? Just another minute and you can go back to work."

Jorge nodded. "I don't know any of the people who belong here," he said. "We're not allowed to talk to people in there, so I'm not sure who he was looking for. But he kept yelling shit about the same two people—Judge and Bishop." He shrugged. "I guess they might be members?" An idea occurred to him. "Are they who you're working for?"

"You're a bright guy, Jorge. Do you remember anything he said about Mr. Judge and Mr. Bishop?"

Jorge dropped his eyes. "It was pretty foul. Real nasty stuff."

"Such as?" Evan prompted.

Jorge shrugged.

"You can tell me," Evan encouraged. "I won't be offended."

"Okay." He looked at her. "He kept calling them a couple of lying cocksuckers and yelled something about collecting the rent. A lot of what he said was pretty hard to understand—he was really drunk. Club security got in there pretty fast and drug him out. Nobody talked about it after it was over." He shrugged. "That's the way things work here."

"Do you know if either of the men he was pissed at were in the dining room that night?"

256

"No. But like I said, I don't know any of the members. We're not allowed to talk to them."

"Right." Evan gave him a big smile and reached out to shake his hand. "That's just fine. Thank you, Jorge. You've been very helpful." She pressed a folded hundred-dollar bill into his hand.

He stared at Evan in surprise before taking the bill and stuffing it into his pocket. At the doorway to the pantry, he stopped and looked back at her before heading to his station. "Do you need help getting back out of here?"

"Is it okay to just go out the way I came in?" she asked. "My car is out there."

He nodded. Evan followed him back out into the kitchen.

"Hey," he asked before she left him, "did anything happen to that drunk guy?"

"Yeah," she said. "Something happened to him."

"I figured." Jorge scratched at his neck. "They don't like shit like that around here."

"No," Evan said. "I guess they don't."

Julia was tarrying by one of the reflecting pools when Evan found her. She looked lost in thought. Evan didn't have to wonder about what. The discoveries she'd made about her father and his trust had exploded in the middle of her world like a hand grenade.

It was either that, or she was comatose from listening to the annals of the Portly grandchildren . . .

Evan checked her watch. She'd been gone less than twenty minutes. It was barely 8 p.m. With luck, they could request Julia's car and be back at her townhouse in half an hour.

"Hi there." She touched Julia's elbow. "I hope I wasn't gone too long."

Julia leaned into her. "No. But I'm glad you're back."

"Me, too. Wanna blow this pop stand?"

"I thought you'd never ask."

Evan was relieved by her answer. "What's the quickest way outta here?"

257

Julia pointed to a distant bank of French doors. "Right through there. That sunroom is fairly close to where we had our cocktails."

"Our reverse martinis?" Evan teased.

"You seem pretty impressed with those."

"Impressed? Hell . . . that thing changed my life."

Julia smiled. Evan thought that was a hopeful response, so she decided to pursue the topic.

"I think you've been holding out on me. I have to wonder what other things you've got up your sleeve."

"I don't believe I'm wearing sleeves tonight." Julia's literal reply was tinged with irony.

Evan tugged at her velvet coat. "Not unless this counts."

"I suppose it could."

Evan considered Julia's sleeves. "I'm guessing you *could* artfully conceal a few things in there."

"Believe me," Julia said. "I gave up on hiding things from you a long time ago."

Evan offered her arm, and they started walking toward their entrance to the club.

"Did you get the information you needed?" Julia asked casually—probably in the event anyone passed by them close enough to over-hear their conversation. There were still several couples milling about.

"Yes. I met a most obliging fellow in the kitchen. He was very helpful."

"I'm eager to hear about it."

"No more eager than I am to get these shoes off."

Julia laughed. "I think they look charming."

"You would. They're Stevie's."

"You know," Julia pondered, "it does amuse me that your daughter is such a . . ." She paused in an apparent attempt to find the right word.

"Girl?" Evan offered.

"Well. That's not exactly where I was going with my observation. But . . . yes, that's also true."

"I don't get it, either. I blame the Cohens."

"You *always* blame the Cohens."

"I know, right?" Evan bumped into her playfully. "It's a great system."

"While I was waiting on you, I found myself pondering something."

Evan thought Julia had an easy baker's dozen of things to ponder tonight, and most of them were things she'd just learned about. "What's that?" she asked.

"My father's trust. I remember when I found out about it, not long after he died. I thought the name of it was curious but I just attributed it to his snobbish affectations. He never lost an opportunity to pontificate about the superiority of his 'classical education.' But now I think I understand the abhorrent significance behind his choice of the name, *Ganymede*."

Evan's curiosity had been mildly piqued by that mystery, too. But she wasn't yet prepared to tell Julia about her own discoveries about Lewis Donne—and the name of his trust didn't hold any particular meaning for her.

"It's an odd name," Evan suggested. "What does it mean?"

"It's from Greek mythology," Julia explained. "Ganymede was the boy who carried water for Zeus."

Evan stopped dead in her tracks and jerked Julia to a halt in the process.

"He *what?*"

"What is it?" Julia laid a hand on her arm. "Is this significant in some other way?"

"You might say that." Evan's mind raced at light speed. Miller had rambled about being punished after carrying water for . . . *someone*. She tried to remember what he'd said. It wasn't Zeus— it was another name. Something occurred to her.

"What's the Roman name for Zeus," she asked. "I can never remember that shit."

"Jupiter. And the Roman name for Ganymede is Aquarius."

"Oh, Jesus Christ." Evan directed Julia to a nearby bench and promptly sat down on it. "I need a minute."

259

"What is it?" Julia took a seat beside her. "Evan? You're scaring me."

"I'm sorry," Evan took hold of her hand. "It's something Miller said to me when I went to see him. He droned on and on about how he'd carried water for '*them*,' and how Jupiter punished him. I just thought he was nuts."

"You think he was talking about the club?"

"I do now. He was working this jigsaw puzzle—of the Homer painting, remember?"

Julia nodded.

"He kept calling the boys in the picture 'little stars.' And then he said something about Aquarius coming out when it's cold."

"*Ganymede*," Julia said. "Dear god . . . Evan? What were they doing? What was my *father* doing?"

Evan didn't answer her question. She didn't need to.

"I asked Miller if he meant Judge Cawley when he said Jupiter punished him," Evan continued. "But he just kept talking about Aquarius, and how Aquarius was the one who got punished."

"Zeus raped Ganymede. He fell in love with Ganymede's beauty and abducted him." Julia was speaking in a near monotone. Evan feared she might be going into shock. "After Ganymede served him as a cupbearer, Zeus turned him into a constellation." Julia met Evan's eyes. "Aquarius."

"I guess Miller wasn't crazy, after all. He was just communicating in the only language left to him."

"I want to leave now." Julia gripped Evan's hand like a vice. "I want out of this place."

"Me too." Evan stood up. "We're finished here."

Once they got inside, a black-coated steward assured them that Julia's car would be brought up in just a few moments. He apologized for the slight delay and told them the valet was delivering another car. They elected to wait outside on the steps for Julia's Audi to arrive.

The valet appeared shortly, delivering a silver Maybach. The big entrance door opened and a very well-dressed man emerged.

He was small in stature, with an expanding waistline and hair that matched the color of his car. He had a craggy, scarred face and appeared to be in his late seventies.

The valet held the driver-side door open for him. "Here you are, Ambassador. I hope you enjoyed your evening."

The man grunted at him and tilted his head at the steps. "She'll be right along."

The valet nodded and rushed around to open the passenger-side door to the large car.

When the door to the club opened a second time, Evan's jaw dropped.

A striking woman wearing a flame-colored satin halter dress and pointed-toe pumps stepped out. She was exotic: tall and elegant, with olive-toned skin and jet-black hair. She looked like a perfect synthesis of wealth and privilege.

She also looked lethal as hell . . .

She should. *She was Maya fucking Jindal.*

Evan cursed the damn stars that had brought them all there on the same night.

When Maya saw Evan gaping at her, she changed direction and approached where they stood.

"Why hello, you two," she all but chanted. "Isn't this a lovely surprise?"

Julia didn't see the woman approach, but she seemed to recognize the British accent right away. She whirled to face Maya in horror. "What are *you* doing here?"

"Same thing as you, I'd imagine. Tell me," she lowered her voice. "How was your chateaubriand?"

Julia seemed to recover her composure. "I'll assume we have you to thank for the lovely Pauillac?"

"Did you enjoy it?" Maya asked. "I do love a nice Bordeaux. They're always so reliable. Don't you find that to be true, Julia?"

"I tend to reserve rankings of reliability for people, not beverages."

"Dear Julia. You always were such a stickler." Maya regarded Evan. "Tell me," she laid a manicured hand on Evan's arm. "How is that shoulder? Bother you much now that the weather has turned colder?"

Evan fought an impulse to smack her hand away. "I feel it from time to time."

Maya's grizzled escort for the evening tapped the melodious horn on his Maybach. Apparently, the ambassador wasn't used to being kept waiting.

"I'll be right with you, Edgar," Maya called out to him. "I'm just saying hello to some very old friends."

"Don't let us keep you." Evan took a step back so Maya would release her arm. "I'm sure Edgar is impatient to be enjoying the rest of the evening he paid for. I feel certain a woman with your—*moxie*—isn't easy to come by here in the provinces."

Maya didn't flinch. "You do enjoy your petty word games, don't you, Evan?"

"Whenever possible."

"It must be nice to have such a rich fantasy life." Maya shifted her gaze to Julia, and took her time looking her up and down. "I confess that I sometimes amuse myself by indulging in a few fantasies of my own. But then, our fantasies always pale in comparison to the real thing, don't they, Julia?"

Julia's blue eyes blazed and Evan had to grab her arm to stop her from slapping Maya.

"It's good to see that your memory serves you as well as mine does me. Let's do lunch, shall we?" She waved goodbye and began her descent toward the idling car. "I'll be in touch, Evan," she called out before climbing into the car.

Edgar pulled away as soon as the valet closed her door.

Evan and Julia looked at each other.

"That was fun," Evan said.

Julia's Audi pulled up and stopped precisely where the Maybach had been.

"Let's get the hell out of here," Julia muttered. "I need a shower."

Julia had to maneuver around an enormous town car when she made the turn into the alley behind her townhouse.

"What the hell is that doing parked there?" Evan asked.

"It's for me."

"For you?" Evan was confused. "What for?"

"I hired it earlier. It's taking me to the airport for my flight."

"To Paris?"

"Yes."

"You're leaving *tonight?*" Evan was incredulous.

Julia parked her car in its customary spot beside Evan's Forester. "Yes. At midnight."

Evan didn't know what to say.

Julia opened her door. "Would you come in with me while I change?"

"Do you want me to?" Evan wasn't sure about anything right then.

"Of course, I do. I think you should stay over here, too. Drive home in the morning."

"And leave Stevie alone?"

"I think you can trust her. Besides," Julia climbed out of the car, "she'll probably just spend the night on the phone with Desiree."

"Thanks for reminding me."

Evan got out and followed Julia into the house. Julia had a different handbag, a small valise, and a lightweight overcoat positioned near the door. Evan didn't know how she'd missed those items when she'd arrived earlier. She figured it was probably because she'd been so gaga about how gorgeous Julia looked.

"Why don't you get us something to drink?" Julia suggested. "I'm going to grab a quick shower and change my clothes, but I'll be fast."

"What about your ride?"

"He won't leave without me," Julia quipped. She gave Evan a quick kiss. "I'll text him before I hop in the shower." She kissed Evan again before heading to the bedroom.

Evan went to a cabinet in Julia's kitchen to retrieve a bottle of cognac and two small tumblers.

Maybe it'll help her sleep on the plane?

She splashed some of the cognac into the glasses and considered them, before deciding to give them each a more generous pour.

What the hell? It's not like I'm driving anyplace, either.

She sent Stevie a quick text message, telling her she'd be spending the night in the city, then proceeded to drink most of her cognac while she waited on Julia to reappear—which took exactly thirteen minutes. Julia had changed into a pair of slacks and a dark blue cashmere sweater that matched her eyes. Her hair was slightly damp, but still looked great.

"That had to be the fastest shower on record."

"I was highly motivated," Julia explained.

Evan handed her a tumbler. "You look more comfortable."

"I *feel* more comfortable. Why haven't you taken your shoes off yet?"

"I was just getting around to that."

"Let's go sit down for a few minutes." Julia led the way to the living room, where they took their customary places on the big sofa."

"How long will you be gone?" Evan asked.

"Not long. Overnight maybe? I haven't even packed a bag."

"*Overnight?* Julia . . . you're going to *Paris*, not Orlando."

"I know that. My mother isn't expecting me. I don't imagine this will be a protracted visit."

"So why right now? Why tonight?"

"Why *not* now? I see no reason to prolong this. It isn't like more time will change the facts or make things less true."

"But," Evan argued, "you must be *exhausted*."

"Sweetheart?" Julia rested her hand on Evan's knee. "Make your peace with this. I'm going. Tonight. Besides . . . it isn't like I'll sleep if I stay at home."

Evan covered Julia's hand with her own. "Okay."

"Is it okay? Really?"

Evan could tell that Julia needed for it to be okay—for both of their sakes. Evan could see that in her eyes.

"Yes." She leaned toward Julia to kiss her. Julia met her halfway.

When they parted, Julia scooted closer and rested her head on Evan's good shoulder.

"It's okay," Evan muttered into her hair. "Really."

Chapter Eleven

Julia's nonstop flight landed at Charles de Gualle Airport at 11 a.m. local time. She'd already arranged to have a private car pick her up outside the international terminal so she could drive directly to her mother's Saint-Germain-des-Prés apartment in Paris as soon as she cleared customs.

Julia had been surprised to realize that she'd actually managed to sleep on her lie-flat seat. She supposed that she'd nodded off someplace over the mid-Atlantic, about two hours into the flight. She woke up when the plane began its initial descent into de Gaulle. She was still bone tired, but relieved she wouldn't be a complete ghoul when she finally reached her mother's home.

She deliberated about whether or not to call her mother when she landed. What if she'd traveled all this way and her mother was not at home? It had been a reckless impulse just to jet off and show up this way, but she was determined to carry through with the plan once she'd set her mind to it. Besides, Katherine Donne was a creature of habit, and Julia knew her habits. She wouldn't be leaving the city until she traveled to Annecy to spend Christmas with Binkie and Albert.

After passing through customs without incident, Julia opted to compromise: she'd send her mother a text message to tell her she'd just arrived in Paris on business. Her mother would know the real reason for her sudden appearance soon enough.

When she exited the airport terminal and crossed over to the island where private cars were queued up, she spotted a placard bearing her name right away. The old-fashioned, hand-lettered sign stood out in stark contrast to the sea of iPads other drivers were displaying. For some reason, she found that comforting. It was a folksier and more genuine welcome than she could ever imagine getting from her mother.

The driver snapped to attention as she approached.

"Miss Donne?" he asked in nearly unaccented English.

"Yes. Thank you for your promptness."

He looked dismayed. "Your luggage?"

"No," Julia tried to dispel his concern. "*C'est bien*. I don't have any."

He appeared confused.

"I keep things at the apartment in Paris," she stated. "*J'ai d'autres choses.*"

"*Oui, Madame.*" He opened the car door on his Peugeot sedan for her. "Of course."

Julia settled into the luxurious backseat for the ride into Paris. With good luck and no traffic jams, they should make it to the 6th Arrondissement in about forty-five minutes.

She withdrew her quad-band travel phone from her bag so she could message her mother. Once her phone successfully connected, she received a barrage of alert tones informing her that she had new messages. Several of them were from Evan.

This absurdly large bed is pretty empty without you.

Julia smiled. That was followed by four more messages, sent at different times during the night. Apparently, Evan had spent some time awake, too.

I don't suppose you have any frozen waffles in this joint?

Hey there. You should be landing soon. I know it's a lot to ask, but could you let me know how you're doing? Just whenever you can? You know I'll worry. It's a thing.

One other thing. I know it doesn't feel like it from your vantage point right now, but I promise everything will get better. I promise. We'll survive this.

Oh. Forgot to add I love you.

Julia sat holding her phone with what she knew was a ridiculous smile on her face.

Evan was right. They *would* survive it all—and not just because they loved and supported each other, although that reality certainly sweetened the odds and made the inevitability of the process a lot more enjoyable. But it was more than that. They survived because surviving was what their species was programmed to do. It was how they were made—to keep going against any kind of odds or any set of obstacles thrown up in their paths by hostile environments. They'd keep going and persevering until old age, disease, or a stronger predator finally took them.

Yes. She would survive this. She knew that. What she didn't know was what shape that path to survival would take, or where it might lead her.

She wrote a quick message back to Evan.

Landed at 11 local time. Now in the car, headed for Paris. I'll take you out for waffles when I get home. I love you, too.

Before putting her phone away, she sent a second message— to her mother, this time—announcing her arrival and ETA. After that, she spent the remainder of this final leg of her journey watching the scenery along the A3 slowly dissolve into the outskirts of Paris.

By the time Evan got back to Chadds Ford on Tuesday morning, Stevie was all packed and ready for her stay with Dan and Kayla.

Evan was sad that she'd be gone for the next few days, but brightened up when she realized that Stevie had left a hefty portion of her cookies behind.

"What'd we do to earn these?" Evan asked.

"I felt bad about interrupting your reindeer games the other night. I figured you and Julia could make good use of them while you have the house to yourselves."

"Okay ... that's just kind of creepy."

"You think having sex with Julia is creepy?" Stevie asked.

"No. I think talking about it with *you* is creepy."

Stevie huffed. "I wasn't born yesterday, you know."

"Trust me. I know exactly when you were born. If you'll recall, I was there."

Stevie made a capital *W* with three fingers on her right hand. "What-*ever.*"

"I see you've learned the alphabet. It's good to know those tuition payments are being put to good use."

"Very funny, Mama Uno. Oh," she seemed to remember something. "Tim called. He left a message for you on the house phone."

"You didn't talk with him?"

"No. I was on the phone with Des, and didn't get to it in time."

"Okay," Evan said. "What time is your Dad getting here to pick you up?"

"He said around 3:30."

"I need a few minutes to talk with him when he gets here. Privately."

"You're not gonna make him throw a rod again, are you?" Stevie asked.

"I promise I'll try to behave."

"Cool." Stevie shifted gears. "Did you two have fun on your date last night? What'd Julia say about your outfit?"

"I think it was a hit," Evan said. "I gave you all the credit."

"I'd be flattered if I didn't know that you'd also give me all the credit if she said you looked like a dork."

"True. But then, Julia would never say that."

"Is she coming over here tonight?" Stevie asked expectantly. "So you can have your uninterrupted sex romp?"

"You don't really expect me to answer a question like that, do you?"

"No." Stevie sulked. "But I keep hoping."

"Well, the answer is *no,* just the same. Julia had to take a last-minute business trip. She'll be gone for a day or two."

Evan didn't see any reason to fill Stevie in on the reason for Julia's sudden trip to Paris. It probably wouldn't remain a secret for long, so she wanted to give Julia as much space and time as possible to figure things out. That went for her report to Dan, as well. She'd already opted to omit any details about Lewis Donne and his "charitable" trust. She'd share that information with Dan verbally, but not include it in her written report. He might balk at that, but Evan was determined to remain firm about her reasons for withholding it. Donne might've been involved with Cawley and Bishop Szymanski in what appeared to be an institutionalized pedophilia scheme. But even if that proved to be the case, Cawley's own sins would be sufficient to sink his nomination. However incriminating what Evan now suspected about Lewis Donne was, it remained uncorroborated. As of today, there was a lot of smoke—but no smoking gun.

At least, not yet . . .

Stevie disappeared to finish up her load of laundry, so Evan took advantage of the quiet to start compiling what she had for Dan. She knew he'd bitch about wanting the written report from her ASAP.

When she sat down at her desk, she listened to the voicemail message on the house phone from Tim.

"Hey, Evan. I had a pretty shocking conversation yesterday with a guy named Mark Atwood. We were teammates at St. Rita's. He now runs a bar in the Gayborhood and he was very open about Father Szymanski. He pretty much confirmed what we already knew. It sounds like there were more members at that private club involved than we realized. He also said some exotic woman approached him a couple weeks ago with a big cash offer to keep quiet—just like Joey. He didn't take it because he's already decided he's not coming forward with anything about what happened to him. He didn't name any names, either. But I think it's possible your guy was involved with what happened to him and the other kids from the team. I know you'll want to talk more about this. So, give me a call when you can, okay? We'll figure something out."

Damn it. What the hell was Tim doing still going around talking to these guys?

She dialed his number back. It rang four times before rolling to his voicemail.

Shit. Phone tag... She'd have to settle for leaving him a message. "Hey, Tim," she said to his machine. "It's me. I got your message. Why don't we meet for dinner tonight? Julia is out of town and Stevie is headed to Dan's for a few days, so I'm on my own. How about I come by the church and pick you up around six or so? We can grab something to eat and you can fill me in. Maybe I'll even take you out to that bourbon bar after dinner? That's if you can promise me you'll quit playing amateur detective. Call me back if this doesn't work for you; otherwise I'll see you at six."

She hung up and started outlining the information she had for Dan. The more she worked on compiling it, the more surreal the whole scenario seemed.

This is going to read like the plot of a Wes Craven movie.

She'd asked Ping to organize the information she'd gleaned from their raid of the PAC attorney's office and transmit it to her in electronic form. That material hadn't arrived yet, but Ping knew Evan was under the gun to turn everything over to Dan today or tomorrow, so she expected to get a Signal message from her with the attachments at any time.

Her cell phone beeped. She picked it up.

"New Signal message from Moxie."

Great. Can't wait to read this...

Hello, dear Evan. How lovely it was to see you and the sainted Julia last night. I suppose, since we've had the big reveal, there isn't much reason for me to keep my identity concealed any longer. My reasons for tarrying in your province (as you so charmingly called it) are all but concluded anyway, so I'll be moving along to greener pastures very soon. One last item of business I have to resolve does, coincidentally, touch upon something that concerns you. Your bumbling friend, "Father Dowling," does seem to have a propensity to stick his nose into areas it does not belong. A word of caution regarding this: if he persists, it will end badly for him. I can assure you that I am not the only party distressed by his recent conduct. I, however, am

271

only peripherally involved and have neither the time nor the inclination to school him about his continued interfer-ence. Alas—I cannot say the same for others who may be less well tempered. I am sure you take my meaning. Please do give my warmest regards to the lovely Julia. It's grati-fying to see that she has achieved a modicum of constancy where you are concerned. Brava for that accomplishment. Enjoy it while it lasts.

  —Affectionately, M.

Sonofabitch...

How could she have been stupid enough not to make this damn connection with Moxie from the outset? Even in those fleeting moments when she flirted with the idea, she'd dismissed it as impossible.

So why was Maya Jindal involved in this, and who the hell was she working for?

Marcus? Possibly.

But Dan denied that Marcus had any role in the Cawley matter.

And what had Maya been doing at the Galileo Club last night?

Evan wasn't naive enough to think it had been an accident. Maya didn't operate that way.

And now she was warning Evan that Tim was in the crosshairs. From whom? She said it wasn't from her—or her client. But somebody had tipped her off that Tim was in danger.

She found it hard to believe that Maya would be working to protect anyone. That wasn't her *métier*.

Tim said that Mark Atwood told him an "exotic" woman had tried to buy his silence—just like Joey Mazzetta. Well, "exotic" could be stamped on Maya Jindal's damn calling cards.

What a perfect cluster. She had no idea how to parse all of this out.

But she knew one thing for sure: she needed to rein Tim in, and fast.

She picked up the phone and called his number again. Same deal. Four rings. Voicemail.

"Tim? It's Evan. If you're there, pick up." She waited a few beats. "Listen. I really need to talk with you. Call me back ASAP about tonight. And don't make any other plans, okay? I'll see you at six."

She hung up.

Fuck. Fuck. Fuck.

She was tempted to grab her keys and head back into the city right now. She could catch up with Dan later. That prospect evaporated when she heard the nagging rumble and drag of Dan's Chrysler, groaning its way up her gravel driveway.

"Dad's here!" Stevie yelled.

Great, Evan thought. *A nice little ass-ripping is just what I need right now.*

She got up to meet him at the door.

Julia's mother was anything but cordial when she opened the door to her extravagant Left Bank digs and saw her haggard-looking daughter standing there.

"Where are your bags?" her mother demanded.

"It's wonderful to see you, too, Mother. May I come inside?"

Her mother stepped back to allow Julia to enter. Julia was impressed by how unchanged the apartment was. She hadn't been there in more than two years, not since before Andy's murder. Her parents had flown to the States to attend the private funeral service for Andy in Delaware. They stayed on in Philadelphia at the Delancey Place townhouse for several days, but Julia saw very little of them. If they minded, they didn't bother to express it. She now assumed that her father had used the trip back as an excuse to renew acquaintance at his club.

The thought sickened her.

That visit had been the last time Julia would see her father before his death, seven months later.

Her mother was now striding about the room in a clear display of agitation, absently straightening things that didn't require adjustment. Julia had noticed when she arrived that her mother appeared to be dressed for going out—impeccably attired, as was her custom. That wasn't uncommon. She doubted that Katherine Donne took *any* meals in her apartment, although its kitchen was impressively equipped with every culinary requisite.

Evan would love it. *Even though it had a dearth of cast-iron pots.* Katherine Hires Donne was the author of Julia's disdain for unrefined cookware.

"I fail to see why it was impossible for you to let me know your plans." Her mother continued to catalog her expressions of umbrage. "I could have been away overnight. As it is, I'm already committed for the evening." She slammed the lid of an ornate cigarette case shut with so much energy, it made the water inside a crystal vase full of white Peruvian lilies pitch and roll in protest.

Apparently, everyone in France still smoked.

"I apologize for that, Mother." Julia dropped into a chair without waiting to be invited to sit.

"Just showing up like this is most inconsiderate of you, Julia. And your appearance is frightful. You look so . . . *unkempt*."

"Mother, I just spent eight hours on an airplane and another three quarters of an hour in a car getting here. Do you think it's possible we might try and at least feign civility for a few minutes before lapsing into recriminations and discussions of appropriate fashion?"

Her mother glared at her for a few moments before sitting down on a love seat that sat opposite Julia's chair.

"What do you want from me?"

It was an odd question, considering the reason behind Julia's visit—an almost prescient one. At least her mother's voice was . . . not exactly *kinder*, but lacking its initial tone of haughtiness.

"I need to talk with you," Julia said, simply.

"You flew over here in the middle of the night—without telling me you were coming—because you wanted to *talk* with me?" Her mother plucked at a nonexistent speck of lint on the empty cushion beside her. "I have a telephone. You sent me a message not thirty minutes ago, so I am able to deduce that you still know the number."

"You always were a quick study, Mother."

Katherine Donne actually started to smile, but managed to rein it in at the last moment.

"If you're here to discuss business, I already made it clear that I have no interest in that."

"It's not business," Julia corrected her. "At least, not publishing business." Julia didn't bother to share with her mother that some of her plans actually *would* have a significant impact on the family business. That could all come later—depending, in large part, upon the outcome of this visit.

"What is it, then?"

Julia could detect a tinge of wariness in her mother's question. She resolved to allay the suspicion that lurked behind her mother's query. "I'm not here to discuss my relationship with Evan Reed, either."

Her mother seemed to relax. *A little.*

"Why are you here, Julia?" She asked in a softer tone.

Julia realized this was as close to empathetic as her mother could get. It reminded her of her mother's first question when she'd heard the shocking news about Andy's death: "But, what will you do?" Even in the throes of her own jumbled haze of shock and confusion, Julia noticed that her mother's initial response wasn't to ask, "How are you?"

There was no reason to put off their conversation. But Julia thought it might go better if they at least engaged in some kind of convivial activity. Something that might help level the emotional playing field and hint at memories of a shared past. Good memories.

"Could we make some tea?" She asked. "Some of grandmother's Earl Grey?"

The exotic, bergamot-scented tea was the first one Julia had ever tasted. On her sixth birthday, her mother and grandmother, both wearing hats and white gloves, had taken her for her first afternoon tea at the Crystal Tea Room in Wanamaker's Department Store. Julia recalled sitting very stiffly on her chair and the struggle she had had to imitate her hostesses, who seemed to have no difficulty manipulating the small cakes and fig sandwiches with their gloved fingers. Julia marveled at the delicate French china teacups, ornamented with pink asters and gold-trimmed ribbon handles. That had been one of the happiest memories of her childhood. She recalled the easy conversation between her mother and grandmother—how they talked about the right time to set gladiolus bulbs in their flower gardens, and predictions that spring weather would arrive earlier than forecast.

Julia carried those memories with her. And ever since, especially during times of uncertainty or discord, she had taken respite in the sweet simplicity and civility that were always delivered inside a cup of hot tea.

Her mother didn't question her request. Julia took that as a hopeful sign as the two of them made their silent way to Katherine Donne's small but well-appointed kitchen. The single window in this room faced west, and afforded a view of the sixth-century Benedictine abbey.

Julia set the kettle to boil on the blue-enameled La Cornue range. She recalled when her parents bought the coveted apartment on Saint-Germain-des-Prés, and promptly began upfitting everything in it. Julia had visited Paris to tour their new home, and she remembered how the kitchen designer had rhapsodized to her mother about how the range's electric oven could "bake a more stable and precise chamomile cake" than any other designer range in its class. Julia's father had scoffed and remarked that for €49,000, it should do the dishes, too. Julia's mother had simply blinked at the overzealous designer and asked if the range were available in blue.

While they waited for the water to heat, Julia's mother opened a mahogany tea box and set about scooping a generous portion of the fragrant leaves into an old china pot that had been in the family for generations.

Julia retrieved two porcelain cups from a china closet and took a seat at the small kitchen table. Her mother carried a pitcher over to her dark blue Smeg and filled it from a container of cream, before joining her at the table. She made no comment about why Julia chose to sit there instead of returning to the living room.

The companionable quiet they shared was a welcome change from the terseness of their interactions when Julia had first arrived. It was so easy and unaffected that Julia hated to shatter it with her questions. But there was little benefit to be gained by putting off the inevitable.

Once they both held their steaming cups of Earl Grey, Julia steeled her determination and opened the discussion.

"How much did you know about Dad's trust when he established it?"

Her mother seemed unfazed by the question. "He told me about it, of course. He wanted to have control over where some of his assets went."

"Did you know any details about its specific provisions?"

"Not really. As I told you, I never had an active role in business decisions."

"But this wasn't about business, Mother. It was about Dad's desire to fund . . . things that mattered to him personally. Did he ever share any information with you about those? Or ask for your input?"

"No. But I don't find that unusual. Apparently you do, so would you like to share your reasons for asking these questions?"

Julia chose her words carefully. She knew her mother had instincts like a wild animal, and would flee at the first hint of anything that threatened the stability of her environment.

"I spent some time with the estate attorney on Monday, reviewing the specifics of some of the trust beneficiaries. There were some things I found . . . *confusing*. I wanted to share them with you, to see if you could shed any light on what his motivation might have been for some of these."

Her mother picked up on one detail of Julia's explanation. "Did you say you reviewed the documents on *Monday?* As in the day before yesterday?"

Julia nodded.

"And what you discovered concerned you enough that you flew to Paris to see me? Immediately and without warning?"

"I suppose so."

"You *suppose* so?" her mother asked somewhat pointedly.

"Yes," Julia admitted. "What I found concerned me a great deal—enough to know that I needed to talk with you about it. And that is why I'm here."

"Why the urgency? Surely, there can have been nothing in your father's estate plan that warranted such an extreme response."

This was getting her nowhere. She needed just to come out with it.

"Mother, did you know that a significant portion of Dad's trust—the lion's share, actually—is committed to support certain . . ." She searched for the right word—something innocuous enough not to alienate or antagonize her mother. "*Projects.* Projects confined to a small circle at his club?" Her use of the benign word to describe a horrifying and contemptible practice sickened her.

"No. I was unaware of that. But I see nothing untoward in it. Your father was devoted to his club. As you know, his work allowed him little enough time to develop or nurture other interests."

Dear god . . . "other" interests?

"There were some other peculiarities, as well," Julia added. "It appeared that Dad sometimes used the fund to pay for . . . expenses— sometimes in large amounts of cash—to . . ." She hesitated. "Men. Young men."

Julia's mother abruptly pushed back her chair and got to her feet. "I will not listen to this."

"Mother . . ."

"*No.* I understand what you're trying to suggest and it's . . . *repugnant.*"

"I'm not trying to 'suggest' anything, Mother. I am asking you if you knew anything about these payments. I'm trying to find a context for these disbursements that makes *sense.*"

Her mother walked to the sink with her teacup and emptied it. She faced Julia with an icy expression.

"There *is* no context for it that makes sense, and you understand that as well as I."

"But . . ."

"But, nothing. I discovered your father's illicit, private . . . *tendencies* years ago—when you were just a baby. The discovery was devastating to me. I had little choice but to do what I had to do to save my reputation—*and yours*—and spare us both the ruinous effects of a heinous disclosure. I never allowed myself to think about any of those behaviors, or about the time he spent indulging himself at his precious club—and I refuse to do so now, just to satisfy your prurient curiosity."

"*Prurient curiosity?*" Julia's temper flared. "How dare you suggest that I might derive some kind of twisted pleasure from this discovery?"

"Why should I think otherwise, based on your recent revelations about your own proclivities?"

Proclivities? Julia was outraged. "How can you possibly equate my honest avowal of my sexual orientation—*or anyone's*—with pedophilia? That is an ignorant and offensive comparison with no basis in fact."

Julia's mother had regained some of her composure, but her frozen countenance did not change.

"You sound as if you've researched the topic. If so, then perhaps you'll discover, like I did, that it's preferable to look the other way. My advice is to let the dead lie buried, Julia. What he did has no bearing on our lives."

"How can you say that? How can you *believe* that? Especially if you *knew* what he was doing all those years?" Julia was staggered by this callous expression of her mother's dismissive attitude toward her husband's horrific behavior. It was equally disgusting that her mother admitted to adopting a tacit indulgence of it because it mattered more to her to preserve her life of privilege.

But Katherine Donne had had enough of their conversation. She held up a hand to halt Julia's tirade.

"I am finished with this discussion, Julia. I will listen to no more of this. You are welcome to rest or shower or do whatever you wish while you remain here. I am going out." She left the kitchen.

Julia stood up belatedly and followed her mother into the living room.

"Where are you going?" she asked.

"*Out.* I honestly do not care where." Her mother withdrew a heather-colored Lolë jacket from her foyer closet, and retrieved her handbag from a shelf. "I have dinner plans tonight. Do not expect me back here before ten." She strode to the front door, and exited the apartment without looking back.

Julia stared dumbly at the back of the carved, French colonial door until the sonorous ding of the elevator bell brought her back to reality.

She sank onto the arm of a chair.

Now what?

Tim called Evan back a few minutes before he had to head over to the church to hear confession. Her phone rolled to voicemail so he left her details about connecting in Center City for dinner, instead of meeting up at St. Rita's:

"Hey, Evan. It's me. Tonight works fine, but you'll need to meet me at the DoubleTree on South Broad Street. I got a call from another former basketball team member, Mike Duffy. I don't think you knew him, but he was only at St. Rita's a little while. He lives in Phoenix now but is back in town on business. He says he saw Mark Atwood after I was there. He wants to talk with me about Father Szymanski, so I'm meeting him at the hotel at 6. We'll be in the lobby bar if you get there early, or I can text you when we finish up. I'm on my way to hear confession right now, so I'll be offline for a while. Catch up with you in a bit."

By the time Tim got back to his quarters, he was already on the cusp of running late for his meeting with Mike Duffy. He hadn't been scheduled to perform the sacrament today, but Father Langley was sick with a sore throat, and the parish priest, Father Joseph, had asked Tim to take his place. It was just Tim's luck that there was a larger than usual turnout.

He thought old Mrs. Magill would never finish . . .

She was legendary at the parish. They all joked about how she used the confessional as her primary social outlet. It was poignant and irksome all at the same time.

He changed out of his vestments as quickly as possible and was on his way out the door when he noticed the message light blinking on his phone. He deliberated about whether or not to take the time to listen to it. He checked his watch. *Damn.* With traffic, he'd be doing good to make it to the hotel on time. He knew he couldn't call Mike, and he didn't want to leave him stranded for too long, waiting in the parking garage.

He decided he'd check the message later, after he got home.

As predicted, Dan had been pissed at Evan's reluctance to include everything she'd discovered about the Galileo Club in her report.

"Why the fuck not?" he demanded. "It's not up to you to decide what's relevant and what isn't. You just need to report the facts."

"That's what I've been trying to tell you for the last half hour," Evan asserted. "The rest of this—the stuff about other club members—is *supposition*, not fact. None of it is corroborated yet."

"So what?"

"Whattaya mean, 'so what'? Aren't you the one who told me not to bring you anything you couldn't take to court?"

Dan looked up from the pages of notes from Ping. "Not when it's this fucking salacious."

"Since when is the creep factor a gauge of what is and isn't admissible?" Evan huffed.

"Since it started including the names of assholes who have been personally financing regressive political agendas in this country for a goddamn quarter century. That's when."

"I will not let you use this, Dan. Not now."

"Not *now?*" he repeated her caveat. "Why not now?"

"Because there are certain to be a lot of innocent people who will be tainted by all of this. We don't have all the facts yet."

"Who are you protecting?"

"No one."

"Bullshit. I know you." Dan looked over the pages from Ping more carefully.

Evan gave up. It had been insanity to think she'd ever be able to stonewall him.

"Julia's father," she said without preamble.

He looked up at her. "What?"

"Julia's father, Lewis Donne. He was one of Cawley's cronies at the club—along with the bishop and a few other blue-blooded scions of the city."

"Jesus H. Christ, Evan."

"Tell me about it." She nodded miserably.

"How the fuck did you find out about that?"

Evan opened her mouth to explain about their second-story work on Sunday night, but Dan held up a hand to stop her. "Never mind . . . I don't wanna know."

"Wise decision," she said.

He sat down. "How much time do you need?"

"I don't know." Evan shrugged. "A week maybe? Julia is in Paris right now, talking with her mother."

"Julia *knows* about this?" Dan was incredulous.

"Yeah. She found out on her own."

"How?"

"She was the one who identified her father—and the Galileo Club—in the photo you got from Marcus, the one with Cawley and Miller."

Dan raised an eyebrow. "I never said that picture came from Marcus."

"Seriously?"

"Yeah, okay. So what if it did come from him?"

"Dan. He had a reason to give that to you. And it wasn't philanthropic."

"Why do you think he sent it to us?"

282

"Precisely so I would do what I did: dive down a useless rabbit hole and waste most of a week trying to track it down. He knew exactly what he was doing. He was buying time for Cawley."

"Cawley? Why the fuck would Marcus want to help Cawley?"

"Jesus, Dan." Evan's frustration began to overflow. "Why the hell do you keep wearing blinders around him? Remember the Miller campaign? Didn't that teach you anything about this scumbag's moral compass? Marcus will help anybody who pays him enough. I'll give you one guess who that might be."

"Who?"

"Take your pick." Evan handed him the list of names attached to the Citizens for Integrity in Government PAC. "But if we're taking bets, my money is on Cawley."

"Fuck." Dan lowered the list to his knee.

"Everything I found is in the report I'll be sending you this afternoon. Take my word for it, Dan—Miller was murdered to protect Cawley. And so was Joey Mazzetta."

"Mazzetta? What did Mazzetta's death have to do with Cawley?"

"Joey was one of the boys on the St. Rita's basketball team who the bishop and his cronies at Cawley's club preyed on. He was going to meet Tim the night he was killed—to spill his guts about all of it. But first, he made a side trip to the Galileo Club. He was dead drunk, but he managed to sneak in through a service entrance. He made his way to one of the club's dining room and made a hell of a scene, sounding off about Cawley and the bishop in front of everyone who was there—and it was a Friday night, so the place was teeming with people. Joey said to tell the bishop and the judge he was there to 'collect the rent.' Club security tossed him out and the police responded. But guess what?"

"They never pressed charges?"

"Bingo. Joey ended up dead an hour later. Killed by a bullet fired from a Tokarev 7.62." She let that sink in. "Ring any bells?"

"Should it?" Dan asked.

"Yeah. It's Maya's weapon of choice—the same one she used to kill Andy Townsend."

"Maya *Jindal?*"

"The one and only," Evan said. "And here's another little happy coincidence for you. Julia and I ran into her last night, when we were scoping out the Galileo Club. And this morning, she sent me a Signal message outing herself as my little pen pal, Moxie."

Evan couldn't remember a time when Dan was quiet for so long.

Finally, he got to his feet.

"Send me your report," he said. "It sounds like you've got enough to derail Cawley's nomination—at least long enough to give Julia the time she needs to figure out her plan for managing the fallout about her father."

"Okay." Evan nodded. "Thanks, Dan."

"Don't thank me," he said. "I'm sorry I got you into this mess."

"There was no way for you to know what we'd uncover."

"Yeah," he said morosely. "But that doesn't make the stench of it any easier to bear."

"No. It doesn't."

"Come on." He put an arm around her shoulders. "Let's go see if that kid of ours is ready to go."

She leaned into him, and they left her office to go find Stevie.

Evan was exiting I-95 onto South Columbus Boulevard, driving as fast as she could without risking an accident.

Come on, Tim. Pick up. Pick up.

She'd been calling his cell phone repeatedly since finding his voicemail message after Dan left.

No dice. He'd obviously already left to head to the DoubleTree. He'd called her back while she was walking Dan and Stevie out. As soon as she got back inside and listened to his message, she did a quick LexisNexis search on "Mike Duffy, Phoenix." There were only four hits, and three of those she was able to eliminate immediately because of their ages. The fourth, Michael Joseph Duffy, was age appropriate and had lived briefly in Philadelphia in the '90s, but he was deceased. Evan found his obituary listed at the site of the Whitney & Murphy Funeral Home in Phoenix. Mike Duffy had been active in the St. Catherine of Siena Roman Catholic Church, and was survived by his wife, Gloria, three children and four siblings. The family requested that memorial contributions be made to the Fight Colorectal Cancer Fund and Solace Hospice of Maricopa County.

Son of a bitch.

Maya's warning was right. This meeting was a setup, and Tim was on his way to an ambush.

She thought about calling J.C. Ortiz. But what could she tell him? It would take more time than she had to convince him about why she was persuaded that Tim was in danger.

No. All she could do was get to the DoubleTree as fast as possible and pray she could head Tim off before he went inside.

She tried Tim's phone again. *No dice.*

Shit.

She knew he had his phone turned off. He *always* did when he was driving. He was such a damn stickler for driving safely— a nerdy godsend when it came to his patience teaching Stevie the rules of the road, but a total pain in the ass right now.

The exit for Washington Street was right ahead. Then it was a straight shot to South Broad and the entrance to the Double-Tree. Evan checked the clock on her dash. 5:58 p.m.

Maybe he's only just getting there? He'd hit worse traffic getting up here from St. Rita's. Maybe I can still catch him before he goes inside . . .

She floored it to make the next two intersections before the lights changed, and took the turn onto South Broad Street on two wheels.

Jesus, if I don't lose my fucking license it's gonna be a miracle.

She turned into the entrance to the DoubleTree Parking garage and stopped to grab a ticket from the automated kiosk. The Standing O bar was located in the lobby, so she needed to grab the first parking space she could find.

Level One was a write-off. There was nothing.

Level Two wasn't looking much better and she'd just about

determined to ditch her car and damn the consequences. Then she saw Tim's Subaru, parked in a space near the entrance to the elevators.

Fuck.

That had to mean he was already inside . . . or wherever else the bogus Mike Duffy chose to take him.

She parked her car behind his and prepared to head inside.

That's when she heard the gunshot and saw the back window of a nearby SUV explode.

Jesus Christ!

She threw open her door and stood up on the rocker panel. Then she saw him. Tim was running like hell, ducking in and out between cars, heading for the exit ramp. There was another man chasing him—and he was gaining fast. Evan reflexively laid on her horn—then started shouting at the top of her lungs.

"Hey? Asshole? Over here you worthless piece of shit!" She blew the horn again. "That's right—I see you! Come and get me, fuck stick!"

Her taunts worked. The man stopped and looked right at her. Evan dropped down behind her car door as he fired again. The bullet hit a support column directly behind her car.

"Tim!" She yelled from her crouch. "Hit the deck! Stay down!"

She stayed low and crept away from her car, trying to work her way around behind the gunman by weaving in and around parked vehicles. When she thought she could, she risked taking a peek at him. He was scanning the area where she'd been and was slowly backing his way toward her still-running car.

He was only about thirty feet away from her now.

Evan ducked down again. *Shit. I need something—anything— to hit him with.* She inched backward to move farther away, but her foot connected with an empty Diet Coke can and sent it clattering.

Shit. He had her now.

He shifted direction and headed straight for her.

"Come on out, Reed," he yelled. "Lemme see your pretty face before I fucking waste you."

Okay . . . this guy was a talker. Maybe she could leverage that?

It was worth the risk. She slowly stood up with her hands held high in the air.

"I think it would be rude for you to kill me before introducing yourself." She said. "Don't you?"

He actually laughed. "Pleased to meet you," he said, as he trained his weapon on her. "You can call me Billy."

What happened next was a blur. Evan saw a swirling flash of bright red, and suddenly Billy was lying flat on his back in a puddle of motor oil.

Evan's jaw dropped.

Someone else had joined their party . . .

Maya Jindal was bending over Billy's unconscious body, retrieving his firearm . . . *her* firearm, no doubt. This, of course, was after she'd appeared out of no-*fucking*-where and nailed Billy with a perfectly placed roundhouse kick.

"Oh, my," she cooed at him, waving her Tokarev back and forth in front of his unseeing eyes. "What a bad boy you've been, playing with Maya's gun. Marcus should've known better than to give you such a grown-up toy. Pity you have to find out the hard way how dangerous these old relics can be."

Evan walked toward them.

"Why, hello." Maya straightened up and faced her. "We do seem fated to keep running into each other, don't we?"

"What the hell are *you* doing here?"

"Now, is that any way to express gratitude? I did just save your life—*again.*"

"I'll be sure to add your name to my Christmas card list."

"Dear Evangeline. I do seem to keep cleaning up your messes, don't I?"

"Don't feel you have to do me any favors."

"Oh, the pleasure is all mine. Unfortunately, it seems this cretin just broke my heel with his face."

Maya calmly trained her gun on Billy, and shot him between the eyes.

Evan lurched backward and stared, stupefied, as Maya bent

down and methodically set about relieving Billy of his wallet and car keys.

"You *killed* him," Evan muttered. "You just fucking *killed* him."

"What a bright girl you are." Maya got to her feet. "Oh, look," she made an oblique gesture with Billy's wallet, "here comes Father Dowling."

Evan looked over her shoulder to see Tim running toward them. When he reached them and saw the dead man, he dropped to his knees.

"What . . ." he panted. "What . . . *happened?*"

"She shot him," Evan said, simply. There was no reason to belabor the point.

Tim looked anxiously up at Maya, then back at Billy. He swayed for a moment, but managed to remain upright. Then he crawled over to Billy, took hold of his hand, and began to pray. "May you rest in the arms of the Lord who formed you from the dust of the earth . . ."

Maya gave Evan a quizzical look. "Whatever is he doing?"

"Praying."

"How very singular. Well. As much as I'd love to stay and watch this fascinating demonstration, I have another small errand to take care of. And thanks to dear Billy, I now have to go and change my shoes."

She removed her heels with practiced ease, as if she were standing near a rack in Ferragamo's, instead of beside the body of a dead man in a parking garage.

"Gotta dash now, Evangeline." She cut her eyes at Tim. "I suggest you two do likewise."

"Trust me," Evan told her. "It's next up on the itinerary."

Maya gave Evan a coquettish smile, followed by a royal wave. "Tutty byes."

She walked briskly away. Seconds later, Evan heard a car start, followed by the screech of tires as she left the parking garage.

Evan knew they only had seconds to follow suit. She stepped closer to Tim and laid a hand on his shoulder.

"Tim. C'mon. We have to go . . . *now.*"

He continued to pray. "May Christ who was crucified for you, bring you freedom and peace."

"Tim? I'm not *kidding*, man. I need you to do the expedited version of this. We gotta go. *Now.*"

Tim still didn't budge. It was clear he was going to finish his errand.

Evan's frustration reached apocalyptic proportions. "I don't know why the fuck you ever doubted whether or not you should stay a priest. If *this* doesn't answer that question for you, nothing ever fucking will. *Now come on!*"

"May Christ who died for you admit you into his garden of paradise." Tim made the sign of the cross and struggled to his feet. His face was ashen.

Evan took hold of his arm and hauled him over to her Forester, which was still running.

"Get in," she commanded.

Once she had him safely stowed, she hurried around to climb into the driver's seat.

They'd be able to return and retrieve his car any time. Right then, what they needed was to put some fast distance between them and what remained of "Billy."

The exit kiosk was unattended when they approached it. To avoid having a time stamp applied to her parking ticket, Evan crashed through some blaze orange cones that blocked off a service vehicle lane and turned out of the garage onto South Broad Street, and made a beeline for The Twisted Tail.

She knew Tim wouldn't be going back to St. Rita's that night.

The other thing she knew with certainty was that they both needed some time, some space, and some goddamn good bourbon before making the fifty-minute drive back to Chadds Ford.

Julia embraced one of her mother's parting suggestions, and took a shower.

She stood beneath the spray until the hot water scalded her

skin. Only when she couldn't stand the heat any longer did she turn the taps off and remain riveted in place until the steam evaporated and her body grew cold. That was when she stepped from the shower, wrapped herself in several thick towels, and curled up on the bed in her mother's guest room until her shivering stopped.

The experiment worked.

She'd needed to feel something. *Anything.* Just to know she was alive, and could still recognize the difference between pain and pleasure.

There was nothing left for her in Paris. There was nothing left for her at all—not in this apartment, not at her grandmother's house in Philadelphia, not at Donne & Hale, and not anywhere else connected to this part of her life or history.

Her mother had made the choice clear for her. It was uncomplicated. There were no variables. There were no avenues for negotiation. No compromises. It was binary. Black and white. One and done.

No . . . one and undone.

Julia understood it all now. It was why she had come here, after all. To learn where the parameters lay that divided love and truth from fealty to self-interest.

It was shocking how simple it had been. With a few declarative sentences, her mother had managed to lay waste to all of Julia's carefully crafted paradigms for the ways they could persevere, could recover, could go forward and salvage something from the carnage that would soon overtake their lives.

That had already claimed hers . . .

There was a kind of giddy release that came with acknowledging the epic scope of her failure.

Julia felt like a character from a Charles Dickens novel.

She was Miss Flite, the half-delusional, faded spinster in *Bleak House,* who wasted her life awaiting judgment in the Court of Chancery. After scores of years, when her verdict was finally returned, Miss Flite released her captive birds from their cages— the same creatures that had been her constant companions and spiritual guardians. Julia had memorized all of their names: Hope, Joy, Youth, Peace, Rest, Life, Dust, Ashes, Waste, Want, Ruin, Despair, Madness, Death, Cunning, Folly, Words, Wigs, Rags, Sheepskin, Plunder, Precedent, Jargon, Gammon, and Spinach.

Judgment had at last arrived for Julia, too—and the time had come to set her own disappointed hopes free.

She dressed and wandered aimlessly through the apartment, looking for anything familiar.

There wasn't much to find.

L'Étranger. She had become the stranger.

She hesitated at the doorway to her father's study—the one room that had always been his private sanctum—whether located here, or in any other of their houses.

She crossed the threshold into the immaculate space. It was clear that her mother kept it up exactly as it had been. The shelves that lined two walls were filled with books. Reference books. Histories. Biographies. The Classics. There was even an entire section devoted to books published by Donne & Hale—all of them from his era, or that of his father, or his father's father. *None from hers.*

She wasn't surprised by the omission.

He had an elaborate desk covered with a leather blotter and a vintage brass lamp with a black shade. There was a caddy containing the routine things a businessman would need: a letter opener, a small stapler, paper clips, a book of postage stamps. Julia picked those up. They featured tiny portraits of Catherine De Médici.

Strangely appropriate . . .

Her father also had a small box containing sticks of blue sealing wax and a heavy brass embosser with his monogram, JLD. The thing had a soft patina. It had seen a lot of use.

She gazed down at his chair. It occurred to her that she'd never dared to sit on it—not this one, and not any of the chairs at his offices in New York or in Philadelphia—not even after he'd retired, and she took over the firm.

She had no desire to sit in it now, either.

Instead, she chose a wing chair upholstered in dark green leather that sat in the corner of the room, near a floor-to-ceiling window overlooking the Seine. There were some books stacked on a low table beside the chair. The top volume had a bookmark in it. She picked it up. *The Decameron.* She returned it to the stack, regretting her impulse to look at it.

It would remain unfinished. Evidence of a life interrupted.

The room was quiet, except for the subtle click, click, click of a Limoges porcelain clock sitting atop a Louis XIV chest near the door. Julia watched its second hand make its slow but measured progress around the painted numbers. She watched it for a long time.

There were several paintings in the room, all perfectly displayed on the boiserie-paneled walls. Most could have been exact replicas of the artwork they saw on display last night in the dining room at his club. *Hunting scenes.* She found his taste for those odd, since, as far as she knew, her father had never hunted for anything—except upstart smaller presses that he could gobble up and make disappear.

There was another painting, only partly visible behind the carved door that led to his bedroom. The edge of its gilded frame flashed in the sunlight streaming in from a nearby window.

Julia didn't recall that painting, probably because the door to his bedroom was rarely open.

Her curiosity was piqued. She crossed the room and inspected it. What she saw when she closed the door stopped her heart.

The painting was a smaller version of "Snap the Whip."

She reached out with shaking fingers to touch the canvas. It was authentic. She was certain of it. Homer had signed and dated it "1872."

Homer painted quite a few of these as studies, Evan had said. There were many practice paintings, but only one original—*the original that had been on display at the Galileo Club.*

"Little stars," she quoted.

She ran her fingers across the faces of the boys in the painting.

On impulse, she took hold of the frame and lowered the painting so she could inspect its back for any telltale gallery markings or inventory data that might suggest where her father had acquired it. She was surprised to discover a fat, booklet-sized envelope attached to the back of the frame with clips.

What on earth?

She carefully detached the envelope and propped the painting against the wall, then held the envelope for a few moments without opening it. It was thick. Heavy. It was clear that it contained many sheets of paper or folded documents.

She began to feel wary.

Maybe she shouldn't open it?

It had been hidden for a reason. Wasn't this trespassing? What if it contained things that belonged to her mother? Secret things? *Letters from a lover?* Things she wouldn't want Julia to know about.

Things Julia *didn't want to know about . . .*

What right did she have to look inside?

She looked down at the painting again.

Little stars . . .

She returned to her chair and sat down with the envelope on her lap. She opened its flap and withdrew a thick stack of . . . *photographs*—scores of them in various sizes and orientations. They were starkly lighted, graphic images—all in black and white. Julia began flipping through them robotically before her tired mind could process the horror of what she was seeing.

Once it did, she recoiled from the photographs in revulsion. They fluttered to the floor and spread out around her feet like a dark wave.

Her breathing became ragged. Blood hammered in her temples. The room began to spin. She knew she was going to be sick.

She clapped her hands to her mouth and stumbled over the images as she fled.

◊ ◊ ◊

Maya waited half an hour for the old geezer to show up.

When, finally, he did arrive, he was shocked to see her.

"How did you get in here?" he demanded.

"It wasn't all that difficult," she explained. "Unlike many establishments, your lock accepts American Express. You really should improve security at this place."

Maya watched an easy half-dozen expressions flicker across the Bishop's sagging features. They ran the gamut from fear to outrage to guarded suspicion. He was a smallish man, which seemed at odds with the entrapments of power and influence exuded by the opulence of his wardrobe. Her overwhelming impression of the man was that he looked . . . *soft*. Pampered. Like he'd never lifted anything heavier than the pectoral cross that hung from his neck at the end of a heavy chain. He had pale skin marked with age spots and eerily white hands that now clutched at the folds of his dark cassock.

"I have no further business with you, Miss Jindal. And I do not appreciate seeing you here."

"I rather suspect we'd be hard-pressed to find any circumstances where you'd appreciate my company. But then, your standards are quite different from those of your colleague the judge, aren't they, Bishop?"

He sat down behind his imposing desk. It was ridiculously tidy. No papers in evidence. Just an ornate leather blotter, a bound folio of some kind, a small bronze replica of Michelangelo's Pietà, and a telephone. He cleared his throat.

"Mr. Zucchetto has informed me that our relationship has been terminated. I believe you've already been paid the full fee for your services."

"Mr. Zucchetto informed you correctly."

"Then why are you here?" He sat back and folded his hands.

Maya crossed her long legs. "Did Mr. Zucchetto also inform you that part of his plan was to have me killed?"

The bishop seemed unfazed by her remark.

"No. But I don't know all the details of his intercourse with you."

Maya laughed. "Touché, Bishop. Well played."

"What do you want?" His tone was icy.

"Contrary to opinion, I'm really an old-fashioned girl." She reached into the messenger bag that sat on the table beside her chair, and withdrew a sleek pair of black leather gloves. She took her time putting them on before completing her thought. "All this is to say that I believe turnabout is fair play."

"I'm not sure I take your meaning."

"Oh," Maya reached back into her bag and withdrew the Tokarev, "don't you?"

That finally got a rise out of the old man. His watery eyes began to show traces of fear.

"What do you expect to accomplish with this?" His voice had lost its imperial tone.

"I'm a cleaner, Your Excellency. That's what I do. It's why you hired me." She cocked the hammer on the Tokarev. "I'd be a very sloppy employee if I left a steaming mess of *your* magnitude behind, now wouldn't I?"

He held up his hands. "Don't do this. It isn't necessary."

"Oh, but I disagree. Think about poor Joey Mazzetta. And sad Senator Miller, who had to swallow all of those tiny nails and wait hours to die."

"I had *nothing* to do with Mazzetta." The bishop was beginning to sound anxious.

Maya chuckled. "It's comforting to know you are still a man of some integrity."

"What are you talking about?"

Maya saw tiny beads of sweat developing on the bishop's pate.

"You're so quick to acquit yourself of only *one* of the two murders carried out to preserve your . . . what shall we call it? Ecclesiastical purity?"

"I didn't have *anyone* target him. That was . . ." he didn't finish his statement.

"Your colleague, the Honorable Justice Cawley, perhaps?"

The bishop did not reply. *That would never do . . .* Maya needed him to elaborate. Otherwise, her visit here would be wasted.

"No matter," she said. "It's all *pro forma* now, anyway."

His eyes grew wide. "What do you mean?"

Maya made an elaborate display of checking her watch.

"By now, I'd imagine the judge is on the phone with the White House. One can only wonder at the story he'll have to tell about your role in this sordid business. As you know," she leaned forward and rested her elbow on the edge of his desk to set up her shot, "the early bird catches the worm."

"Cawley panicked." The bishop was desperate now. "He had that man, Goldman, take care of Mazzetta after his disgusting performance at the club. And Goldman's people dealt with Miller, too. I had *nothing* to do with either of those incidents. They weren't about me."

"Well, the perfect symmetry of this is that you're in the enviable position of being able to forgive yourself for the sins you *have* committed. Isn't that right, Bishop? All of the nasty things you and the judge did to those innocent little boys?"

"That was all over *years* ago. Another life. *A different time.* I haven't broken my vows."

"Which vows would those be, Your Excellency? Shall we tally them up? Let's see . . . poverty, obedience, chastity . . . did I get them all? Oh dear. It looks like you might have a problem with that last one."

"You can go to hell." He nearly spat the words at her.

"Oh, that's in my long-range plan, I assure you. I'll so look forward to seeing both you and the judge there. We'll have quite a time reminiscing about the secrets we shared, don't you think?"

"Tell me what you want." He was desperate now. "More money?"

"Back to that, are we?" She exhaled. "You're right. I probably *have* tarried too long. Allow me to get to the point. You're up to your sanctified beanie in dung. From where I sit—*literally*—this can unfold in one of three ways. First: I could kill you right now and simplify everything for everyone. A nice little remedy, but I'm not really feeling the magic in it. Second: I could turn the *lovely* recording I just made of our conversation over to the authorities. It would incentivize a lot of lively discussions on the cable news channels, don't you think? And it provides the extra benefit of inoculating me against any future reindeer games by our mutual friend, Mr. Goldman. That leaves us with option three: you can put feet to your own twisted prayers, and go out in a proverbial blaze of glory." She pulled back the slide on her Tokarev. "Your choice, *Bishop*. But I think I'm leaning toward that last option. How about you?"

The bishop was starting to shake.

"I see we've reached consensus." Maya deftly extracted a second, smaller weapon from her bag before placing the Tokarev on the desk between them. She got to her feet. "Do take care to make your first shot count. This weapon tends to be messy. You won't want to try it twice."

She backed toward the door.

"*Deum vigilat*," she chanted, before leaving his office.

She'd reached the elevator doors when she heard the gunshot. It wasn't followed by a second.

Julia didn't often drink by herself, but tonight she made an exception.

Her Norwegian Air flight left Paris at 6:15 p.m. local time, and she'd arranged to have a driver pick her up at JFK outside the international terminal for the trek back to Philadelphia. That choice had been simple. A two-and-a-half hour car ride held greater appeal to her than spending the night at an airport hotel to wait for the first commuter flight home in the morning.

She'd already determined that she wouldn't call Evan. She knew it would be the middle of the night when she got back to Delancey Place—and, in truth, she wasn't ready to face Evan. Or anyone. Not until she could sort out her emotions and figure out what she was going to do.

After the driver dropped her off, she headed straight for the shower, followed by a much-needed change of clothes. She was bone tired, but knew she wouldn't be able to sleep. She'd actually managed to doze a bit on the long flight back from Paris. That surprised her—mostly because she'd stashed the fat envelope of photographs into her carry-on bag, and the damn thing tormented her throughout the entire flight. It virtually banged and strobed from its nest on the floor in an obscene parody of "The Tell-Tale Heart."

Your sins will find you out.

Would this unwelcome record of her father's sins now become her own dark secret to keep?

What should she do?

Had it been possible, she'd have tossed the photos out the window of the airplane, and let them disappear into the cold waters of the Atlantic.

Now? Now the unopened envelope sat in front of her on her grandmother's coffee table.

It didn't belong here. She said a silent apology to her grandmother for bringing the abomination into her house. That thought made her wonder if her grandmother had ever known about Lewis Donne's sick fraternity of pedophiles? Had Katherine Donne ever shared her lurid discovery with her *own* mother? At one time, the two women had been close . . .

No. Julia doubted that she had. It wouldn't be Katherine's style. And in the end, everything came down to considerations of "style" for Julia's mother.

She nursed her tumbler of cognac and stared at the packet containing the photos. The decision to bring it back to Philadelphia with her had been reflexive. Now she wondered why she chose to do so? It wasn't like she wanted more time to review the photographs . . .

Quite the contrary. She never wanted to see them again. She knew she'd live the rest of her life trying to erase the memory of what she'd already seen. The collection of repulsive images was burned into her mind like hidden objects revealed by flashes of lightning.

She closed her eyes. Her father . . . naked and bent over the back of a boy. *A boy.* A boy with a blank expression on his young face. *Vacant eyes . . .*

No. She didn't need to see these again. *No one ever needed to see these.*

What good could come from making them public? Scores of lives would be tainted . . . ruined by their accidental association with these men. Innocent people who'd had nothing to do with her father or his closed circle of . . . *perpetrators* . . . would be tarred by the exposure of what some members of their beloved club had done.

Her gaze shifted to the fireplace that commanded the wall facing the sofa. She'd turned on the gas logs before she sat down. There were no lamps on in the room, and the dramatic shadows cast by the fire undulated along the walls and ceiling like underworld demons. Their frenzied movements compounded her agitation. She felt surrounded—pursued by a posse of every unholy thing that lurked behind the shroud of darkness.

Enough. It was enough. She would not allow herself to become a hostage to her father's diseased and criminal past.

She couldn't will her discovery away any more than she could change the reality of what her father and the other men in his cabal had done. She *knew* about it. And knowing about it changed everything. Knowing about it also implied responsibility. There was no denying that. Hiding from the truth never solved anything. Averting your gaze from things you'd rather not know about simply gave those things greater power and the tacit permission to flourish unfettered.

She drained her glass of cognac and picked up the envelope. There was nothing to be gained by putting this off. She owed it to herself to face the full reality of her father's deeds. She owed it even more to every one of the children he'd victimized. Violated. Their lives had been changed forever.

Just as learning the truth about what had happened to them had now changed *her* life.

She removed the stack of images and spread them out across the top of the table.

The scenes they depicted were abominable. Harsh, graphic scenes of the sexual abuse of children preserved for . . . *what?* Voyeuristic pleasure? Licentious reminders of forbidden conquests? Some profane historical record?

My god . . . Julia forced herself to stare at the images. *This was my father's private porn stash.*

The realization sickened her.

The faces of some of the men—at least the ones she could make out—were familiar to her. Bishop Szymanski. Judge Cawley. Albert. Others were too obscured. She guessed they all were part of the same small set within the club—her father's special *confederacy.* The beneficiaries of his Ganymede Trust.

The boys, however? The faces of the boys were all alike. Their expressions were empty. Vague. Void of any emotion. One face in particular deviated from that. She nearly missed seeing him as he stood in the shadows near the edge of one of the photos. A rail thin boy wearing only his underpants. He stared directly at the camera with a look of terror on his face—like he knew what would happen. *Like he knew he'd be next.*

She swept the images back into a stack and covered them with the empty envelope.

Once again, she thought about destroying the photos. Once again, she resisted the impulse.

Destroying them would be wrong. Destroying them would make her complicit in the crimes committed by her father and his cronies. Destroying them would allow the same abhorrent acts to continue without consequence, without conscience, and without responsibility.

Destroying them would make her like her mother . . .

When you know better, Maya Angelou said, *do better.*

It was now her turn to do better.

She could tell Evan. She could simply hand the evidence against Cawley over and let Evan decide what to do with it. Undoubtedly, Evan would give the images to Dan. Would justice then be served?

Maybe.

She thought about Edwin Miller and the way the Democrats had protected him because they cared more about changing the legislative balance of power than protecting the children he preyed upon. How naïve would she have to be to expect today's Republican majority to behave any differently?

They wouldn't.

Political divisions in the country had moved beyond concern for what was right. There was no longer a shared moral compass that steered divergent political ideologies toward a shared sense of the common good.

It was no longer possible to trust the instincts of a political culture that had lost its center.

No. She couldn't play Pontius Pilate and calmly wash her hands of this before waltzing off to resume the pampered comforts of the rest of her life.

That was all finished now. It had to be.

Monday's unread newspaper sat on an overstuffed ottoman beside the sofa.

Jessica Hayes Marsh. They'd been classmates at Exeter. Jess had gone on to study journalism at Columbia, and now worked as a senior editor at *The Washington Post.* Julia had run into her last year in New York at the Pulitzer ceremony. Jess and her team had just won the award for investigative reporting.

Julia looked back at the stack of photographs. Jess would know exactly what to do with these.

But she'd have to make another phone call first—to the board chair at Donne & Hale.

She got up and headed for the bedroom to retrieve her cell phone.

Chapter Twelve

Evan's text alert tone went off twice before 6 a.m.

She checked it the first time because she hoped it might be a message from Julia. It wasn't.

It was Dan. She ignored his message and rolled over. She knew he was texting to nag her about when she'd be sending him his damn report.

The second time the alert sounded, she ignored it and pulled a pillow over her head. She hadn't gotten much sleep. She'd stayed up with Tim until the wee hours to process everything that had happened in the parking garage. They'd finally made their way upstairs a little after 1 a.m.

Even then, she doubted that Tim had got any sleep. Although he did seem calmer than he'd been in weeks. Calmer and more at peace than he'd been since the night he appeared like an apparition in the snow, to tell her he was thinking about leaving the priesthood. She knew better than to press him on his state of mind where that consideration was concerned. She knew he'd talk with her when he was ready.

Her phone went off again—ringing this time.

Jesus Christ, Dan . . .

She grabbed it off her nightstand. "What?" she barked.

He didn't waste time. "Cawley withdrew."

Evan sat up. "What?"

"Yeah. We got word about half an hour ago. He called the president last night."

"What the hell happened?"

"I was hoping you could tell me."

"Me?" Evan rubbed her eyes. "Why the hell would I know?"

He shrugged. "Wishful thinking, I guess."

"What are they saying?"

"What do they ever say?" Dan scoffed. "The White House is gonna issue a statement saying that Judge Cawley withdrew over health and family considerations. You know . . . one of the old standbys."

"Something spooked him," Evan suggested. "He must've found out everything is about to break."

"I'm guessing you're right. Either way," he declared, "our work is finished."

"Not all of it."

"Whattaya mean? It's over. Now we wait for the next scumbag POTUS spools up."

"Yeah," Evan said. "You can count me out on that one."

"Come on. Where's your sense of adventure?"

"Let's just say I left it in my other suit. Do you still need my report?"

"Oh, yeah. We want a paper trail on this asshole. With luck, he'll resign from the bench altogether."

"Okay." Evan thought about filling Dan in on what had happened last night with Maya and Marcus's goon, but didn't. There'd be plenty of time for that in the days ahead. "How's Stevie?" she asked instead.

"Good. She and Kayla are going to that Alice Cooper concert today."

Alice Cooper? "Dan, that's Alice *Glass*—not Alice Cooper."

"Yeah . . . whoever. They're having a great time."

"Anybody's phone in the freezer yet?" she teased.

"Hey . . . I do *not* put phones in the *goddamn freezer*—all right?"

"Cool your jets, man. It's too early to bust a blood vessel."

"Yeah—whatever. I'll talk to you later."

"Right." She hung up.

Evan figured she might as well get up and go watch the news. There was no way she'd get back to sleep after Dan's news.

She dressed and headed downstairs to find Tim already up and in the kitchen drinking coffee.

He held up his cup when he saw her. "This coffeemaker of yours really sucks."

"Yeah? News flash . . . *not*." Evan got a mug from a cabinet and poured herself some of the nasty brew, anyway. "How long have you been up?"

He shrugged. "I don't think I ever went to sleep, really. I finally gave up and came down here."

Evan joined him at the table and pulled out a chair. "Have you heard the news?"

Tim looked wary. "What news?"

"Relax." Evan wanted to set his mind at ease. "It's not about 'Billy' or Maya Jindal. Cawley withdrew this morning."

"No way! What happened?"

Evan shrugged. "I guess we'll have to wait for that to be revealed. I can only guess that he had a heads-up about what was in the works to derail his nomination."

"So it's over."

"If only."

"Hey." Tim reached across the table to touch her hand. "Julia will weather this. *With you.* Nothing will change what you two are to each other."

"Is this a little pastoral encouragement, Father?"

He gave her a small smile. "I guess it is."

"You're pretty good at it, you know?"

"That's funny. Stevie said the same thing to me on Saturday, when we were out practicing three-point turns."

Evan smirked at him. "Are you sure she wasn't talking about your defensive driving techniques?"

"I hadn't considered that possibility. I suppose she could've been."

"Well, don't waste your time wondering. That kid is pretty damn perceptive."

Tim nodded in agreement. "I guess that comes from the Cohen side of the family?"

"Fuck you." Evan gave him the finger.

He laughed before slowly shaking his head. "This feels good."

"What does?"

"This. Being able to laugh and joke about simple things. Is it wrong? Am I in some kind of shock or denial about what happened last night?"

"I dunno." Evan considered his question. It was a good one. "I suppose you could be. You also could be at a point where you've found some answers to all those questions you had."

"Not all of them. Many of them will take years—and a lot of outside help."

"What kind of help?"

"The expensive kind," Tim elaborated. "The kind that bills for forty-five-minute hours."

"Ah. My favorite."

"But I think I do have an answer to one question—and you get the credit for it."

"The question?" Evan asked. "Or the answer? Knowing me, it could go either way."

"I won't argue with you about that," Tim said. "But in this case, it's the answer. It happened last night, when you were yelling at me after praying for . . . *Billy.*"

"I yelled at you?"

Tim gave her a deadpan look.

"Okay . . . I *might've* yelled at you. But we needed to get out of there before the cops arrived."

"I'm not disputing that. But you said something about how you couldn't understand why I ever doubted that I should stay a priest, because I had tarried to pray for the man sent to kill me."

"I think my version might've been a bit more colorful that that," Evan observed.

"I exercised editorial restraint." Tim took his time getting the next bit out. "I thought about that comment. I thought about it most of the night. The truth is, no other action would've been possible for me. It wasn't just a programmed response. It was what I needed to do—not because I've been trained to do it, but because it *mattered* to me to do it. It mattered more than anything else at that moment. More, even, than getting away."

"Yeah, I noticed that last part." Evan observed. "So, maybe you're close to an answer?"

He nodded. "About this one thing, I am. Stevie said that maybe I was in a bad marriage—to the Church. And that I'd been feeling like the Church had broken its vows to me. I think her word was 'cheated.' Well, her simple metaphor was right . . . at least, it was half right. The Church *has* failed. But I'm not married to the Church—I'm married to God. And one of my solemn obligations is to protect and nurture His Church. And I think that means not turning my back on it when it loses its way."

"I guess I have to agree with your police work on that."

"It's kind of a no-brainer, isn't it? Can I be less charitable to the Church than God has been to me?"

"You?" Evan asked. "Not a chance. Me, on the other hand?"

"Trust me," Tim said. "We don't have enough time or crappy coffee to answer that one."

Evan laughed and got up from the table. "How about some waffles?"

Tim left shortly after they'd finished breakfast. He'd managed to hitch a ride back into town with Father Malloy, who was visiting with a sick relative in the West Chester hospital, about ten miles from Evan's house. Father Malloy was happy to swing by on his way back to St. Rita's and pick Tim up.

Evan suggested that Tim wait a while before trying to get his car. He balked at the fees he'd be racking up by continuing to leave it there, but she suggested he'd be better off paying those than having to sit for an interrogation with the cops, who would certainly still be working the scene for clues about what had happened.

Evan was back at her desk, putting the last touches on her report for Dan and halfway listening to cable news to see if anything else would break about Justice Cawley's decision to withdraw from consideration for the high court. At noon, the local NBC affiliate broke into the broadcast to announce that an auxiliary bishop in the Archdiocese of Philadelphia had been found dead in his office from an apparent suicide.

What the hell?

Evan turned up the volume.

It appeared that Bishop Frederick R. Szymanski's body had been discovered by a custodian who entered the bishop's office at the archdiocese headquarters on North 17th Street a little after 7 a.m. No other details were available. A statement from the archbishop was expected soon.

Evan's cell phone rang. It was J.C. Ortiz.

One guess what he was calling about . . .

"Yo," she answered. "I'm just watching it on TV right now."

"I guess we can dispense with preliminaries, then?" he asked.

"I guess."

"So, Reed? You got anything you'd like to share with the class?"

"Me? What makes you think I'd know anything about this?"

"Well, shit. I don't know . . . maybe the fact that the body count seems to be piling up around your ass like Stonehenge?"

"Oh, come on, J.C. You don't seriously think—"

J.C. cut her off. "I'll tell you what I think. Last night, some güey got capped, execution style, in a parking garage at the Center City DoubleTree. And he was killed with the same kind of fucking bullet they dug outta Joey Mazzetta."

Shit. That hadn't taken long. The Philadelphia P.D. was getting better at its job.

"I guess that means the same shooter is still at large?" she asked.

"Not anymore," J.C. declared. "The bishop shot himself in the head—with a Tokarev 7.62. What do *you* think the odds are that there are two of those commie guns floating around this town?"

Jesus. Maya said she'd had an "errand" to take care of. How the hell had she pulled that one off?

"I got nothin', man," Evan confessed. "It sounds like a paradox to me."

"A paradox?"

"That's what I'd call it."

"Yeah? Well I'd call it a fucking stink bomb with your fingerprints all over it. If you know anything about this, Reed, you better come clean. You owe me," he reminded her.

"I hear you, man. If I find out anything, your number will be the first one I call."

"Yeah. Make sure it is. And, Reed?"

"What?"

"Stay the fuck outta my district. I'd like a goddamn night off." He hung up.

Holy shit. When Maya cleaned something up, she didn't mess around.

Now the cops had the gun that had been used in three homicides. Correction: *four*. Evan needed to include the unsolved murder of Julia's husband, Andy Townsend. And the kicker? She was positive Maya would've made sure that the only fingerprints on the gun would belong to Bishop Szymanski.

Talk about just damn deserts.

After Evan finished her report and transmitted it to Dan, she tried again to reach Julia. She'd sent her half a dozen text messages and had received no response. She understood that even with a good international calling plan, cell service could still be sketchy—but it was starting to worry her. *A lot.* She had no idea what was happening in Paris or how Julia was managing. Nor did she have the slightest idea about when she'd be back. Julia had said her trip wouldn't be long—and she hadn't prepared for a stay of more than a night or two. But this continued radio silence was maddening.

How was she?

Evan didn't do well with worry. She tended to digest her own organs if someone she cared about was in difficulty, and too much time passed without contact. And in this case, Julia wasn't just somebody she cared about. Julia was . . . well. Julia was the apotheosis of that.

Evan was in the kitchen, making herself something to nibble on, when she heard tires crunching on the gravel out front.

Great. What now?

She sneaked out onto her back porch to steal a look to see who it was. She was ninety percent sure she'd choose to pretend she wasn't at home. A black car she didn't recognize was pulled up next to the sidewalk. The driver got out and opened the rear passenger door.

Evan uttered an expletive and took off in a run to reach the front door.

Julia was standing on the porch when Evan threw the door open. Her hired car was already backing out the driveway.

Evan held out her arms. Julia walked into them and the two of them stood there in the cold, hanging on to each other.

"When did you get back?" Evan muttered into her neck.

"Last night." Julia had her face pressed against Evan's hair.

Evan drew back. "Last night?"

Julia nodded. "I managed to snag a space on the 6:15 flight from de Gaulle. I got into Philadelphia a little after 11:00, so I went straight to the townhouse." She shivered.

"Hey, you're freezing." Evan took hold of her arms. "Let's go inside."

"It's supposed to snow," Julia said distractedly. "I guess there's another big storm heading this way from the Midwest."

"That's okay. We don't have anywhere to go."

"No. We don't."

Evan wanted to give Julia as much space as she needed to feel ready to talk about whatever had taken place in Paris. Given that Julia was already on a plane heading back to the states less than six hours after arriving was confirmation enough that things hadn't gone well.

"Are you hungry?" Evan asked. "I was just making myself something to eat."

Julia took off her coat and commenced rubbing her hands up and down her arms. "Yes. That would be great. I haven't eaten anything but a few bites of some painfully indifferent airline food. I haven't had much of an appetite."

"I can fix that. Follow me to the kitchen."

Evan led the way and Julia followed her. When they reached the kitchen, Julia perched on a stool and watched while Evan started pulling things out of the fridge.

"Don't feel like you have to fuss," she said. "Something simple is fine."

"We don't *do* simple here at the house of Reed."

"Silly me. I forgot."

"Did you?"

"No." Julia confessed. "I don't forget much of anything that relates to you."

"Should I take that as a compliment?" Evan pulled the rest of the truffled Gouda out of the fridge.

"You'll have to determine that for yourself." Julia crooked an index finger and wagged it to summon Evan over.

When Evan got there, Julia took hold of her face and pulled it down so she could kiss her.

Really kiss her.

Really, *really* kiss her.

"Okay," Evan croaked when Julia released her. "I guess that's cleared up."

"Let me know if you require more proof?"

"Oh, don't worry. I will. I have some bad news, though."

"What's that?"

Evan held up the hunk of cheese she'd squeezed the stuffing out of during their object lesson. "I think this Gouda is toast."

"Hmmm. Maybe you should just put it *on* some toast?"

"Capital idea."

Julia seemed to relax a bit. At least she looked less furtive than she had when she arrived.

310

"You know what I'd like right now?" she asked.

"No. But if it involves me and a bed, I can stow all of this food in, like, two seconds."

Julia actually smiled. It was a tiny, little baby of a smile, but Evan thought it still counted.

"I think it's safe to assume we'll get to that eventually," she said. "But right now, I'd love a drink."

"Say no more." Evan walked to the cabinet where she kept her liquor stash. "Too bad we don't have any of that French vermouth. I'd make you one of those wacky martini things."

"No, thank you. I think I've given those up."

"Don't like 'em anymore?"

"It's not that so much as it is the 'French' part. I'm not feeling much of a kinship with it right now."

"Yeah . . . about that?" Julia's opening gave Evan the courage to ask about the elephant in the room.

"How about we take our drinks, and that melted hunk of cheese you're still carrying around, into the living room and I'll tell you about everything?"

Evan regarded her fistful of Gouda. "Deal."

Once they were settled on the sofa with their large cognacs, Julia half turned on her cushion to face Evan. "Do you want the long version, or the short version?"

"I want whatever version you feel inclined to share."

"All right. To quote badly from *The Godfather*: today I settled all family business."

Evan looked perplexed.

"Sorry," Julia apologized. "I guess I just ruined the punchline. What I'm trying to say is that my mother and I are . . . *finished*. We have agreed to disagree—and on terms that do no credit to either of us. But the break is complete, and I won't be going back."

Evan was trying hard to follow the gist of what Julia was saying, but it was difficult.

"You quarreled?" she asked. She knew it was a simplistic question, but wasn't sure how else to ask about Julia's mother's response to what Julia had uncovered about Lewis Donne's trust and his involvement with the abusive and predatory behavior of the men in his circle.

"Oh, we quarreled. But not about what you might think. After her expressions of umbrage about my audacity to show up unannounced, I told her what the purpose of my visit was. I asked her some nonspecific questions about her knowledge of why my father set up his trust, and what she knew, if anything, about some of its more suspect disbursements."

"How did she respond?"

"She was enraged—furious with me for bringing any of it up. You see? That was my greatest offense: *asking* her about it. Making her *think* about it. This thing . . . this horrible thing she'd known about my father for decades and had consciously chosen to ignore. *She knew about it, Evan.* She knew about it, and she did *nothing.*" Julia closed her eyes. "It sickened me to realize that she'd known about him—about that place and what they were doing—all those years. She turned her face away and hardened her heart—against him. *Against everything.* All so she could keep her money—protect her historic name and defend her rightful place in society."

"Oh, god, honey." Evan reached out to take hold of her hand. "I am so very sorry."

"No." Julia squeezed her hand tightly. "Don't be sorry for me. Be sorry for *them*—the boys they hurt. The little stars . . ." Her voice trailed off.

Evan handed her the glass of cognac. Julia took a sip and nodded at her gratefully.

"She left me then—just grabbed her coat and bag and left. Told me I could do whatever I wanted, but that she had plans and wouldn't be back until late."

"Is that when you left to come home?"

"No. No, I wish it had been. I wish . . ."

"It's okay." Evan bent forward and kissed her forehead. "Honey, it's okay. You don't have to talk about this right now."

"Oh, but I do. I want to tell you—*myself.* Before . . ." She hesitated. "I just want to tell you myself." She took another sip of cognac before continuing. When she started speaking, she kept her eyes fixed on her glass. "When I was alone, I took a shower. Then I dressed and wandered through the apartment. I guess I knew I'd never go back there again. I went into my father's study. It was exactly the way he'd left it—everything pristine. Everything unchanged. *Everything*. I noticed a small painting, half hidden by a door—one I'd never noticed before. I went to look at it and . . ." She looked up at Evan. Her eyes had darkened. They looked more steel gray than blue. "It was a Homer painting—an original. One of the studies for 'Snap the Whip.' Dated 1872, just like the one in the photograph. I was stunned. I took it down and turned it over to look for any indication of where he'd gotten it, and I . . . I found—something." She closed her eyes again. "Dear god . . . I'll never unsee it, Evan. *Never*."

It took more self-control than Evan knew she possessed to wait for Julia to continue. It wasn't really that long—but it felt like a couple of centuries.

Finally, Julia continued in a steadier voice.

"It was an envelope. Full of photographs. Horrible images. Grown men with boys. Doing unspeakable things. Sometimes, two of them with one boy. Sometimes the men wore masks that were more like hoods. Sometimes not. And, I . . . *I saw him*. I saw him, Evan. And . . . others, too. The judge. Albert. The bishop. All of them engaged in sex acts with children. *With children*. It made me sick. Literally. I ran from the room and threw up so many times I lost count. I sat on the bathroom floor in my mother's apartment until I felt strong enough to stand. Then I called for a car to take me back to the airport. Before I left, I returned to the study and picked up the pictures and returned them to the envelope without looking at them, and brought them back with me." She took a long, deep breath. "I was going to ask you what to do with them. I was going to come straight here from the airport."

Evan felt sick and distraught at Julia's revelation. It was impossible for her to imagine the shock this had been for her—the trauma. She knew Julia was right when she said she'd never be

313

able to unsee the horror she'd discovered—hidden for salacious gratification behind a painting that immortalized childhood innocence. Julia was right: there was no going back. She now had to live with this. And Evan would live it with her.

"Why didn't you come here?" she asked, softly.

"Because I realized I had some things to take care of that could only be done by me. *Alone.* I had eight hours on an airplane to come to that realization. So, when I got back, I went to my grandmother's house, and I settled all family business. Which brings us back to where I started."

Evan started to ask Julia to explain what she meant by her oblique mob reference, but she never got the chance. On the coffee table in front of them, both of their cell phones lit up as long sequences of tri-tone alerts sounded. There were so many she couldn't count them all.

"What the hell?" Evan snapped up her phone. "Good god. I've got about *eight* breaking news alerts."

Julia reached out a hand to stop her from reading any of them.

"That's the other thing I have to tell you," she said.

"What the *serious* fuck?"

Dan was nearly apoplectic.

"I told you." Evan related it all—*again.* "Julia turned everything over to *The Washington Post.* She contacted an old classmate from Exeter, who's now an editor in their Washington bureau, and she connected Julia directly with the reporters covering Cawley. They reached out to Cawley's office for comment before they ran the story. You can intuit the rest."

"What the fuck made her *do* that?"

Evan lowered the phone and addressed Julia. "Dan wants to know, 'what the fuck' made you turn everything over to the *Post?*"

Julia tipped her head back and stared at the ceiling. "Tell him I thought it had more credibility than *HuffPo.*"

Evan repeated Julia's response, only instead of *HuffPo,* she substituted *Media Matters.*

314

Julia glowered at her.

"Well, I'll be goddamned," Dan said. *Again.*

"Look. We're both exhausted. Neither of us got any sleep last night."

"Yeah, all right." Dan picked up the clue phone. "Call me tomorrow?"

"Count on it," Evan said. "Good night, Dan."

"Later," he said.

Evan tossed her phone down on the coffee table. Then she thought better of it and picked it back up.

"What are you doing?" Julia asked.

"I'm turning the damn thing off. Enough is enough."

"I'll second that." Julia retrieved her phone and did the same thing. "I need to get a new one of these, by the way."

"How come? Did you drop it or something?"

"In a manner of speaking. I resigned from Donne & Hale this morning."

"*What?*"

"Okay," Julia said in a placating tone. "Before you light up like a Christmas tree, I promise this is my last piece of breaking news."

"I sure as shit hope so." Evan sat staring at her like she'd never seen her before. "Why the hell did you do that?"

"Quit the company?"

"Oh, is *that* what we were talking about? I thought we were still discussing the Ukrainian diaspora."

"Wiseass." Julia bumped into her. "When I made the decision to turn everything I'd discovered over to the *Post*, I understood what it would mean for any future I could ever hope to have with my mother. I burned that bridge pretty thoroughly. I couldn't take an action like that and keep drinking from the family well. I couldn't do the same thing I repudiated my mother for doing. I had to let it all go. The business. The houses. The money. All of it."

"Holy shit." Evan didn't know what to say.

"Hey." Julia nudged her again. "Don't tell me you're now rethinking our living arrangements?"

"Hmmmm. Well. Now that you're a pauper . . ."

315

"A pauper?" Julia quoted. "I wouldn't go quite that far."

"No? How far *would* you go?"

Julia pushed her backwards on the sofa and crawled on top of her. "About this far?"

"Yeah . . ." Evan wound her hands into Julia's head of thick dark hair and pulled her closer. "I think we might be able to work something out."

Desiree's seventeenth birthday was on Saturday, and Ping put on a big spread for the family. "The family" in this instance included Stevie, Evan, Julia and Ben.

Ben complained about having to wear something other than pajama bottoms, Crocs, and one—or both—of his favorite flannel shirts, but Ping said she'd refuse to let his sorry ass through the door if he didn't clean himself up. Evan was surprised at his appearance when he got there. He'd obviously showered and shaved, and he wore a pair of trousers that nearly fit, and a button-down shirt with a tweed jacket.

"Damn, Ben. You got a job interview after this shindig?" she asked him.

Ben was busy loading his plate up with deviled eggs, pigs in a blanket, baked ham, macaroni and cheese, biscuits and a single stalk of celery.

"Go fuck yourself. Sometimes you gotta pay to play."

"Shirley teach you that?"

Ben had been creating a precarious tower of biscuits, and he paused in mid-stack. "Who the fuck is Shirley?"

"Seriously?" Evan asked. "The blonde with the fake . . . you know."

He narrowed his eyes. "I'm gonna need a little more to go on."

"Yeah. Never mind." Evan eyed his plate. "What's with the celery stalk?"

"Ping will chew my ass if I don't eat fucking vegetables."

"Right." Evan nodded. "Good plan. That should throw her right off the scent."

"Hey?" He asked in a lower tone of voice. "How's she doing?" He inclined his head toward Julia, who was sitting at the kitchen table, having a cup of hot tea with Ping.

"She's okay. It's gonna be a long haul."

"No shit. The news coverage reads like new installments of *Fifty Shades of Gross*."

"Maybe don't share those insights too broadly around her?"

"I won't." He plucked one of his biscuits off the top of his tower and crammed the entire thing into his mouth. It wasn't pretty.

"Yeah, and with *that*—I gotta go." Evan felt a sudden need to change the scenery.

"How come?" Ben asked, displaying a mouthful of flaky goodness.

Evan patted him on the arm. "I think I left the iron on."

She walked across the room, intending to annoy Stevie, who was entirely taken up with Desiree. The two of them had been inseparable all evening. It was sickeningly sweet.

"Yo, kiddo. It's time for us to blow this pop stand."

Stevie's face fell. "Come on, Mama Uno. It's only, like, 7:30."

"I know this will stun you, but I learned how to tell time thirty-five years ago." She held out her arm to display her wristwatch. "And when the little hand reaches the nine, Mama Uno turns into a flesh-eating bitch who does unspeakable things—like hiding the car keys or eliminating all the premium channels on someone's cable package."

Stevie and Desiree looked at each other, before sighing in tandem.

"Twenty more minutes?" Stevie begged. "Please?"

Evan deliberated. "Do you have plans tonight after this party, Des?"

Desiree perked up at once. "No. Not a thing. I mean, besides watching *White Christmas*."

"We *were* going to watch it together," Stevie complained. "We've been looking forward to it all week."

"*White Christmas?*" Evan regarded the pair with disbelief. How

317

could the same kid who was gaga over Alice Glass have her heart set on watching something as smarmy as *White Christmas?*

"Totally," Desiree added. She gave Stevie a playful nudge and grinned at Evan. "She has the hots for Rosemary Clooney."

"Rosemary . . ." Evan blinked at her daughter.

"*Woof.*" Stevie had a dreamy look on her face. "Total spank bank material."

Evan let that one go. "I was wondering, if it's okay with your mother, if you'd like to come home with us, Des—and spend the night? I can take you home tomorrow."

The two girls nearly jumped out of their skins with excitement.

"That would be so awesome," Desiree gushed. "Let me go ask her right now." She squeezed Stevie's hand and hurried off to find Phyllis.

"Mom, this is so freakin' cool. Thanks for doing this. Really."

"Yeah, whatever." Evan said. "But there are rules, Stevie. Des sleeps in the guest room—in virginal solitude. No exceptions. Understood?"

Stevie looked mortified. "*Like* I'd do something like that with you and Julia across the hall."

"I'm so relieved to hear you say, 'Gee Mom, I've decided to wait until I'm really sure I'm ready for such a big step.' That just warms my cold, dead heart."

Julia walked over to join them. She was carrying a fat grocery bag filled with foil-wrapped packages. Evan didn't have to ask what it contained. She caught Ping's eye. Ping flashed her a big smile and a double thumbs-up. She supposed that meant she'd get a call from Ping tomorrow, and a summary assessment of how Julia was 'doing,' post all the traumas of the last few days.

"Are you two ready to go?" Julia hefted the bag. She'd already put on her coat and gloves. "If we leave now, we can make it home in time for *White Christmas.*"

Evan gaped at her and Stevie burst into peals of merry laughter.

"What's so funny about that?" Julia asked. "Rosemary Clooney is totally hot."

Stevie leapt to her feet and hugged Julia. "I love you, Mama Dos."

Mama Dos? Evan was surprised, but moved, by Stevie's new moniker for Julia.

Julia noticed it, too. She positively beamed, as she hugged Stevie back.

Evan threw up her hands.

"Tell Julia about our overnight guest," she said to Stevie. "I'll go start the car."

After they got home, Julia opted to forgo watching the movie with the girls. She explained that the pair should be allowed to create their own Christmas traditions, without parental supervision. Besides, she told Evan, it was the winter solstice, and there was a supermoon to be seen from the edge of the snowy field behind their house.

So once again, Evan trudged through the fresh drifts carrying two campstools and a flask of cognac.

Just like the last night she'd wandered out here and waited for the heavens to reveal their secrets, there was fresh snow on the ground and a shimmering canopy of stars. Only this time, instead of being stuck in Albuquerque, Julia was right there beside her, scanning the galaxy in an ageless anticipation of magic.

It had been the shortest day of the year. And now they were in the midst of the longest night.

Evan thought the fates guiding their stars had a wry sense of humor. The solstice was the universe's great equalizer. For this one night, the sun stood still at its greatest distance from the earth.

A celestial caesura.

But tomorrow, the longer nights would end—and the sun, in its petty pace, would creep closer from day to day.

Macbeth knew some things.

As far as she was concerned, their longest nights had already passed.

It was oddly appropriate that they sat here, huddled together in the cold, watching the sky. It was like the epilogue at the end of a book.

An ironic metaphor for Julia, who'd spent her entire professional life helping other people tell *their* stories. Now it was her turn to speak.

And boy, had she ever commenced *that* new phase with a bang . . .

There was no doubt Julia would figure things out. Land on her feet. Keep moving forward. It was who she was. Any other course would be impossible for her. She'd already proved that.

Evan's shoulder was killing her. But she'd finally made her plans to have the damn thing fixed. She'd made a grand ceremony out of presenting Julia with a printout of her appointment with an orthopedic surgeon at Penn. And much to Evan's chagrin, the surgeon had a damn cancellation, so her appointment date for the procedure got bumped up—to the day after tomorrow.

Hell. She didn't need two arms to lift a plate of food . . . she could always just sit next to Ben Rush. His plates could feed a multitude—with *no* basketsful left over.

And Julia had surprised Evan with a gift, too—a new coffeemaker. It was a doozie, with more bells and whistles than a superconducting supercollider.

Which was not a bad metaphor, when she thought about it . . .

Stevie had teased them about how sappy they were, as they stood together in the kitchen, smiling at each other stupidly over their early presents. She'd said they were like that couple in the O. Henry short story.

"You know," she prompted. "That whole jazz with the hair and combs?"

But Stevie had been right: the exchange of gifts *had* been like making promises—both as commitments to a shared future. Tonight, that future spread out around them as wide as the bright December sky.

"When will we be able to see it?" Evan's voice cracked on the night air. She thought she could see the words travel their short distance to Julia.

There was no context for her question, but Julia was unfazed by it. By now she was used to what she called Evan's "sudden lane changes."

"See what?" she asked.

"Aquarius."

The word swirled between them like a dervish before dissipating into space.

"It's already come and gone," Julia said quietly. "In October."

Evan stared at the sky. "Where would it have been?"

Julia pointed at a place on the horizon, just above the dark outline of their house. "Over there—in the southern sky. That's where Galileo discovered it."

"Over our porch?" Evan quipped.

"You might say that."

The little stars. "I'm sorry we missed it."

"Me, too. But don't worry."

Evan looked at her.

Julia smiled. "It always comes back."

Evan took hold of her hand.

They would wait for it, together. They would wait because the little stars were worth it.

The best things in life always were.

Acknowledgments

"Four" must be my lucky number because I seem to keep making hay during my self-styled Vermont writing residencies. Credit for these small successes goes, as always, to Susan and Mike Tranby, who never fail to welcome me (in room #4) at their little slice of paradise on Lake Champlain. Thank you both for your never-ending kindness, morning coffee runs, and the life-giving indulgences of hot, apple popovers.

Tara Scott is the reason I chose to write this book ahead of some others on my list. "Yes," she said when I shared the story idea with her. "Write *that* book. Write it right now." So, Tara? If this one bombs, I blame you . . .

Sincerest thanks and adoration are heaped at the feet of my two extraordinary editors, Elizabeth Sims and Fay Jacobs. You both pushed me to make this a better book—sometimes with a backhoe. I was humbled by your insights and sage advice—and grateful that I had enough therapy on board to heed it without digesting my organs. Because of you, useful phrases like "search and destroy" entered my editorial lexicon.

Carole Cloud, as always, provided a reality-based

assessment of the story—and did her best to help me right-size Philadelphia. Cloudie? You always tell me the truth. What more can I say about why I'll always trust you. Well . . . except for when it comes to figuring which way to turn on US 29 North. (Don't ask. It's complicated.)

Cathi Jones rendered invaluable resource inspiration when I had no idea where Evan should turn to begin her background research on Judge Cawley. I owe you lunch at the Sonoma Wine Bar.

Lynn Buckingham, my sister-in-law (and surgical nurse extraordinaire), spent hours acquainting me with various effects of gunshot wounds and ensuing complications. Both Evan and Julia thank you for your time and expertise.

Carleen (Cars) Spry did a yeoman's job encouraging me during my self-imposed writing retreat—and checking in on Buddha (likely to update our wine inventory) while I was away. Thanks, Cars, for taking such good care of us. Whenever I grew weary, I heard your dulcet tones chanting, "No handsies!"

Who among us is fortunate enough to boast not one, but two moral compasses? I guess that be me, for I am the beneficiary of the love and constancy of two extraordinary men: Father Jimmy and Father Frank. Together, your combined expressions of grace and good humor encourage me work harder to be a better person.

And as further evidence that God moves in mysterious ways, Father Frank, surprisingly, became my go-to source for selecting precisely the right signature weapon for Maya Jindal. It is because of him that the phrase "single stack, suppressed fire" now occupies a hallowed place alongside "He is risen" in the litany of things he has taught me.

What can I say about my Bywater family? Holy

smokes . . . something must be in the water at this joint. The jaw-dropping collection of books this community of authors keeps churning out pushes me to work harder every single day. I'm giddy to be pulled along in your wake. What a wonderful community you are! Special love and thanks go to Marianne K. Martin, Salem West, Kelly Smith, Fay Jacobs, Elizabeth Andersen, Nancy Squires and Rachel Spangler for helping me put my best foot forward. Anna Burke? Well. Just keep doing what you're doing, Kraken. And don't forget my phone number down the road when you're between films and wanna talk with someone you know will always take your calls. I am so proud of you—existing technology cannot measure the respect I have for your talent.

I draw daily inspiration from the interactions I am blessed to have with readers and writers. Thank you all for your candor, support, and friendship. Special thanks to Christine, Louise, and Sandy for being brave enough to read early drafts of this book. You each should receive hazardous duty pay. And the enduring love and support I receive from my personal "Nurze" and Lodge Sister, Jeanne Barrett Magill, means the world to me.

Not a day goes by that I don't remember and celebrate the too-short life of Sandra Moran. You had a giant footprint, my dear friend—and I will forever be grateful that I got to walk alongside you for a while. You will never be gone as long as we remember you—and those of us fortunate enough to have known you will never forget you. That is especially true for your mother, Cherie Moran. Rumor now has it that Cherie lost her prized role as the lead synchronized swimming understudy for Esther Williams in *Million Dollar Mermaid* when her water broke (creating mass confusion on the set), kicking off a jaw-dropping 16 years of labor pains before giving birth to Sandra in 1968. Cherie? A tired and incredulous world thanks you for your sacrifice.

Buddha Bean? When I think about the debt I owe you, words fail me. You abide at the center of my best self—and whenever I wander off and get how I get, it is your voice that calls me back and calms me down. You remind me of every good thing. I think that's because, for me, you *are* every good thing. Thank you for sharing your life with me. Thank you for your love and patience. Thank you for your hard work, your incredible involvement and investment in these stories, and your keen instincts. Thank you for making everything I do better—the least of which is reflected in these pages, and the greatest of which is reflected in the life I live with you. You mean everything to me. Having said that—no, we are *not* getting a second husky . . .

About the Author

ANN McMAN is the author of nine novels and two short story collections. A Lambda Literary Award winner, she is also a two-time Independent Publisher (IPPY) medalist, an eight-time recipient of Golden Crown Literary Society Awards, and a laureate of the Alice B. Foundation for her outstanding body of work. She lives in Winston-Salem, North Carolina.

dust

AN EVAN REED MYSTERY
Ann McMan

"A definite must read for anyone who likes political thrillers, great characters, and twisty plots with tantalizing climaxes." —*The Lesbian Review*

McMan is the lesbian Armistead Maupin, only better."

—Lee Lynch, author of *The Swashbuckler*

When it comes to finding dirt, Evan Reed is the best in the business. She's a "dust-buster"—a paid operative hired by political campaigns to vet candidates for national office. She's also a foul-mouthed and cranky ex-Catholic, attempting to raise a 14-year-old daughter on her own. When she is hired to investigate the background of a squeaky-clean and charismatic junior senator who might just be the next president, the last thing she expects to uncover is a murder. Evan's life is further complicated when she meets the senator's reclusive wife, who seems to be hiding a few secrets of her own.

Dust available in
Paperback • eBook • Audiobook

www.bywaterbooks.com

Beowulf for Cretins
a love story
ANN McMAN

Winner of the 2019 Lambda Literary Award for Lesbian Romance

English professor and aspiring novelist, Grace Warner spends her days teaching four sections of "Beowulf for Cretins" to bored and disinterested students at one of New England's "hidden ivy" colleges. Not long after she is dumped by her longtime girlfriend, Grace meets the engaging and mysterious Abbie on a cross-country flight. Sparks fly on and off the plane as the two strangers give in to one night of reckless passion with no strings attached, and no contact information exchanged.

Back home at St. Albans, the college rocks Grace's world when it announces the appointment of a new president, the first woman in its 165-year history. Cue Abbie—and cue Grace's collision course with a neurotic dog named Grendel, a fractious rival for tenure, and a woman called Ochre, in what very well might be Grace's last real shot at happiness.

Beowulf for Cretins available in
Paperback • eBook • Audiobook

www.bywaterbooks.com

The Jericho Series
Jericho • Aftermath • Goldenrod
Ann McMan

PRAISE FOR THE AWARD-WINNING JERICHO SERIES

"[Jericho's] hardscrabble characters invoke Dorothy Allison; its provocative humor, Rita Mae Brown. In other words—it's pure Ann McMan."

—Lambda Literary Award winner, KG MacGregor

". . . substantial, touching, loving—at times, laugh-out-loud funny—gathering of evocative characters who lead intricately interwoven lives in a setting as dramatic and full of life as its inhabitants. Ann McMan is a writer with a multitude of unique gifts, and I thank her for sharing them so freely with her readers."

—Lee Lynch, author of *The Swashbuckler*

"McMan's writing is glorious, her wit and intellect as sharp as ever, and her pin-point descriptions are those of a keen observer of the absurdity of human behaviour."

—*The Lesbian Reading Room*

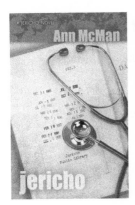  

Jericho, Aftermath and *Goldenrod are* available in
Paperback • eBook • Audiobook

Bywater
BOOKS

www.bywaterbooks.com

Bywater BOOKS

At Bywater Books we love good books about lesbians just like you do, and we're committed to bringing the best of contemporary lesbian writing to our avid readers. Our editorial team is dedicated to finding and developing outstanding writers who create books you won't want to put down.

We sponsor the Bywater Prize for Fiction to help with this quest. Each prizewinner receives $1,000 and publication of their novel. We have already discovered amazing writers like Jill Malone, Sally Bellerose, and Hilary Sloin through the Bywater Prize. Which exciting new writer will we find next?

For more information about Bywater Books and the annual Bywater Prize for Fiction, please visit our website.

www.bywaterbooks.com